Praise

JAGUAR'

G000151370

"A ripping good adventure tale. [Watch as] our hero takes on Mexican cartels, confronts Washington bureaucrats, and heads to Brazil to fight fires and illegal loggers in the Amazon."

> —**Bruce Babbitt, Secretary of the Interior under Bill Clinton, 1993-2001**

"A delightful, character-driven novel with a hero we can root for. Taz Blackwell is wise and knowing with an unforgettable inner voice and a humor that is wickedly accurate. The writing is flawless. This novel is to be read slowly—for the pleasure of savoring each page."

> —**Robert J. Mrazek, award-winning author of the Jake Cantrell mysteries.**

"A vivid tour de force. Taz Blackwell is a swashbuckling antihero the reader can't help but like. Be prepared to follow him from one fascinating intrigue to another, and to delight in Yeager's superb writing along the way."

> —**Judith Mills, Author of *Blood of the Tiger*, Former Director: TRAFFIC wildlife-trade monitoring program in East Asia.**

"Indiana Jones meets Greta Thunberg! This is the action-adventure story for the reader who understands that 'global warming' may be the single most important problem facing us today. Yeager's capacity for describing the finest details of his settings, whether on Chincoteague Island, in the forests of Brazil, or the deserts of Northern Mexico, creates a full-blown "movie-in-your-head," and is it ever fun to watch! [The author's] rare combination of environmental expertise and political/diplomatic acumen provides the essential grist for a story that's at the very heart of the fight to protect the earth."

—Stacy Rhodes, Senior Foreign Serve Officer, U.S. Department of State.

Jaguar's Claw: A Taz Blackwell Intrigue

by Brooks Birdwell Yeager

© Copyright 2022 Brooks Birdwell Yeager

ISBN 978-1-64663-853-6

"Let's Start Again"
Copyright credit: Bap Kennedy
Publishing credit: Lonely Street Music

Published by

köehlerbooks™

3705 Shore Drive
Virginia Beach, VA 23455
800-435-4811
www.koehlerbooks.com

To Brenda Kennedy with my thanks.

jaguar's claw

A Taz Blackwell Intrigue

brooks birdwell yeager

VIRGINIA BEACH
CAPE CHARLES

Pour l'enfant, amoureux de cartes et d'éstampes,
L'univers est égal à son vaste appétit.
Ah! que le monde est grand a la clarté des lampes!

✒

To a child who is fond of maps and charts
the universe is the size of his immense hunger.
Ah! how vast is the world in the light of a lamp!

Charles Baudelaire

THE RUN FROM REYNOSA

TAZ'S ROUTE THROUGH THE AMAZON

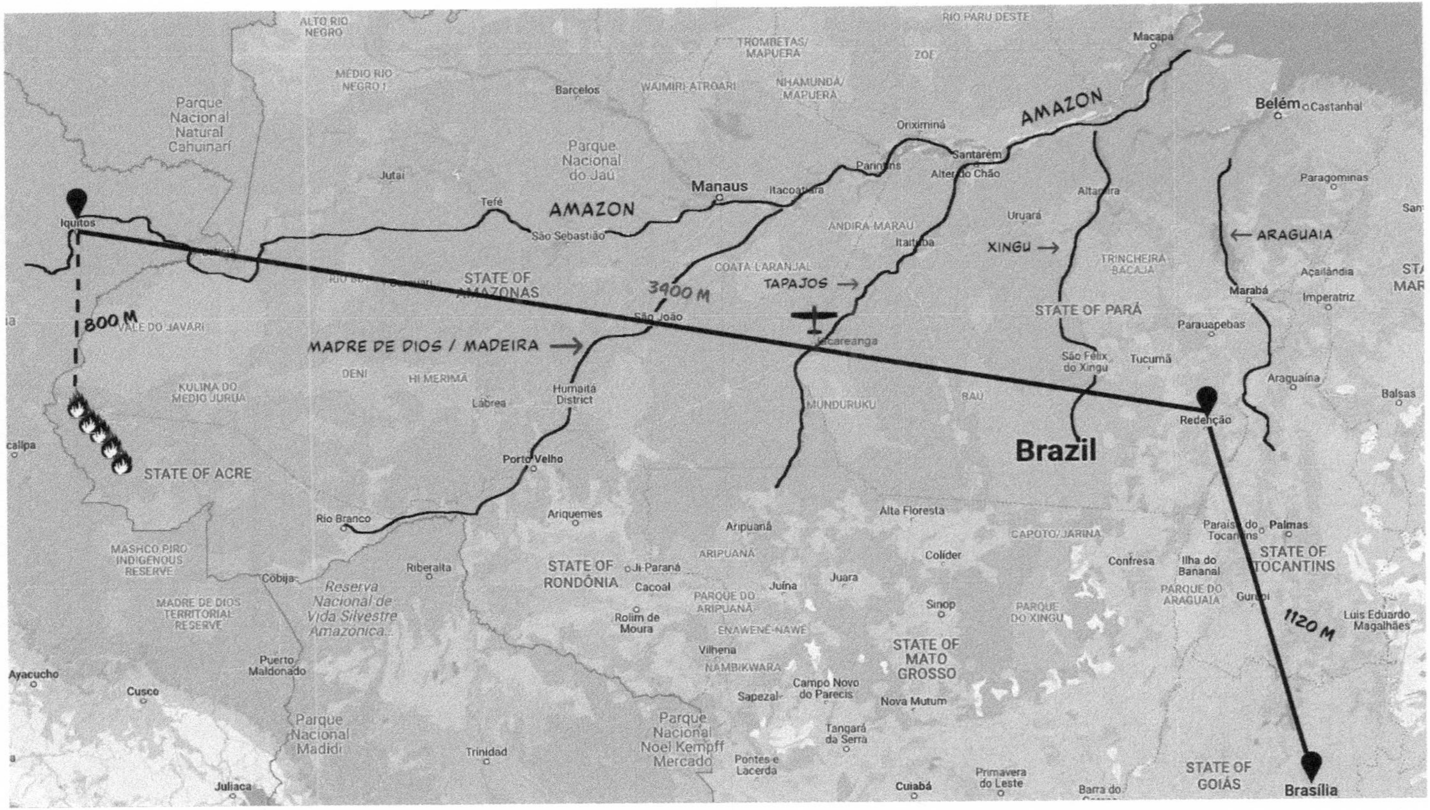

CHAPTER ONE

Hello Stranger

LIFE HAS A WAY OF moving on. The weather changes for better or worse, friends come and go, surprises wait around the corner, realities make themselves felt. You adjust, tacking into the wind or sailing large before it. Heartbreaks recede into memory. Wounds heal. Your wake lengthens behind you. Your horizon still appears far away. And so Taz Blackwell sailed on. Only sometimes it seemed more like rowing.

He had promised himself not to play the romantic fool again. Two times was plenty; the first drove him to the Island, the second nearly drove him off again. The scars from folly number two were still tender.

Taz was counting on a quiet day. He had two reports to finish for State's spooks—the Bureau of Intelligence, Narcotics, and Research. INR's check would cover his immediate expenses, not to mention clearing his tab at the Pony Pines, the Island's only bar of note. As to the mortgage on the waterman's cottage he called *Dachateague,* the next payment would have to wait for the check from the World Bank. The one to pay for the time spent on a report for his friend Valentina Belin, the director of the Bank's environment program. Her request had been urgent—they always were—but the Bank's payment schedule was correspondingly relaxed. Taz had kept her voicemail. Valentina was Bulgarian by birth, and Taz enjoyed the Balkan rhythms and dark tones of her voice.

> *"Taz. Shake the sand out of your shoes. I need your help. An independent look at the final draft of our forest conservation strategy. Looks to me like they're papering over a lot of problems. Our forest loan program in a dozen countries depends on getting it right. You were one of the culprits who got the damn thing started. You owe me. Oh, yeah . . . love, Valentina."*

There were days now when all that seemed so far away. The world of tense late-night negotiations and boring banquets, of deals and runarounds, alliances and deceptions, and words, words, words. The presidency had changed hands and the new denizens of the West Wing were markedly unmoved by his briefings on the country's environmental challenges. Soon enough, the political purge he knew was coming reached his level and he was liberated from the diplomatic grind, perhaps for good.

The interruption in his career had coincided with the dissolution of his marriage and left him little reason to hang on in the nation's capital. He took refuge on the Island. After five years, and despite his second romantic fiasco, he had few regrets. These days, he made his living doing odd carpentry jobs, giving guitar lessons, and consulting, which his local friends dubbed "running errands" for his former colleagues. Sometimes the errands meant producing policy analyses for State's upper echelons or assisting the formulation of diplomatic strategies. Other errands were more operational. The last mission of that kind had pitted him against the Russian ambassador to Iceland, and very nearly cost him his life.

When work slowed, or on the gray and wet days, he read. Napier's history of the Napoleonic war in Spain. The Colombian novelist Alvaro Mutis. Flann O'Brien's Irish comic masterpiece, *At Swim-Two-Birds:*

> *"Is it life? I would rather be without it," he said, "for there is queer small utility in it."*

Taz opened a new recording by Lucinda Williams. He sat at the kitchen table, listening closely as the Louisiana songstress cycled her blues-drenched voice through moods from loneliness and a tired resignation to defiance and a steely determination to go on. He kept looking at the telephone pad with his list of chores. A good day to spend some time ripping out the rotten dock planking that had been nagging at him all winter. Or to load and haul the half ton of broken cinderblock riprap that he needed to protect his marsh grass. He only had about a hundred and fifty feet of shoreline on Chincoteague Bay, but he figured that if he correctly shaped the riprap, it would hold enough marsh grass to shelter at least a small colony of mud fiddlers, snails, mussels, baby blue crabs, and migrating elvers.

First, the dishes. He handwashed the glasses and the few plates and forks. He considered his dog-eared to-do list for a moment, smiled to himself, turned it over, and threw on a threadbare yellow beach shirt. Retrieved his old cherry-red dreadnought guitar and pocketed a bottleneck, a capo, and picks. With his guitar in one hand, he used the other to pour some black coffee, which he carried steaming to the front stoop. He sat on the hard-brush welcome mat; the cracked concrete of the steps was still cold.

It wouldn't be cold for long. The sun had shed its cloud cover and was just beginning to enforce its warmth on the early morning. Taz nestled the guitar on his thigh and fingered the strings. Tried a few scales and then some random noodles, a little Travis picking, some arpeggios. Moved on to a few of Jerry Garcia's solo lines. Jerry had been the melodic and spiritual inspiration of the Grateful Dead, his favorite band after Count Basie. Taz had learned the styles and tunes he played by ear, and the best way he knew to sharpen his chops, as the jazz players would put it, was to get as close as he could to Garcia's free-wheeling sense of melody. When he found a hook, he explored it, relaxed into its groove, then tried a variation or two, enjoying the feeling of happy anarchy that allows a melody to sing, float, trip over itself, and return home.

A flash out of the corner of his eye; two lithe young women in yoga outfits running down South Main in his direction. They smiled and waved as they passed. Short-time come-heres getting their late morning exercise.

Taz raised his picking hand to wish them well. He recalled seeing the duo wandering through the Saturday market on the grassy expanse outside the Church Street Community Center. He had them at their mid-to-late twenties. They had drawn the attention of most of the men in the crowd. That is, until various wives and significant others gave their partners a gentle nudge—or, if required, a strategic elbow. When they left, the blonde slid into a yellow Fiat convertible with blue and gold plates, and the dark-haired one jumped into a shiny, maroon Jeep. Taz's friend Cliff Custis, who sold the middle and top-neck clams he dug at fifteen dollars a fifty-count bag, and often unloaded forty net bags on a sunny market morning, smiled with him as they drove off. "You don't see that every day."

The blonde was running closest to Taz. Just as they reached the corner at Beebe Road, her partner braked, circled back, stopped in front of him, hands on knees, dark eyes on his, breathing hard. "Sorry. How much farther to the end of the Island?" Sweating, catching her breath, trying her best to smile. Her black hair tinged with red and cut just short enough to reveal her neck and shoulders.

Taz's attention remained fixed on a chord progression that he knew damn well he didn't have right. After a moment he looked up. "That's kind of an existential question. Are we talking miles or years?"

She straightened and made the sign of the cross. Rolled her eyes. Took a deep breath. "Save me Lord. *Miles?*"

"Two, maybe a little more. You'll see a little bohemian trailer camp on your right, and a big marina on your left. There's one other hard-to-miss signal. You won't be able to go any farther south without a swimsuit."

She shook her head. "Can't laugh . . . breathing too hard. Gotta run. Maybe later?" She mopped a little sweat off her brow, brushed her hair out of her eyes, trotted back towards her pal, patted her on the backside, whispered something in her ear. A quick glance back at Taz and they were on their way.

Taz tried a few tunes, fingerpicking and shimmying the bottleneck for another quarter of an hour or so. Then he leaned his guitar against the rusty iron piping that served as a rail for his front steps. A little sun wouldn't do the soundboard any harm. He finished the last of his coffee and watched a trawler chug south towards the Chincoteague Inlet. Smiled at the raucous cries of the laughing gulls that trailed the boat like a plume of white and black cinders floating above a burning house. He reflected on the lamentable state of his love life, which had barely risen from the ashes of his romance with Dana Bonner. Dana was Taz's second romantic failure, the one that about blew him off the Island. He hadn't seen anyone in the year since they called it quits, at least not for any length of time—hadn't wanted to. Life was certainly less complicated that way. Sometimes, he even thought he liked it, or at least that's what he told Laney. Laney Langer, his closest friend on the island and the co-owner of Rainy Day Books, a Chincoteague institution for two decades.

Taz's friends, his guitars, and his surroundings kept him well enough entertained. On the hard days, he grabbed his binoculars and biked to the beach to watch the shorebirds or climbed in his truck to explore the backroads of the Eastern Shore.

Taz visited the bathroom and then lifted another longneck from the refrigerator, thinking about which of the INR reports he should turn to first. The beer was reassuringly cold. He found the church key and pried off the top. Caught the sound of women's voices, seemingly close by. He took a look back through the screen door. The two runners, now exhausted, were sitting on his stoop, sweating, still breathing hard, admiring the view. He stood in front of the refrigerator for a minute, weighing the potential entertainment value of joining them against the looming deficit in his accounts. The bottle was beading with condensation as he took his first step towards the stoop.

The two runners looked up as the screen door closed behind him. Using his hand like the bill of a baseball cap, he slowly scanned the horizon. "Any port in a storm?"

"Oh, come on." Deep breath. "You have a nice view." The black-haired one with the ironic smile, looking up towards him and shielding her eyes from the sun. "You should share it. I bet you can do the *welcome, stranger* thing better than that."

"I'm a little out of practice." He glanced at her and pointed to the sign at the entrance to his dock. Six feet off the ground, crimson, the size of an extra-long license plate. A silhouette of a tortoise and the words *Fear the Turtle* etched in black. The symbol of the University of Maryland Terrapins—the Terps, to their fans. Taz wasn't much interested in college football. He had played soccer in college. That and baseball were the sports he enjoyed, but he liked turtles, and the message was occasionally helpful.

The black-haired one rolled her eyes and made a sound halfway between a yelp and a sneeze. "Oh, sure! That will *definitely* keep the bad guys away."

Taz gave her an appraising look. "And the bad girls at bay. At least that's what they told me when I bought it." She shrugged and averted her eyes. Turned again, settled a quizzical gaze on him. Her dark hazel-green eyes showed flecks of gold as the gaze made way for a hesitant smile that was easy enough to return.

"Soooo . . . right. I should've known it wouldn't work. I found it in the hermits' aisle at the Dollar Store." She closed her eyes and gave a polite little snort. Taz rambled on. "Let's start again. Welcome to *Chez Taz!* You must be parched after your run. I'll bet you could use some water."

"We brought our own water." Hazel-eyes again. She made a little duck call out of the corner of her mouth and smiled, pointing to a half-empty Perrier in her hip holder. She wasn't about to make this easy.

"Well, that is a problem." Taz ran his fingers through his hair. "I've got orange juice . . . and . . . I think cranberry." The dark one, eyebrows raised, seemed less than impressed. "Right — two-thirds of a sunrise." He sighed. "Out of tequila." She drummed her fingers lightly on her lips. He could swear her eyes actually twinkled. Two strikes, one more swing. "However, I do make a hell of a mimosa."

The blonde leapt to the bait. "Mimosas!" Hazel-eyes smiled, nodded her assent. Taz headed back to the kitchen, wondering at the detour his day appeared to be taking. He pulled a bottle of cava and some grapefruit juice from the refrigerator. Found a glass beer pitcher in the lower cabinet, opened the ice drawer, and started ice-mining; his freezer tended to cycle up and down around the freezing point, and the ice frequently congealed into unwieldy clumps. He used a screwdriver to wedge two large agglomerations off either side, tossed them on the cutting board. Called in the direction of the front door, "I could use a little help in here, you know."

The feisty one appeared in the door frame. She walked slowly through his rather simple wood-paneled living room, casting a quick gaze here and there. Over the winter, Taz had replaced the old pine slat walls with birds-eye maple fitted on a forty-five-degree slant. The maple shone in the morning light from the two windows facing the side of the front stairs. She brushed the satin surface with her fingers, looked his way with a smile. "You?" He nodded, eyed the ice, reached in the bottom drawer for a hammer. "You have a good eye for wood."

She paused on the dividing line between the old oak flooring of the living room and the linoleum in the kitchen, as if she was unsure he'd want her to enter. Taz turned her way, dipped his head towards the little round kitchen table. "Despite what you may have heard, I don't bite." She smiled hesitantly, stepping to the right to avoid blocking his way to the refrigerator. Stood on the other side of the table with what Taz figured was an unfortunately good view of his bedroom, past the louvered sliding doors that his friend Jimmy had helped him install two years back.

Which were wide open. *Not much to see,* Taz reflected, except a cheap chest of drawers, a yellowing poster from *Les Enfants du Paradis* that he had found in Paris years before, and a writing table piled with books. At least he had straightened the bedcovers.

He pulled a glass beer pitcher from beneath the sink. Made himself busy bashing the ice clusters with the side of the hammer, a process he hoped might distract her from further investigations. His third hammer blow launched a cluster of ice cubes off the cutting board and sent it skittering across his little round breakfast table like a hockey puck. She caught it one-handed as it flew off her side of the tabletop. Without thinking, Taz tossed out the line old-time baseball announcers used when a fan of the female persuasion caught a foul ball. "Gold glove for the lady in the front row."

An arch smile as she came around the table to slide the chunk slowly into the pitcher: "So how can I help? I mean since you have the ice thing so well under control."

"Yeah." Taz grimaced, using the hammer to point to the upper cabinet above the kitchen sink. "There are some champagne flutes up there." She stretched unselfconsciously to reach the top shelf, the easy arch of her back flexing as she plucked the glasses one at a time. A graceful turn as she placed them on the table with more care than they deserved. He trained his eyes on the pitcher while he poured the juice and the cava. She smiled, aware of his interest, then turned and gently rubbed the back of the nearest of his wood-slatted kitchen chairs, watching him mix the mimosas, swirling the chunks of ice that had actually managed to make their way into the pitcher. Straight stance, shoulders back, she was within two or three inches of his five-foot-eleven. Dark eyes with a hazel tint, keenly intelligent. An ironic but attractive smile. Not at all nervous. She carried herself with a certain confidence that suggested she could be fierce. A narrow waist leading to slim hips and long legs. Exquisite standing there, supple when she moved. He did his best to resist smiling.

She lowered her gaze briefly, amused by the evident impact she was having on him. Then she continued her visual tour, allowing her eyes to linger on his corner cabinet, where he had a heavy copper ashtray with a small collection of carved birds, a turtle carved from ironwood, and a hand-cast golden raven amulet that had been given to him by a friend from Norway's far north. He followed her progress with an amused smile. "Do I pass inspection?"

She brought her eyes back to him. "Totally charming. Home away from home?"

"Just home."

For a brief moment, their eyes locked. Hers held a question. "You've done a lot of work on it."

"It's pretty quiet here in the winter."

She raised her eyebrows, then continued survey. Her sweep was arrested by the gallon-jug of Tabasco on the corner of the counter nearest the stove. "There must be a story behind that."

"There is. But it's a long one."

A short laugh. "Of course. The deepest, darkest, spiciest Tabasco secret of all. You can't reveal that to just anyone." Her voice was infused with a kind of comic sarcasm, and a smile had just begun to light the corners of her eyes.

Taz handed her mimosa number three, took the first two in either hand. Bowed slightly and swept his left arm low and backhand to suggest that she take the first steps to the door.

When they got back to the stoop, the feisty one's pal was fingering Taz's guitar, trying to strum a few basic chords. Her straw-colored hair was fixed in a slightly ragged bun. Blue eyes. Freckles. Nice smile. She had the build of a serious athlete—strong arms and shoulders, a runner's calves. "Sorry, I was just curious. But I can't make the chords work." Frustrated. "I didn't think you would mind."

Taz placed his mimosa on the brush mat, put hers on the step next to her. "I don't. But she's in a different tuning than you're used to."

"There's more than one? Tuning, I mean?" She strummed another discord and grimaced. The feisty one found a place next to her on the second step.

"Sure." He smiled. It wasn't the time for a long explanation. He sat back on the upper step, tasted his mimosa with a smile. Glanced at the blond. "The mimosa—you're meant to drink it." He bent and cupped his ear to listen. "It's feeling unloved." Took a long sip from his, his eyes on her. She laughed and followed suit.

"So, you speak mimosa?" Hazel-eyes, smiling, pert. "Or who knows? Maybe you're multilingual."

"I'm fluent in martini. But I've only just begun flirting with negroni." Her eyes went beyond a smile to something more like merriment. "It's really quite complex. Grammatically, I mean. Maintaining correct syntax becomes almost impossible after three."

She rolled her eyes again, but she couldn't entirely suppress a laugh, covering her mouth with the back of her hand. Her friend—Taz had decided she would be called Sandy—was watching the exchange, her arm resting easily on the guitar. "I'm just starting lessons. You sounded good as we were passing by. How long have you been playing?"

"Since high school."

"Wow, that's a long time."

He winced. "Ouch."

"That didn't come out quite right, did it?"

The dark-eyed one rescued them, gently lifting the guitar out of Sandy's hand. "Play us something?" With great care, she handed him the Guild D-25 dreadnought that he'd been playing since he was seventeen, bought with summer money made driving pilings in creek bottoms for the Palo Pinto County survey crew. All mahogany, a little worn and nicked, particularly around the pickguard, with the dark cherry finish that Guild bestowed on a few of their better models.

"Sure." Taz thought for a few moments. He caressed the guitar, tapped a random rhythm on the pickguard. Hazel eyes was having difficulty disguising her doubt that he'd be any better than the college boys who built entire repertoires on three folk chords.

Taz scratched his neck, still undecided. Finally strummed a modified D chord, then the opening of "Hello Stranger." He played it fingerstyle, using a church lick, the way Mother Maybelle did in her famous 1930 recording session.

> *Hello stranger*
> *Put your loving hand in mine*
> *Hello stranger*
> *Put your loving hand in mine*
> *You are a stranger*
> *And you're a friend of mine.*
>
> *Well I'll see you*
> *When your troubles are like mine*
> *I'll see you*
> *When your troubles are like mine*
> *Yes, I'll see you*

When you haven't got a dime.

Raven. Somewhere after the second verse, Taz decided that was what she should be called. She had the crooked smile of a trickster. So, there were only three choices, really. *Fox, Coyote, Raven.* It had to be Raven. The subtle flashes of red in her black hair shone, and she was light on her feet, as if she could take flight at any moment. Now she looked down, then turned to meet his eye.

"So. A girl makes one snarky comment. And you come back with that? For God's sake don't tell me you just made it up!"

"It's a Carter family tune. Doesn't get much airtime on top-forty radio."

"Which is what you imagine I listen to?" Indignant.

Taz shifted his guitar under his left arm and leaned forward so that his chin rested on the heel of his right hand. He pondered the question. "Actually, I see you more as the techno type."

"You know, if I could reach you, I'd pop you one."

Taz laughed, thinking he might get to like her. Except she'd be gone by the weekend. He'd be better off not wading in too deep. "Seriously, I doubt if you'd know most of the tunes I play. They're from the Dustbowl—the Depression era."

"The Depression? Really? Wasn't that kind of a long time ago? I mean, there's been a lot of music since then, you know, soul, rock, roll, punk, hip-hop, all of that. The Beatles, for God's sake."

"I just like the style."

"Hate to tell you, but you're not that old."

"Maybe I'm older than I look."

She snorted delicately. "Oh, for sure. You've got at least three years on me, practically grandfather material. And your guitar is a *she?* Now that's old." Wagged her finger at him, the way a soccer player denies a foul. "You could be tagged with a gender *faux pas*—and being a senior citizen won't protect you."

Taz turned to Sandy, with a back-hand hitchhiker's thumb in Raven's direction. "You didn't tell me your pal was with the gender police. But I guess it figures, being from California and all."

"How did you—"

Raven jumped in. "Right. That'd be the coast that's actually made it out of the nineteenth century." She shot him a dirty look. Taz continued fixing his eyes on Sandy.

"You're a long way from home."

"Tell me. Seems like we've been through every state in between." Nodded at Raven. "She's never seen a detour she didn't want to take."

"Me either. The most interesting paths start as detours, don't you think?"

Raven seemed at a loss for words. "You don't seem like an Easterner all that much. You're not uptight enough. So does your guitar have a name?"

"Big Sister."

"That's kind of an odd name for a guitar, isn't it? Aren't you supposed to give it a real name? I mean BB King called his Lucille."

"She's the eldest member of my little guitar family, you know, the bossy one. I'll introduce you sometime, I mean if you're really interested."

She raised an eyebrow at the challenge. "You don't trust me at all, do you?"

"I didn't want to presume."

"Maybe you're being a little too careful."

"After a good enough sunburn, you can't blame someone for using sunscreen."

She looked him in the eye. "I wonder. Maybe, if you ever *deign* to tell me about the sacred Tabasco, we could discuss the ups and downs of sunscreen. I've heard that if a person uses too much, it can have some unintended side effects—even freeze you right up."

Sandy piped up: "Any chance of an encore?"

"Sure, if you want." Taz looked over his shoulder and lifted the bottleneck, put it in the pocket of his shirt. The cloth was so threadbare it barely disguised the bronze color of the glass. He thought for a second and pulled it back out.

Raven looked at it in horror. "Wait. Did you get that out of a dumpster? That's not even a real slide. You're going to play that beautiful guitar with something that looks like it came off a broken wine bottle?"

Taz shook his head, suppressed a smile. He slipped the bottleneck on the ring finger of his left hand, swept it up the neck to get the high shimmying tones he was looking for and then began double thumbing a blues scale for the bass. It was a sound he'd liked since he first heard Blind Willie McTell as a teenager.

> *If I lose, let me lose,*
> *I don't care how much I lose*
> *If I lose a hundred dollars*
> *while I'm trying to win a dime,*
> *'cause my baby,*
> *she's got money all the time.*

Raven grinned. "Ooh, I like that one. Cavalier."

He played another verse or two. "From the thirties. Charlie Poole and the North Carolina Ramblers. *Cavalier* is a good word for them."

Sandy, staring at him, open-mouthed. "How . . . where did you learn to play like that?" Her cell phone lit. She listened for a few seconds, then turned to Raven. "We've got to go."

Raven was sitting on the first step, Taz on the third. She looked up at him with a question in her eyes. "I don't even know your name."

"Taz. Taz Blackwell." He was about to ask hers, thought better of it. Didn't really matter; it wasn't like he was going to see her again anyway. "And by the way, where I'm from, both coasts look pretty good."

"Okay, I have to ask."

"Mineral Wells." She was completely at a loss. "Texas—*west* Texas. The Brazos country—out where it starts to get dry."

Raven, somewhat abashed, said, "Aren't you a surprise." Regaining her composure, she continued, "Well, Señor Taz from Texas, let's say I'm actually interested in antiquarian music. Where do I go? I mean to slake my thirst for your catalog of happy tunes from yesteryear?"

Taz liked how quickly she coined a phrase. "There's an eight o'clock jam on Friday at the Rainy Day bookshop. South end of the downtown business district, just by the old bridge. That's why I'm practicing."

Sandy reappeared, snapping her cell phone shut. "Doesn't seem like you need a lot of practice."

"Trust me, we all do."

Sandy put her lips to Raven's ear, whispered something that Taz didn't try to work out. Raven pulled herself up, took the first step to the street. A glance over her shoulder: "We're having dinner with some friends that night. So, if we don't make your jam, it's not that we aren't—I'm not—interested."

Taz offered a silent toast with the remains of his mimosa.

Raven and Sandy exchanged a private look, sprang off the stoop, and trotted up Main Street. After they had run past at least twelve houses, Taz watched to see which one they were staying in. He was pretty sure they turned in at the driveway of the only other yellow house on his end of the Island.

CHAPTER TWO

Getting to Know You

A GULF FRONT HAD MOVED in overnight, and Wednesday dawned warm and damp. The temperature hit the eighties by seven, and Taz found himself devoutly wishing that he had done the damn chores yesterday, as he'd meant to. If not for his unexpected visitors, that is. Their momentary diversion had scotched his interest in pounding nails or pulling weeds, and the two mimosas had made writing a report on the security implications of the EU's recent maritime directive totally out of the question. After they left, Taz had bicycled to the beach and taken a long run. He found a palm warbler, a Louisiana heron, and two little blues who had flown in early from the Carolinas. In retrospect, the day looked more worthwhile. But now, on an April morning that was already ten degrees hotter than the average for May, he was kneeling on his dock listening to the sporadic rattle of a clammer's skiff on the other side of the Queen Sound marshes and using a cat's paw to pry rusty nails out of over a dozen warped and rotted planks. He had a stack of new two-by-six pressure-treated boards leaning on the bulkhead. He had sweated through his T-shirt, which had once been red but was now a mottled pink from too many washings. His khakis were dirty, he had torn one leg of his pants carelessly kneeling on a half-pulled nail, which nicked his knee as well, and now there was a little trail of dried blood down from the tear.

He finished nailing the first of the new planks, dropped the hammer, and settled back on his haunches, sniffing the marsh reek, and watching little wisps of steam come off the water. It was slack tide, and the channel was as still as a pane of glass. There was a sound behind him. A little cough, hard to hear over the distant burst of the clammer's engine. He looked back towards the cottage. Raven stood at the edge of the street, watching him.

"Hi." Her Jeep was parked straddling the sidewalk two houses up towards town.

"Hi." He wasn't sure what else to say.

"Looks like maybe you could use some help again."

"You're too well dressed." She looked almost cool in a loose pink short-sleeved cotton blouse over well-worn blue jeans. "And what I need is to cozy up to an air conditioner. You could join me if you like."

"I don't know. Suzy thinks we're going out to lunch." *Suzy.* Taz filed the name away. "Really, I just dropped by to thank you for your hospitality yesterday. The conversation and all. I enjoyed meeting you, but I probably shouldn't." He looked at his watch, raised his eyebrows. He was curious about this one. She had a way of making his best-laid plans fade into the background. "No kidding. I only have a few minutes."

They ended up in the kitchen, enjoying the cool air and talking over the occasional rattle and hum of the window unit in his bedroom. Taz had changed into a pale olive short-sleeved button-down, and was now leaning over the aluminum sink, splashing cold water on his face. He turned in her direction.

"There's wine in the fridge. The glasses are . . . well, you know where they are."

"If I didn't know better, I'd say you're trying to get me to stay."

"I just thought you looked thirsty."

"You know, I am."

He opened his hands. "Yesterday, that was the last of the cava." She looked positively grief-stricken. "Come see for yourself." The miscellaneous collection on the rack of the refrigerator door included a bottle of vermouth, a Chablis, a Riesling with German lettering so archaic it couldn't be read, and a pinot grigio from the Alto Adige. He was still holding the handle. She reached and pulled out the Italian. Turned it to read the label.

"I don't know, they all look good. But what's the Alto Adige? And why not?" Taz felt a little rush of relief. he had been saving the Chablis for Saturday evening, when the attractive thirty-ish woman who owned the bakery on Maddox—Ava—had said she'd drop by with one of her famous apple tarts. Sort of an extra-curricular delivery.

He reached for the bottle, spotted the glasses on the table. Raven watched him, smiling. Taz's initial vexation faded in the face of a growing sense of amusement. "It's the landscape between Venice and the Austrian Alps." He retrieved his waiter's corkscrew—the kind with a double-jointed lever. It took him about twelve seconds to strip the foil and open the wine.

"Why don't you use one of those horrible things with wings, like everybody else? You're not an amateur at this, are you."

"Of course I am. A pro would be able to tell the wines apart."

She giggled, put her hand palm-up above her eyes as if to shield them from the sun, and hiccupped. Once. Twice. Once more. Bent over and coughed out, "Water, please." Another hiccup. Her cheeks glowed pink.

"I can do better than that." He poured a glass of the wine, placed it carefully in her hand. She looked at him with watery eyes and that slightly crooked smile.

Taz found himself gazing back. *Pretty* was not the right word. Maybe *striking.* Her hair was curly and attractively disheveled, parted on the right side, cut short enough to highlight her neck in the nicest way. She had the straight and delicate nose frequently encountered in Persian women. Her deep almond-shaped eyes shaded imperceptibly from a dark brown to hazel, under carefully trimmed black eyebrows.

She finally caught her breath. "Come on, really. If you didn't know what you're doing, your refrigerator would be filled with plonk, just like most of my boyfriends."

The plural caught his attention. "So, where are all these boyfriends, and why don't you have two or three with you?"

"Oh, I didn't mean it like that. I'm just pals with a whole crew in California—Davis and Sacramento. Most of us went to college together at UC Davis. Quite a while ago." She put her hand on the back of the chair by her side and asked a question with her eyes.

He nodded, twisted the cork off the corkscrew and slipped it back in the drawer. "And you still hang out together? Must be a fun bunch."

"Most of the time, yes. Lately I've been waking up desperate for a change of scenery."

"I guess that explains why you've put three thousand miles on your pal's odometer just to get to a beach where the waves are about half the size of the curlers at Pescadero." A cold little beach off Highway One halfway between San Francisco and Santa Cruz. "And that's right after a hurricane."

Raven gave him a puzzled look. "I thought you said you were from Texas."

"I am."

"How does somebody from Texas know about Pescadero? It's hidden so well even half the folks who live on that stretch of the coast can't find it."

"I once built a sweat lodge on the bluffs above the beach. With a Paiute friend named Charles Kills-Enemies."

"A sweat lodge? Right off Highway One?"

Taz just smiled. "On that big rise about a half-mile north of Duarte's restaurant, so it couldn't be seen from the road."

She squinted as if he had lied under oath. "So, if you like waves, why Pescadero instead of Half Moon Bay?" Chin up. A challenge.

Taz chuckled, turned to the window. His friend Teddy was nailing trim on the house next door. The previous adornment had been blown halfway to China by last year's fourth nor'easter.

"Pescadero is the only place I know north of Santa Cruz where you can get outside the surf line and swim without freezing your ass off in the California Current. Also, when I used to surf I did it without a board, and the waves at Half Moon Bay, well, I have this strange desire to stay alive."

She lowered her head to the right, smiled knowingly. "Let's see, you live on an island. You're an ocean guy. You've got too much edge for La-La Land, but you've spent time on the northern California coast. You must have been studying out there. Oceanography? Maybe at Santa Cruz. Some of my grad school friends started there."

"That probably would have been a better choice, but I couldn't deal with a school with a banana slug for a mascot."

"So now we know where you didn't go and what you didn't study there...."

Taz rolled his eyes. "Philosophy at Stanford."

"Jesus. That must have been a barrel of laughs. Particularly with those snoots."

"Trust me. There was no way to survive if you didn't have a good sense of humor."

"So, shouldn't you be a professor somewhere?"

"Do I look likely?"

She regarded his faded shirt and his ragged-leg khakis with a supremely skeptical eye. "Not even close."

"What, then?" He waited for the quip that would lay him low.

"Not sure. Maybe a river guide. Or a drug smuggler." Glanced away, as if she felt a little vulnerable. "Or a bad guy in a B movie. Even better, a rodeo clown—okay, without the makeup."

"I like the range of possibilities."

"I guess that's the point."

He pulled out a chair for her, sat on the other side of the little round table that served him for breakfast and dinner—and as a computer stand. "Meanwhile, you're sort of a cross-country beachcomber—an *Endless Summer* type. Either that, or a travel writer, or a nomad queen. You're three thousand miles from home. And judging by the red clay on the carriage of that Fiat, you didn't get here in a straight line. You're looking for something. Have you found it?"

A quiet smile, eyes on her wine. After a few moments she got up and began a more leisurely scan, brushed her hand lightly over the surface of his small quarter-circle corner stand. Her fingers stopped at the heavy copper ashtray. Looked a question at Taz. He nodded his assent, watched as she examined a coin and then picked up the raven.

"What a wonderful . . . what do you call it? A pendant?"

"It's missing a necklace. Without it, I guess it's an amulet." She smiled, placed it back with care. Then she picked up a hand-carved turtle. Its shell was just a little too big to fit easily into her palm. She hefted it, surprised at its weight. Shot another quick glance at Taz.

"Florida Ironwood. One of the densest woods in the world, right up there with South African leadwood. A friend carved it for me from a tree that lightning had killed, just outside the Loxahatchie Refuge." She caressed it, ran her finger over the shell, feeling the indentations that marked it as a diamondback. Put it back and stepped to the refrigerator and retrieved the wine bottle. Handed it to Taz. Sat at the table once again. He filled their glasses, waited, then raised his eyebrows to renew his question.

"Not yet. I'm looking for someplace where I can do my work. Someplace with a university nearby that I could use as a home base. It would have to be easy to fly in and out of. Better if it's near the ocean. I didn't get much of that where I grew up. And it wouldn't be bad if there were some people I was going to like. I mean, at least one." She said the last totally deadpan, looking steadily at Taz. "In a pinch." She ventured a tentative smile, then quickly changed the subject. "You made that bottleneck, didn't you? You didn't just find it in a dumpster."

"My dumpster-diving days were some time ago." She arched her eyebrows, wondering. "The slide used to be attached to a bottle of port—a tawny from the Rojas vineyard on the Douro. Port bottles tend to have nice long necks." He glanced down, caught her eye. "Like yours." He took a moment; watching Raven blush was its own reward. "It's simple. You score the neck with a diamond cutter, soak a string in lighter fluid, wrap it around the score mark and light it on fire, plunge the bottle into an ice-water bath, and then snap it off."

Raven caressed her neck slowly, as if to make sure it would not be available for Taz's broken-bottle process. He refilled her glass.

"What sort of work do you do?"

She looked surprised. "I'm a wildlife biologist. I study panthers."

"So, you're a wildlife biologist and you like the coast. Shouldn't you be talking to dolphins?"

"We didn't have dolphins where I was raised—the Pit River country—northern California. But we did have cougars."

"Just don't tell me you were talking to them."

"Well, actually—"

Her cell phone growled. Once, twice. She gave a wan smile and found it in the back pocket of her jeans. Listened for a few seconds. "Suzy. I have to go. Nice talking to you. And thanks for this."

She drained the rest of her wine, smiled, and walked out the door.

CHAPTER THREE

Thirsty Boots

A QUIET MORNING. TAZ ENJOYED the early hours with the help of a hot cup of black coffee. He had spent the evening before reading the first volume of Napier's *History of the Peninsular War* in a losing effort to divert his attention from an annoyingly persistent replay of little bits and pieces of his conversation with Raven, of her voice, her smile. Napier had finally done the trick—put him to sleep.

He finished what passed for breakfast, put an LP by the Dixie Chicks on the turntable he had bought to cheer himself up after he and Dana split. He took a perverse pleasure in referring to it as a *phonograph* in company, perhaps as a way of acknowledging a certain fondness for relics. He liked the song where Natalie Maines spits fire at the Nashville music czars. Her lyrical anger carried him through the ritual morning dishwashing. Then the sound faded, and he found himself thinking back yet again to his conversation with Raven. She was a walking self-contradiction—sharp and yet ingenuous, fierce in one moment and fragile the next. A good sense of humor, but with a current of sadness that seemed to flow somewhere behind those smiling eyes. That made him wonder. Still, she wasn't going to stick around. He thought for a second about Ava and Saturday night. What he liked most these days was a good pastry. He wasn't looking for a full-course meal.

The sound of crows interrupted his train of thought. His cell phone, back in the kitchen, lit up like a Christmas tree. He walked slowly over to the little round table, now serving as a computer stand, and answered.

A woman's voice. Taz made out the Portuguese phrase for *please hold*—"*Por favor, espere,*" and then the name Martins, or, as the dusky voice pronounced it, "*Marteens.*" After a pause and some random clicking, he heard a familiar baritone. Everton Martins, who had led the negotiation of the Biodiversity Convention's forest conservation protocol for the G-77—the Group of Developing Countries—a powerful negotiating bloc in the UN system and in global negotiations. Taz had led the negotiations for the US. Everton was a senior envoy for the Brazilian foreign ministry, a specialist in global environmental issues—the Wizard of Itamaraty. Pronounced *Itamarachi,* the name referred to the ministry's building in Brasilia. Think Foggy Bottom, Whitehall, Quai D'Orsay. He was one of the most subtle counterparts Taz had ever tangled with, and occasionally, a highly effective ally. Taz much preferred the ally mode. It had been at least four years since they last talked.

"Everton, to what do I owe the honor?"

"*Meu amigo*, I just had a most disturbing conversation with your new undersecretary of state, a Ms. Jessica Lansman."

Taz had heard about the appointment from his friend David Dalton, the State's lead negotiator on fishery issues. "Disturbing, why?"

"She informed me, and in quite a brusque manner, that you were no longer with the Foreign Service."

"Don't take it personally, Everton. She's brusque with everybody. Just give thanks you're not married to her. I worked with her when she was at the National Security Council. And she's right, I'm no longer at State. I had to resign when the new team came in. I thought you knew."

"I'm sorry to say I hadn't kept track. As you know I'm just back from my post in Geneva. I imagined you had been reassigned to a more important portfolio."

"There is no more important portfolio. You and I both know that."

"Well, that is of course increasingly obvious by the day. But for some reason, not everyone shares our opinion." Everton went on in his excellent if slightly formal English. "In any case, I hoped to ask Ms. Lansman to lend your services to us—to Brazil, that is. Since you're no longer in government, I'm calling now to ask you whether you would still be open to such an arrangement, if an agreement can be reached."

Taz thought about that for a few moments.

"Taz, are you still connected?"

"I guess, Everton, you better tell me what you have in mind. Even if I would be interested, I'd still have to check it with State."

"Please, Taz. I don't want to 'go around' Undersecretary Lansman. So just a preview if that's acceptable."

"All right."

"Taz, I'm hoping you might be willing to help us put together a program to combat wildland fire. You understand we have a new problem with fires on the margins of the Amazon, where the forest is broken up and the soils are drying. You worked with the senior managers of your government's wildland fire management team. The best in the world, and we all know it."

Taz thought through his list of commitments and consulting projects, of which there were far too few—at least ones that paid. That was bad enough, but he was bored as well. Reports and paperwork were not what he wanted to be doing; they were barely enough to keep him awake.

"Everton, my friend. Building a wildland fire response system is a long-term project—very long-term. But I'm willing to see if I can help you get something started, provided we can get the clearances we'll both need. We can review the details later."

"Excellent. I will arrange a call, perhaps at the end of next week? It would help if you would be willing to take the call in Ms. Lansman's office."

One thing was clear. Taz would have to talk to the senior managers at the Interagency Wildland Fire Management Team before he offered a full commitment. They were headquartered in Boise, Idaho. Taz had worked with them in his days as policy advisor to the secretary of the interior. Without their expertise, what Everton was asking for could never be accomplished. Taz would need to spend a few days in Boise before the call to the new undersecretary. He thought for a few seconds about who he should contact to arrange a visit. Then he returned to his dock and dangled a hand line for a while, but it seemed the crabs were just as bored as he had been before Everton's call. Not even a bite. Maybe time to head down to Rainy Day to see if he could find Richard or Laney.

Richard Langer pretended to be a curmudgeon. He was gruff, and sometimes it seemed complaining was his favorite sport. But he enjoyed talking about the news of the day and he could shed that hard shell faster than a peeler crab in the presence of new music or conversation with good friends. The last two qualities ensured that Taz would keep returning to Rainy Day's chessboard despite losing two-thirds of their games.

Coffee with Richard's wife was Taz's other addiction. Laney managed the bookstore's business side. Taz regarded her as the older sister he'd never had. It was Laney who sheltered him under her wing when he first came to live on the Island, trailing the shattered dreams of a broken marriage, and it was Laney who succored him after his relationship with Dana Bonner hit the rocks. But there was more than that. The two of them had something else in common—a view of the world as a place where comedy and sadness were inextricably entangled, and where a warm sense of irony could at times be the only salvation from the cold rigors of reality.

◆

A critical mass didn't gather at the Saturday jam until almost seven-thirty. Taz brought his guitars in through the back door. Richard sat behind the counter in case any music fans got bored and decided to go on a literary spree. Laney was reconciling accounts in the little first-floor office.

Taz made to take off his baseball cap, thought better of it. It struck him that the cap was appropriate for a night of the blues—waxed canvas crown the color of garnet, dark blue crab with the words *Suicide Bridge Restaurant* embroidered in copper on the front beneath the crease.

He parked his guitars by the romance novels. Retrieved his capo and bottleneck from the little compartment in Big Sister's case, slipped them in his pocket. Wiped his darling guitar down with the shammy cloth that was a permanent case fixture. Did the same for Teensy, his little acoustic cutaway, almost always tuned in open-G, what the old-timers called Spanish-style.

The crowd, a mix of come-heres and locals, had been good-humoredly twiddling their thumbs for at least a quarter of an hour. An ideal time for gossip and culture commentary.

There was a soft stir in the audience as Dan Whipple quietly made his way into the room. The deputy chief of the Island's small police force was a tall, angular man with buzz-cut white hair and a smile that could warm all but the most hardened hearts. He wore blue jeans and a checked shirt with the sleeves rolled up. Taz nodded towards an empty fold-up chair in the inner semicircle facing the chairs and sofas that their audience was starting to fill. He looked over the crowd. "Everybody. Welcome to the Swamp Possums' weekly skirmish. And please give a hand to our new mandolin player, Dan Whipple. I don't think he needs an introduction." Whipple smiled, opened his case, pulled out a vintage Gibson mandolin. Fingered it a few times. It was in perfect tune.

The Possums weren't so much a band as a revolving cast of friends. Newcomers were welcome as long as they could keep up, or better, lend something new to the mix. The core players had worked each other out pretty well over the years. Tom Axton, an ace harp player, with his hair swept back and looking a little like a skinny version of Paul Butterfield. Ronnie Ripton, in his sixties, who played guitar for the services at First Baptist. Riley Lapham, a young bluegrass fiddler with bright blue eyes and a blond ponytail.

Taz figured they should open with something up-tempo. Whispered to Tom behind the back of his hand, the way catchers do when they don't want the other team to read their lips or their signs. Tom nodded to Ronnie. He made a sign to Riley, who had a quiet word with the deputy chief.

They started with a Blind Willie McTell tune, "Love Changing Blues." Taz played lead on Teensy, sliding the blues notes with his bottleneck. They played a dozen bars just to get the tune's groove:

Get me one more glass
pour me some more good booze
My woman done left me
I got these love changin' blues.

The Possums were halfway into the tune when Sandy and Raven sidled through the crowd at the door and found the little available space along the back wall. Jesse Wilkins was making his way through the crush as well, carrying his ancient Epiphone bass guitar over his head. Taz's evening had just brightened considerably.

While Jesse was setting up, Taz surveyed the scene. Caught Raven's eye, tipped his cap in her direction. She was wearing a pair of red denims and a loose-sleeved black silk shirt. Sandy stood next to her in blue jeans and a pink cashmere sweater. The two of them could've stepped out of a Sundance catalog.

Ronnie had played with a rockabilly band before Riley was born. He suggested a Buddy Holly tune he was fond of. It fit Taz's mood perfectly. He launched a Bo Diddley rhythm on Big Sister and started singing the refrain:

You know love's made fools of men
You don't care, you're going to try it again
And when you're feeling sad and blue,
you know love's made a fool of you.

Taz was technically a baritone, but with a little medication he could push his voice up the register to a bluegrass tenor.

It can make you feel so good,
When it goes like you think it should,
But it can make you cry at night,
When your baby don't treat you right.

Tom and the deputy sheriff came in on harmony.

Time's a'goin,' it's passing fast

you think true love has come at last.
But when you're feeling sad and blue,
you know love's made a fool of you.

Happy applause and friendly hoots. Some "Alright's." Raven gave a wolf-whistle just loud enough to draw the attention of a few of Taz's friends in the audience. Sandy wore a big smile. She was eying Tom. Taz made himself busy tuning his already-tuned guitar.

He lifted his gaze to the folks standing at the back and played the first chords of a song he had just learned. It was by Bap Kennedy, a talented young songwriter from Belfast.

Let's not talk about the old days
You'll just make me cry
Sometimes love has no reason
And no rhyme
We have all the things we need
You and I,
But baby, baby,
We don't have much time.

Tom waited to let that one sink in and then started riffing on his harp. He was homing in on "New Minglewood Blues," one of the more stellar in a long line of '30s hits by Gus Cannon and His Jug Stompers. First covered thirty-five years later by the Grateful Dead, whose version was electric, hard-hitting, and yet totally faithful to the original. There wasn't another rock band on either side of the Atlantic that could've pulled it off. Taz picked it up on the second bar:

I was born in the desert, raised in a lion's den
I was born in the desert, raised in a lion's den
And my number one occupation is stealing women from their men.

Well I'm a wanted man in Texas, busted jail and I'm gone for good

I'm a wanted man in Texas, busted jail and I'm gone for good
Well the sheriff couldn't catch me, but his little girl sure wished he
would.

Yes and the doctor call me crazy, some says I am some says I ain't.
Yes and the doctor call me crazy, some says I am some says I ain't.
The preacher man call me sinner, but his little girl call me saint.

Taz knew he had no hope of replicating Jerry Garcia's tripling guitar solo, but he did manage a decent version of Gus Cannon's bridge. And it was Cannon who wrote the damn tune back in 1927.

The time had come to take a break. Ronnie had to play at a wedding party. In his honor, they struck up the first chords of "Angel Band." Circled through the chorus to the opening:

My latest sun is sinking fast,
My race is nearly run
My strongest trials now are past,
My triumph has begun

Oh, come angel band
Come and around me stand
Bear me away on your snow-white wings
To my immortal home
Oh, bear me away on your snow-white wings
To my immortal home.

Taz waited until the clapping died down, looked around. "Time for a coffee break, folks. The coffee maker is just on the other side of the back wall. And while you're at it, buy some books!" His deal with Richard.

A few of the band's friends and most of the come-heres wandered back into the main room of the store. Sandy and Raven had already made themselves scarce. *Oh well.* The locals were talking in little knots, occasionally moving from one conversation to another—the way a community works.

A few wandered outside to smoke or enjoy the cool night air. One or two of the early spring visitors did their best to talk up the band.

Taz found Richard at the counter, nodded meaningfully. Richard quickly surveyed the crowd, pulled a bottle of Knob Creek from under the register. They went out to the gravel back alley.

A dazzling clear night. The only ground light was the warm yellow emanating from Rainy Day's door and an indistinct blue shine inside the cabin of a fishing trawler tied up at the wharf. Taz looked up and found the Big Dipper, followed the curve of the handle to Arcturus, then Cassiopeia and the Milky Way. He let himself be absorbed by the beauty of the night sky. Taz found it miraculous and somehow reassuring.

We are—all of us—Earth, the lands, the seas, all sentient beings, formed from stardust. From dust we are formed, and to dust we shall return. Taz recalled a saying from a poet-friend in California: *It's all cosmodegradable.*

Richard was used to his friend's reveries. He smiled, offered the bottle to Taz a third time. Taz waved it off at first, then reached out his hand with a muttered, "Thanks." Richard winked at him, headed back into the store to see if anyone needed help, or if anybody, God forbid, actually wanted to buy a book. Taz took a pull on the whiskey and was getting ready to go in himself when Tom stumbled off the porch step and made his way out to join him. He handed Richard's half-full bottle to Tom. "Do your worst. I'm already past the legal limit."

Tom was happy to oblige. Just as he finished his second swig, Sandy and Raven swung around the bookstore's rear corner, giggling, and leaving a trail of herbal smoke in their wake. Tom jolted as if he had been startled out of a dream. He winked at Taz, touched Sandy's elbow, whispered in her ear, walked with her back inside. Taz just shook his head and smiled, muttering, "That was quick."

"So, you think romance is comic?" Raven, looking quizzical, with her hands on her hips.

He dropped his voice down a fifth. "Comic? No. I think it's very, very serious. Occasionally fatal."

She rolled her eyes. "Do you take anything seriously?"

"Not if I can help it. I reckon if it's serious enough, it'll take me."

A glance. "Not if you won't let it, it won't."

Taz smiled up at the Milky Way. "It's just I've never liked the idea that my script has already been written."

"So now you're going to go all philosophical on me?" Irate. Then softening, looking thoughtful. "Or . . . maybe it's just that you don't like risk."

"Is that a diagnosis, doctor, or just an insult?"

"I don't know yet."

"Thank heavens for small favors."

She stepped to her right and put her finger to her cheek and her thumb under her chin, as if to view an abstract sculpture from a different angle. "Let's try a different approach. Your singing's not so bad. Sounds like you might have done some before. What's your favorite love song?"

"You first."

"Love makes the World Go Round." Hands back on hips, eyebrows arched. "And I want a straight answer."

He imagined her as a bobby soxer in Alturas, or wherever, listening to Broadway show tunes and dreaming of life in the big city. "'Bye Bye Love'—the Everly Brothers."

"That's not about love, it's about loneliness."

"Okay then, the Buddy Holly song I played in there," Taz said, pointing back towards the porch, and," He thought for a moment. "'Long Black Veil.'"

In the dim yellow light of the porch windows, he saw her rueful smile. "You know, I was thinking it would be fun to get to know you, but now I'm not sure. I don't throw pity parties."

"With the luck I have, I'd miss mine anyway."

She hmphed and rolled her eyes. He sensed she was enjoying the gentle push and pull. The joust, when he came on too sharp, the exploration when the possibility showed up. She stuffed her hands in her pockets, leaned back against the store's wood-slat wall.

"Okay, smart guy, let's try a Rorschach test. I say *love* and you give me three descriptions off the top of your head."

"I'll need an example of what you mean by a description."

"Oh, right—a philosopher. Hmmm. My first boyfriend said, 'Love is like a song in your heart.'"

"Let me guess. You broke up with him."

She swatted at an imaginary fly. "Irrelevant. No more stalling— *Love*—"

"A dangerous side effect of sex."

"Jesus, I don't know if I can get through this. Two more."

"An expensive cheap thrill."

Hands back on hips. "You are hopeless."

"Well, that's the point, isn't it."

"Last chance." Chin up, arms crossed.

"What angels order for dessert."

Raven turned her head, put her hand to her lips and just barely shut down a giggle, and then a snort. Just to make up for her slip, she shook her head like a schoolteacher reproving an errant child. "You've earned one more chance—just one. Do you read poetry?"

He looked back at the light from the door, hoping that Richard or Tom might show up to rescue him. "Don't tell me you're a poet."

She shrugged as if in surrender. "I've tried my hand. But don't worry, *Mister Depression*. I won't commit any poetry around you."

"You had me worried there for a second."

A call from inside. "Taz! Time to roll."

Raven stepped from the wall, eyes on the ground. The audience was calling for more. Taz gave her a quick look over his shoulder. "I have to duck back in to play a few more tunes. Be sure to let me know when your *lariati* hold their next poetry bash." He wanted to take it back before he had even finished the sentence.

Raven opened her mouth in astonishment, slapped her forehead with her palm. "Don't worry. I'm sure you'd have better things to do." Taz was struck by the edge in her voice, the dark beauty of her eyes, her anger. It would have felt better if she had just slapped him.

The Swamp Possums' second set was mostly chestnuts. "Mr. Bojangles,"

"Stay all Night, Stay a little Longer;" "Whisky River;" "Stealin' back to my good old use-to-be;" "Not Fade Away." Applause and friendly hoots. No claps from Raven. She just leaned her back against the wall and looked around, avoiding Taz's eyes.

They ended with "Black Muddy River," the deep and somber Garcia-Hunter ballad. Taz sang the lead:

> *When the last rose of summer pricks my finger,*
> *And the hot sun chills me to the bone,*
> *When I can't hear the song for the singer,*
> *And I can't tell my pillow from a stone,*
> *I will walk alone by the black muddy river,*
> *And sing me a song of my own,*
> *I will walk alone by the black muddy river,*
> *And sing me a song of my own.*
>
> *Black muddy river, roll on forever,*
> *I don't care how deep or wide, if you've got another side,*
> *Roll muddy river, roll muddy river, black muddy river, roll.*
>
> *When it seems like the night will last forever,*
> *And there's nothing left to do but count the years,*
> *When the strings of my heart begin to sever,*
> *And stones fall from my eyes instead of tears,*
> *I will walk alone, by the black muddy river,*
> *And dream me a dream of my own,*
> *I will walk alone, by the black muddy river,*
> *And sing me a song of my own, sing me a song of my own.*

What was left of the audience clapped, collected their purses and packs, and headed out, chatting as they went. As did Riley and Jesse, who had a lot less difficulty getting his bass out than he'd had bringing it in. Raven stood her ground until the last of the back-row couples had sidled by her. Sandy glanced Taz's way, scowled and wrapped her arm around

Raven's shoulder. The two of them slipped back into the main part of the store. Taz and Tom started stacking chairs. Tom left to have a smoke while Taz packed his guitars and did his best to clean up the coffee table.

He had just finished when he heard the creak of the stairs that led to the second-floor annex.

Sandy's voice, "He can't have meant it that way."

"Don't know about that. I was trying so hard to be pleasant, actually having fun for once. But talking with him is like fencing. He wasn't going to let me in, not even a little. And then he had to say that stuff about the *lariati.* Like I was talking about cowboy poetry! Rude is one thing. I can deal with that, but him! He practically threw it back in my face!"

The footsteps stopped midway down. Sandy: "I kind of doubt he meant it to hurt. The other morning, he couldn't get enough of you."

"Yeah. Apparently, that was Doctor Jekyll. Now I've met Mister Hyde."

"Remember what you said to me when we first hit the road? You wanted to meet someone different from the little boys we went to college with."

"Whoever I was looking for, it certainly isn't him!"

"You can't have it both ways, darlin'. A grown-up, you said. Well, you found one. Okay, it turns out he's got a few dents—and you're surprised?" A series of creaks from the stairs. "You wanted—" Taz was just getting snatches. "I'm here to tell you the shiny new models from the TV ads aren't all they're made up to be." More footsteps. "Even if he does look a lot like his truck." Sandy's voice. She was talking about Old Faithful, which had been in his driveway the morning they decided to camp on his doorstep. A beaten gray-blue Toyota Takoma. Taz smiled. *That truck has more personality than a lot of the people I know.* He heard a peal of laughter. "Alright, Tommy does too—but look at their trucks! I'm definitely getting a better deal." A hoot—they were at the bottom of the stairs. The sound carried.

Raven, giggling. "Oh, that's cruel. You just like shiny trucks...and movie-star hair. Anyway, who says I'm looking for a deal? Just because I've outgrown the boys scene in Davis . . ."

"I know, right? Either they're mooning around sharing their feelings or they're pretending to be Mr. Macho."

"That's the thing. He's sure not a share-your-feelings type, but he's not macho either. I mean he couldn't be bothered to pretend. I get the feeling he just doesn't care how other people see him. Including me. That spells trouble, don't you think?"

"Soooo cautious! Come on, *Cherie,* loosen up. You're not that bad a fencer yourself. It's way too early to worry about the deep stuff. Gamble! You can't win if you're afraid of risking anything. He's really not bad looking at all, from a certain point of view—if you like them a little dangerous— and he sang that Muddy River song like he wrote it."

A long breath. "I know. But what if it's his theme song? When he put his guitar away, I didn't know whether to kick him or kiss him. I still don't. Sometimes I really think men are more trouble than they're worth."

Richard had left the keys behind the counter so Taz could close the register and lock up. The register, the old ornate kind that bars sometimes use as ornament, still worked. Taz smiled as he stepped over and began ringing out. Hearing an unvarnished feminine review was bracing, at the very least—as long as you were properly pre-medicated.

Sandy and Raven showed their shock as they turned the corner from the stairwell. No doubt they had expected Richard. Sandy was holding a Marcella Hazan book on Italian cooking. Raven carried a small chapbook, which she was now doing her best to hide. Taz recognized the vermilion color that Jonathan Cape, the publisher, had for some reason decided should adorn it. *Twenty Love Poems and a Song of Despair.* Pablo Neruda. Taz put on his best poker face.

"Sorry—I've just closed out. Let me write down the prices, and you can pay in the morning."

Sandy lay the Hazan on the table. A hardback. Richard had it priced at $7.50. Raven, still trying to cover the title of her slim volume. "So, you're a book clerk as well? The pencil price is three seventy-five."

Taz smiled and wrote it down. "Well, I'm pretty damn good with a pencil and a cash register. Too bad nobody uses cash registers anymore." He shook his head, wishing he could reach back and say anything but the stupidity he had blurted outside. "I did used to work in a bookstore—right out of college. You'll laugh—I was the book buyer, but the owners had me arrange the poetry nights too. The saving grace was that part of the gig was to take the authors out drinking afterward."

Raven shrugged in resignation. Then she straightened and looked him in the eye. "Am I supposed to be impressed? Why would you waste your time sweet-talking poets? I mean when you think so little of them. For being naive, and actually trying to say what's in their hearts?"

Her tone cut. He really had hurt her feelings—and why? Because he'd been hurt too? But so long ago. No matter. Ever since, talk about feelings was just play, the words like badminton cocks, with no weight at all, not things with an edge that could cut or cause pain. He spent a few moments watching her stand fierce, realizing that he didn't know her or what her life was like, what she'd been through before arriving on his doorstep, so saucy and light. He's seen the sadness behind her smile and then skated right past it. He lowered his gaze to the counter and bent to look for the paper bags. He slipped the books in, making sure the logo was properly folded. As he rose to put their bags on the counter. He smiled, trying to catch Raven's eye. "I hope you have me wrong. I really didn't mean to insult you." He held the bag towards her. "This one's on me."

The two women stood stock-still. Out the front window a police cruiser crawled by with blue lights flashing. Sandy watched Taz. Raven absorbed herself in the patterns on the floor beneath her feet. The three of them were lit periodically by the blue light.

Taz tore his gaze away from the police car long enough to catch Raven as she raised her eyes to look his way. He smiled. Quietly, "You know, if I thought I could impress you, I'd probably be fool enough to try. Just now, I'm tired of reaching for the impossible. So, no. Don't worry. I just didn't want you thinking I was *Bartleby the Scrivener*. That's all."

CHAPTER FOUR

Back at the Pony Pines

BLESS HIS HEART, RAINY DAY'S back door crashed open, and Tom came strolling in. He winked at Taz and placed a light hand on Sandy's arm. "It's only ten thirty. How about we hitch it to the Pony Pines?"

"Bless you, my son." Taz turned away to rearrange some books that didn't need re-arranging. Pulled the Neruda out of the bag and wrote quickly on the title page. *To Raven: From Bartleby.*

Raven seemed more than a little distracted. "The Pony Pines?"

Sandy looked at her friend. "Who can tell? Let's just go and find out." Then she linked arms with Tom, who was sporting a shit-eating grin.

Raven gave Taz a questioning look. She was chewing her lip. "Still willing to give a girl a ride?" Taz nodded and summoned a smile. "Of course."

Tom peeled out of the gravel parking lot in his shiny green Dodge Hemi. Taz pointed Raven to his scratched blue Toyota. "Your limo tonight, I'm afraid. Half the size of Tom's Dodge and twice as rusty."

Raven was having trouble with her seat belt. The passenger-side buckle had frozen up a couple of weeks back. He apologized, asked if it was okay for him to help. She nodded, exasperated. He reached across her, brushing her shirt as he drew some extra belt out of the holder. She flinched. Taz pretended not to notice, pulled the belt, set it in the buckle, banged it down until it clicked. "Sorry." He pulled onto Church Street, turned in the direction of the East Side Road by the Assateague marshlands. Finally, there was nothing but the road and an oyster house across the street.

"Taz, who wrote that one song?" She started to sing, somewhere between a whisper and a hum:

> Sometimes love has no reason
> And no rhyme
> We have all the things we need
> You and I,
> But baby we don't have much time.

"It was so—I don't know—wistful. And sad."

He glanced her way. "His name was Bap Kennedy. Young singer-songwriter from Belfast. Mostly light, comic kinds of songs. But then he came down with cancer. When he wrote that, he knew it was only a matter of months." Raven looked like she had blundered into the worst blind date of her life.

They pulled into the gravel lot. Parked near Tom's Dodge and two hopped-up pickups sporting South Carolina plates. Taz came around to help Raven with the seatbelt. One of the pickups was bright shiny and red, the other was tan and covered in olive-green camouflage markings. The red one sported a Confederate flag that covered the entire rear window of the cab, a slew of bumper stickers, including a *Don't Tread on Me* coiled viper, a blue, black, and white American flag, and a vulgar denunciation of *dimocrats and libtards*. Taz motioned Raven towards the entrance while he marveled and snapped a quick picture. The viciousness of the right wing never ceased to amaze him. Raven waited for him, standing just outside the refracted colors of the giant neon fish bolted under the peak of the roof.

Before they crossed the threshold, while they were still bathed in the red-and-blue neon light, she faced him, searched his eyes.

"Jesus! Why do I feel like this?"

"Like what?"

"Like I just set fire to a bridge."

Taz paused, scratching the back of his neck. "There *are* other ways to cross a river. I always liked skipping from stone to stone."

"Is that what you're doing now?"

He took a step back so he could get a better view of her. "The man who wrote the little poetry book you just picked up? He put it like this: 'I want to do with you what spring does with the cherry trees.'"

Raven leaned back against the door; arms crossed. "Damn you, you don't even want to know my name, but you already know how to reach me. Okay . . . and how to piss me off, too. Maybe there's something ahead for us, I don't know. But if you've been burned so badly that you . . . you know . . . that you really can't try again, if it's not possible for you, I'll steer clear." She moved through moods and emotions like a grand prix driver shifting gears. She was determined not to be taken lightly, and she wasn't afraid to show anger, yet she also had a certain tenderness. He was as sure as a man could be that she was cloaking a deep vulnerability under the joyous challenge she tossed out at life. All he could do now was to watch, to see her on the other side of an entrance they had to go through—or not. For over a year he'd been telling himself and his friends he felt fine, but the truth was that his own life had gone gray. Now there was a little color seeping back into the picture. He gave her elbow a gentle touch. She nodded and let him walk her in.

*

There were a few couples at scattered tables. Three women in one of the back booths. Taz thought he recognized some friends of Laney's. In the half dark it was hard to make out with any certainty. Roxy Lopez was polishing the bar. A petite sand-colored woman with a minimalist Afro, a smile that on the right occasion could light up the room, and a glare that could melt most men, no matter how macho they thought they were.

Tom and Sandy had already found their places at the bar. The Carolinians were sitting three stools down the bar from Sandy. The older, heftier one chewed a wad of tobacco, spitting into a beer can. The driblets that missed had discolored his wispy blond goatee. He had his sleeves rolled

up so onlookers could admire—or fear— his biceps. The second was a
good deal younger and going to fat. His head was polished like a cue ball.

The two of them had apparently bought the next set on the jukebox.
Mostly techno and White rap. Taz considered the first a travesty, and the
second a contradiction in terms. The two toughs were singing along, loud,
and off-key.

Roxy nodded to Taz, reached behind the bar. Turned to the second
rank of bottles just below the mirror and picked out a bottle of Tanqueray.
Taz had once told her that Bombay was even better. She had told him to
fuck off. Now she pulled two glasses out of the freezer, squeezed a lemon
twist over each of them, waved a small bottle of dry vermouth in their
direction, and filled them to the rim.

Raven said, "I like mine dirty, please."

Roxy glared. "Girl! Why ruin a perfect martini when you can drink a
whole ocean of saltwater just out the door? Why not try the kind I make
for the troublemaker you're sitting next to?" She glowered at Taz.

Raven ventured a quick look at Taz. "Okay. I'll try it." A stiff swill.
"Mmmm." Turned back to Roxy. "The dirty kind was just what an old
boyfriend always asked for."

"Girl, I wouldn't follow that boyfriend to the next corner." Winked
at Taz. "Hey, cowboy. You don't call, you don't write. Was it something I
said?" Gently slapped her own cheek.

Taz pulled down a very chilly swallow of dry martini. "Roxy, in my eyes,
you can do no wrong." Raven was observing the exchange with interest.

"You liar. I thought maybe what's-her-name, the one who sits in the
back booth having Laney tell her fortune, maybe she stole your voice."

"Like in the Garcia Lorca poem?" Raven shifted her gaze Taz's way.
His was on Roxy. "Nah. It wasn't her fault. I'm a lot to put up with. She
was just looking for someone who was maybe a little more predictable."

"Yeah? You can blame yourself all you want. What I know is she lit
you like a sparkler and then she broke your heart." Roxy turned on her
heel and strode down the bar.

Raven said, "I like her. And she likes you." Still looking to splice the broken connection? "But it sounds like there's a Casablanca-style backstory hidden in a piano somewhere. You know, 'We'll always have Paris.'"

Taz stared deep into his martini. He knew.

Roxy had a short conversation with Tom, ducked through the door behind the bar and returned with four shots of añejo tequila on a small wooden tray. The Carolinians looked on, confused as to why they weren't getting the same attention. The two pairs of friends stood in a tight circle behind Sandy's chair, trying their best to agree on a collective toast. It was slow going— Tom and Sandy were the only ones in the mood to celebrate. Finally, Taz looked at them and then at Raven, raised his shot glass. "Here's to crooked paths and unexpected destinations."

Tom winked. "And bullet holes in stop signs." The women laughed and slid onto stools next to each other. Taz just smiled, relieved. Tom said something about nature's call and headed back to the men's room.

The older of the black-leather pair spit in his empty beer can. He pushed his stool back and sauntered self-consciously their way. Taz watched as he slowed to admire his own image in the mirror behind the bar. Taz had him at about six foot-two, maybe thirty. He sported a blond buzzcut and a mullet. Taz found it all amusing, until he saw the swastika tattoo carved on his neck, just below his shirt collar. Chewbacca was a homegrown Nazi.

The Nazi put his right hand on the back of Sandy's neck. Made some rubbing motions. "Come on, pretty thing. I'll teach you how to dance to today's music."

"Get your hand off my neck." She tried to shrug him off. He kept his grip on her shoulder and started to pull her toward the jukebox.

Roxy reached behind the bar. She held a barbeque fork that she had been using to break up some ice clumps. She put it down on the low narrow shelf just in front of Taz.

Sandy reached for the brute's wrist again. "You're hurting me." Louder this time.

Raven was climbing off her stool, eyes blazing, voice low but intense.

"Are you hard of hearing? Get your hand off her!"

Taz caught Roxy's attention, nodded at Raven, and whispered, "Hold her if you have to." Raven looked his way with a fierce question in her eyes, then turned and continued to scowl at Chewbacca.

The lug sneered, pushed Sandy out of the way and took a step towards Raven. "You think I care what you say, bitch? You want me too, don't you?" Taz gradually reached his right hand over the bar until he found the two-pronged fork and nestled it against the inside of his forearm. He rose slowly, stepping between Raven and the Nazi. The hulk gave him a derisory glance. "Now I get it. The bitch is *your* whore." Raven was glaring daggers, struggling to push Taz's arm out of her way.

"I don't know who you are, jackass, but your courtship style needs some serious polishing."

The brute spat a gob of tobacco juice on the floor. "And you think you're the man to do it?"

"Actually, I'm just trying to keep the spitfire here from tearing you to pieces. If you weren't so fucking stupid, you'd thank me."

Taz's insult had the effect he was looking for. The big man's eyes went wide, and he swung a wild right-hand roundhouse. Taz ducked. The slugger's momentum threw him off balance. He lurched to the bar, slapped his meaty hand down to steady himself. Taz whirled and plunged the fork right through the pliant flesh and into the wood, deep enough that pulling it out would take a pair of pliers. The Nazi screamed in pain, straining to pull his hand up. He grabbed the fork with his left hand, tried to yank it out of the wood. That fork wasn't going anywhere. Blood flowed over the bar in all directions. The tough guy fainted, fell backwards, dislodging the fork with the force of his fall and smacking his head on the closest table.

His companion pushed away from the bar, glaring at Taz, and muttering something undecipherable. Taz faced him and partially blocked a hook to his ribs. The blow landed with enough force to convince Taz to avoid another. He put up his fists and blocked the second hook with a jab to the skinhead's cheek. Suddenly something yellow whizzed past Taz's shoulder and hit the wall behind the punk's head. A second flash of yellow;

the skinhead yelled, and his hand flew up to his ear. He ducked behind his arm just as a third lemon sailed over his head. When his head came up again, a glass saltshaker caught him right on the bridge of the nose. He howled and backed up a step, shaking his head. His nose flowed with blood. He put his hands back up and stepped uncertainly towards Taz. He looked dizzy. An equal opportunity lime grazed Taz's cheek on its way to the far wall. Taz swiveled quickly to see Raven pick two more lemons out of the plastic bin on the bar. The punk was still shaking his head and listing drunkenly from side to side. Roxy reached underneath the register, pulled out a sawed-off shotgun, aimed it directly at number two's most vital equipment. "Don't worry, friend. It's not steel shot—just rock salt."

Tom was strolling back from the bathroom. He took one look and quickened his pace. When Taz looked again, he had a seven-inch switchblade in his hand. He waved it in the direction of the neon fish, made sure the young Nazi got a good view of it. "Collect your fuckbuddy and get the hell out of here. I mean off this island. I see you again, you're dead." The kid grabbed one of the bonehead's wrists, took a few uncertain backward steps, turned, and dragged him away from the bar and finally over the threshold, limp as overcooked linguini.

Taz slapped Tom on the shoulder as he was folding up his blade. "Thanks, brother."

"Not a problem." Sandy was standing beside him, eyes wide with a mixture of fear and desire. Tom put his arm around Sandy's waist.

Taz had already turned his gaze to Raven. She was watching him in disbelief. Smiling, he plucked the last lemon out of her hand and tossed it back in the basket. She looked about to protest. He rubbed his cheek and whistled. "Where'd you learn to throw a fastball?"

She took a deep breath, lowered her eyes and smiled. "In high school. I was a pitcher."

"I thought girls used an underarm delivery."

"It was a small school. I pitched for the boys' team. Varsity." Her smile widened. "I've got a slider, too. Want to see it?"

Roxy piped up. "Not with my lemons. I won't be able to make another martini until the Monday delivery."

Taz cast a glance over his shoulder. "My tab good for a round of shots?"

Roxy pulled down a bottle of Herradura and poured four. Handed one to Tom. Slid the other Taz's way with uncanny accuracy. Placed the last two carefully in front of Sandy and Raven. "On me. Those two have been causing problems here, and at PJ's too. I talked to Jenny is how I know." PJ's was one of the island's better restaurants. Jenny was PJ's top bartender. Roxy bored in on Taz. "Wipe that smirk off your face, *Mister* Blackwell. If you try to play that language police thing on me again, you won't have to wait for some revenge-hungry Nazi to kill you!"

"Not *revenge-hungry . . . vengeful.*" Blew her a kiss. Raven shook her head, staring at him. Taz turned his gaze back to her. "Next time I get in a bar fight, remind me to line up on your side." He rubbed his cheek. "And to stay away from your curve."

Taz reached for Roxy's arm, leant over the bar, kissed her on the cheek. "Thanks, sweetheart. I don't think I would have enjoyed getting the shit beat out of me by two Nazis. The young one was bad enough."

"Shit. You must have been one hell of a diplomat!" Sarcasm dripped from her voice instead of honey. "You're so blind, I want to smack you. I will always have your back—but really, it's exhausting."

The four of them started on the second round of tequila. Raven weaved towards the nearest table and very carefully slid the chair back. Sat down with great deliberation. Taz downed his shot. Roxy gave him a meaningful look. Raven was leaning somewhat unsteadily on her elbow, watching them.

Tom put his arm around Sandy's shoulder and headed to the parking lot. Winked at Taz. "Make sure to phone if you need help."

Sure. You and Sandy are going to achieve carnal bliss before I even get Raven home. Just my luck.

Taz's ribs were sore, and the pain was growing. He finished his tequila, turned, and reached for Raven's hand. She stood, straightened and glared his way. "I'm okay. You don't have to look after me." She took an unsteady step. He wrapped his arm around her waist and started towards the door.

She slid just a little down his side, righted herself, flashing a vague smile.

A pleading look at Roxy. She parried with a glower. "I will, but you'll owe me. And double not to talk about it." Working together, they drew Raven's arms over their shoulders, walked her like an injured soccer player to the passenger side of Old Faithful, and helped her into the passenger seat.

Then it was just Roxy and Taz. "Taz, why is it that every time you come here, a fight breaks out? You've got some anger in you, is what I think." She faced him and came closer. "Doesn't matter to me. I've always liked your style." Stood on tiptoe to brush her lips across his cheek, then his neck, then his lips. Gradually intensified what had started as a light buss into an open-mouthed kiss, with her hand on the back of his neck, making sure he couldn't pull away until she was good and ready. "But right now, you better get lost. Do me a favor and don't cross paths with the police. Jenny says the Nazi-weenies have some friends out there."

*

By the time Taz got to South Main, Raven was fast asleep. He had to make sure he was taking her to the right house. Imagined the delight if he deposited her in the wrong one—the one where the teenage boy trots down the stairs in the morning to find the best birthday present ever. He recollected that the target house was the same canary yellow as his cottage. Then he spotted Tom's truck parked in the yellow house's driveway. He parked straddling the sidewalk.

There was still the matter of getting Raven in the door. Out of other options, Taz lifted her over his shoulder and carried her in like a sack of flour. She mumbled something under her breath. He couldn't make it out. He found the couch and laid her down as gently as he could. Looked around, saw a quilt carefully folded in the corner, tucked her in. He was sure he had been totally stealth until a door to his right creaked open. Sandy sneaked out, holding a bathrobe closed in a mostly unsuccessful effort to hide her nakedness. "Is she okay?" Tom's steady snore was drifting in from the bedroom.

"Yes. But she's up against a tough morning. Do you know how to make a good Bloody Mary?"

Taz kissed Raven on the forehead. She managed to utter a single word, in a soft, warm voice. "Stay?" He found himself smiling as he started the ignition and headed home.

CHAPTER FIVE

Every Silver Lining Has a Touch of Grey

MORNING. TAZ HAD TO DRINK a full pot of coffee before he was capable of driving into town. He slowed as he passed the yellow house. Sandy's Fiat was the only car in the driveway. He stopped off at the bookstore to see if Laney wanted a coffee before she opened. He quickly discarded the idea when he saw Richard outside the store with a bucket of off-white paint and a brush. His friend was in a decidedly foul mood. Someone had sprayed the word *Commie* on the wall in bright red three-foot letters and painted a jagged black lightning bolt over the middle of it for good measure.

"Got another brush?" Richard pointed to the paint tray. Taz wet the brush and settled in to work alongside him.

"When did it happen?"

"Fuck. Sometime last night. They hit the library, too. Somebody's idea of a prank."

"You better hope so. Otherwise, we've got an entirely different kind of problem. There were two Nazis at the Pony Pines last night."

Richard gave him a baleful look.

When they finished, Taz dropped his brush in the can of kerosene and stepped quickly around the corner, pushed open the front door. Laney stood stiffly behind the counter. Her lips were sealed in a grim version of a smile. "You saw it?"

"Hard to miss. Richard almost has it painted over, though."

She came around for a hug. "Who would do such a thing?"

"Someone who doesn't like books. Richard said they got the library too. I was going to head over there next, but I wanted to see you first." He kept her folded in his arms for a moment more, then disengaged, with his hands on her shoulders. "Have you talked to Maddie or Cass?" The long-time couple who managed the town's small library, one of the best on Virginia's Eastern Shore.

"They're up in Philadelphia visiting museums. We were going to clean up over there this afternoon."

"Why don't you let me do that."

"You'll need blue paint to match their door. Enough to cover the upper front panel. We're commies and they're queers. Quite a progressive message."

"Says more about the cretins who left it than it does about either of you. Have you told the police?"

"Whipple's out of town. The ones who came took a look around and scribbled in their notebooks. Didn't seem that interested though—just another teen graffiti prank. The chief was busy in meetings. So, I called the mayor. He's in Fort Lauderdale, on a golf trip."

"There might be something I can do to wake them up. Permission?"

"As long as I'm not the one saying *sorry* later."

Taz pulled his cell phone out of his back pocket. Scrolled through his contacts until he got to the C's. Eliza Clarke—a young, spirited reporter for the *Salisbury Times*, the only serious newspaper on the peninsula. They had met at a Shorebirds game the summer before. She was Eliza Burkett then. Taz had been a source for a series of stories she wrote about a Chinese company's bid to mine ore under a mostly Black township on the shore of Chesapeake Bay. He had been invited to Eliza's wedding but had to be away on travel for the State Department. A year later, he had read about her divorce. He was glad for the chance to renew their friendship. He told her what had happened and emailed a picture of the wall that Laney had taken when she first saw it. Just as he hit send, it occurred to him that he had the license plate of the Nazis who caused the ruckus at the Pony Pines. Maybe they had something to do with the paint job as well. He scrolled through his pictures and sent Eliza the one he had taken that night. It would be easy for her to trace the South Carolinian's license plate.

Instead of resolving the nation's differences, the last election seemed to have deepened them. Talk radio wasn't helping. The garbage jockeys were in full cry. Some folks ignored it. Others absorbed it all like sponges. Last night's graffiti wasn't an isolated incident. Hate crimes seemed to be sprouting like noxious weeds. But this was the first one Taz knew about on his island.

A blistering round of telephone tag occupied most of the morning, as Richard and Laney's friends woke up and heard the news, struggled to learn, or explain what had happened or, God forbid, interpret it. Taz was back on his dock, tying down the Adirondack chair that had gone overboard during the winter's final nor'easter. His personal interpretation was that whoever defaced the buildings should be found, hog-tied, and hung by their heels until they squealed for mercy.

By noon, many of Richard and Laney's more progressive and artistic colleagues had gathered at the store to mill around and express their sorrow and outrage. Taz showed up at one with the intention of checking on Laney. He stood at the back until he had heard all the sympathy he could stand.

Taz caught Laney's eye, gave her a thumbs-up, headed out the door to Marcy's wine store, and from there to Church Street Supply to pick up the blue paint and a honing stone he had ordered. After he had painted the library door, he was going to take care of a patch of phragmites spreading on the edges of his marsh grass. The honing stone was to sharpen up his rusty scythe, a relic from his teenage days on the road crew back in Palo Pinto County. The crew boss, a codger named Benny Jones, had taught him how to use it. "*When you hone the blade, keep your thumb down! Unless you want to jack off with just your four fingers, and good luck with that.*" Sharp enough, the scythe would slice through the stiff phragmites stems while the green spartina shoots ducked.

A Gulf front had come in overnight. April's unusually warm days were becoming the norm. Taz honed the scythe blade until it shone and stepped through the marsh mud to confront his unwanted vegetation. Another Bennyism came to mind. *"A scythe is for cutting—it ain't a fucking golf club!"* Backswing had nothing to do with it. You just started with a slight twist to the right, and swung the scythe left through the green shoots. Some of them were already two feet tall. But the scythe cut them cleanly, and if you got 'em early, you could stop the invasive bastards from using the sun's power to feed their evil and all-too-happy rhizomes. After two hours, Taz was mopping sweat from his brow, and his anger about what happened at Rainy Day had subsided, at least temporarily.

He gathered the green and brown stems for the burn barrel. He was honing the scythe for the next cut when his friend Teddy Robben pulled his pickup around the corner from Beebe Road. He honked, then stopped. "Who are you? The grim reaper? Don't believe I've ever seen a scythe on this island. What the hell are you up to this time?"

"Come get a beer and find out." Teddy pulled up behind Taz's old Toyota truck and climbed out of the cab. Teddy was a third generation Teaguer, a sometime carpenter, and rest-of-the-time clammer. He made his real money mowing lawns; had a lock on most of the lots within a quarter mile of Beebe and Main.

They walked together into the cottage. No need for small talk. Taz grabbed a can of Miller Lite from the fridge and handed it to Teddy. Teddy protested—said he had a few in the cooler in the truck. He was used to the Teaguer way: bring your own.

Taz looked at him in horror. "Jesus. Why do you think I have my coolerator stuffed with this crap? You know I won't drink it. If you won't either, I'll just have to toss it in the bay." He found a Pacifico, and they headed out to sit on the dock.

"Looks like you been working on your phragmites."

"I hate that shit. Invasive. Even the birds don't like it. No self-respecting swamp sparrow would go in there unless it was being chased by a sharpie.

That's where the scythe comes in."

Looking at the stubby remains on the near edge of the marsh. "Well, that's not bad, son. But you're going have to poison it in the end."

"What do people use?"

"Damned if I know. I'm sure it's bad, though. But not as bad as phragmites." Took a pull of beer.

Taz pushed up the bill of his cap. "Been downtown lately?"

"Nah. Warm days, it's too crowded. Cold days, been sitting around Nicky's burn barrel, pulling down silver bullets, shooting the shit."

"I'm shocked."

"But I heard." Teddy didn't say what. Taz didn't spend a lot of effort guessing.

"What are folks saying?"

Taz meant the Islanders. The ones whose great-grandparents moved to the Island from Assateague in the late 1800s.

"Well, they don't know. But nobody thinks it's a Teaguer."

"I reckon not. But it would be good to find out who it is before things get nasty."

Teddy knocked the rest of his beer down in one long, easy motion. "I'll ask around."

Then he was off up the dock and climbing into his new black Dodge Ram 2500. It shone like a Marine's spit-polished shoes.

CHAPTER SIX

Rotten Dock

ELIZA'S FRONT-PAGE STORY ABOUT THE White Power paint job hit like a bomb. Her editors had put her lead dead center above the fold. Somehow, they had scrounged up a grainy cell phone photograph of Richard painting it over, which made for a more than usually exciting morning at Rainy Day.

Police Chief Rainey, looking more careworn than usual, hurried in to tell her how sorry he was that this had happened in his town, and to reassure her and everyone else that he was personally committed to finding the culprits. Laney looked him in the eye. "You mean *our* town."

Stammering, "Of course, of course," the Chief tipped his cap and scurried back out to his patrol car. The chair of the town council brought flowers, said she was going to badger the mayor and the chief until the issue was "put to bed." The town manager called to let Richard know the mayor had interrupted his vacation to express his concern.

Taz spent the afternoon on his back in the crawl space under his house, cleaning and securing his air ducts. Messy work. The flood tide from the last nor'easter had pulled the ducts out of their brackets and filled them with mud and sea wrack.

He showered to get rid of the grime and sweat. Heated up a frozen chicken potpie for dinner. They were usually pretty good, though most of the commercial brands could use more dark meat. Taz sat at the round deal table in his kitchen and ate appreciatively, listening to the evening news on the radio. If there was anything positive happening out there, they sure as hell weren't talking about it.

The sun had set behind a cloud bank hanging on the land side of Chincoteague Bay. The humid air beneath spread a maroon dusk on the western horizon. A riotous crowd of gulls squawked and swirled just in front of the burnt orange stretch where *El Sol* had decided to travel on to other locations.

He was still enjoying the post-sunset glow when his cell phone blared. It was Suzanne Bonner, Dana's thirteen-year-old daughter. Even though Taz's hopes for a future with her mother had gone up in smoke more than a year back, Suzanne and her younger brother, Moyer, had maintained, and even strengthened, the bond that they and Taz had begun while he was courting Dana. Taz thoroughly enjoyed being their honorary uncle.

"Taz, Moyer's in trouble. You need to come." She was trying to stifle a sob.

"Where are you? Are you with him?"

"We're on the old Landmark dock."

"I'll be right there."

The Landmark Plaza had been torn down three years past, its dock now a rotting collection of planks around the shell of what used to be Captain Fish's Grill. It balanced precariously over the Chincoteague Channel, on top of a shaky set of barnacled pilings. And ever since they closed the Dream over in Wattsville, it was the only platform the kids had for skating.

Taz hopped in Old Faithful and sped into town. Past the bookstore and three blocks of storefronts. Don's Restaurant, the fisheries sheds where the trawlers unloaded. Turned into the old Landmark parking lot, spitting gravel as he stopped. He found Suzanne first. She was waving at him, crying, trying hard to pull herself together.

"Moyer fell through!"

"Fell through what?"

"Taz. Moyer and Frankie were roller-skating on the dock, and Moyer fell through!"

The light was fading fast. Taz hadn't brought a flashlight.

"Show me where."

She was trembling. Parts of the dock were still flat and minimally stable, but there were also broad areas of rotten planking. Suzanne pointed to a jagged hole big enough for a grown man to fall through, let alone a thirteen-year-old boy.

Taz kneeled, trying to scan the water. He couldn't make much out in the murk. All he could locate were some nearby pilings and the diagonal support struts that had been jury-rigged to keep the dock from collapsing. He heard the lapping of the tide, and then, faintly, what sounded like shallow breathing and an occasional cough.

He called down. "Moyer, can you hear me?"

He heard a muffled cough and a groan.

He looked over his shoulder at Suzanne. "Call your mom. Tell her what's happened."

"I already tried! Before I called you."

"Okay. Try Laney. Tell her to bring a flashlight. I'm going down to get Moyer."

Taz knelt on what was left of the decking, feeling the dew through his khakis. Reached down until his fingers felt the slime of the closest diagonal strut. Wet and slippery but solid. He sat and pushed his feet down through the hole, scraping his shins, feeling for a cross-strut or at least a little purchase on one of the diagonals.

"Moyer, I'm coming down. Stay put, okay?"

He tried to avoid putting too much weight on the strut while he felt for another possibility with his left hand. His right hand gripped the edge of the wet dock planking. He couldn't hold onto it forever. With his head below the deck, he was now completely unsighted.

"Moyer? Are you hurt?"

To his relief, Moyer started to speak. His voice was soft and hesitant.

"I don't think I broke anything, but I can't seem to get a foothold. I don't know if I can make it back up." Judging by the sound, he was somewhere down by the water line, at least ten feet below the deck.

"Are you still wearing your roller skates?"

"Yes."

"Take them off."

"But Mom will kill me if I lose them."

"Moyer, she'll kill me if you don't."

Taz heard one splash, and then another, as the skates went to their watery grave.

"Okay, Moyer, now feel around. Can you reach the next strut above you?"

"Maybe. . .Yes. But it's too slippery."

"Okay, look for a joint. Anything you can wedge your hand into."

Taz heard a grunt. "Okay, I got something."

"Pull up on that and feel for a higher foothold. Then use your free hand to find the next one. Just like climbing that pin oak you like."

Labored breathing, then a panted, "Okay." Taz lowered himself and found a cross strut that seemed likely to sustain his weight. He let go of the deck planking and found a rusty bolt sticking a foot out of a wet piling joist and grabbed that. Heard more panting. Holding on to the bolt, he lowered himself down again and found a loose strut that gave him a precarious foothold. The dark was near total. Now Moyer's panting was closer, but still below him.

"Moyer, can you get up to where I can reach you?"

"Not yet. I'm going to try and shimmy up this strut. Maybe that'll do it."

He was less than ten feet away, but still out of reach.

A few moments passed, punctuated only by heavy breathing and the slapping of the tidewater from the wake of a passing fishing boat. Then the breathing sounded closer, and more labored. Moyer was shimmying up a strut not more than two or three feet away. Taz reached, touched a belt. Yanked up as hard as he could. Moyer used the leverage to climb another two or three feet.

"I can feel the decking!"

Suzanne called, "Moyer, grab my hand! I've got you!"

Taz sagged with relief. He stretched to feel for the bolt but found nothing but wet wood. He started working hand over hand up the strut towards the deck. The strut was slick with sea-slime; the only holds were sharp-edged barnacles that cut his hands. Still, he was making slow progress—until his right foot slipped entirely and his handhold gave out. He ripped through a lightweight crosstie and landed on his back on a piling that was floating in the water eight feet below, hitched to a sturdier companion by an old hawser. He thought he heard Suzanne call his name. He didn't have the breath to answer. His ribcage ached, and pain shot through his back. He blacked out.

The water was cold as the piling rolled and he went under. Taz struggled up and up until he finally broke the surface. His mouth and nose were full of liquid. Gasping, coughing, he spat out a stream of bay water. He could see the lights of town over the wooden bulwark of the wharf. He tried to swim, but his right arm was close to useless. Ended up with a crooked sidestroke and finally reached the bow of *Crazy Nellie,* an aged wooden trawler that was moored at the old fish plant. Using his left arm, he pulled himself around the bow to the wharf and then worked his way down the bulkhead until he reached the small boat ramp that the town had put in after the fish plant closed. He pushed himself up until he was kneeling, water lapping on the cement under his knees, his chest wheezing. Starting to fold sideways, he forced his shoulder against a tarred piling. He reached and dug his fingers into the top of the piling and levered himself up to stand, struggling up the ramp until he reached dry concrete.

Taz could hear voices off to his left, a siren passing on Main Street. The blinking red light almost blinded him. He started to walk unsteadily in the direction of the voices. He heard his own steps on the wooden boardwalk, and then on the rickety stairs at the end. He leaned against a piling and breathed awhile, shivering, feeling his wet shirt cling to him in the cold. Pulled himself to the wobbly railing on the steps and dragged his way up one at a time. He was back on the dock, and heard Suzanne calling his name. Two male voices were arguing. He worked his way forward until he could see them. They were pointing bright flashlights towards the hole in the dock.

Moyer's voice—high, strained, choking off a sob. "I told you twice already! He slipped! He has to be down there somewhere. He has to be."

Laney was standing a little off to the side with another woman. The scattered light from the flashlights and the police cars' beacons made it difficult to see. Dana was hugging Suzanne, who had stopped calling and started crying. Two or three firemen were talking some way behind them.

Feeling light-headed, Taz took two steps towards a rail and managed to hold himself upright. In the process, his arm hit a loose piece of steel pipe and knocked it ringing to the deck. Dead silence as the two flashlights swept towards him, and a dozen faces turned his way. He tried hard for a smile. Did his best to shout but ended up croaking. "I heard someone was looking for me." He tasted his own blood and crumpled to the deck. The world went black.

CHAPTER SEVEN

World of Pain

TAZ TRIED NOT TO FOCUS on the pain, which started just below his shoulder blades and extended down his spine to his lower back. And then there were his ribs, the ones on the left that the younger Nazi thug had battered. And his head, which was throbbing like a drum.

A woman's voice, soft, with a Piedmont lilt. "Mr. Blackwell, can you hear me?" She repeated it three times for emphasis, gradually raising her pitch each time.

Finally, to swat away the sonic mosquito, he coughed out a yes.

"Well, that's something."

The room was blue. It was also very jagged, almost cubist. He closed his eyes, hoping he might go back to sleep.

Other voices, one male. "Keep a careful eye. He's been heavily sedated. Let me know if he starts to get too active."

He couldn't escape a disturbing dream. An airplane hangar. A number of men, working, but not on anything he understood. He walked the length of the hangar to reach a door. Opened it with great difficulty. A white hallway—leading where? He felt terribly alone. Still, he walked, found a side passage, down a half flight of stairs, opened another white door, and finally emerged. He was on the bank of the Brazos River, just above a little riffle he liked to wade in when it was hot. He took off his shoes.

The image faded, making just enough room for rudimentary perception in the present tense. Taz looked around, gradually putting the room together. It was all planes and quadrilaterals, splashes of color, and a face—Laney's.

He struggled to say something witty, but it wouldn't come. Finally, "Laney."

She was sitting at the foot of his bed, holding an open book. She reached to touch his hand. "What were you dreaming about? You were muttering and whimpering. Then all of a sudden you started to laugh. You ended with the nicest smile."

He told her what he could remember. Asked for some water. She handed him a cup. "Do you need help?"

"I sure hope not."

She watched him as he drank, greedily. Gave her back the cup. She filled it again.

"See if you can sit up."

He could, if he ignored the pain in his back and propped himself up with his hands.

"I want to see your back." She opened his hospital gown. God, how he hated these things. "Jesus, Taz."

"You're supposed to say it doesn't look that bad."

"But it does. Worse. How does it feel?"

"It's okay, with whatever painkiller they're giving me."

"It's a strong one. We've got to get you off it as soon as we can."

"It's an opioid, right? How about we just go to the opium?"

"Yeah right. I'll fly to Afghanistan tomorrow and pick some up."

"No? I guess there's always Plan B." Laney smiled, her eyes raised in a question. "A fifth of whisky and a brick of hash."

Laney snorted. Taz began to swing his legs over the side of the bed. Got halfway before the searing pain stopped him cold. She gripped his shoulder, helped him back on his pillow. "Taz, remind me why half our dates are in a hospital? By the way, in case you care, you're in the Peninsula Urgent Care Clinic in Salisbury."

He looked around the room, remembering their visit after his little dance with the Russian ambassador's goons in the Meadowlands, when she had read him the farewell note that was his last communication from Irina Tsolkin. It could've been the same room. "You're going to spring me, aren't you?"

"Day after tomorrow, the doc says. Meanwhile, enjoy the food. The brochure says it's really good."

"If you like lime Jell-O and dead chicken."

Her eyes blazed. "Quit carping. At least you aren't dead . . . not because you didn't try."

Taz couldn't even catalogue all the reasons he loved Laney. Start with her knack of summoning the tough love he needed, leavened with just the right touch of sarcasm. Her pride. If she cared about something, she did something about it. The way she had his back in the most difficult stretches of his path. Her absolute refusal to take shit from anybody. Her easy willingness to let others take credit for achievements and performances that wouldn't have been possible without her. And yes, her beauty. She had a few years on Taz and almost a decade on Raven. She also had a yoga teacher's body, maybe because she was a yoga teacher. Her gray-green eyes were deep and penetrating. Her hair was starting to go silver, which bothered her not at all. To put it plainly, she was every college boy's fantasy of the older woman who would teach him all he needed to learn about love. As for Taz, she was the older sister he had needed all his life.

"Dana called this morning, while you were still out. She's taking Suzanne and Moyer up to Cherry Hill so they can meet Stewart's parents, but she said she'd like to stop by to see you when she gets back, if that's okay." Stewart Padget was the arrow-straight church mouse who had proposed to Dana some months before. He was a banker with a future. Taz had stopped trying to figure out what she saw in him, except that he was everything Taz wasn't.

"Sure. I mean—it's okay. But how's Moyer doing?"

"He's fine, if you ignore the fact that Dana's grounded him for a month, and that he feels personally responsible for getting you into this mess."

"It wasn't his fault, Laney. You have to tell Dana that. He was just being a boy."

"He's going to give us all a heart attack. So are you."

"And Suzanne?"

"She's swooning. Over you! The great Taz, who can do no wrong!" Laney rolled her eyes.

He shook his head, delicately. "If not for her, Moyer would still be under that dock. She's the one who put the alert out. Dana needs to know that as well. And I can't meddle, you know?"

"I know it's hard. You two were so close."

"They say time heals all wounds, but you know what they don't tell you? It's done by cauterization."

"Ouch. I almost forgot. Your friend Tom came by the store. He was with a new woman—blond, good looking. They seemed quite fond of one another. He had already heard about what happened. The island grapevine, I'm sure. Her name's Suzy, I think. She wanted to hear everything, said she and a friend had been with you and Tom the night before at the Pony Pines. When were you going to tell me about that? When you faced down the Nazis, I mean. Or about your new romantic interest?"

"I'm not so sure she's a romantic interest. I've only seen her twice. As for the night at the Pines, I meant to. But I kind of got sidetracked by everything else that was going down."

"Do you think your little set-to might be related to that lovely greeting card that somebody left on our wall?"

"I guess it's possible, but the *commie* splash makes me think whoever did it just doesn't like the books you stock. It could've been them, but I'm not sure I see how those jerks could link me with you or the store. Can you?"

"Not offhand. Anyway, Suzy is staying the week. She said her friend is coming back over the weekend. I gather she's in DC for work or some kind of meeting."

CHAPTER EIGHT

The Undersecretary's Request

TAZ AWOKE JUST BEFORE FIVE. An orderly came in to tell him he had a phone call at the nurses' station. He climbed out of bed and hobbled down the hall, swinging his left leg like Long John Silver. Breathing hard, he picked up the phone. The female voice at the other end was clearly doing at least two things at once, an indistinct hubbub behind her.

"Is this Taz Blackwell?"

"Last time I looked. To whom do I owe the honor?"

"You probably don't remember me. It's Jessica Lansman."

Taz blanched for a moment. Jessica had been a young presidential assistant when he and John White, the assistant secretary in charge of INR—State's Intelligence Bureau—worked together to undercut a corrupt Russian bid for a rare earth mine in Greenland. Ms. Lansman had been less than impressed by his methods, though she appreciated the result.

"Of course, I remember you, Jessica—I mean, Ms. Undersecretary." Undersecretaries are the cardinals of the State Department. There are only six of them. Jessica Lansman was now *G*— Undersecretary for Global Affairs. "I gather congratulations are in order."

"Or condolences, as I'm told you used to tell those you promoted.

Your ghost seems to haunt these halls. Well, at least this wing."

"Well, that was then. What can I do for you?"

"You know I've been talking with Everton Martins, Itamaraty's top environmental envoy."

"I've heard just enough to get the basic outline."

"The call was supposed to be this week, but Everton and I agreed to put it off until you could participate."

"I'm honored, but that might be a week or two. Or so they tell me."

"The issue won't hold 'til then." A trace of her imperious tone. *Keep an open mind.* "Taz, we can't really do this over an unsecured phone. You can't come to me. I have half a day tomorrow. Where can I find you?"

"I'm in the Peninsula Hospital in Salisbury. The roundtrip would take most of your day."

"Don't worry about all that. I'll see you before noon."

"I'll block my schedule. These days, that's not very hard." He thought he heard an "Aha."

"Taz, your friend from the bookstore—Laney? She told me what happened. I trust you're on the road to recovery."

"The doctors tell me I'm going to get better whether I want to or not."

A genuine laugh. "You have an interesting sense of humor, Taz."

"Well, Ms. Undersecretary—"

"Call me Jessica."

"Okay. May I ask what we're going to be talking about? The only thread I have to work with is a hint from a friend at the World Bank." He didn't see any reason to tell her about his *ex parte* discussion with Everton.

"I can't tell you much just now, but our friends in Brazil seem to think you could help them deal with some high-priority issues. 'New challenges in the Amazon,' were the words Everton used. We can go into all that when we meet. But there is something I have tell you before we talk with him. Taz, I asked if he was sure you were the right person. I told him how I knew you. I expressed some surprise that he would pick an Arctic specialist to help him with a conservation issue in the Amazon."

Taz choked back a laugh. "I'm just trying to imagine his reaction. I'm sure you've already run across the sense of humor underneath that oh-so formal diplomatic persona."

"Oh great! You sound just like him—he found it amusing too. Now I really am embarrassed. I only knew you from our Greenland discussions when I was at the NSC, and I know I was harsh . . . perhaps unfairly so. I thought you were a freelancer. Nobody briefed me about the work you did when you were still at State. Now I'm trying to build a relationship with Everton, and I'm going to be involved in whatever you cook up together. Will that be a problem?"

"No. Look, Jessica. I got my back up for a moment, that's all. You had every right to question our approach. If you hadn't, you wouldn't have been doing your job."

"Now I understand. Everton called you a *navegador.*" Navigator. "He also told me about the forest negotiations. He said you had pulled the agreement out of the fire."

"Everton's a good friend. He may be gilding the lily."

Taz recalled the frantic last seventy-two hours in Johannesburg when he and Everton and the EU's lead negotiator, Geert Ronk, outflanked a particularly pompous stiff from the British Foreign Office and hammered out the final deal.

"Sometime when things aren't so rushed, I'd enjoy hearing more about that. See you Thursday, then." The line clicked silent. Taz made his slow way back to his room.

Couldn't sleep. Skip James sang it best:

> *I lay down last night, looking to take my rest, but my mind was ramblin' like the wild geese from the west.*

He woke swimming in currents of moods, from contented to anxious and every stage in between. He was trying hard to forget a torturous dream, which resurrected itself every time he nodded off. His legs still tingled, and the neurologist wanted to do a few more tests to see if his back injury had damaged his spinal cord.

Laney had come Wednesday morning with a book she thought Taz would benefit from: *The Idiot's Guide to Rest and Relaxation.* Outside his window, a helicopter was settling onto the tarmac of one of the hospital's parking lots. The concussion of the long rotor blades rattled the window for a minute before they finally slowed to halt. Laney stood fixated, her eyes wide. When she came to herself again, she reached into her bag and handed Taz a tin of homemade cookies. He recognized the tin. He had seen it the last time he was in Dana's kitchen.

A tall man in sunglasses and a charcoal suit jumped out of the copter, pulled out a step, and held out his hand for a woman in a perfectly tailored blue pin-stripe pants suit. *Jessica.* The man pressed a finger to his earbud and reached for the handle of a brushed aluminum briefcase. They strode quickly towards the hospital entrance and were soon out of sight. Taz and Laney returned to their conversation. That is, until the man in gray appeared at his door. Taz waved him in. While Laney watched with a smile and an air of amusement, the suit put the briefcase on Taz's bedside table, unlocked the combination, lifted out an Iridium 9555 satellite phone, put it in its cradle, and set up a speaker.

"That's pretty cool."

The suit looked Taz over briefly. "The newest model. It has a mike that can pick up ten different voices in a room this size, and it can conference up to two dozen other phones anywhere in the world, all on satellite transmission. It probably has more RAM than your desktop." He smiled at Laney, turned back to Taz. "I think the Undersecretary is outside."

Taz pulled a comb through his hair and straightened up in bed. "Please show her in."

Laney gave Taz a quick kiss on the forehead. "I need to check in at the bookstore."

Less than ten seconds after she left, Jessica Lansman entered and stood at the foot of Taz's bed. "Glad to see you're still among the living. From what the doctor told my staff, we're lucky you're here at all. They must have you on some powerful painkillers."

"You talked to my doctor."

"We had to see whether you were really up to the conversation." *Making sure I wouldn't embarrass them or say something Everton shouldn't hear.*

"Of course."

The suit pulled out a small tape recorder and set it on the table next to the SAT phone. "Do you have a cell phone? We're going to designate this room as a SCIF for the next hour." *A Sensitive Compartmented Information Facility. So the Brazilians didn't want to broadcast the fact that they were asking for help.*

Taz handed the man his cell. He turned it off and put it face-down on the little shelf by the bathroom. Jessica looked at Taz, nodded quickly in the direction of the hall.

"Was that your friend from the bookstore? I wanted to meet her. I enjoyed our phone conversation." She eyed her helicopter through the window, sighed. "Everton should call within the next five minutes."

Taz rubbed his chin. He hadn't shaved in days and his beard itched. "Laney. She's my best friend."

"She knows you very well. She has that Western look. Colorado?"

"Montana. She ran cattle there for a few summers. What about you?"

Her eyes widened ever so slightly. They were blue, and not at all hard to look at. "Massachusetts . . . Not what you think, though. My parents had a sheep farm in the Berkshires."

He smiled. "I'm trying to picture you shearing lambs."

"Don't be so patronizing. I'd like to see you try it! I was good. I knew all our sheep by name. I can still feel the lanolin on my hands."

"My apologies. The NSC was the only context I had for you before now. How did you get from sheep shearing to the White House?"

"By way of Yale Law and a presidential internship."

"That makes sense."

"Makes sense? Why?"

Taz wondered if he should say what came next. "When I first met you, my read was, smarts off the charts, but could use some seasoning."

Now wait for the boom to fall.

Surprisingly, she responded, amused. "And what do you think now?"

"Well, I've been hearing good things from the folks who count. Not just your policy guys. Also, the senior Foreign Service players. They say you've 'got a few crises under your belt,' and that you back up your troops. That's something they respect."

Another smile. "Is that a compliment?"

"When your colleagues give you a review like that, you don't need a compliment from me."

The satellite phone buzzed like an angry bee. They both shifted their attention to it. The suit picked it up and punched in a key. "Undersecretary Lansman's office." Handed it to Jessica.

She put her hand over the mouthpiece and turned to Taz. "The Brazilians are very sensitive about this—asking for our help. That's the reason for the hush-hush." Lifted her hand. "Hello, Everton. How are you?" So, Everton hadn't made her wait for the connection at his end. After a pause, "I've got Taz Blackwell here with me. Is it all right if I put you on speakerphone?" The suit put the phone on the table between them and punched another button.

Everton's voice boomed loud and clear. "Greetings, Madame Secretary! You are so gracious to make the time to speak with me." Jessica flinched at the "Madame Secretary."

Then, "*Ola, meu amigo!* Taz, my friend. How is your recovery proceeding?"

"My recovery?" Taz's voice betrayed his perplexity.

"A private matter, of course. But I understand your actions were quite courageous. I hope you're feeling better. Soon, with Jessica's permission, we'll have you dancing the samba."

Taz rolled his eyes, gave Jessica a thin smile. She kept her gaze on him for a moment, then turned to the phone. "That I'd like to see. Perhaps we should discuss your idea."

"Yes, of course. Jessica, as I think I mentioned in our last call, Brazil is facing a new and difficult challenge. I am hoping that we might find a way that your government can help us with this. The problem is fire—fire in the Amazon. The Amazon Forest has always been immune to fire. The forest is so vast that it creates its own weather, and that weather is for the most part wet. Hot, but wet. But over the last four years, we are seeing disturbing changes. The soils on the periphery of the forest are drying, and the number of fires in the western and northern Amazon is increasing. We have taken the conclusion that concerted action is necessary." *Yes. To get the ranchers under control, reduce fossil fuel emissions, and slow the rate of global warming.* Taz had heard such commitments from the Brazilian government before.

Jessica said, "So, Everton, my friend, how can we help you?" Taz could almost see Everton's eyebrows lifting. Maybe Jessica was a little too familiar and quick to the ask, but she had good instincts. She was trying to get on the playing field where the real conversation would take place.

"Despite our good luck with offshore oil, we are still a developing country. There is no way the government at this stage can afford to fund a major fire monitoring and response system without international support."

"Everton, budgets are stretched everywhere, even here. Congress just cut our foreign aid budget by almost twelve percent." *Too quick again.* Everton would know all about her budget constraints. And he hadn't asked for anything yet.

"I'm aware of that unfortunate decision. But we're not talking about US foreign assistance."

"No? What are we talking about?"

"Two things. Technical assistance from your government, and help in obtaining a special loan from the World Bank, which would allow us to set up a national wildfire program like yours."

Jessica looked at Taz. He struggled closer to the phone. "Everton, what do your fire managers think you need?"

"Fire managers?" Everton laughed. "We have none of those, by your standards. We have the *bombeiros*—very brave on the fire line, but few in number. Picks and axes, shovels, and those foil blankets you invented to save them when a fire blows over. From the Rockefeller Foundation. In some Amazon states, we don't have any *bombeiros* at all. On the technical side, we need basic help in every area, from monitoring to the kind of advanced fire suppression techniques you use."

"And on the funding side?"

"The World Bank has a special environmental fund under which we could apply for a loan to build a fire program. But we must draft a detailed proposal, good enough to persuade them to give us the initial money out of their emergency fund."

Everton, always two steps ahead of anyone he was talking to. Particularly if he was preparing a request. Now Taz understood why he was trying to inveigle him into his scheme. He had experience with the US wildland fire program from his time as a senior assistant to the Interior secretary, and he had good contacts with senior staff at the World Bank from his time at State.

Jessica eyed him, waiting to see what he would say.

"What do you see as the timeline for this effort, Everton?"

"One year, at most. That's the window we have to tap the Bank's environmental emergency fund."

Taz looked at Jessica. She nodded vigorously. He did his best to wink at her.

She spoke into the phone. "Everton, the US government regards Brazil as an important friend. We would like to help you in any way we can."

"So, you'll lend Taz to our effort?"

Looking again at Taz, this time with an arch smile.

"Taz is a private citizen. But if he's willing, we could call him back in and second him to you, under whatever arrangement you and he work out."

"Thank you so much, Madame Undersecretary. This has been a very positive and, I must say, a very genial call. I look forward to meeting you in Geneva." They were both going to be there for the annual human rights meetings.

Jessica leaned back in her chair and drew a long breath. Then she reached sideways with an almost feline stretch and touched his arm. "Taz, are you sure you're willing to do this?"

He made a mental note to find out if she had been a dancer, and what kind. "Well, it will take me some time to get back on my feet. I'm not looking for a full-time job and I don't want to move to Brasilia or São Paulo. But as long as we can deliver what he needs short of that, yes, I'm willing."

"It would mean a lot to me, Taz, and I think it would benefit our relationship with a very important friend—a potential ally." Now she was thinking like a good *G* should.

CHAPTER NINE

Maps and Charts

TAZ'S X-RAYS SHOWED A SLIGHT concussion, badly bruised ribs, and a hairline fracture of his right collarbone. It would take a few quiet days to make sure his headaches were gone and a couple of weeks for his ribs to mend. Laney got him set up in bed at home and left to attend the customers who were already piling up at Rainy Day's front door. He watched her leave, struggling not to give into despair. Taz hated being bored. But one way or another, he was looking forward to at least three or four days sitting idly around.

The answer dawned as he was stirring his scrambled eggs. As a boy, Taz had loved maps. Later, one longtime friend swore that he had drawn a map of his mother's womb before the doctors dragged him into the real world. He loved to explore the Brazos country—*his country*. Spring, summer or fall. Armed with a pair of beaten-up Army surplus binoculars, a dented aluminum canteen and a peanut-butter-and-jelly sandwich. And sometimes, when there was friction with his father, his Army surplus cotton sleeping bag as well.

On the winter days when the frigid clippers from Alberta drove horizontal snow and the schools closed, or in the summer when the thunderheads swept across the plains, carrying tornadoes, and his Aunt Betty wanted him near the shelter, he spent the time drawing and mapping the wild country of the Brazos headwaters—the draws that led to the eroded ravines, their progress to the creek. The places where water first appeared, and at what time of year; the stream, where it ran under the damp surface, and the spots where it bubbled up through the sandstone and the surrounding scrub oak, and mesquite country where he conducted his explorations.

On the margins of his maps, he noted when the days began to cool, and the sun first slipped towards the horizon. The series of sandstone ledges where you had to keep an eye out for rattlers. The location of the oldest live oak—the one you could climb up and hide in. The outline of the low escarpment that declared the limit of Uncle Ray's range. The canyon on the other side that started as an eroded arroyo and ended as a chasm with a cool shady stream at the bottom. The path from there to the river.

When he tired of going over his local maps, he imagined the places he could go. Faraway cities. Paris. San Francisco. New York City. Cape Town! How it might be to live in those exotic places instead of the hardscrabble mesquite lands of Palo Pinto County. And when he ran out of cities, he drew maps of imaginary places. The Island of the Outcasts. The Black Forests of Nowhere. Routes and paths along which he could find his way. The Trail of Bitter Truth. The Path that Follows the Full Moon. The Track that Loses Itself in the Forest.

His favorite book in those days was Ransome's *Secret Water,* in which a trio of misfits, two boys and one girl, enjoy all kinds of adventures in a remote bay where their parents have taken up residence for the summer, and spend their evenings mapping their exploits. He loved the idea that you could live life on the water. The maps of the trio's adventures were included in a folding pocket on the inside of the back cover, which Taz used as a secret envelope for his notes as well.

It was getting towards evening. Just now, with time on his hands, not-so-great weather, and no possibility of outdoor work or even of a long walk, he was sitting on one of the hardback chairs at his round kitchen table, studying an obscure monograph on the origins of European cartography.

The monograph had as its subject the *Vienna-Klosterneuburg Map Corpus,* the most comprehensive source of the early maps and cartographic materials that guided European explorers. In short, a priceless gem. Taz had once seen an original in the Bibliothèque Nationale.

In case he tired of fifteenth-century geographic disputations, he also had, on the other side of the table, a twelve-foot length of double-plaited nylon rope. He had been using the rope in a mostly futile effort to learn to tie some particularly complex marine knots. Taz liked the names: Carrick bend, timber hitch, Spanish bowline, Tarbuck knot, and best of all, the square Turk's head.

The pain sporadically radiating through his sides and back made it hard for him to keep his concentration for very long. So, he listened to his little boom box. Cooped up as he was, his taste ran towards music high on the depression scale, the saddest fado he could find, Dolores O'Riordan, Fred Neil, Lucinda Williams, Leonard Cohen.

Bless her heart, Laney visited every day. Always with soup and some new magazine she figured he hadn't seen. Richard, for the occasional game of chess. Tom, to demonstrate his latest harmonica lick. Marcy, who brought him a rare aged barbaresco that she claimed would cure all his ills, or at least induce him to forget them.

The days seemed long, but the doctor had been right. By day four he felt markedly more like himself. His bruising had started to turn yellow and subside. He applied the package of frozen peas as an ice bag religiously, and the pain and tense muscles in his neck and back finally started to relax.

Right now, he was listening to the Cranberries, Dolores O'Riordan's band. He began to nod off somewhere between "Dreams" and "Linger," and there came a medley of images of Raven. Bending towards him, hands on her knees to ask the distance to the south end of the Island. Sitting on his front stoop. Laughing and hiccupping by his open refrigerator door, glaring when he accused her of being a fan of techno rock, her fascinated gaze as she looked at his little collection of totems. Her triumphant trickster smile when she asked him if he wanted to see her slider.

He stepped to the cabinet and picked up the gold raven, imagining how it would look on a delicate gold chain, the pendant just above the light curve of her breasts. After rummaging in his closet, he found a small wooden jewelry box just the right size. He thought he'd write a short note to accompany it. At which point it occurred to him that he didn't know who to address it to, or how to get it to her. *To Raven, via extraterrestrial pony express?* Not exactly.

He needed to do a little research. He started with a one-handed internet quest—*wildlife biology—panthers*. No luck. *Wildlife scientists—panthers*. No hits. *Wildlife conservation*. A blizzard of useless information. *Panther conservation*. The third entry gave the name of a group—the Panther Conservation Society. He went to their homepage. Scrolled through the exciting pictures and the *How to Contribute* section until finally reaching *Upcoming Events*. The PCS was preparing a conference. There was a call for papers, and a list of those already submitted for consideration. Taz combed through the list, not even knowing what he hoped to find. But find it he did: "Conservation status of the panthers *(puma concolor)* of Northern California." The author, Dr. Lucia Turan, University of California at Davis. A small photograph, like a yearbook portrait. *Raven*.

Her name in hand, Taz decided to look a little further. Another site turned up a sidebar about "The Girl Who Tracked the Shasta Cougar" in an old *Wild West* magazine, and a short interview with the outdoor editor of *Sunset* back when it was still published in print. Wild West's editor expressed some degree of awe that a young woman, "who doesn't even hunt," brought home such stunning photographs of a cougar that experienced hunters had been trying to find for two years. Despite the complaints of several local ranchers, the editors agreed that the young woman's refusal to identify the locations where she took the shots showed a remarkable sense of sport.

Sunset's outdoors editor, a middle-aged woman named Robyn Ochs, asked a number of predictable questions, and got mostly predictable answers—with one exception. "Is what you do dangerous?" Ms. Turan replied, "It would be, if I didn't know what I was doing," and then told a story about being charged by a cougar who got within ten feet of her, hopping forward two feet at a time on its hind legs, screaming and baring its claws. "I had this terrible urge to run, which is exactly the wrong thing to do. Then I saw two cubs behind her and realized she was bluff charging me to protect them. After that everything was okay, except maybe for my blood pressure."

Taz smiled, closed his computer, and poured himself a rye. Somewhere around his third sip, he recalled that Suzy—*Sandy*—was staying the week. Maybe Laney would know how to reach her. Or maybe not, but she would for sure know how to reach Tom. Taz began writing.

Lucia,

It was unkind of me to make light of your love of poetry the other night. I didn't intend to hurt your feelings, but I know I did. I can only say that your beauty struck me as the kind that could easily leave a trail of conquests and broken hearts. So, to echo your words under the Pony Pine's neon fish, perhaps I was also trying to protect myself. Considering your sterling pitching later that night, I hope you'll accept this small token of my interest in another turn at bat.

In friendship, I hope,

Taz

As if on the rim of a cloud, I remember your words.
And because of my words to you, night became brighter than day.
Thus, torn from the Earth, we rose up, like stars.

Anna Akhmatova, 1945

He wrapped the note and the box in his favorite kerchief—the yellow one from St. Lucia that celebrated the local beer, called "Amazon" after the island's endemic parrot. When Laney stopped by later in the day, he asked her to give the package to Suzy with a request that she give it to her friend when she got back from her meetings in the nation's capital.

CHAPTER TEN

Truth and Consequences

IT WAS JUST AFTER SUNSET on Saturday, exactly a week since Taz's unfortunate encounter with the Landmark dock. He had spent the morning making preliminary arrangements for his trip to Boise, and the afternoon sitting on his deck, inviting the sun and the bay breeze to finish healing body and spirit. He was finishing cleaning the pots and dinner dishes when he heard two gentle knocks on his front door. He recalled that Laney had said that Dana wanted to thank him for fetching young Moyer from under that damn dock.

Taz limped through the living room to welcome her, show her in, thank her for the cookies; it had been so long. She stood on the stoop just outside the screen door with her back to him, looking at the remains of sunset. She spun around when she heard the door. It wasn't Dana after all. It was Raven, uncertain, and holding a bottle of whiskey. The sun left a maroon and gold glow behind her. Her dark eyebrows above hazel eyes and her hesitancy hit Taz all at once. She wore a faded blue cotton work shirt with the sleeves rolled and the top two buttons undone. A light gold chain like a parabola around her neck. Laugh lines just outside those wonderful eyes. The smooth melody of her voice, asking him if he was going to invite her in. She giggled at his stumbling effort to make her welcome.

"I hope you like rye." Taz reached for her hand, led her in. She followed him through the porch and the living room to the kitchen.

"Are you sure it's alright for . . . for me to be here? Maybe you don't want company right now—I'd understand. It's just, well, I really wanted to see how you're doing." Taz pulled out a chair for her at his little round table, reached into refrigerator and found the bottle of white wine he had opened the night before, poured two glasses and pushed one of them over to her.

"You know how to charm a girl, even when you're all broken up. Your friend at the bookstore—Laney—she told me what happened . . . what you did. Looks like you're mending, though. I hope so."

"I'm fine. Really, it wasn't that big a deal."

"That's not what Laney said."

"How in the world did you cross paths with Laney?"

Lucia sipped her wine. "Suzy introduced me to her when I got back yesterday. She's terrific, but I guess you know that. At first, she was kind of poking around with me. Asking questions like an older sister would, you know, if she was worried about her brother." Another sip. "We ended up talking, and pretty soon a couple of hours had gone by. She told me the whole story, Taz." She drained the flute. He poured her another, then topped up his own. "So don't try to pretend it was nothing. Plus, she said folks have been ringing her phone all week to see how you're doing."

"Mostly people who've been waiting a long time to see me go. They were probably disappointed when they learned I was still breathing. Oh, and the undertaker—to find out what's taking me so long. They haven't had much business lately."

"You really are a surprise." If there was anything like a gentle glare, she threw him one. "You're getting all twitchy because you don't like to admit that anybody cares about you." Another sip. "Laney said that's what you do."

"Now I know why I was hoping you two would never meet. What other nonsense has she been feeding you?"

Her smile returned. "That you're impossible! Which I already knew." Another, longer sip, looking at him over the rim of her glass. "That you can't look away from trouble. That you 'need to be bailed out more often than a blind cat burglar.' Her words, not mine." She idly toyed with the necklace. Pulled the fine gold chain to her mouth and held it between her lips. She was wearing the raven pendant.

Taz drained his glass as well. "Enough about me. What would your blond friend say about you if I asked?"

"Changing the subject? Nice try. You know perfectly well I'm going to come back to this. Anyway, it's too late for you to grill her. She left this morning."

She looked down, embarrassed or maybe just uncertain. "I should've come by last night." Then, with a tone of surprise, "I wasn't ready."

She looked out the window. Came back to meet his gaze. "Weird, right? I hardly know you. You barely know me. Doesn't seem to matter— I'm all wrought up anyway. I didn't think I could stand to see you all busted up." She fingered the pendant, looked down. "I was so sure you didn't know my name." She raised her chin in defiance. "You never even asked."

He studied her face. "I didn't imagine we would see each other again." She flinched. "And knowing your name would have just made it harder to forget you. You probably think that's pretty strange."

"No, it's just . . . why is it so important to me? To have you know who I am?"

"Turned out it was important to me, too. I ended up Googling *panther conservation* ten ways from Sunday. I finally found your paper on the Shasta cougars. Other than the fact that I'm no good at statistics, I thoroughly enjoyed it." He thought it better not to mention the article in *Wild West*.

"You found me on the web? I should be flattered. But really, I'm a little freaked out."

"I didn't pull up your rap sheet. I just wanted to find your name." He rolled it over on his tongue. "Do you pronounce it the Spanish way? '*Lu-see-ya*?' And it would mean *light* from the Latin *lux.*"

Her eyes lit with amusement: "You really *have* been doing some research. Now I'm flattered. I pronounce it the simple way, *Loosha*. But the root is Syrian, not Latin. In the old country it would be spelled *L-u-*

j-a, and it means *great depth.*"

Taz rubbed his forehead. "I'm not doing very well at this, am I?"

"No, but your persistence is admirable. I don't blame you, it's hard. My great grandmother fell in love with a French soldier who was stationed in Beirut. They both died before I was born."

"So where did you come by your Irish side?"

"What makes you think I even have an Irish side? French, Lebanese, Irish? That's three sides. Which is weird."

"You want the tells? Your sense of humor, your sharp tongue, the slightly defiant walk, the hazel eyes that can smile with all the heart in the world or pierce like a Druid arrow. Shall I go on?"

Lucia's blush crested at the top of her cheekbones. "You're a glib one, aren't you? My grandfather married a girl from County Sligo. I guess you've redeemed yourself after all. But it'll be a special day when I live up to that description." She shook her head, leaned into the palm of her hand in the universal expression of wonderment and incomprehension.

"So, what brought you back? To our little island, I mean."

"Despite the mosquitoes and its perverse devotion to mediocre food? I like the water, and the folks I've met. They remind me of home."

"Even the hermits?"

Her eyes twinkled. "The jury's out on that. But Laney and Richard for sure. Cliff, your clam guy—a great storyteller! Roxy. I like it that she tells it straight. They remind me of my friends on the river." His eyebrows raised in question. "I know—that's high desert, and this is an island with its head barely above high tide. But the people, well, they're not that different—good-hearted, hardworking, proud. The boys at Ferraro's Auto Repair. I had to get an oil change. I know, it's a guy's scene. But it's kind of cute, and they let me hang out for a while. And by the way, they all knew about the scene at that bar last week. The one they call Scooter said the Nazis had it coming. They seem to think you're okay."

They sat for a while, absorbing the quiet.

"Taz, Laney said you needed a fresh start."

"I will love Laney until the day I die. But she spends an inordinate amount of energy planning my future." Changing channels would be his only out. "And while you're listening to Laney's blarney about me, I'm an open book, but I'm in the dark about you."

Lucia gave him a piercing look. "If you're an open book, it's one nobody but Laney can read." Looked anxiously around the kitchen. "Where do you keep your cocktail glasses?" Taz pointed. She opened the cabinet and took down two old-fashioned glasses. Twisted the top off the Sazerac and poured an inch of rye in each glass. Downed hers in one hit. The very last thing Taz was going to tell her was that he usually took a little water with his.

"Okay. I really do study panthers. They're probably the only thing that could have pulled me away from my Pit River country. We have cougars there. Cougars and panthers are different. The cougar is smaller and it's officially a puma. But they're a lot alike otherwise. Panther is actually a family name. It includes real panthers, tigers, leopards, and jaguars. Lions too, technically. By the time I was in high school, I had gotten to know our local cougars well enough that I could track individuals. I even gave them names—Splayfoot, Queenie, and Hopalong. They helped pull me through some rough times. I thought if I got some wildlife biology, I could study them for real, maybe even make a contribution. So that was college, and after, I started doing field research. But for the bigger cats that everyone knows as panthers, it's either Florida—the Fakahatchee Strand—or Texas. The lower Rio Grande. And on the Rio Grande, who knows? You might even run into a jaguar."

Taz drained the rest of his rye. Spent a few moments staring at his pine ceiling, considering his situation. She had a mysterious ability to magnetize his gaze. Now he sought her eyes. "No big cats on this little island. I'm sure you knew that. So, really, what brought you here?"

"You already know the answer to that, too. I came to get away from work, to laze around a different beach, to hang out with my bestie."

"I don't mean the Island. I meant why here, to this broken-down old waterman's cottage? My little *dacha*. It's not exactly a tourist attraction. I'm not sure how to say this, but if you're looking for someone, the whole Island is yours for the taking. DC too, for that matter. Every young wannabe, all the eligible bachelors, and half the used-to-bes as well. They'd flutter around you like moths to a flame."

She looked at him steadily. "Who says I'm looking for anything? And if I was, has it occurred to you that I might be interested in something more than a fling? Besides, what do you think I am, a twenty-year-old undergrad looking for a sugar daddy? Or for a boy-toy who's mostly equipped with outsize ambitions and an adolescent libido? Earth to Taz. I'm thirty-three. I got my doctorate six years ago."

Taz flinched. "It's not the first time I've been a fool. Honestly, I was guessing you were in your twenties. I didn't mean to . . . you know . . . "

"If there's one thing I know, it's that you're no fool. And by the way, that's not a mistake most women would take as an insult." She sniffed her empty glass, poured them both another two fingers. Bent forward so she could look up at his eyes: "Taz. That first conversation—the one when we surprised you on the stoop. You were so . . . I don't know . . . amused? Okay, so at first you were mostly irritated that we had the gall to invade your little hideaway. But you were still the gentleman. Wanting to see something more than my boobs. You were more interested in who I was than in what I was. I was struck by that."

"If anyone was struck, it was me—when you told me off. I've only had that experience once before. I mean to have a beautiful woman stranger tell me what for."

"Tell you off? I did no such thing."

"Let me quote: 'Come on—you can do a better *Hello Stranger* than that'."

Another belt of rye. "No, no, no. You started with 'Any port in a storm?' And I just tried to suggest—that was all I did—tried to suggest that you might have considered a warmer, I mean more warm, you know, a more warm greeting. That's all."

"I think we're having our first spat."

She glowered at him. Pulled her chair closer to his, picked up the bottle. It was already down a quarter. Poured them both another two fingers. "Okay, you bastard. Then—well, then you had to pull out your guitar and turn into the only dust bowl romantic I've ever met! How many of you are out there? Do you have club meetings where you compete to see who can play the most obscure song? Just asking."

He was about turn that one around, but there was no stopping her. "Then, okay, you pissed me off, and so I blurted out the most hurtful words I could find. I wanted to take you down a peg for your quip about the *lariati*. I was paying you back. I'm embarrassed even now."

Taz reached and stroked her hair. She gradually leaned forward, let her head slowly list his way until it was resting on his chest. He kept stroking. Her hair was silky.

She pulled herself up. "And if that wasn't enough, I had to let you drag me into joining you and your pal—well, my pal too, I guess—no, Tom was her charm—to that crazy-ass bar with the neon fish. And you froze me out so hard on the ride that I couldn't wait to get inside where it was warm. Then you decided to teach a lesson to that bonehead who was groping Suzy. Taz, he was twice your size! Didn't matter, apparently. I'll never get over the image. Bigfoot with his hand nailed to the bar, and then you still had to take care of junior!"

"Yeah, well I wasn't the one pegging lemons at his head. Although I think it was the saltshaker on the nose that did the job."

Lucia smiled. "Just a little chin music." She said it in a light singsong. She looked around. "Where's your bathroom?"

"Through the bedroom." Taz pointed her in the right direction. He waited, dropped a couple of ice cubes in his whisky, swirled them with his finger. Heard the bathroom door close with its usual squeak and moan. Licked his finger for a little taste. Sat, alone with his thoughts, which were, at best, confused.

Lucia burst back into the kitchen, arms up, shaking a book in either hand. "You were gaslighting me!"

"What?"

"Totally! That night outside Rainy Day. You acted like you hated poetry—just to get my goat! So, what are these doing here?" She looked up at one hand, then the other. "Garcia Lorca? Rimbaud? The others in that little stack on top of your dresser? Gary Snyder? Yeats? Kim fucking Addonizzio? That Russian woman from your note?" Fierce. Glaring.

She wasn't close to finishing. "So first you gaslight me. You must have thought I was ridiculous! Then you go out of your way to piss me off. Then you do that Prince Valiant thing at the bar. Wait, wait, and then, when I was finally drunk off my ass, you had to carry me home—I must have been one hell of a prize, about as tasty as a bag of wet cement. And tuck me, for Christ's sake, *tuck me in,* on my own damn couch. And part of me was saying, 'Lord, please tell him to fuck me,' but then you were already walking out the door. Fortunately for both of us, I blacked out."

Taz looked her over. Her eyes hazel, with shards of green. Deep enough to be serious. They crinkled when she smiled. Her hair, which threatened to fall over her eyes but never quite did. Black, hints of red in sunlight. Just curly enough to produce some delightfully loose tangles. Her nose, straight and delicate. Her lips, soft and delectable. Her collarbones. Her elegant neck. Her shoulder, which was becoming ever more visible as her blouse slipped down her arm.

She got up from her side of the table. "Taz, would it be okay if I kissed you?"

"I could probably stand it." She glowered. Then she bent, brushed his lips with hers, smiled a private smile, came back, and gave him a gentle but marvelously sensual kiss.

His back had started to ache again, and his head was spinning. He got to his feet a little unsteadily. "But there's something I still don't understand. I just can't think what it is."

She pulled herself up with a hand on his forearm. "What I think is we're both swizzled, and you're still not exactly a hundred percent. Maybe I should tuck *you* in this time."

That's pretty much what happened. When Taz woke up, he was still clothed, and Lucia was gone. He could still smell her, sweet and dusky, where she had lain beside him, her knees pressed into the back of his, her arm wrapped over his side.

CHAPTER ELEVEN

Lucia Farewell

TAZ NURSED HIS MORNING COFFEE, blearily eyeing the next stage in his most recent consultation for State. A knock at the side door. Lucia on the other side of the screen. He struggled out of his chair, opened the screen door just a crack. "You selling Bibles? Unless they cure hangovers, I don't need any."

Four fingers slipped through the crack and pulled the door open just enough for him to get a glimpse of an eye watching him behind a curtain of dark tresses. "Hair of the dog?"

"Tip of the iceberg? First serious adventure? Bloody Mary? You could've just come in, you know."

She wore a blue-gray pants suit with a pink blouse. The pendant complemented her look perfectly. She held out her hands in imitation of a Buddhist with a mendicant cup. Taz pointed her towards the little round table and started clearing off his laptop and papers as she sat. She moved the gray-bound book on top of the remaining stack and slid the top document her way—a draft of a paper with the properly officious title, *Outlining policy options for negotiating a Global Forest Conservation Funding Agreement with the Council of Europe.* Lucia looked at it for a moment, then turned the book so she could see its title. *Developments of International Law in Treaty-Making,* Rüdiger Wofrum's latest tome. She gazed at Taz, eyebrows raised, then smiled and shook her head.

Taz stepped to the refrigerator to get lemon, horseradish, and V8. The vegetable drawer for olives and celery. Then to the cabinet for the vodka, the drawer below it for Tabasco and Outerbridge's. Old Bay to coat the rims. He glanced over his shoulder at her.

"I didn't even ask if you had time."

"I'm not in a hurry, if that's what you mean. I have some meetings in DC that I have to get ready for, that's all."

Taz stirred the pitcher, poured two. Dropped a green olive and a celery stalk in each. Put Lucia's on the table in front of her.

She sampled his work. "Why don't you just give it up and be a bartender? This is beyond good. Is it that little magic bottle?"

He brought his Bloody over and stood opposite her. "The Outerbridge's? It's a sherry pepper concoction they make in Bermuda. Like Worcestershire, only better. I should have put in a little more." She shook her head vehemently. "I'd get back in cocktail practice if I had more customers."

That smile. "Oh, really. How many customers would you need?" He put his glass down in front of his chair and turned to close the refrigerator door, giving her a quick look over his shoulder.

"I think one more would do the trick." He pulled his chair out. "But she'd need to be a regular."

She pinched the toothpick and pulled off the olive with her teeth. Her wide eyes and a little sigh said she was enjoying it. "Well, I do come this way once in a while."

"You can't mean here. I'd have to have been blind not to notice."

"No, more to Washington. I have business there sometimes." He raised his eyes in a question. "I ended up here because of Suzy. We often travel together. She came out to visit, and she'd heard of the Island. I think maybe Misty and the pony stories. She wanted to see it for herself. And so, voila." She took a long sip of the Bloody Mary, wiped her lips with the back of her hand. "I got here because of a girls' story book. How about you?"

He let out a breath. "Broken marriage, busted career. Nothing to keep me in DC, and no place to go back to. I needed a place to rebuild. I thought I could do that here."

"So, when you said, 'just home,' that's what you meant. But," She swept her hand over his paper and the gray book. "It doesn't really look like your career is past tense. Unless all this is just a hobby."

"I was the State Department's environmental negotiator in the last administration. The new bunch couldn't care less about all that, which is good, because if they did, they'd be taking us backward. So now I try to help some of my old colleagues—senior foreign service types who are doing their best to keep the country's promises and make whatever progress they can." He sighed. "The life of a consultant. I end up travelling a fair amount. It's nice to have an anchorage." He sipped his Bloody Mary, added a dash of Tabasco. "Mobility, it's our gift, and our curse. The lucky ones manage to touch down someplace where they can contribute and find work where they can make a difference. Something tells me that might ring a bell for you."

"Well yes. I mean I still go to see my grandmother Tillie in Alturas, but all the rest of it . . . I've kind of left that behind."

"Do you miss it?"

"Miss it? No. There wasn't that much to miss, to tell the truth."

"So, where's home base now? Where do you hang your hat when you're not gracing our sainted isle? California's a little far away to be part of a monthly commute to DC."

"Monthly? Where'd you get that?"

"I don't know, maybe Tom? Does it matter?"

She looked at him steadily. "I love Suzy, but she couldn't keep a secret if her life depended on it."

Taz wondered why Lucia's monthly schedule would need to be a secret. He felt as if he were trying to solve a difficult crossword and must have shown his confusion.

"I couldn't keep track of my cats on the Rio Grande without an easy way to cross the border—at odd times and sometimes outside the official crossing points. That means a special passport amendment and a visa note from the Mexican consulate. Not hard to get, but they both have to be renewed every month. So, back and forth, back and forth." She stiffened. "But why would any of that matter?"

She likes her privacy, for sure. "I don't know. Maybe I like the idea that you have to come up once in a while. It's a long way, I know. I used to spend a little time on the border when I was at Interior. Haven't been down there since. But I've been thinking about going south to do a little spring birding. There are a few places that are totally spectacular in March—the San Pedro River in Arizona, the Everglades. The lower Rio Grande is the third. I've never tried Laguna Atascosa, and I hear it can be sensational. If that's where I end up, it would be nice to know how to find you."

Her eyes dilated ever so slightly. "I have a little place upriver from there, not far from the Santa Ana Wildlife Refuge. That's where we've had the most panther sightings over the past few years. When I have to observe at night, I camp. But I generally do my field work alone."

"The risk doesn't bother you?"

"Not any more than it would bother you!" He realized his miscue. She quickly placed her hand on his. "I . . . I don't mean it the way you think. It's just that even if I liked the idea, I'm probably not such good company. When I have to observe at night I camp. I get pretty absorbed. Not only that, but I get up all the time to check the infrared cameras. I make it as safe as I can. I sleep in the research van, and I stay away from places I don't know." It was as considerate a brush-off as Taz could recall.

She put her handbag on the chair to her right and rummaged around in it for almost a minute. Her expression changed from calm to alarmed. It was like watching a cuttlefish change color from blue to red as it recognized a threat. Taz was flipping through his mental Rolodex of the towns near the Santa Ana other than McAllen itself. Had to be Hidalgo, a small border town right on the river.

"Oh God, Taz! I meant to give this back to you long before now. In the shape I was in last night, I'm lucky I remembered my own name." With a sigh of relief, she held up Taz's ironwood turtle. "I'm really not a kleptomaniac!" Rolled her eyes. "I was playing with it that day we met, and then—" Her voice trailed away. She turned it over as she put it in his hand. "The inscription . . . I was curious. I wanted to see if I could find a translation." Holding it closer, "It's not any language that Google can find. What does it say?"

"It's in the language of the Nanticoke. It reads, *'Yu 'uta rezki tu kulum u'uk.'*"

"And that means?"

"Talks with owls."

"Talks with owls?" She gave him a quizzical smile.

"The strict formulation is, 'He who talks with the owl.'" She was about to ask a question. Gave up with a slow shake of the head, gazed out the window. He stood to add some vodka to the pitcher, caught her eye when she turned to see what he was up to. "Could you stand a little more? Or maybe we should switch to a border favorite—like *chamoyadas.*"

"Too sweet for me." He nodded. "Anyway, how do you know about *chamoyadas?*"

"Like I said, I spent quite a bit of time on the border when I was working for Interior Secretary Talbot."

"And what was your job at Interior? Clearly not a Bartleby. Yes, they made me read Melville—third year."

"Kind of you. There was a fancy title, but those are a dime a dozen. Basically, I was Talbot's utility infielder."

"Let me guess. The problems nobody else could solve?"

"Mostly the ones no one else wanted to pick up."

"On the border?"

"Yup. And Arctic Alaska and the Everglades. Sometimes I think he liked me better when I wasn't close enough to give him a hard time. So I was negotiating a joint resource mapping agreement with the Mexican Environment Ministry. I had to know what was at stake. Not just minerals and oil, but also wildlife, endangered species, all those things. So, I ended up sitting down with most of the refuge managers from Brownsville to San Ysidro."

She looked at her watch. They made their way through the living room and out to the stoop. They watched the channel for a bit. When she turned back to him, her expression had become hard to read, her eyes searching his face.

She blinked. "Okay, what?"

"You have that look."

"What look?"

"Like you're getting ready to tell me something."

"Well, I really enjoyed last night. And just now, too. Earlier this morning, not so much, but it was worth it."

"And?"

"You really can be insufferable, you know that?" He just smiled. "And I'm headed back the day after tomorrow."

"Isn't it a little early to be breaking up? We haven't even had our second date."

"Very funny, Mister Quip. We haven't even had a first date, unless you count that riot at the Pony Pines."

He raised his glass in a mock toast. *"Touché."*

"Anyway, it's two separate things, so it'll probably take some time. I don't know how long. I'm trying to raise some local money to support our conservation education program. And two days ago, one of my grad students spotted a panther without a tag pretty far up the river, near Eagle Pass. If we don't tag it soon and transport it back down at least as far as the Santa Ana, it'll probably get shot by some fool rancher."

Taz studied her face in silence. His grandfather CL always said, "Two excuses is like two alibis, it's one more than you need." Taz wondered what she wasn't telling him. He stood. "Got to keep those ranchers in line. I'll bet you're good at it."

She stood, put her hands on his shoulders, went up on tiptoe to plant a kiss on his cheek. Moved her lips to his, all too briefly, whispered, "I'm glad I got to meet you." Spun on her heel, climbed in her Jeep, backed out of the driveway, and turned so she was headed up the street. She paused there, opened the passenger window, and called out to him. "How often does someone have to show up to be a regular customer?"

Taz stepped down off the stoop and walked to the car, resting his hands on window slot on the door. "Often enough to keep an open tab." Then he stood in the street and watched her drive up South Main towards town.

Once she was out of sight, Taz walked dazedly to the shed, brought back some sandpaper wrapped around a short cut of two-by-four, and spent a few quiet hours sanding the windowsills on his front porch. The ones that took the worst beating in the last nor'easter—or, really, any time the wind whistled and blew the salt spray across Chincoteague Bay from the west, which was most of the time. Once they were smooth to the touch, a first coat of spar varnish. There was a lot of sanding and layering ahead of him, but he had plenty of time.

❧

Three hours later, just as he was finishing the first coat of varnish, Laney called. "Richard's taking the counter at five. It'd be a good time for you to invite me over for a drink."

"I can do better than that. How about staying for dinner? It won't be anything fancy. I'm just going to pan-sear a couple of steaks."

"Sounds great. I'll bring a side or two. Be there by six."

He had an hour and a half. Time enough to leave messages for a few friends at State, until he finally hit a live one—Becca Scoresby, who had been a young star on his Stockholm Convention delegation and was now a senior attorney for the consular service.

After some glad greetings and mutual reminiscences, she asked the purpose of his call. He needed to know how hard it would be to get a passport amendment to allow frequent trips across the Mexican border, outside the official crossing points.

"Taz, how do you know about this? Even the existence of those waivers is closely held. I shouldn't be talking about them. But I guess you already know more than you should. Have you still got your classification?"

"Yep."

"If I remember right, it's high enough that I can read you in. How hard are they to get? Almost impossible. They only go to people working intelligence or enforcement. Every senior ICE special agent and DEA criminal investigator wants one, and we don't give out more than three or four a year."

"Thanks, Becca. What would it take to get one, if you met the right criteria?"

"An extremely convincing demonstration of need, and the endorsement of someone serious on the seventh floor, either an undersecretary or an assistant secretary with unusual clout." Another little piece of the jigsaw puzzle. Taz hoped she could find time to have dinner with him soon; it would be on him. She thought that was a fine idea.

Taz rounded up the seemingly random facts he had collected and pushed them to the back burner, where they could continue to simmer until he figured out how they all connected. Meanwhile, he'd do his best to pick up his own trail again. Lucia was tracking panthers in the Rio Grande Valley, but maybe she was also tracking something else— something more to do with the border than the river. She was an unsettling challenge, a mystery and a delight all rolled up into one dangerously beautiful package. Hot and cold and as hard to resist as fried ice cream. And here and gone. He needed to forget her.

*

Laney had brought red wine and a homemade Caesar salad. They started on martinis at six-fifteen. Once they had drained the first round, Taz lifted his cast-iron frying pan out of its drawer and put it on the grill to sizzle.

She replenished them, held both martinis by the stem, motioned with her head to Taz. They went to sit on the wicker love seat on the front porch, where they could feel the cool breezes from the north.

With great care, she put her martini down on the wicker table, worked it around until she found one of the few places where it could stand perfectly straight. Then his.

"So. Lucia's headed back to the Rio Grande?"

"That's what she told me this morning."

"We talked a little bit—maybe she told you. I like her, Taz. How could I not? I mean, come on, she's a home-grown girl who's fun to hang out with, and just to complete the picture, she makes a living doing field research on subjects who could kill her if she isn't careful. And she seems genuinely fond of you. What I'm saying is I think you need a fresh start, and you deserve one. That's why I did what I could to help her get to know the Island. I love you, and sometimes I put up my guard for you. Or at least I'm tempted to. Not this time."

Taz gave her a sideways glance. Took a sip. "It must be hard being my guardian angel. I'm not so sure about the new start thing. She's like a butterfly. She doesn't like to be pinned down. She has more ups and downs than a yo-yo. And it doesn't seem like she's in the market for anything more than a friend. Still, I enjoy her. I can't help it."

"Of course, you can't. You're a man, and she's a knockout. But I'm sure that has nothing to do with it." Laney's eyes twinkled.

"She is easy on the eyes. It's her spirit, though— that's what catches you. She can be soft one moment and steely the next, and she's downright fiery when she wants to be." Turned his head and took a little sniff. "Smells like the steak is ready."

They talked through dinner. The local arts organization had asked Richard to join its board. The city was going to spruce up the park by the wharf. Tourists were everywhere downtown, but they were also buying books by the bushel, so Laney couldn't exactly object. The irony that Teaguers can't vacation in summer because that's when everybody else comes to the island. On the other hand, the money—Marcy's wine store would never survive without them. Taz poured more wine.

"I'd like to see her again. But there's this little doubt. It feels like there's a lot I don't know. And part of me says don't go there—she's never coming back."

"And you're saying *she* has her ups and downs?"

"Okay, okay. I admit it, she's got me good and turned around. Not exactly what I need right now."

"Stop whining. Every man on the island would like to be in your shoes. I mean, at least she gives you the time of day."

Taz winced. "Yeah, we've gone a little beyond that."

"That's kind of what she said to me this morning before she left. She'll come back, Taz. And if she doesn't, you're just going to have to go and find her."

He thought about that one for a little bit. "In the meantime, it looks like I'm going to be doing some travelling of my own—to Brazil. Work. . . fire stuff. For a week or two, likely. Maybe the trip will give me a chance to sort things out."

"Fine for you. But who's going to buy my coffee?"

"You have this husband person. I'm pretty sure he can carry two cups at once. Not only that, but he's also smarter than me, and he's luckier than me too. You want proof? He found you first."

"Here's some advice, Prince Charming—save the good lines for Lucia. She's not going to be an easy catch. In the meantime, try not to get yourself killed, okay?"

"Okay, but what makes you think I'm trying to catch someone?"

Laney rolled her eyes and laughed with a sound like a wiener dog's bark. Kissed him on the cheek and headed home.

CHAPTER TWELVE

No Good Deed Goes Unpunished

HE SHOULD HAVE KNOWN IT couldn't last. The softness of those early days of April, the breezy bike rides into town, the joy of crabbing with Suzanne and Moyer on their spring break. Dana had lifted Moyer's month of house arrest after two weeks, and Taz was still on his list of acceptable destinations. Jessica and her team at State were finally ready to assemble an interagency group to help design the Brazil strategy. It had taken them two weeks, which was good, since it took Taz just that long to return to anything like top form. The fact that he spent half his time wondering what was up with Lucia didn't do much to speed the healing process.

The late afternoon sun angled for the western horizon. Taz was deep in a game of chess with Richard when the call came from Arthur, Jessica's gay factotum. He was inquiring, delicately, whether Taz would be available for a meeting at State on Thursday. It was Tuesday. Taz sighed, said, "Sure." Arthur gave him the details, and some background. He was going out of his way to be helpful.

They finished the game with a bang. Taz made a clever move, after which Richard took his bishop and then his queen. Taz waited a suitable length of time, then toppled his king.

"You're distracted."

"Sorry, not at my best."

"I would still have beaten you. Tough opening."

"For sure."

"So that was your pal at State, I imagine."

"You are just a master of perception. Anyway, it's *pals*. There are more of them than there are of me."

"Now what?"

"Boise and Brazil, in some combination I haven't quite figured out yet. They're going to want me to go sooner than I thought. And between now and then, I'm going to be pretty hard to find." Taz scratched his head. "And there are some questions I need answers to before I leave. Don't tell Laney quite yet, okay? I don't think I told her how soon I have to go."

"All I can say is you better tell her soon. You're still not a hundred percent, and you and I both know she'll kill you before she'll watch you kill yourself."

"Richard—even for you—that's a new low in hyperbole."

"And that's a contradiction in terms."

Taz held his hand in a gesture of peace and stepped out the back door to make a call.

"Secretary White's office. Can I help you?" Not Ellie, but he recognized her assistant's voice.

"I hope so. I'd like a few minutes of John's time on Thursday, if that's possible. I'm going to be meeting with his new undersecretary in the morning, but I could do any time in the afternoon."

"And may I ask your name?"

"Taz. Taz Blackwell."

A few moments of silence. "He'll be glad to work you in, Mr. Blackwell. I'll call back with some possible times."

John White was the assistant secretary of Intelligence, Narcotics and Research at State. He and Taz had been colleagues over the years when Taz led the negotiation of the government's environmental agreements. Taz had once declined John's invitation to undertake an undercover operation during a global negotiation. His decision led to a number of predictable consequences, which only stiffened Taz's resolve. White eventually saw the futility of his efforts and, in his own cryptic way, made a peace offering. The clash left a bad taste in his mouth, but Taz still respected White's intelligence and expertise.

The store's back door banged open and in came Tom, a bag of harmonicas slung over his shoulder. "I've been playing with Ronnie at a church social. God, do I need a beer."

Taz got off his stool, saluted Richard, looked at Tom. "Pony Pines. I need to thank Roxy for her help the other night."

"Meet you there. I'll be the one with the tailpipe dragging on the ground."

"I imagine I'll recognize you. Better yet, get me a wire coat hanger and we'll tie it up, so it doesn't get jammed right up your butt the next time you put the damn thing in reverse."

The fix only took ten minutes. They were on their second beer when Laney walked in. She made a beeline for Taz's stool. "I hear you're going gallivanting again." Taz sent a sideways look in Richard's direction. Richard held up his hands in the universal gesture of "What the hell was I supposed to do?"

The four of them sat at the bar. Roxy glowered at Taz, then at Tom. Took their orders without a hint of a smile; neither of them had stopped by for over a week. Lots of talk about local doings. The scallop fleet was arriving from North Carolina one boat at a time. The major dredging operation to clear the outlet channel south of the marina had to wait to get started until the Corps could bring their heavy dredge up from the Oregon Inlet on the Outer Banks.

Roxy filled their glasses, exchanged pleasantries with Laney. Gave Taz a long look. "Been a long time, cowboy."

"Not for lack of wanting to. I was told I needed some bed rest."

"I heard some cockeyed story about you dueling a dock. The way I understand it, the dock won." A slightly warmer smile. Taz looked down the bar at the old, filigreed silver cash register.

Two couples came in, sat at a table near the end of the bar. Taz didn't recognize them. He caught Roxy's attention. "Doesn't matter. I should've been by to thank you. Are you ever going to forgive me?" She scowled again, grabbed a dishtowel, and came around the bar to wipe down the foursome's table. Paused just behind him and whispered in his ear, "Maybe. But when I do, it sure won't be in front of your little booster club. It'll have to be a one-on-one kind of thing."

Taz smiled and watched her as she swayed towards the table. He was debating whether to stay or go when his cell cawed and changed the course of his evening.

Liza Clarke's number. "Taz, remember that Carolina license plate? Well, it turns out to be quite a story."

He got off his stool, winked at Roxy, and headed out to his truck. The sun had already gone down. "Tell me."

"The plate belongs to a miscreant named Jimmy Slater. Twenty-seven years old. From some little 'burg in the hill country above Greenville. Quite a rap sheet: burglary, assault, history of domestic violence. On top of that, the Edgecomb County prosecutor thinks he's mixed up with some White supremacist group. He and a pal named Daniel Carr did some time for stealing guns from a dealer in Spartanburg. Thanks for turning me on to this. If I can get a decent picture and find a better link to the graffiti at your friends' bookstore, maybe I'll do a profile for the Weekend section."

Without thinking about it, Taz headed Old Faithful for the cottage. "You might want to wait until we've got him locked up. These guys are mean as mules."

✦

Dusk had settled over the western lands across the bay. Taz slowed in front of the cottage, thinking about Liza's news. Maybe he should pay Deputy Chief Whipple a visit in the morning. He decided he might head up to Rainy Day and see if either Richard or Laney were still there.

Just after he pulled out again, a red pickup jumped from the stop sign at Beebe Road with its tires squealing and came rapidly up behind him. He looked in his rearview mirror. The pickup was a Ford 150 with South Carolina plates.

Taz was driving twenty-seven miles per hour, just two over the legal limit. The local constabulary were famous for citing the smallest infractions. Even at the speed limit, he had to slow to keep from coming up on a station wagon with Pennsylvania plates, its driver searching addresses on the way into town. The Ford revved and closed the distance between them until it was only a few inches off Taz's rear bumper, headlight over taillight for about half a mile. Taz hated tailgaters. A panel truck and an RV had pulled in off Bunting and were now behind the Ford. At last, there came a string of RVs, trucks, and SUVs heading south in the other lane. Taz slowed to a stop, reached into the toolbox on the passenger side floor and slid a cat's paw under his belt, where it would be held tight against his left hip. Opened his door and walked back to the truck. He recognized the license plate from the parking lot at the Pony Pines. Took a quick look in back and saw a dozen paint cans and a splattered drop cloth. He motioned for the driver to lower his window.

Of course, they were listening to "Sweet Home Alabama," the only pop song Taz was aware of that actually celebrated Lester Maddox, the little cross-eyed governor who held back integration in Georgia for a few years. The window came down. The driver looked familiar. He stared at Taz with scorn. "What the fuck do you want?" His passenger snickered, stared determinedly at the dashboard.

The memory came to Taz in a flash. He was looking at Chewbacca's companion from the fight at the Pony Pines. He took a step closer to the window. "If you want to kiss my ass, maybe you should pucker up."

The driver squinted in his direction. "Oh, I'll fuck you up, that's for sure. You're the one who stabbed Big Dan at that stinking bar."

"That was his name? Big Dan? Seriously? Big Dan the ladies' man! Daniel Carr, right? Then you must be Jimmy Slater. I hear you have quite a record. Maybe we can add a few charges to your rap sheet." Slater was wide-eyed, a purple flush spreading north from his chin towards his hairline. "You know my name? You been tracking me?"

"I don't care about you enough to track you. But I guess the FBI does."

Jimmy flushed even further, sputtered something unintelligible. Reached for his door handle. "You just stay right there, fuck-head, and see what happens." He opened his door, put his left foot on the step-up. The van behind them started honking.

Taz drew the cat's paw from out of his belt and showed it. "Come on ahead, jackass." A semi back in the line pulled on his air horn. It was soon joined by an RV one place behind, and then by the panel truck, whose horn sounded like an enraged tuba. The cacophony brought a smile to Taz's face. He reached in his shirt pocket with his free left hand and retrieved his cellphone. "Mind if I take a picture?" Jimmy scowled, blinked at the flash, and pulled himself back into the driver's seat, muttering under his breath. The second he pulled the door closed, Taz swung the cat's paw and shattered the Ford's driver's side headlight. That was his backhand. For good measure, he used a forehand to smash the driver's side rear rear-view. Smiled at Slater through the window and tipped his cap. Slater jammed the pickup back until it kissed the panel truck's bumper, pulled into a driveway to get around Taz's truck, and sped off up Main. The last RV headed south had already shown its taillights. Taz waved to the truck driver behind him, motioned him to pass on by. The driver looked a little startled as Taz realized he was waving with the cat's paw.

Rainy Day was dark as Taz passed by. He pulled off onto the gravel lot behind one of the Island's few remaining oyster houses and called Richard's mobile. "Are you two decent? I'm headed your way, and I've got some news."

◆

They were sitting in their living room, Richard leafing through a copy of *Wired*; Laney reading Isabelle Allende. She put it down. "Well look who's here. I just got off the phone with your friend Lucia. She said she had tried you, but the call wouldn't go through." *Probably because I was busy popping Slater's headlight.*

"How'd she sound?" His mind was still on what he had to tell them.

"Not exactly full of joy. She kept saying things weren't going the way she hoped."

"Maybe I'll give her a call and see what's up. In the meantime, I'm pretty sure I've found out who left that calling card on your wall. When Whipple calls, give him this name." He wrote it down on a scrap of newspaper. "Tell him that he was the ringleader. He's a White Power punk with a rap sheet as long as his arm."

"He's going to ask how we know," Richard pointed out. "What are we supposed to say?"

"It's better if I stay out of this. Just tell him you got a tip. It'll be a cinch for him to pull up Slater's rap sheet, and he can find him pretty easily. I'm ninety percent sure he's still on the Island. He's the one with a jacked-up red Ford 150 pickup with South Carolina plates and a broken driver's side headlight. That ought to be enough to bring him in for the moment."

CHAPTER THIRTEEN

Great Expectations

WEDNESDAY'S OVERCAST WAS SO HEAVY that the transition from darkness to light was almost imperceptible. Taz woke up trying to remember various fragments of the conversation from the night before. Richard and Laney had lots of questions, most of which he couldn't answer. So, they had drunk wine and talked gloomily about the new fascism rising in the fringes of the American conservative movement. Somewhere along the way, Laney showed him a note Lucia had sent her. Laney was going to be in town for the National Book Festival and had been hoping to take Lucia out for dinner. Taz couldn't remember all of it, but the gist was that her work along the river had gotten a little more complicated than she expected, and that she wasn't going to be able to meet Laney in DC as they had planned. Missing from Lucia's explanation—no mention of her effort to raise money for panther conservation in the valley, or even of the missing panther that she had been so worried about.

Taz spent the rest of the morning reading briefing material for the Brazil trip, and most of the afternoon in his shed, sharpening tools and knives. He had found a little hand-cranked grinding wheel at a flea market down in Bloxom. It fixed on his workbench with a screw clamp, and even though the wheel was slightly out of true, he could use it to do the first rough sharpen on chisels, hatchets, and oyster knives. The process required attention. Took his mind off other things.

For dinner he had an almond butter and jelly sandwich. Laney had told him almonds were better for his health. He had promised her to pay more attention to such issues. After a second bottle of Beck's, he spent a few hours googling the Brazilian press and NGO reports on soil conditions in the Amazon. Then he called Everton.

"They've called me in again. I figure it's about you."

"I'm afraid so, my friend."

"What can you tell me?"

Everton told him a lot. The Brazilian government had just submitted the application to the World Bank for a hundred-million-dollar loan to develop, from scratch, a national wildland fire program. This was not Everton's work, not at all; he thought it was premature, and besides, as Taz was fully aware, he had just requested technical assistance from the US government to put together a serious program, not the comic opera version that came from the Environment Ministry. The application was moving through the system, but the green eyeshade folks at the World Bank wanted assurance that they weren't being asked to fund yet another contribution to the Brazilian president's slush fund.

"Taz, the fools at the Environment Ministry have no idea what it means to develop such a program! But now that it's been proposed, we can't afford to let it fail. Our credibility is at stake." In other words, they needed muscle on the bones and soon.

"Everton, I'm not a fire control expert."

"I know, I know. But to paraphrase the well-known negotiator Taz Blackwell, 'I don't need an expert, I need somebody who knows how to build a team of experts.' We need a designer, Taz, an architect. Somebody who can impress the World Bank. Who has credibility with Valentina." *So, my reputation is going to be on the line, too.*

"Everton, it will work out. I've already put in a call to our top fire people. They're going to help me put together a team."

"Thank God. We have to move quickly."

✐

When Taz finally made his way through security at Main State late Thursday morning, it became apparent that Jessica had arranged an extremely thorough briefing. He was chaperoned to a medium-sized seventh-floor conference room, where he surrendered his cell phone. Arthur was there. Also, two rather fidgety young men from the OES science staff, and two relatively senior officials from NASA and NOAA, the National Oceanic and Atmospheric Administration. Taz said a quick hello, shook hands with everyone he could reach.

At the last minute, Undersecretary Lansman strode in, all business. She called the meeting to order. "We're here to acquaint our new special environmental envoy with the elements of the upcoming Brazil mission." Taz tried hard to hide his amusement. There was no such title, as far as he knew. Still, he appreciated the spirit of her introduction. There were three PowerPoints. Fortunately, the room was darkened, so he didn't have to pretend to be interested. He just had to avoid snoring. The outline of the challenge was roughly similar to what Everton had told him, but not as detailed in picturing the divisions within the Brazilian government.

The gist of the briefing was that the White House expected State to put together a priority effort to respond to Brazil's request for assistance in monitoring and responding to wildland fire. NASA and NOAA were working on the assumption that the Brazilians was looking to ramp up their remote sensing capabilities. Satellite monitoring was clearly a specialty of the two skinny OES scientists, but bureaucratically, it was the exclusive province of NOAA and NASA.

Taz listened, said nothing. Thanked all for the briefing. Stood and opened the door to let the specialists leave the room.

"So, what do you think?" Jessica was excited.

At this point, it was just Taz, Jessica, and Arthur.

"They've got it all cockeyed."

"What do you mean?" Incredulous. "They're the best aerospace engineers and climate scientists we have."

"I know. That's the problem. They're like doctors who always think you have whatever they know how to treat. Here's the issue. Brazil already has top-of-the-line remote sensing. Lockheed designed their system seven years ago. On top of that, you can't actually fight fire from satellites. The satellite sees lightning strike a blaze in Roraima, up by the Venezuelan border. So what? There's nobody to read the satellite data for fire occurrence, and even if there was, there's nobody to make the call, and there's nobody to pick up the phone at the other end. At least nobody who would have a remote chance of doing anything about it. And if there was, Roraima is fifteen hundred miles from Brasilia, and there isn't a single fire company in between."

He had crossed Jessica's exasperation threshold. "Okay! That's just great, just great! So, what do we do? We need to deliver for Everton."

The question of what she hoped to get in return would have to wait. "Let me rejigger the delegation. I'll keep at least one senior guy each from NOAA and NASA, so their directors won't be giving you any pissed-off calls."

Jessica looked skeptical. "I assume you know who you'd want to add."

"Our wildfire management program costs seven hundred and fifty million dollars a year just to maintain readiness. A bad fire season will add as much as a billion dollars for fire crew pay, smokejumpers, planes, and all the response logistics. It takes three agencies to run it, and we're not talking about NASA and NOAA. BLM and the Forest Service are the main players. It operates in all fifty states. There's a system of state and local contacts all the way down to the county level. Protocols for everything from who you contact to how you grade fire danger and response priorities. I'm going to take some folks who can teach them about all that."

Arthur said, "But they can't match our program. And anyway, they're only looking for pocket change from the World Bank."

Taz was irritated, but also impressed. Arthur was clearly more than a gofer. "Right on both points. But even if their program is smaller, it still has to be systematic and effective. And we're going to have to help them get it through the Bank, as well."

"Taz has a point." Jessica said. Then she shot a questioning look at

Taz. "Where are you going to find the rest of your team?"

"Boise, Idaho."

"You're making fun of me!"

"Not at all. That's where the interagency wildland fire team is based."

Jessica yielded her only smile of the day. "You do know what you're doing, even when you're being a pain. Keep me updated."

Taz's next stop was on the INR corridor. John White stood outside his door to greet him. Offered his hand. "Taz, it's good to see you." Taz's recent work with White had been much more productive than their relationship when they were on the same hall at State. Together, they had discovered a Russian effort to control a key deposit of rare earth minerals on the southern tip of Greenland and used the information to undercut the Russians with a better offer. White received a commendation for that one.

Once seated around the assistant secretary's little coffee table, White smiled. "To what do I owe the honor? I've never seen you call a meeting without an agenda."

"Only one agenda for this one, John. Lucia Turan."

"Who?"

"Oh, come on. I thought we were friends. I'm not going to hang our discussion out on social media. We're talking about the young panther biologist who you've got gathering information about the cartels just across the border. She's been meeting with your office once a month for almost a year."

White's eyes widened. "And what's your connection?"

"She showed up in Chincoteague a few months ago. We hit it off."

"So, you started to snoop around to see what you could learn."

"You know perfectly well I don't snoop. At least not well enough to make it a strategy."

"Admitting your rather iconoclastic style of information gathering does not constitute a denial."

"I know."

"Taz. You've never fit in with most of the people in our line of work. You observe patterns and the occasional detail, then you apply some mystical method to link up the dots. You confound the folks I report to, but they've seen the results."

"So here are the dots. There's this woman I'm interested in. She studies panthers along the Rio Grande. Except when she's shuttling monthly—sometimes weekly—to our nation's lovely capital or taking the occasional side trip to our little marsh island, which is growing steadily fonder of her. She also makes periodic visits to the Mexican Embassy to renew her visa. And she requested and received a US government pass that allows her to cross the border at any point, rather than just at the authorized ports of entry."

White's left eye twitched twice. "Permits like that are closely held. They're exceedingly rare and mostly reserved for the DEA and our own narcotics investigators."

"Right. Unless the request comes from you or one of the only three people above you in your chain of command, right? Or maybe the DEA? And, last but not least, her friends on the Island are getting notes from her that don't say anything specific but leave them with a worried feeling. I think she might be in danger. So, John, who endorsed her request? And what have you got her doing down there?"

"I did, with the undersecretary's concurrence. Your friend Doctor Turan came to State to ask for support for her panther conservation effort. A staffer in the environmental office looked at her application and realized she would be in a perfect position to pick up bits and pieces of news that might help us understand the border situation a little bit better. Passive listening. That was all."

"Was?"

White wiped his brow with his hand. "She surprised us. Started bringing in some grade-A intel. My folks couldn't figure out how she was getting it. She came through with some information—leads we were able to verify—that pointed to cartel influence high in the Reynosa police, and in the ranks of the political leadership as well. How, I don't know. A few weeks after that, DEA took control of the operation. They're managing it from their intelligence office in El Paso. They promised they would keep us in the loop, but they've cut us out. That's all I know."

Taz knew just enough about DEA's operations on the border to know that the El Paso DEA office reported to the assistant administrator of the intelligence division. He needed to find the person on that staff whose responsibilities included covert operations on the border. In the meantime, he had a plane to catch.

CHAPTER FOURTEEN

Double Trouble

BRAZIL AWAITED. TAZ ARRIVED AT Andrews Air Force Base two hours before the departure time listed on the itinerary Jessica's staff had emailed him the night before. And there he cooled his heels.

The waiting room wasn't much. Cinderblock walls painted gray. Posters listing current safety regulations. Benches instead of chairs. A picture of the new POTUS and his VP, both looking like real stand-up guys. Also, the secretary of defense. No generals, though, which caught Taz's attention. Since they were the ones with the real day-to-day responsibilities, they didn't need their portraits on the wall.

The duty officer ran him though a cursory security check. The dispatch office at State confirmed that his name was on the manifest. The officer checked his backpack, which held only his dopp kit, extra socks and boxers, T-shirts, a light poncho, and various incidentals. A slender Mac with a portable CD player and a selection of Brazilian CDs—Gilberto Gil, Gal Costa, Caetano Veloso and his little sister, the great Maria Bethânia. His Portuguese-English dictionary, a detective novel by Javier Marías, and a copy of Wallace's travels on the Amazon and the Rio Negro, bound in leather by Ward and Lock in 1853.

His duffel and computer bag were trip-tagged, X-rayed, and loaded. All he had left was the clothes he was wearing—ultra-light hiking boots, khaki pants, a light cotton shirt, a tan water-resistant jacket, and an old baseball cap. He stretched out on one of the benches, using his backpack as a pillow, tipped the brim of the cap over his eyes, and dropped dead asleep, Wallace open on his chest.

A woman's voice, not one he recognized. "Shall I wake him up?"

Then Jessica. "Let's let him sleep for a few more minutes. He looks like he's enjoying it."

Time elapsed. A cool hand on his shoulder. "Taz. Time to straighten up and fly right." Jessica in a cream-colored, tropical-weight pantsuit, the very image of what one of Taz's old friends had christened "East Coast clean-smart." It wasn't hard to manage a smile.

The jet was a chartered Embraer 1000. Only the secretary of state was allowed to use Air Force Two. There was a reasonably well-stocked bar just in front of the swivel chairs. The captain stepped out of the pilots' cabin. "Hi folks, welcome aboard. We have a short takeoff window today, so let's review the safety procedures." Definitely military. They all found seats. Taz ended up next to Jessica in the first row. She gave him a quick glance as she was buckling up her seat belt.

"You know, Taz, there's a lot riding on this trip. We need Brazil's help on a whole range of issues. Everton has a lot of respect for you. I need you to help us put our best foot forward."

"You've already done one thing right."

"What's that?"

"The jet. It's an Embraer. They're made in São José dos Campos, in São Paulo State. Their executive director is good friends with the president."

"Ours or theirs?"

Taz laughed. "His name is Paulo Cesar de Souza é Silva. He and Carvalho go back to grade school. And it doesn't hurt that he's one of the richest men in Brazil."

She turned. "Arthur. Is Paulo de Souza in my briefing book?" Arthur reached to the seat next to him, brought up a tabbed binder the size of an old Manhattan Yellow Pages, and began anxiously flipping the pages. "I don't see a tab for him."

"Well, there should be." She still had the claws. Turned back to Taz. "I forget myself. I should offer you a drink."

"What are you having?"

"A gin and tonic."

"That'll do just fine."

Jessica got up to serve him, slid out of her jacket. She was slim, especially at the hips. The top button of her light blue blouse was open. As she bent to put the drink in his hand, Taz kept his eyes on the plane's emergency instructions, then looked up and smiled ever so briefly.

A handsome young woman appeared from the galley just behind the cabin and swayed up the aisle to his seat. She was holding a white notepad in her hand. "I'm Sylvia Jaquard, Jessica's senior assistant." Taz gave her a quick glance; he could have sworn that she winked at Jessica. The moment passed, and she directed her attention to him. "What would you like for dinner? We have beef or chicken. They both come with potatoes and salad."

Taz asked for the chicken. The sun was going down. They appeared to be off the Florida coast. He watched for a while, but the dusk hid most of the detail. He went to use the restroom. When he returned Jessica was deep in a novel. He couldn't see the title.

Sylvia announced that the food was ready. Taz slotted his plate into the tray in front of his seat, stepped to the bar and pulled out a bottle of red wine and two glasses. Looking inquiringly at Jessica, he poured for both of them. She nodded her thanks, then peered over his shoulder. "That's a great cap." Motioning to the bulkhead where Taz had hung it alongside her dark-blue Red Sox cap. "Can I see it?" He pulled it down for her to take a closer look. It boasted an Otter floatplane and the words *Katmai Air* embroidered on the maroon waxed-canvas crown. The bill was brushed leather. The cap was distressed, as the fashionistas would have it, but not because it had been scrubbed in the factory. It had been with him hiking and birding along stream sides and in bramble thickets all over Alaska's Kenai Peninsula, and in every cedar swamp on the Delmarva. He had long ago concluded that the cap would probably outlast him. She twirled the cap on her finger.

"Do you spend a lot of time in Alaska?"

"As much as I can. Like the saying goes, a bad day in Alaska is better than a good day at the office."

"But you don't really have an office, do you?"

"My place is pretty small. Just an old waterman's cottage. I do have a workspace though. It's just that it doubles as a bedroom."

"You don't really. Work in bed, I mean."

"No. But I really do have my desk in the bedroom, so I'm being legit."

"I don't see you as caring much about being legit."

"That's just one of many things about which I'm oblivious, at least according to my ex."

"Exes are tough like that. I know from experience."

Taz raised an eyebrow.

"You didn't know?"

"My staff apparently did a superficial research job."

"You didn't research me at all."

"I'll come clean. I don't have a staff."

She gave him a quizzical look and a polite laugh, tilted her head back and closed her eyes. She had a nice neck.

Taz said, "The itinerary says we touch down in five hours. We must be going in through Belém?" They needed to return to safer ground.

"To refuel and stretch our legs for a few hours. It will be morning when we get in."

"I know a good café along the wharf. They serve a terrific breakfast, strong coffee, and the best fish you'll ever taste."

"I grew up on fish. Good fresh haddock and cod. You're going to have trouble topping that."

"Trust me. You be the judge. I'll explain after you've tried it."

CHAPTER FIFTEEN

Ribs of Tambaqui

THEY LANDED AT *VAL DE CANS* at six-thirty in the morning, all bleary-eyed, but it was nothing a gallon of high-octane coffee couldn't cure.

"So, about this mythical breakfast place?" Jessica asked.

"Let's commandeer two taxis, and I'll show you."

"We only have three hours."

"We can make it with time to spare."

"Okay." To all, she said, "We're headed to the great Taz's favorite breakfast nook. If it's weird, you know who to talk to."

Taz just smiled at Sylvia and Arthur.

Their little quartet from State had been joined by the international deputies from NOAA and NASA, a sop that Jessica had thrown to keep the peace. Taz corralled two cabs, and by the time he made his way to the curb the first was already fully occupied. He knocked on the cabbie's window. Told him they were headed to *Yasmin's* on the wharf. The cabbie smiled. "*Boa escolha.*" Taz knew some rudimentary Portuguese. His face must have betrayed the uncertainty of his translation. The driver smiled. "Good choice."

Taz joined Arthur and the remaining crew in the second cab. They wound their way through Belém's cobbled streets to the harbor. Taz recognized the location by the houseboats. Just upriver, the fishermen and the fishmongers held sway. Boatloads of cupuraçu, bull shark, terrapin, armored catfish and, last but best, tambaqui. Taz was the last out of the cab. He enjoyed watching as his colleagues reacted to the facade of his favorite restaurant in Belém—or, for that matter, anywhere north of São Paulo. Mostly wide eyes and open mouths.

Yasmin's facade was not imposing. A mildewed wooden sign hanging from rusty chains pointed the way to a somewhat dubious wooden gangway that bridged the harbor waters to an empty entry hall under a corrugated tin roof. The main dining room was on a barge anchored by chains and attached to the land side by hawsers. All open to the rain and the wind, the cooling breezes, and the humidity of high summer in the tropics.

Taz ushered them in. Jessica gave a skeptical look, which made him smile all the more. A teenage boy pointed them to a table and brought water, asked if they would like anything to drink before they ordered. Taz ordered caipirinhas all around. "As the Brits say, 'A little sharpener for the morning.'" Jessica noted tartly that it was an early start. Then she took the first sip and smiled.

They were still savoring lime and cachaça when a tall woman appeared from the kitchen, surveyed their table from a distance, and had a quiet word with their server, who immediately disappeared into the kitchen and came back a minute later holding a teak tray of shot glasses full of a dark purple liquid. *Açaí*. Taz smiled, remembering his old friend Regiao, the Rasta man of Ipanema, who would stroll the beach selling the drink from couple to couple, family to family, growling *"Aaah-ça-eee!"* in a bass tremolo that even Nicolai Gedda would have trouble topping.

The tall woman watched quietly. Her sheath was cut high above the knee and adorned with black-trimmed slashes starting high on each hip. The neckline plunged just enough to be enticing. Her smile, as she approached their table, was warm and inviting. She gazed at the table, turning her head to see each of her new customers.

"Welcome to Belém! The most special river city of Brazil." She pronounced it *Braaazeel* in a pleasingly hoarse voice and with the emphasis on the first syllable.

Having welcomed them all, she glided to Taz's end of the table. Bent and kissed him on his left ear, caressing his cheek with her right hand. "Taz. Why so long for you to come back?"

Taz looked at his companions, who were riveted. "Friends, I'd like to introduce you to Yasmin Oliveira, the chef and owner of the best restaurant in Belém." When Yasmin beamed, it was as if the sun had come from behind a cloud. She looked them over again. "The plum-colored juice we call *açaí*. Very tasty, very good for your blood."

Taz raised his shot glass and saluted her. His friends followed suit. *"Mms"* and *"Aahs"* all around. Yasmin looked directly at Jessica. "What can we offer you?" She had already sorted out who was in charge.

Jessica replied, "Your restaurant is beautiful. This is my first time, though, so perhaps I should ask Taz to order for us."

Taz looked around the table. "Eggs, everyone?" They nodded. Looking back at Yasmin, "Just your usual egg breakfast, strong coffee, and ribs of tambaqui, if you have them."

"If I have them?" Imperious. With a glare that would light a fire.

All this had transpired without any further input from those most at stake. They continued looking on. Finally, Arthur said, "What's the usual? And what in the world is ribs of tambakee?"

"The usual is eggs your style with the crusty bread they call *pao de sal,* maybe some rolled ham and cheese or a little grilled meat. As for the tambaqui, let's just say I bet your boss I could find her a fish from the Amazon that would equal her Cape Cod favorites." He threw a look to Yasmin, who murmured, *"Não se preoccupé."*

Jessica looked on, skeptical. Sylvia smiled, taking it all in, including Jessica's reaction. She winked at Taz.

Taz pinged his glass, looked to Jessica to offer a toast. She lifted her glass. "Here's to a successful alliance with our Brazilian friends."

All agreed. Then Sylvia looked up. "Taz has been here more than once. Maybe we should ask him to propose a toast."

"I think Jessica said what needed to be said." Murmurs from the table.

"Oh, come on." Taz smiled and made a shooing motion, his hand shaped like a brush. At which point, their server brought plates of poached eggs over bitter greens, with stringy dried beef and crisp-fried onion straws. They ate silently, concentrating on tastes and textures. When they looked up, it was with expressions of delight.

Sylvia said, "Maybe I was just hungry, but that was fabulous." General assent, followed by excited talk and speculation as to what other surprises this trip might hold.

"Now for dessert," Taz announced.

Yasmin and her cousin approached, each carrying a platter with what looked like long white pork ribs. The ribs were seared, and the edges brown, but the meat was pure white, firm, and just beginning separate into natural slices. The way only perfectly cooked fresh fish can be.

When each of them had been served two ribs, Yasmin addressed the table in the voice of a samba singer, which she was. "Any friends of Taz are friends of ours as well. So, to our friends from North America. I am very happy to serve you ribs of tambaqui, the fruit-eating fish of the Várzea—the flooded Amazon. I feel sure you enjoy."

Taz took the first bite. It had the wonderful sweetness he remembered, redolent of apricots and kiwi. Sylvia took a long look at Yasmin. "Wow!" Which seemed to speak for the whole table.

Taz waited for all to finish. As they looked up from their momentary comas, he stood and pinged his glass for another toast. Looked around the table, doing his best to make eye contact with each of his colleagues.

"Let's drink to Brazil, to its rivers, its wildlife, and its people. To Yasmin," raising his glass in her direction, "Who sings brilliant *forró* and samba at night and runs the best restaurant in Belém by day. And to the tambaqui, a miraculous fish, which, like so many Brazilians, excels in enjoying the sweetness of life." Another nod to Yasmin, who was now standing just off the corner of the table, blushing and smiling, with her hands in prayer mode just below her chin. The table clapped in unison, with appreciative calls to Yasmin, who opened her arms in a virtual embrace. Taz drained the remainder of his caipirinha. Jessica just smiled, gave him a silent *"cheers."*

As they were reboarding the plane, Sylvia sidled up to Taz. "Tell me about Yasmin. How did you meet? I think I'm in love."

Taz smiled. "Better take a number."

CHAPTER SIXTEEN

Everton's Magic

AFTER A ONE-BUMP TOUCHDOWN ON the tarmac in Brasilia, the team was picked up by a trio of black Suburbans and dropped off at the post-modernist Parthenon that housed Brazil's Foreign Ministry, otherwise known as Itamaraty. Pronounced Itamarachi, but not by the ever-irreverent Cariocas and Paulistas. Ignoring their own chronic conflicts, the residents of Rio de Janeiro and Sao Paulo happily joined forces to oppose and, when possible, obstruct the edicts that emanated from the bureaucrats in Brasilia. Even better, to have a laugh at Brasilia's expense. They called Itamaraty "the ship of fools." Meanwhile, the poor and dispossessed, trapped in their hillside favelas, with their tin-roofed shacks and open sewers, called it "the Golden Palace," halfway believing the rumor that the nation's gold reserves were stored there.

A rectangular moat festooned with water lilies surrounded the building. As you walked over the narrow-railed bridge towards the giant mahogany doors, you could see golden carp and, God knows, tilapia, disporting in the artificial lake. Taz had occasionally wondered whether there were piranhas in there as well.

Jessica observed the double doors, which were at least fourteen feet tall. "Magnificent!"

Taz imagined her wishing that State's old, Stalinesque building on the edge of Foggy Bottom could be transformed in the image of the Palace of Itamaraty. "There's enough high-grade mahogany there to make a thousand Martin guitars." Jessica looked a question at him. "The most resonant guitar backs are either mahogany or Brazilian rosewood. They're both being decimated by illegal logging."

"Don't think for a second that you're going to make me feel guilty for admiring," Taz smiled and peered at her through lowered eyebrows. "Okay, for lusting after these magnificent doors. Can we just appreciate them for a moment?"

Taz crossed his right arm over his heart and bowed softly. "Yes, Madame Secretary." Jessica glared, and then snorted good-humoredly.

Sylvia, meanwhile, had turned around and become transfixed by the larger landscape. The palace, the moat, and then the seventeen ministry buildings, row after row, separated by a perfectly mowed grass meridian the width of two football fields.

None of the other capital buildings was quite as magnificent as Itamaraty, of course. And yet, standing in series, on one side of the grassy mall, with an identical set of office towers on the opposite side, the collectivity was magnificent, in its own perverted way.

Sylvia turned to engage Taz. "This is like something out of *Doctor Who*!" This time Taz snorted.

When they pried open the great doors, Everton was descending the broad spiral staircase to the lobby to meet them. He was of average height, with the beginning of a pot belly, and a hair line that had been receding steadily since the day he and Taz had met. Nonetheless, he carried himself with an inescapable gravitas, which might have been overbearing if not for his evident sense of humor and his obvious delight in being alive for yet another day.

They talked in his office. He gave them two hours—an extraordinary chunk of time out of his day. Jessica did her best to fill the time, working from her briefing, and Everton did his best to look interested. Occasionally he gazed at Taz, with an odd smile over his rimless glasses. Sylvia caught it all, which Taz found quite amusing.

At the end, after some whispered conversations with Taz, Jessica had agreed to bring a larger delegation down to look at the fire issue in the northern and eastern Amazon, to assess what, if any, technical assistance the US could offer the *bombeiros*. Most importantly, to help Everton and his staff develop an effective proposal to the World Bank to help fund a national wildfire management program. She left it to Sylvia and Arthur to work out a proposed calendar and to identify staff contacts for further work.

Everton was distraught when he learned that Jessica's plan was to fly right back to Belém and exit Brazil from there. Since it was her first visit to Brazil, he insisted in the politest fashion that Jessica, "the highly admired—and beautiful—undersecretary," allow him to host a short visit to his home city of São Paulo before making the U-turn to the United States. So, their next plane ride took them to Brazil's biggest city, at the Brazilian government's expense..

CHAPTER SEVENTEEN

São Paulo from On High

THEY DIDN'T RECONNECT WITH ONE another until early afternoon the next day. Everton was to meet them at the hotel at three to show them the city. With Jessica safely at the consulate, and Sylvia glorying in the boutiques on Alameda Lorena in the Jardins, Taz had time to amble over to the university to find some good coffee and see the library. He spent the rest of the morning leafing through a rare first edition of Spruce's *Notes of a Botanist in the Amazon.*

A little before the hour, Taz wandered over to the hotel bar. He returned to the lobby with four caipirinhas on a tray. Jessica and Sylvia emerged from the elevator and made a beeline in his direction.

Jessica asked, "I don't suppose one of those is for me?" She was clearly getting more used to Taz's way of doing business.

Taz handed her one with a smile, then did the same for Sylvia. "Here's to a successful first meeting. I believe Everton really wants this to work."

"Of course. But no doubt he will expect something in return!" Jessica said it sharply, to show her diplomatic sophistication. And maybe to set a marker down regarding Taz's seeming loyalty to a friendship beyond the diplomatic protocols.

"I don't know... I think he's putting himself in your debt. He wouldn't do it if he didn't need to, or if he didn't trust you to treat him fairly."

Scowling, Jessica turned to sipping her caipirinha. Sylvia smiled and turned her wide eyes to Taz. "That's the way it works, isn't it? There's always a ledger of sorts."

"Yes, but it's not like an account book. It's intuitive. You're considering how critical your need is, how willing your counterpart is to help when called on, what level of sacrifice was entailed in the counterpart's commitment to help, and things like that. Everton is asking for a substantial favor, but nothing earthshaking. He'll choose his time, but I'll guarantee he'll find a way to be of help when he sees we need it." Jessica was looking away, listening intently all the while.

Sylvia took another sip of her caipirinha and gave Taz a long look over the rim of her glass. Jessica looked at her and then at him. "I hope he's not planning to drag us to every museum in the city. I bore easily." Taz reckoned that was true, for better or worse. At which point Everton strolled into the lobby. He spotted them almost immediately, swiveled, and strode their way, waving away the greetings offered by the hotel management. Taz picked the fourth caipirinha off the tray and held it out.

"You of all people should know I'm still at work!" Then he gladly accepted the drink.

Once they got past the pleasantries and finished the caipirinhas, Everton smiled at Jessica and swept his arm towards the hotel entrance. Instead of a ministry limo, he ushered them to a bright red Tesla. It was an eye-popping ride. Rush hour hadn't hit yet, and that was apparently the only thing that was capable of slowing Everton. He booted up the car, depressed the pedal, and, in a sweeping, smooth, silent motion, they were on the avenue. Within seconds, they hit seventy miles per hour. Fortunately, Avenue Parada Pinto was straight and wide. That was fine, until Everton turned up the hill on Santa Ynez. Now it was only two lanes, with lots of climbing curves, which Everton took at nearly the same pace.

They followed Santa Ynez until they reached an area of forest close to the top of the hill. Everton pulled over on a little dirt siding, by a clearing with a rough granite substrate poking through the red clay. Looked at Jessica and said, "So now I show you São Paulo." They all got out and walked over to a little promontory a short distance down. There was a fair amount of trash. Then the view appeared in its full glory.

The late afternoon was darkening prior to the equatorial sunset. The Earth was spinning—a living top in an indifferent cosmos. The quartet stood a few hundred feet from their red Tesla, each immersed in their own questions, fears, and musings, as they were driven inexorably towards sunset, along with a whole mega-city of twelve million souls. They were looking at São Paulo from a height of about twelve hundred feet, and they had a panoramic view of the throbbing metropolis below. If any of them were conscious of the irony of their journey, it wasn't apparent to Taz.

They turned and began to walk uphill to the Tesla. Sylvia, shoulder to shoulder with Taz. "You've been here before?"

"It's my favorite park in São Paulo."

"So, where next?"

"Next? It's only a short way to the best traditional Brazilian restaurant this side of Minas Gerais—*Tias*."

✑

They arrived quite early, at least by Brazilian standards. The rough dirt parking lot held a dozen cars scattered at odd distances and odder angles. Everton found a spot with space to open all four doors and room to spare.

They were looking through the windshield at a dusty brick wall that appeared to have needed a lot of work, say, fifty years ago. There was an archway to the right, leading into a dirt courtyard as big as half a soccer pitch. Scattered around the periphery were various carpentry and masonry shops, and a rudimentary hardware supply store. All were made of the same red clay bricks, covered by a gray stucco, with rough wood lintels and open doors. None had signs; the only way to tell what they were was to peek inside and see sawhorses, workbenches, bricks, or plumbing supplies. Some still had dusty lumber piles, piping, or other evidence of ongoing work lying around. Others were empty, in various states of disrepair, open to the sun and rain.

Everton took Jessica's elbow and turned them to the left, where a hardened dirt path led to what looked at a distance like a slightly more presentable porch, with lights behind it.

He turned to Taz, as if to explain why his two female colleagues weren't getting the full tour. "The *Tias* have made a special *feijoada*. And you and I need a little time to talk."

As they topped the little rise above the south wall of the courtyard, they found themselves at the edge of a patio lit with soft oil lamps hanging from rough rafters. The rafters supported a sloping tin roof at least twenty feet above their heads. There was an old mahogany and teak bar to the left, and scattered tables to their right. If you looked through a narrow opening just behind the bar you could see the open-air kitchen, with homemade brick hearths and cast-iron pans hanging from cast-iron stanchions, all lit with low flames, waiting to grill or bake the next order.

Everton started them with cocktails. Once he was sure that Jessica and Sylvia were on the road to true enjoyment, he stepped back to the bar and asked the bartender to bring one of the *Tias* out. She appeared after a minute, an elegant woman of girth, and Everton greeted her effusively, then spent several minutes conferring with her. She then returned to a back area next to the kitchen where there were some open stainless-steel vats and a few old wooden casks on racks. She tapped one of the casks and filled two shot glasses with a whisky-colored liquor.

She walked slowly towards the two of them and, with great solemnity, offered each a shot glass. Everton thanked her with a kiss on both cheeks, eyed Taz, smiled, and said, *"Lentamente."* The second *t* was pronounced as *ch*. Knowing Everton's wide circle of friends, Taz figured this was his polite way of saying, "Don't drink this like a Russian, all in one gulp."

Taz took a sip. The taste was amazing and complex, and kept changing the longer he held it in his mouth. And then there was the afterglow. Taz was astonished. "Everton, where is this from? It's amazing. It reminds me of Ardbeg." An Islay Scotch best known for its medicinal, briny start and its herbal ending, and in between a rainbow of tastes playing hobnob with your senses.

"You see those vats over there, and the casks?"

Taz nodded. "I wish I had known to ask for this the last time I was here." Everton shook his head, clapped Taz on the shoulder, took another sip.

They walked back to check on Jessica and Sylvia. The two were in an animated conversation that had something to do with a recent controversy at the Organization of American States.

Everton cocked his ear, listened for a few seconds, turned back to Taz. "I think we are better off on our own, at least for the moment. So, what is your review?"

"What do you mean?"

"Of your beautiful undersecretary, Ms. Lansman. Apparently, I'm to be dealing with her for the next four years, at least."

Taz considered how much he could say. He was, after all, being asked to help the deputy minister of Itamaraty better understand the US undersecretary of state. Fate and national interest might require that they be allies on some issues and determined adversaries on others. Still, allies or adversaries, they were better off if they had a feeling for each other's principles and motivations.

"Well, she's very smart. It doesn't pay to underestimate her. Studies her briefs thoroughly, asks the right questions, gets things quickly. Started as a twenty-five-year-old deputy assistant to the president, which is almost unheard of. Perhaps her intelligence leads her to seem a bit arrogant at times, although it seems she has mellowed with experience. Can be sharp when crossed, and she's good at keeping score. What else?"

"All that squares with my own assessment. I'm hoping I can convince her to see our point of view on a few key issues. For instance, on the need for a forest conservation chapter in the Climate Convention."

Taz couldn't agree more, aware Everton was ultimately pointing towards the need for a fund of some kind to support carbon reductions through forest conservation. Still, not out of the question since the US and Europe had their own reasons to want credit for reforestation efforts.

"Or with regard to the prerogatives of coastal nations under the Law of the Sea."

Both countries had thousands of miles of coast, and so a similar interest to protect. On the other hand, the US Navy had a powerful institutional interest in the doctrine of the freedom of the seas. They wouldn't support any assertion of authority over innocent passage if, for instance, it might later be used by Indonesia to close the Malacca Straits. So that one would require striking a very creative balance.

"And on the intellectual property challenges in the Convention on Biological Diversity."

Taz looked at Everton like he had just opened a jar of dead worms.

"All right, all right. But certainly, on the adaptation chapter of the Climate Convention."

"With or without South Africa and Mexico?"

"With them, if possible. But definitely without the Philippines." The Philippine delegation was led by a doctrinaire Third-World advocate who simply could not be negotiated with.

Maybe, with the right exchange of interests.

"I see that you're at least willing to think about it, which means it's not out of the question."

Taz clinked his glass with Everton's. They each took a long, appreciative sip.

Everton turned to smile at Jessica and Sylvia, who were sipping the last of their caipirinhas. They had moved from a somewhat one-sided discussion of Latin American politics and were now discussing which of Rio's beaches they'd most enjoy visiting. Taz was trying to picture both of them on Ipanema. Sylvia seemed the more likely.

Everton touched Taz's elbow and guided him along a little stone path into the greater darkness. "Taz. The region with the worst fire challenges, the western margins of Amazonas State. I want to take the full delegation there. But I need you to know that it's a dangerous place. It's not just the fires. We think something else is going on, but we can't prove it."

"What kind of thing?"

"We're not completely sure. Illegal mining and timber theft, absolutely.

Rosewood, mahogany, even *pau brasil*. But something else. We're hearing that locals are being forced to cut trees illegally. Often in the indigenous reserves."

"Forced?"

"It's just as in the days of the rubber tappers. They were slaves. The Manaus Opera House was built with the sweat of their backs."

"What makes you sure what you're seeing isn't just a spike in random settler attacks?"

"The same pattern has shown up in five distinct indigenous areas, hundreds of miles apart: Putumayo, del Vaupés, Pacaya, the northern border of the Vale do Javari, and the Paraná, right under the Araracuara escarpment. In each case indigenous villages are burnt; women and girls are kidnapped. When the men come to rescue their wives and daughters, they are slaughtered. Now the area is empty and open to gypsy loggers. It's not random, Taz, it's a strategy."

"But what kind of poachers' syndicate would be big and well-organized enough to cause that kind of trouble over such a wide area?"

"Nobody we've ever encountered thus far. Our intelligence people are working on it."

"Okay. If I remember right, our government and yours have an intelligence cooperation agreement."

"Yes. If our people will allow me to request a joint initiative under the agreement, can your undersecretary help us pursue it?"

"She's certainly high enough up to have her views taken seriously, and her time in the White House won't hurt either."

Jessica called in their general direction. "Are you two ever going to join us?"

They walked quickly back up the path towards the light.

Taz placed his half-full shot glass carefully down on the woven place mat. It was easy to get lost in what to him was an almost magical environment, to be magnetized first by the kitchen, then the bar, then the distillery. Not to speak of the aged beauty of the Tias, the mystery of the surrounding forest, amplified by the call of howler monkeys and the croak of toucans, and the wonderful history of the place itself.

He found his chair and turned his attention to his companions. The Tias, walking a little unsteadily, brought out four burnt-orange ceramic bowls, and ladles the size of fireplace tools. They ladled the feijoada into the bowls from a cast-iron pot hung over a crackling wood fire. The pot was big enough to hold a pig's head, which it did on occasion. It must have weighed two hundred pounds. The rusty chain that held it hung from a wrought-iron bracket that was bolted through one of the rafters, and probably weighed as much by itself.

The Tias placed a steaming bowl in front of each of them, and a wooden tablespoon. Black beans, salted bacon, smoked pork ribs, bitter greens, bay leaves, onions, garlic, and broth. All topped with farofa—toasted cassava flour. Usually not much more. Except the Tias made an even more traditional kind, from family recipes going back three generations. They added pigs' ears and feet to the stock, and *carne-seca* and hot peppers to the stew. The result was unworldly.

They finished their drinks. Everton excused himself and stepped to the bar. Came back with two bottles of red wine from the Douro River Valley in Portugal. They went very well, indeed.

Everton was an excellent conversationalist, and the discussion flowed easily from topic to topic. They turned to music, which pleased Taz. Everton, all innocence, asked Taz a rhetorical question— what country, in his view, enjoyed the best popular music. There followed a friendly verbal joust as to the relative merits of polka, rock, blues, and samba.

Taz laughed. "*Meu amigo.* Why don't you just put some on? Carlinhos Brown. Or better yet, Gilberto Gil or Zélia Duncan?" Everton moved to the little boom box on the bar and found the stack of CDs in a stack under the liquor shelves. The old speaker crackled, and then began thumping with a wonderful beat played on what sounded like timpani of different sizes. Then a voice, hesitant at first, reedy, singing a lyrical melody.

Jessica was watching Everton intently. She turned her eyes to Taz, then to Sylvia, reaching to caress her hand. Back to Taz. "I am *completely* magnetized. Gilberto. Is it '*jeel*'?""

Taz quickly abandoned the thought that the magnetization was related in any way to him. "I thought you might like it, considering you were a dancer."

"I never told you about that."

"You didn't have to."

The last shards of sunset were fading in the São Paulo haze. Everton had a dessert in mind and asked them to forgive him in advance. Taz begged off, walked back down to the courtyard, meaning to check in with Laney. He got her message.

He was just turning back to his companions when his cell cawed. One, two, three. He took a few more steps away from the table, struggling to fish it out of his pocket. Lucia's number flashed on the screen.

"Taz! Laney told me you were in Brazil. I'm so glad I caught you! How are you?"

"Lucia, I don't know what to say. How are *you?* Where are you?"

There was a faint sound of other voices. "I'm back up in DC. Had to do the permit thing, you know. That's how I hooked up with Laney."

"Well, I'm glad you called. I was just starting to think you might have been a pigment of my imagination."

"A what? Ah, I forgot, it's Mr. Quip."

"Careful what you say. I'm not going to be gone *that* long."

"Tough luck for you. I'm headed back to the valley tomorrow."

"In that case, you're going to miss tasting my *feijoada.*"

"Are you getting fresh with me?"

"What did you expect? Okay, I'll 'fess up. Right now, I'm at a restaurant in São Paulo, and I've just eaten the best bowl of *feijoada* ever made."

"*Feijoada?* Whatever you call it . . . is it even in the food pyramid?"

"It's an amazing bean and meat stew seasoned Brazilian style. Since I can't give you a taste over the phone, I'll see if I can make a reasonable version of it for you when I get back."

"Taz, I won't be on the Island for quite a while. There are some things that need taking care of before I can leave the valley again. That's why I called you. That, and to tell you that I'm sorry we're going to miss each other."

"Oh. Well, I guess I am too. The things that you need to deal with—"
The phone crackled. "Is there any way I can help?"

"No. Really, I'm fine."

Taz was thinking of his conversation with John White. *Maybe DEA is pressing her too hard.* "Are you sure? I'd be glad talk to some friends in DC, if that would do any good."

Silence on the other end. Then a long sigh. "Taz . . . I like you; I really do. But I'm starting to get tired of the men I know thinking I'm in over my head. You know, I *can* handle myself. I'm *fine*. But thanks anyhow."

"Okay, then. Take care of—" A crackling sound again and the call dropped. *'The men I know'? Dammit, John, tell me you didn't call her right after we talked.*

It was a multiple-choice question. Either it was just what she said, and she was simply tired of the men in her life offering help she didn't need, or she really was fine, maybe sunbathing on the famous non-existent beaches of the Rio Grande. Or she was telling him that it had all been very enjoyable, you know, but she didn't want his company all that much anymore. Or, perhaps, she was in real trouble and for some unexplained reason didn't want to talk about it. Or couldn't.

The abrupt end to their conversation left Taz frustrated. He found himself juggling a strange mix of feelings, for which there is a word in Portuguese, but not in English —*saudade*. Brazilians pronounce it *saodahjay.* Very softly. Not only is there no translation, but there is also no definition, either in Brazil or in Portugal. Some quipster tagged it as "the untranslatable word that everyone sings about," and for a time that was on everybody's tongue. The Portuguese writer Manuel de Mello said simply, "A pleasure you suffer, an ailment you enjoy."

Brazilians, rather than using words whose meanings only refer to other words and evaporate like morning mist, define it musically. So, if you asked your friend Braulio, as Taz had done, he would smile and put on a CD of Luciana Souza singing "He Was Too Good to Me." Or if you asked Viviana, the college co-ed with the pink punk haircut whom you met late one night in an anonymous bar in the lower city of Salvador, she would sing you the melody line of "*Lamento Sertanejo*," the beautiful ballad from Brazil's salt-dry northeast made famous by Gilberto Gil.

Taz decided that the best English equivalent was "homesick, with love." Thinking about it doesn't get you there. Feeling it does. *Saudade.* There was no other name for the tide of emotions that swept through him that night, sitting at the hotel bar, staring at what was left of a glass of Ballantine's best. No use fighting it. He couldn't stop the ramble of images and thoughts streaming through his mind, nor the questions coursing through his heart. Lucia bright and insouciant on his front stoop. Glaring daggers at him in the dark lot behind Rainy Day. Murmuring sleepily with her head snugged on his shoulder. Laney with her arm around his shoulder, explaining all the things he didn't understand about love. Which, Taz reflected, took a very long time, and at least two bottles of wine.

CHAPTER EIGHTEEN

Too Far Away

TAZ WOKE EARLY, THREE DAYS after their plane took off from Sao Paulo. The flights and cities in between, Belem and Miami, were no more than a blur. He luxuriated in a long, hot shower. His first thoughts as he toweled off were of the work in Brazil. What they had learned. The issues needing consultation with the Boise fire boys so they could chart the next steps. His next thoughts were all about Lucia. It had been five days since the dinner at the Tias. Five days since the call when she had not so jauntily told him to stay out of her business. He had just finished unpacking groceries when he noticed the light on his cell phone blinking. He stepped over to his table to check the message. Waited for the little signal, pulled up voicemail. An area code he didn't recognize. Then the voice. It was Lucia.

"Taz, I really hoped I'd catch you. Maybe you're still in Brazil. That call . . . sorry, I was just a little stressed. I can't call again, at least for the next few days, and you won't be able to call me—at least not on my personal phone. Laney has another number you can use. Try me tonight or tomorrow—say nine o'clock? I really hope you do." Taz thought her voice had a different tone than the one he'd heard on the last call, nothing obvious, just a little less certain, less confident.

He figured he'd better check in with Laney. "Hello, sweetness. I'm back."

"Don't you try to sweet-talk me, Mister Smooth. You know perfectly well I've grown fond of her. Now you've left her dangling for what? Ten days? Okay, a week. Either way, you're in Brazil dancing the samba, and she's down in Bumfuck, Texas, trying to make sure the local alligators don't decide she looks like lunch. And now that I've got that off my chest, you never had time to call here and let me know whether you were dead or alive? Although, come to think of it, you couldn't very well call to tell me you were dead."

Taz sensed an opening. "How about we have some coffee?"

Still irate. "Fine. You're buying."

"And how's that different, exactly?"

"Just drag your skinny little butt down here. We'll see how it goes from there."

Yow! He slipped barefoot into his sneakers and aimed Old Faithful downtown.

He sidled into Rainy Day as quietly as he could. Laney was shelving upstairs. Richard sat behind the counter, his head resting uneasily on his palm, which had some mystical connection to his elbow, and therefore to the actual desk.

"You're back." With his usual baleful gaze.

"Yes. If you look carefully, you'll notice that I'm standing here in front of you."

Richard's eyes were fixed on the desktop he used to manage inventory and record sales. He twirled his forefinger.

"Okay. What's going on?"

"Actually, we're all a little worried about your friend Lucia."

"There's news?"

"We haven't heard anything from her for almost a week. Laney says they usually talk every couple of days. God know about what, but still."

Taz heard Laney's footsteps on the stairs. She blew Richard a kiss, and she and Taz headed up the street. Their conversation began with the usual espressos and continued over a couple of glasses of Richard's whisky on the wharf just up from the store.

"So, have you heard from her? Because I sure haven't."

"We managed one broken call while I was in Brazil. It cut out before she had much chance to tell me what was going on. Actually, when I asked, she kind of told me to mind my own business. But this morning I picked up a message."

"And?"

"Well, it was very cryptic. She can't call me for the next few days. And I can't call her on her usual number. She said she had left a different one with you?"

"Oh, right!" Searching through her bag. She pulled out a crumpled piece of newspaper. "I brought it for you. Here it is."

Taz pocketed the scrap. "Meanwhile, I have to do some prep for the next Brazil trip—this one was just reconnaissance. I'll be back in not too long."

CHAPTER NINETEEN

Accidents Happen

WHEN HE TOLD LANEY THAT his preparation the next Brazil trip was going to take place in Idaho, she laughed out loud. It did smack a little of the theater of the absurd.

"Why don't you come with me? Spend a little time out West. You know you'd love it." She gave him one of those Laney laser stares. "I'd have to leave our little mosquito infested marsh island. Besides, who'd mind the store? More importantly, who'd take care of Richard, not to mention Suzanne and Moyer?" Dana was in New Jersey with her fiancé. Laney or Taz were the usual designated hitters when she was out of town.

"So, this is why Suzanne calls you their fairy godmother."

"Their Wicked Witch of the West, more like. And you're their knight in shining armor. I'm almost jealous."

He looked at his feet.

"Taz, wake up! You saved their mother from a bullshit relationship. I know you lost her in the process. And you rescued Moyer. That would be reason enough. But you also taught them how to hand-line for crab and plant marsh grass. Plus, they earn real money working outside with you. Though they'd do it anyway just because you make it fun. You're their inspiration."

Looking in her eyes, in all seriousness. "You don't understand. I'm not their inspiration. They're mine." Tough older sister started to tear up, said she had to get home to start dinner for some guests from out of town.

He had dinner at the Chincoteague Inn, watching the channel that the trawlers used to reach their moorings just a hundred yards north of Rainy Day. Nine o'clock finally arrived. He couldn't find his cell. Checked the bedroom and the porch. Muttering curses when he decided he had left it at the Inn. Just as he was climbing into Old Faithful to go back and get it, he saw it on the passenger-side floor. He punched in the number Laney had given him. Heard Lucia's voice for the first time in what seemed like a month. "Taz, is that you? How are you?"

"A lot better, now that I know you're still alive."

"Don't tell me you were still worried. Even after I told you not to?" She sounded almost coquettish.

"Well, not *really* worried—it's just been a while since anybody's heard from you."

"So, you really *weren't* worried. Did you at least miss me a little?"

"What I missed was having somebody of the female persuasion around to give me a hard time."

A quick laugh. "How about Laney?"

"That's a different kind of hard time. Let's get back to you."

"I've had my ups and downs. Things can be a little complicated down here."

"So, you're still down in the valley. How're your cats?"

"That's the problem. I've been spending more time finding donors than panthers. It's been a long three weeks. But things are looking up. I got a call last week. The Panther Conservation Society. They want me to speak at their annual conference in Denver next week. They said they've been trying to reach me for more than a month. And I can actually get the time. The folks I'm working with pretty much have to let me go if they want to keep me credible. I'm going to go home for a day or two first. It's a chance to see my grandmother Tillie in Alturas. Sorry I'll still be so far away. I'd really like to see you. I don't suppose there's any chance you'd be willing to give up your futile attempts at crabbing to come out to see me?"

Keep her credible? Taz slipped that one into the mental file he was keeping about all the oddities surrounding Lucia's work on the Rio Grande. "There's only one problem—I have to be in Idaho that week. At the Interagency Fire Center in Boise. I need some volunteers for a delegation to help the Brazilian government deal with the wildfires they're seeing on the margins of the Amazon."

"So that's what Laney meant about you having friends in Brazil. And here I thought you were an ocean guy."

"I'd rather be playing in the surf than slogging through a rainforest, if that's what you mean. But work is work. We're still juggling dates, though, so maybe I can find some wiggle room. How can I reach you?"

"I better call you. I'll ring you when I get to Alturas."

Taz decided he'd like to know a little more about Lucia's panther group. He had bookmarked their website. They seemed to be a pretty straightforward collection of panther biologists and some conservation activists; nobody he had heard of. He was just about to close his browser when he noticed a note in the members' pull-down menu that said that they were proceeding with the conference as scheduled, even though their first-choice venue in Denver had fallen through. They would be notifying participants as to the new venue promptly.

Two days later, Lucia called again, this time from a Northern California area code, sounding remarkably like the woman he had met back in April. "Taz, you won't believe this—I ran into an old buddy of yours at the airport in Alturas—Billy Dorsey." Billy was the top Wildland Fire Manager for Northern California and Nevada when Taz and Secretary Talbot were working to get the wildfire program some badly needed emergency funds during an unusually intense fire season. He was one of the best frontline managers in the program. Taz had asked him to come to DC for the congressional hearings on the issue. After just a little coaching, he had done a brilliant job. His stories of life on the fire line saved the program's budget.

"Somehow, maybe from my grandmother, he had heard that you and I knew each other. He couldn't stop talking about your work together back in the day. You never told me you worked with the fire guys. That's pretty cool. Anyway, Billy's wangled an invitation to your get together in Boise. It will be good to spend some time with him again."

Taz was puzzled. Lucia was so excited. Had she and Billy been more than friends?

"But that's not all, Taz. Our Denver conference hotel threw us overboard for an antiabortion group, so the Fund had to move the meeting. All the other hotels in town were booked. Salt Lake City's dry—can you imagine the horror? Five hundred wildlife conservationists and no freaking alcohol? So, I don't know if our dates overlap, but we're coming to Boise too!"

*

On Sunday, Taz landed at the Boise Airport—*Your Gateway to Adventure*. He left a message for Lucia while the plane was still on the taxiway. As they waited for the crews to clear the gate, he checked the WPC's website for the conference schedule, thinking he might be able to treat her to lunch. The conference had apparently been a tremendous success. Taz noted the past tense with a sinking feeling. The conference had wrapped up early so attendees could enjoy at least a part of their hard-earned weekends. He was surprised by the depth of his disappointment. The idea that he and Lucia would be together in a faraway city had rooted itself deep in his imagination. He wanted to see her, to tease her, to watch her smile. Not to speak of the darker desire to plunder her charms and carry her away. It was a particularly savage irony that his dream was crashing and burning at the same time his plane landed in the city where he'd counted on making it come true.

There was no sight of her in the terminal. Life would be so much simpler if he could just forget how much he enjoyed her company.

He was staying at the Cabana Inn, a glorified motel just west of the city center. It appeared that Lucia's conference had filled up every decent hotel room in town. He took a quick look at his room. Habitable. He dropped his bag on the bed and went out for a walk. Ended up on the north bank of the Boise River, where he found a concrete bench with tired wood slatting. He used his windbreaker for a pillow and settled in to watch the clouds. He was just coming back to consciousness when his cellphone began cawing. Probably someone from the fire center.

"Taz! I've been trying to reach you. Are you finally here?" *Lucia.*

"I am. You must have called while I was in the air. Then I heard the conference had ended, and I thought you'd be long gone."

"I agreed to take a half-dozen high schoolers on a hike tomorrow. Why don't you come with us? It's been too long."

"I really wish I could. But tomorrow's my day with the fire managers. I don't know how long it will go. Maybe I could grab Billy and the three of us . . . but what an idiot I am. You two probably want some time to yourselves. I know how excited you were to see him."

"Taz! Did you get a concussion under that damn dock? Billy might as well be my uncle. He and Tillie are old friends. It would be nice to spend some time with him, but that isn't why I was all excited when they moved the conference. Can't you understand? It's you I want to see." Her voice descended to a darker shade. "I thought maybe you'd feel the same way."

Softly. "I do. That's why I'm hoping you'll stay another day. I was thinking it might be fun to drive down to the Snake River Canyon, to take in the views by the Raptor Center. Any chance?"

"I . . . I don't know. I'd like to, but I'll check."

"Okay, but how about you at least let me plead my case? I'm told I can be very persuasive. Over dinner tonight?" They agreed to meet at Bar Gernika, a little bistro in the Basque block downtown.

⸾

Over a dinner of pintxos, grilled chorizo, a spinach fritatta and vino tinto, they traded stories: her visit with Tillie, happenings on the island, the latest from Laney. It was late. He ordered coffee. "Dessert?" Lucia shook her head no and crossed her arms over her chest.

"Tell me about Brazil. Laney said your companion was a beautiful woman from somewhere high up in the State Department." She lit the table with a smile. "Should I be jealous?"

"I'd be flattered. Actually, it was *two* women. Unfortunately, they're in love—with each other."

"Must have been quite a come down. Sorry!"

"You're not, really."

Lucia put on a wonderful fake smile. "You're so full of yourself. It's really annoying. Okay, no, I'm not sorry. But I wish I could have seen your face when you realized what you were up against."

"Such sympathy. I'm touched. Where are you staying?"

"At the Hilton."

"I'm just a few blocks up the street from there. Shall I walk you home?"

She glanced quickly down at her lap: "If you'd like to."

When they got under the little cupola over the front doors, he gave her a quick kiss, stepped back, and turned to go. "Taz? Would you like to come up?"

"Do you want me to?"

"Ummm . . . yes. At least for a little while. I have to get up early. But I have a bottle of wine I haven't finished. We could share it."

Her room was on the seventh floor. She fumbled with her key. She seemed anxious. Taz wondered why. He opened the sliding glass doors to her little balcony, and they stood in the cool evening breeze looking out over the city lights at the Boise River and the more scattered lights on the far bank. The wine helped her regain her balance. She was excited to take the kids into the hills, but shocked at how insulated they were—just like city kids anywhere, but here? In the middle of such a spectacular landscape, with so much to experience? Maybe she could help them open themselves to the wild all around them.

"One way or another, I want them to have a day they'll remember."

Taz laughed. "That sounds a lot more fun than what I'll be up to. You're going to be out gallivanting around in the hills, and I'm going to be stuck inside trying to convince a bunch of grizzled fire managers that they want to go to Brazil, but not to vacation in Rio. No—to do exactly what they do here, except in a country they don't know and a language they don't speak. Don't you think I deserve a little company on the day after?"

"I wish I could . . . really. But—"

"But aren't you the one who makes the schedule? Just give yourself the day off."

She stiffened. "It's just a little complicated is all. They do need me back. I guess I was lucky to be able to stay as long as I already have." Taz didn't ask who *they* were.

✦

In the morning, Taz drove his rental to the fire center in the flats just south of the Boise River, a stone's throw from the airport. There was no traffic to speak of and he got there earlier than he had planned. He locked the car and stood for a while with his back to the door, watching the sun struggle to surmount the Sawtooth Range. His mind wandered back to the night before. It must have been something he'd said. After they had come in off the balcony and Taz had closed the sliding doors against the chill, Lucia went to freshen up and Taz stood watching the city lights through the glass. She reemerged and stood next to him. Her hand sought his. The city lights gave way to her reflection in the window—a beautiful black-haired woman in a loose cream-colored blouse and blue jeans, with a single tear making its slow way toward the little valley between her nose and her cheek.

Taz turned her way and drew her towards him, watching her eyes the whole time. Their lips nearly touched. Suddenly she reached her arms behind his neck and closed the distance. He felt her lips, her breath, then her tongue searching his mouth. His left hand was under her shoulder blade and his right was finding its way down to the small of her back. He pressed her there to bring her in closer and felt a tremor run through her. And just as suddenly as she had begun, she broke the kiss, using the flat of her hands on his chest and shaking her head in desperation. Surprised, he stepped back. She reached for him, rubbing the back of his hands with her thumbs. She looked up, trying to smile. He asked if she was okay. She brushed a lock of hair out of her eyes and turned away.

"I can't, Taz. I can't afford to get involved—not now."

"I enjoy you, Lucia. You're beautiful, but it's beyond that. And you feel it too, I know you do. I know how important your work is to you. Trust me—I'm not looking for a lifetime commitment. I just want to enjoy whatever time we have together. Why don't we take it one step at a time and see where it goes."

"Because, dammit, if we start, I don't think I'll be able to hold back. And you'll eventually learn that maybe I'm not the pretty girl you think I am. Trust me. And then I'll crash and burn, and I can't afford that either."

Taz couldn't find words. She faced him, a second tear running down her cheek. She took a deep breath that ended in a sigh and let her head rest on his shoulder. He was holding one of the most beautiful women he'd ever seen, and she was telling him that no matter how far they climbed, there was one summit they weren't going to reach, at least not any time soon. He kissed his fingers and stroked her cheek, then turned and walked out the door. One more reason why he couldn't sleep that night.

*

Taz walked across the modest interagency campus towards the fire headquarters. It was a spartan place, except for an extremely well-equipped communications center adjoining a spacious, if plain, conference room. He poked his head into a few offices. A large digital watch above the door registered 7:45. 9:45 in Washington. Staffers chatted in the hall. The fire season hadn't started in earnest yet, although it had been a dry spring in parts of the West, including in southern Idaho.

Some of the senior fire managers who had been there when he was playing utility infielder for Interior Secretary Talbot had retired, but the ones who had remained greeted Taz warmly. Billie Dorsey stood to shake his hand and exchange a few words. The group, which had grown to seven, spent the morning talking about how this year's wildland fire budget was shaping up—that was one of the things Taz used to take care of—then waded into the Brazilian issue. Besides Taz, only one of them had been there, and that was for a vacation in Rio de Janeiro.

At three, just as they were wrapping up, the center took a call from a local fire warden. A fire had started in the tree belts somewhere behind Shafer's Butte on the southern margin of the Payette National Forest.

Carl Pettin, BLM's senior fire manager, stepped over to a younger man who Taz had noticed sitting quietly in a corner by the door off and on during the day, listening intently.

"Pete, is the rig ready to go? I think we'd better take a look." Then he clapped his hand on Taz's shoulder. "We need to do an aerial scan—it's protocol." Raised his eyebrows in a question. "Just for old times' sake?" Taz nodded. "And we'll need one more—Billie?" Billie hustled out to his truck to retrieve his gear. Pete led them out to the Sikorsky, an old military castoff, an H-34, probably from Vietnam, that could comfortably carry six.

It wasn't until they were buckling up that Taz put two and two together. He felt a sudden pain in his stomach, and before he could even open his mouth to alert the others, sweat streamed down his face.

Pete turned a key. The engine coughed twice, and the rotor began rotating slowly, then whirling and thumping for all it was worth. Taz jammed on his headphones and adjusted his intercom mike. "Carl. Shafer's Butte. Are there hiking trails up there?"

His headphones crackled. "You bet."

The helicopter lifted itself off the ground, dipped its nose, and started moving forward with increasing speed. Taz centered his microphone: "Cougars?"

"More'n likely."

They were over the Camel's Back and headed towards a range of mountains to the northeast. "Okay. Lucia—my friend—the one you were going to meet tonight; she went hiking with a bunch of students today. She could be up there."

Carl flipped his mike to talk to the pilot. "Change of plans, Pete. Let's comb the part of the back side where the hiking trails are before we check the fire. And can you call the Forest Service center and see if a woman hiker with a bunch of kids left any route information?"

Pete swung the nose gradually to the right until they were over a series of wooded hills that marched up towards the higher peaks. They flew that way for a minute while Pete talked on the radio. He switched it off and quickly banked to the left, straightened out, and cut the curve close to a ridgeline trending up and to the left. "Carl! I've got something. They said a woman teacher and six high school kids headed up to the Mores Peak loop this morning."

They were flying over a series of eroded, brushy ravines. Taz had been assigned to ride shotgun on the right-side window facing the top of the hill. He was scanning the area just below the slope where a number of hiking trails spidered through the lodgepole pines. Nothing. He turned to Pete and shook his head.

They kept following the wooded side of the ridge. It was cut by gullies and rockfalls that fed the creek at its base, extending to the north, climbing until it was at least a thousand feet above the creek. After a few minutes, Taz got a whiff of smoke. It was another minute before either of them saw the flames. The fire seemed to be burning in an area about two ravines over. Pete was already turning the rig uphill to get a better look.

As they approached, Taz watched the fire leap entirely over the next ravine to the north, and light up a brown grass hillside above it. That was when he spotted Lucia and her little band—three boys and two girls. They were struggling up a talus slope about fifty yards above and to the right of the blackened ravine. Lucia was waving her arms at them, semaphore-style. He elbowed Pete, found his mike switch, flipped it. "Can you land up here to the right? We'll need to pick them up."

Pete took a long look. "No can do, compadre. There's no place to put down. Those rocks are so jagged, we'd be tumbling downslope before we knew what hit us."

Pete was right. Taz scanned the area as far as his field of vision would take him. There were now flames coursing up three bushy ravines, and the grass had ignited on a hill about three hundred yards above Lucia's position. The thing could erupt at any time. No good. Lucia didn't even have a fire shelter to cover them if they were swept by a burn over. There was one possible escape route—a rockfall leading to a talus pipe that branched away downslope for about three hundred yards. No fuel there to feed the fire. The top of the rock fall was only about fifty yards away from where the group was standing. It was separated from Lucia's band by a low granite hogback.

Taz tried to remember the training he had been given at the Bitteroot Lookout years before. He tapped Pete's shoulder again.

"You have a drop ladder?"

"In the back, behind Carl." Billy was already pulling it onto the seat next to Carl. He got busy unwrapping the ties that ensured it was ready to deploy.

Taz whipped his headphones off and climbed back from his seat into the main well. Shouting against the rotor. "Can you hold it here?"

"As long as the fire winds don't buffet us too much."

He leaned out the door and waved frantically, pointing Lucia to the top of the talus. Carl took hold of Taz's wrist to pull him back in. "I used to do this for a living. So did Billy."

"I'm twenty-five years younger than either of you. How about if Billy belays me and you tell us both what to do?"

Carl's grim smile was a recognition of the limitations imposed by age. "Okay. Wait 'till we're about thirty feet above her, and just roll it out. Leave five feet to spare so it doesn't catch. Try to keep it away from trees or brush. Get the throw end as close to her as you can and then lower it to where she can help the kids up."

They waited impatiently as Pete moved closer to the rock outcropping where Lucia and the students stood. Lucia was pointing towards the talus slope and shouting something he couldn't hear. That was when Taz realized he had counted five students. She'd told him she was taking six.

Finally, Pete managed to position them above her. Taz rolled out the drop ladder. At sixty feet it was still too short to reach the ground. Billy motioned to Pete to lower the copter. Pete looked worried. Billy waved down again, hard.

Pete managed to put the ladder within four feet of the ground. Lucia reached for it, got her right hand on the third rung. She was holding the arm of one of the girls with her left hand, trying to boost her to the ladder. She couldn't push the girl high enough to get a grip. She tried again. Same result. She shook her head, looked at Taz with a plea that should have gone to heaven. The smoke was getting thicker by the minute. Standing at the open cargo door, Taz was already having trouble breathing. He shouted to Carl, "I've got to go down. Will it hold two at a time?" Carl nodded vigorously.

As he took his first steps down, he reminded himself to keep three points of contact, the way you do in a cliff descent. But this was more like climbing down the ratlines of a sloop in heavy seas. By the time Taz got halfway down, Lucia had lost her hold on the bottom rung, and he was swinging like a pendulum. He tried not to look down, just to keep descending, foot after foot, hand after hand. He could already feel the heat from the fire, which was now only a couple of hundred yards downhill.

He finally got his feet on the second-to-last rung, within jumping distance of the rocks below. Just then, a blast of hot wind swung him wide. Lucia stretched for the rope ladder but couldn't reach it. A few seconds later, Taz swung back, holding on with his left hand and reaching out for her with his right. As the ladder got close, Lucia yelled above the din, "Grab my wrist! Hard!"

It worked. He grabbed and she held on with everything she had. Taz at last found rock with both feet. He looked into Lucia's eyes. Her face was streaked with soot and tears. She was yelling above the din of the helicopter blades. "I lost Jenny! I'm going down to find her. You take the others up."

Taz shook his head vehemently. He was sure he would never see her alive again. He held the rope ladder with one arm and grabbed her sleeve with the other: "You've already taken too much smoke. I'll go!"

"Taz! I know the route we took. You'll never find her! Take the kids up!" She turned, running, climbed swiftly up the hogback, and headed down the rockfall.

Cursing a blue streak, Taz kept his hold on the rope ladder and waved the five students to him, helped them get a sure foothold and hustled them up one by one. "Remember, three holds all the way!" They were frightened, but they did as they were told. Just as the last—an athletic young girl who thanked Taz politely for his help—climbed into the cargo bay, he locked eyes with Carl, who was making a slash under his chin. They were already full, and they were running out of gas. Billy threw down a silvery bundled package about the size of a rolled-up sleeping bag. A fire shelter. Taz tucked it under his arm and headed over the hogback and downslope to the talus chute. He could hear the copter lifting off behind him.

Lucia was nowhere in sight. The going was tough. Every rock was a different shape and size from the ones beside and below it. The occasional head-high boulder was interspersed with jagged half-size rocks that were piled on top of the scree. He marveled that Lucia had made it down so fast. Taz had descended about two hundred yards when he caught sight of them. They were clearly struggling. It looked like young Jenny had sprained or broken her left ankle. As Taz made his way towards them, he kept his eyes alert for any place that could shelter all three.

When he reached them, Lucia helped Jenny onto a rock, then stood and hugged him, with her face to his neck. She pulled back. "I was so sure . . .I—" Her voice was drowned out by a sound like twin jet engines. She tensed, pulling on his sleeve, yelling against the hot wind. "We have to get Jenny somewhere safe!" A series of small explosions cut her off. The trees on the edge of the fire burst like popcorn. The heat suddenly intensified. A curling jet of orange flame shot over their heads and spiraled up into the smoke.

Taz let the rolled shelter drop. "Take this. Put Jenny on my back." The girl was badly frightened and only barely mobile. Once she had her arms around his neck, Taz held her to his back with his left hand, used his right for support, and made his way as quickly as he could up the talus towards a depression he had noted on his descent.

Their hide was an open space the depth of a two-man foxhole, downwind from a giant eccentric boulder and surrounded by heaps of talus rock and smaller scree. It was just big enough to accommodate the three of them. Lucia lifted the terrified girl off Taz's back, knelt and placed her on the ground with care. Taz started unrolling the shelter. She helped him stretch it over them and jammed the corners in between some good-sized rocks. Then the two of them crouched on either side of the girl and waited.

Within minutes the first wave of heat and flame rushed over them, with a sound like a freight train derailing at seventy miles an hour. Cinders and chunks of debris rained down on the shelter. Taz and Lucia tried their best to knock them off from inside. Taz heard a thunderous whoosh as the trees standing on either side of the talus ignited. Within seconds they too were popping and crackling. After an indefinite period in which every minute seemed like an hour, the winds slackened, and the noise died down. Taz peeked out. The most intense flames had passed to their east side. He stood to fix the shelter more securely. A crosswind picked up a small tornado of ash and brick-sized embers. Taz felt a gouge and then a burn on his left cheek. The talus beneath him was still hot enough to burn his feet through the soles of his boots. He boosted the girl onto his back a second time, and they made their painful way slowly up the slope to a flat granite platform not far from where they had first seen Lucia. There they sat while the first drops of an approaching thunderstorm splattered around them. They were breathing too hard to talk. Then Taz heard the welcome beat of the Sikorsky's rotors.

It took less than twenty minutes to reach the fire station, but it seemed like hours. The Sikorsky's enormous drooping blades were still tickling the rain puddles on the apron as Taz wrapped his arms under Lucia's, lowered her down to the cement. She was liberally sprinkled with soot, as if Jackson Pollock had painted her using a palette that ranged from black to gray. He handed Jenny down to her, then jumped down himself. A fire crew hurried towards them, put the girl on a stretcher and ran it to an ambulance just off the landing apron. They took off with sirens blaring. Taz hitched Lucia to him with one hand around her waist as they gimped together towards the helicopter hangar. The fresh air stirred up by the rotor wash seemed to revive her, at least a bit. She was murmuring something, but he couldn't quite make it out.

They crossed into the shadows under the hangar's tall roof. The other five students had already been taken to a nearby clinic. Carl and Bobby were sitting on a side bench, calling the students' parents. Jenny had a badly sprained ankle, and all of them had suffered some effects of the smoke, but other than that they were in decent shape. Carl waved his phone in Taz's direction. Taz gave him a thumbs up, bundled Lucia into his rental car and headed to the local walk-in clinic. The doctor gave her fifteen minutes of oxygen. Once she was breathing more easily Taz led her out of the clinic and sat her on a bench in a small park across the street. The wood was slightly wet and cool to the touch. Over their heads, an aspen tree's green leaves fluttered in the gentle breeze. He placed his hand gently on hers.

"Are you okay?"

She shivered. "I guess so. I mean I'll be alright." She was shaking.

Taz put his arm around her shoulder, taking care not to touch the scratches. "How about this—I'll take you back to the Hilton so you can shower and take a little rest. I'm willing to bet we'll both be hungry by sundown." He recalled a sports bar downtown with decent food and billiards tables. They agreed to meet at the bar at eight.

CHAPTER TWENTY

Even Cowgirls get the Blues.

IT WAS STILL DUSK WHEN Taz stepped out into the cool of the evening. The shower and shampoo and a change out of his smoke-fouled clothes had done wonders for his frame of mind. The bar was closer than he remembered. The first floor was crammed with gigantic TVs showing a bunch of bizarre pseudo-sports: truck dragging, obstacle racing, motocross, golf. Country music provided a backdrop for the hoots and hollers of fans at tables scattered around the central bank of TVs. Taz stepped stiffly down a large staircase to a lower level dominated by pool tables, with cocktail tables scattered around them. Blues tunes hung in the air. A full, old-style bar with a mirror running the full length above two racks of liquor, and a kitchen that served mostly appetizers. The televisions above the bar were on a football game. The audio had been snuffed in favor of a blues-rock song led by two women with smoky voices and good harmonies. Except for the buzz of conversation around the bar, the room seemed quiet after the sonic storm upstairs.

Taz surveyed the bar. Cocky college boys out for a good time, couples eyeing themselves in the mirror as they talked, trios of men talking sports and women talking about men, and one or two solitaires, probably regulars.

He watched as a quintet of young bartenders and waiters scurried, bent, and twirled to take care of the tables between the bar scene and the adjacent rectangular world of pool tables, chalk dust, yellow lights and men and women with long pointed sticks in their hands.

Behind the far corner of the bar, a tall auburn-haired woman moved fluidly, directing traffic, chatting up customers, smoothing feelings, sliding pints towards waiting hands, mixing cocktails, yet never seeming in the least hurried. Probably on the light side of her thirties. A calm center in the swirling storm. Just now, she was conferring with her college-age colleagues, dealing directly with some of the more obstreperous stool sitters, and still finding the time to greet the newcomers who came in out of the blue.

Stools were coming empty and refilling rapidly. For a moment, the calm one appeared deep in thought. Then she swiveled in Taz's direction. Touched one of her ducklings on the shoulder. He appeared in front of Taz seconds later. Taz ordered a gin martini, straight up with a twist. He nodded his thanks her way, then turned to survey the action at the pool tables.

The martini was beyond good. Scents of juniper, lemon, herbs, fresh, savory wafted from his glass. A delicate hint of bitters, swirling in shards of ice. He was savoring his third sip as the calm one turned from rinsing a shaker. She wiped her hands, walked in his direction with a wary expression.

"Here from out of town? Or just an unrepentant football addict with a broken TV?" She had a point. If the upstairs was about sports, this bar was about hooking up. Most folks weren't even casting a gaze at the game.

"True on both counts. But as to the football, I'll take the kind with the round ball."

"Really. So, who's your favorite team?" Testing him.

"Our women's team, then Ajax Amsterdam. How about you?"

With a smile. "What makes you think I would even care?"

"Well, let's see. Something tells me you played. You have that sense of balance. Agility. And then there's the trophy above the register. That's kind of a telltale sign. Shall I quote it? 'Boise Arrows—Idaho State Champions. MVP Idaho and Golden Boot: Fiona Macoun.'"

"I never should've let the owners put that ugly thing up."

"For God's sake don't take it down. Tipsy sports fans love champions." She turned away. "My guess is that it was you who mixed the martini."

A concerned look over her shoulder. "Sure did. You didn't like it?"

Taz chuckled, giving her a sideways look. "It was delightful. What gin did you use?" She took two steps down the bar, pulled up a stepladder, climbed the first step and, in one fluid motion, pulled a bottle from the top shelf, stepped down, turned back to Taz, and placed it carefully in front of him. Caught his eyes and smiled.

Taz smiled back. "Mind if I take a look?"

She leaned towards him, elbow on the bar, a nice smile slowly widening. "Well now, I guess that depends on what you're going to be looking at." Taz did his best to keep his eyes on the bottle. Fiona raised her eyes to look over his shoulder: "Too bad. I think your girl just came in." Taz fished in his jacket pocket, slipped a twenty under her hand. She began to protest, but he had already turned to greet Lucia. She was walking uncertainly in his direction, nervously scanning the room. She finally spotted him as he threaded his way through the crowd. She was having difficulty summoning a smile. Every time she got halfway, she ended up wiping tears from her eyes.

He led her towards a recently vacated table. Her skin was tender and cool, her hair still damp from the shower. Her scent could have come from fresh moss in a fir forest.

While a skinny young man brought them menus and ice water, Taz reached for her hands, stroked them gently. Lucia looked into his eyes— hers were still red from the smoke. "Taz, how could I have been so stupid? I put those kids in danger. If I were one of their mothers, I'd be coming after me with a pitchfork!"

"Lucia—stop. Those kids wouldn't have stood a chance if they'd been out there on their own. Carl told their parents how you risked your life to save them. And he wanted me to tell you that the burn had started early in the morning, probably from the remains of a breakfast fire some lunkhead left without making sure it was fully doused. From its location, it would have been impossible for you to see it."

"It's nice of him to say that, but I . . . I should have been more careful. And I put you and the fire crew in danger as well." She looked down, shaking her head. "I fucked up, Taz."

Taz found a pitcher of ice water and two clean glasses on a wall platform. He brought them back to the table and filled the glasses, handed one to Lucia. "How about we order some starters?" She nodded. He stood and sidled through a few tables to the bar. Fiona was pouring two pints of beer for a rhinestone cowboy and his platinum blond. She disengaged and drifted down the bar in Taz's direction. Looking over his shoulder. "Lucky you. She's beautiful."

"She's a little upset just now. Would you be willing to make us two of those marvelous martinis?" Fiona nodded her understanding and smiled.

"You better go keep her company. I'll bring them over."

A few minutes later, as Taz was trying his best to lighten Lucia's mood, Fiona appeared and set a frozen martini glass in front of each of them, dropped in two lemon peel twists, produced a silver shaker, and gave them each a full pour. Taz pulled out his wallet, made to thank her. She put her finger to her lips to shoosh him, winked at Lucia. "On the house." Turned gracefully and strolled back to the bar.

Lucia gave him a quizzical look. "You know each other. From other trips?"

"Actually, I just met her tonight."

"You seem so easy with each other."

"Fellow martini fanatics. We hit it off."

She spared him a wan smile. He raised his glass for a toast. She seemed not to notice. He watched her face, put his glass down with care. "Lucia, are you still with me?"

"Sure. But you'd be better off if I wasn't."

"Why would you say that?"

"I'm saying you could be happier, that's all. If you were with someone . . . easier. Maybe with your martini friend instead. Someone with fewer problems. I only get you in trouble, cause you pain. I'm a complication. Haven't you already got enough of them?"

"Lucia, don't. You've been through a hell of a day."

"Really? That's twice you've nearly gotten yourself killed trying to protect me from my own stupidity. First, I put you at risk in that damn bar, and now this. By now, you should be running away whenever you see me, and we've only known each other for a few months. If I were you, I'd make sure it didn't go much further."

He reached to hold her hand. "That was on me. I'm the one who lost my temper. And you're not responsible for what happened today, the idiot who left his fire burning is. So, half the time, I'm the one that's gotten *you* in trouble. I figure the least I can do is to stick around so I can fix my mistakes."

She pulled her hand away. Looked at him, eyes clouded. "You're such a bullshitter."

"Occasionally. But I'm not bullshitting you now. You were great out there. You scared me to death when you ran back down that slope . . . but Jenny's alive now because of you."

She turned away, hands twining. "Don't. Don't try to make me feel better." She swallowed half her glass in one quick move.

Taz considered his martini, thinking about his next words. "You're being so hard on yourself. Why? I guess that's what's got me worried. The way the world is – it's not because you did something wrong. You're punishing yourself for things that aren't your fault. Is that what you're doing down in Mexico? Expiating your sins?"

She was shaking her head. "Taz, that isn't your business. Please don't press."

It was time to get it out on the table. "You're in trouble, Lucia. If someone has put you in harm's way, I want to help, but I can't, not unless you tell me what's going on."

She glared at him, straightened her back. "I'm not worth worrying about. Like I told you, I can take care of myself."

"You say I'm a closed book, but were you ever going to tell me what you're really doing on the Rio Grande?"

"What I'm really doing? How do you get off—"

"Lucia, I know the antinarcotics team asked you to keep your eyes and ears open for information on cartel activities across the border. By itself, that wouldn't make you a target. But now you're in deeper. People are worried about you; they think you're risking your life. Who put you on the spot, and why?"

Lucia's eyes widened. "Who made you my guardian?" Her voice raw. "Who gave you the right to rummage around in my life? To call John White behind my back? He's the one who told you, right? I should have known. You must have been buddies at State. And now you're trying to pin me down like one of Nabokov's damn butterflies? In case you hadn't noticed, they're all dead!"

Taz sat back, just trying to absorb her anger, her anxiety, her fear. Was it just the tension of the past few days? Or maybe it was something more. Something that threatened her sense of herself.

"I'm new to Chincoteague, okay?" Calmer, but her tone almost bitter. "I wanted to make friends, so I've tried to let folks get to know me. Are you telling me I have to lay myself open for examination like a cadaver? Because if that's the price of your or anybody else's friendship, I'll skip it."

Taz trained his eyes on hers. "Okay, Lucia. You can have it that way if you like. I get it that I made you uncomfortable last night, and I'm sorry. But I'm not one of your friends in Chincoteague. There's something else between us, and it scares you—or maybe I've just got it all wrong. I've done that more than once."

"Taz, I didn't mean—"

"Oh, but you did. Maybe I'm wrong and everything is just fine . . . I sure hope so. I'll stay out of your life if that's what you want. But if you do end up in trouble, for God's sake don't let your pride stop you from asking for help. And take care of yourself. I really don't want to see you get hurt."

She was tearing up. "Okay, Taz. I have to go back to the hotel. Pack my things. I'll be on the road early. Just don't— Oh, Jesus. You're right, it was all a fantasy. I just need to be by myself." Wiped her eyes with her sleeve. "Goodbye."

She ran up the stairs. Taz stood slowly and drained his martini, reached for his wallet to pay the tab. It slipped out of his hand and spilled most of its contents on the floor beneath the table. He stared at the litter for a moment, then knelt on one knee to retrieve his credit cards and driver's license. Slipped two twenties under the glass and headed towards the stairs.

Fiona was watching him while she wiped down the bar. Her gaze lingered in his direction a few more moments. "Your main squeeze? Fiancée?"

Taz stepped to the right and put his hand on the bar. "Too early to tell. Either way, more a hope than a reality."

"My advice? Don't give up on her yet. She'll be back."

"What makes you think so?"

"Because, Mr. Blackwell, I saw her look at you when you brought her up that rope ladder, and again when she came in tonight."

Taz was stunned. He must have shown it.

"It's a small community, Taz. Nobody's been talking about anything else all afternoon. Your buddies at the wildfire center put a video up on their website earlier today. Looked like it was from a fixed ground camera mounted on the helicopter. It's the best entertainment anyone here's had since the Broncos won the college football regionals. The only debate is whether you're a suicidal romantic or just plain crazy. You know—Evel Knievel's mad brother." She smiled, kissed her fingers, and lightly touched his cheek. "See you around." A simple gesture, but it lifted his spirits.

❧

Whatever schedule Taz had imagined for his last day in Boise had been scrubbed clean by Lucia's early departure. He slept late. Skipped lunch to transcribe his notes from the meeting with the fire managers. He would ask Arthur to put them in cable form for Undersecretary Lansman.

When he was finished, he took a walk along the river and reflected on the unraveling tapestry of the past three days. The morning's cotton puff clouds had flattened, spread, and turned dark and brooding. A damp chill flowed around him, and a welcome drizzle. He walked slowly, enjoying the smell of wet grass and the feel of the droplets on his face. Back in his room, he rummaged in his duffel and found his copy of *The History of the Murder of Charles the Good, Count of Flanders*, Henri Pirenne's pathbreaking edition of the manuscript composed by Gilbert de Bruges in the bleak winter of 1127. He had finished Napier, and he figured De Bruges' riveting tale of the brutal crime that transformed the Netherlands in the twelfth century might at least absorb the rest of his afternoon. His flight to Norfolk left at five-thirty.

CHAPTER TWENTY-ONE

Sorting Things Out

TAZ SPENT THE FOLLOWING MORNING sorting himself out, as Tommy Sokutu, his South African brother, would have put it. Cleaning up the mess in his cottage. Tending to his garden. Assessing the so-called progress of his *spartina* plantation.

By four-thirty, he was sitting on his front steps in the sun, drinking gin and lime. Somewhere around five, after his second, it occurred to him that what he needed was a good swim. He took off his watch, left it on the top step of the stoop that was his headquarters for sunset. The water would be cold. He knew that. He felt sure it would refresh him. Maybe even sober him up. Waited for his opportunity, crossed the street a little unsteadily, heard the blare of a truck's horn. He wasn't sure where it emanated from. He stood, stepped to the edge of the dock, and dove, fully clothed.

The outgoing tide pulled him towards the mouth of Chincoteague Bay. In two hours or a little longer, the current would discharge him into the broad Atlantic. It occurred to him that a losing battle with the tide was actually not the way he wanted to go, so he turned and started back to the dock. The weight of his wet flannel shirt made swimming difficult. He made gradual progress, but it took a bloody long time, as Tommy would put it.

After fifteen minutes that felt like forever, he was sitting back on his stoop in the late afternoon sun. He was dripping wet from his feet to the top of his head when Laney showed up and stepped out of her red Toyota truck.

"Jesus, Taz. What the hell are you doing?"

"Just trying to clarify my thinking, you know, sort it out. I mean how I feel. I don't really know, do I? How I feel. Not so good, actually. Three strikes and you're out, you know? Three strikes and you're out."

"Taz. Stop. Are you *trying* to kill yourself? It's almost six. The sun's about to go down, and you're as wet as a dishrag." She grasped his wrist, helped him get to his feet, and walked him into the cottage.

She stripped him and pushed him into the hot shower. Handed him a towel. He sat at the little round kitchen table while she made coffee. It smelled good. He was glad for the warmth of the tin cup he was holding with both hands. Laney busied herself in the kitchen, warmed him up a can of chicken soup. He sipped it appreciatively. She poured herself a bowl and sat across the little kitchen table, watching him.

"Taz, you can't do this to yourself again. And I can't watch you do it. I really can't, Taz. There's no point in numbing the pain by hurting yourself even more. You have to go on. You just have to."

He reached over, touched her cheek with the back of his fingers. "Okay, Laney. Thanks for the rescue."

They sat and talked a little longer. She had to take care of her cats. After she left, he poured the remaining gin down the drain and tossed the bottle into the recycling bucket.

❧

Taz's head was still banging as he walked into Rainy Day the next morning. The door's creaking sounded like the scream of a lamb being torn apart by wolves. Laney took one look at him, ducked into her office, and came out with two cups and a thermos of hot coffee. "Let's take a walk." Out the back door and over to the deck above the channel.

"Have you heard from her at all?"

"Not a word."

"She called me last night while you were drying out. She was so upset, Taz. What's going on? Please tell me she's not running away and you're not about to get yourself killed by poison arrows in the Amazon."

"I don't know. At this point, I'm just praying that she doesn't pull a Dana and tell me she can't do it anymore."

"Don't give up, Taz. She told me a little about what happened in Boise. Said she and her high schoolers would have died on the mountain if it weren't for you. And she was miserable about your argument in the bar. She didn't mean to hurt you, but she knows she did. It wouldn't matter if she didn't care for you, but she does. And I really want to see you happy for once. I mean before we all cash in our chips."

"Help me out then. I think she's in trouble down at the border. Richard said you were worried too, so you know. That's what we quarreled about. I wanted to see if there was a way I could help. But she decided I was prying into her private life. She went ballistic."

"I know you're hurting, but you have to give her some room. She said you made her feel things she hadn't felt before. But it's come on so fast, and it's new for her. She's had other relationships. She told me about some of them. But whatever's going on between the two of you is completely different, and strong enough that she's a little scared of where it might take her. There were some difficult things she had to get over to trust you, or any man. She does trust you, Taz. But she also craves her freedom. And she's trying as hard as she can to figure out a way to reconcile the two."

"Trust? Did somebody hurt her?"

"There's something you need to hear, Taz, and it's not going to be easy. I had to coax her even to share it with me. I'm going to share it with you because I know how much you care for her. And if you don't know, if you stay in the dark, you won't be able to help her when she needs you the most.

"Lucia carries a terrible wound, one that may never completely heal. She may not be able to bear children. That's the thing that scares her most, because it has already cost her one relationship. One that she thought might work.

"She was raped, Taz. She was only fourteen. The perp was her father's boss, a 'trusted uncle'. A Type A corporate CEO who had put up the money for her dad to join an experimental trial to cure his melanoma. Her father was in a hospital in Houston, more than a thousand miles away. Her mother was an alcoholic. She left Lucia to take care of the house while she was on a binge with friends in Hawaii. She called Lucia exactly once, to tell her that she had decided to extend her trip. 'Uncle Mike'—the CEO—offered to let her stay with him and his wife, a woman Lucia trusted and admired.

"The wife was actually out of town for a business conference. As soon as he locked the door behind her, Lucia knew something was terribly wrong. It didn't take long for it to begin. First the door locked, then caresses, then the groping. She told me she tried to scream to the neighbors. He put his hand across her mouth. She bit him, Taz. Drew blood.

"He raped her twice a day after that. Threatened her if she ever said anything. It was three days before she found an unlocked upstairs window and used sheets tied together to reach the ground. She ran to her best friend's house and told her everything.

"But she couldn't tell her parents. Her father would have had to withdraw from the medical trial and leave his job."

Taz stared at Laney, jaw set, wide-eyed. He put his head in his hands.

"Not long after, she found out she was pregnant. She couldn't tell anyone about that, either. She borrowed the money for an abortion. That was when she moved west to stay with her grandmother in northern California.

"Years later, when she was in grad school, she found someone. 'I threw myself at him because that's what I thought love was.' Her words. She thought he loved her just as much. What he really wanted was a nice nuclear family—you know, two and a half kids, a dog, and a house in the suburbs. He sucked her right into that dream. She told me she was halfway to becoming his little homemaker. She can laugh about that part now. Then she learned that she couldn't get pregnant. Maybe ever. What the boyfriend wanted most, even more than being waited on hand and foot, was kids of his own. He treated her like dirt. Berated her for lying to him. Like she had planned it all. She tried so hard, Taz. When she told me it broke my heart. She asked how she could fix it, talked about adoption, begged him to come with her to counseling. The asshole told her that if she really wanted to fix it, she should go find herself another sucker to con. Six months later he married some poor girl he had dated in high school. And three months after that word got around that his wife was pregnant. And he was parading around like it was time to hand out cigars. That's why she's scared, Taz. She couldn't tell anyone then and she can't tell anybody now."

Taz cradled his face in his hands. "Jesus. If I don't kill him, it's only because he's got his damn family. Is there anything I *can* do?"

"My advice is don't push her. Even last night, when we talked, and she was so upset, she told me you liberated something in her. Lucia's the one who has to figure this out. Let her."

Laney stood. "I've got to go back. It's my turn at the counter." She put a hand on his shoulder and locked eyes with him. "One other thing, Taz. Respect her freedom. What you love about each other is the freedom that frightens you both."

CHAPTER TWENTY-TWO

Existential Questions

TAZ RETURNED TO THE COTTAGE to find his cellphone on the kitchen counter with a new message on it. Arthur's voice. The gist of the call was that Everton had told Jessica that Brazil could be ready to accept a full US fire team in three weeks, and that Jessica wanted to be sure Taz could have their team ready on time. The schedule seemed about right, and Taz didn't see much point in protesting the lack of consultation. He called Carl to set things in motion in Boise and turned to his two most urgent tasks—outlining the team's in-country strategy and replacing a rotten joist under his porch. He decided to start with the joist, a job that would have the advantage of requiring enough concentration to take his mind off Lucia, and, equally important, might help him sweat off the black cloud that had followed him ever since his return from Boise.

Taz spent the afternoon at the supply store collecting the brackets, hangers, and eight-penny nails he would need to toe-in and fix the joist to the sill plate. It took him a little while and a long conversation with the lumber manager, whose name was Delbert, to select a two-by-twelve with the right length and a crown that assured it wouldn't bow under the weight of the porch's floor. Having learned a great deal about Delbert's family history and views on Island politics, he finally unloaded his materials just as the sun went down.

In the morning he borrowed a circular saw and router from his clammer friend Cliff, who lived just up Main, and began to work. It was five o'clock when he finished bolting the joist to the north-side bracket. A white van pulled up in front of the house. The driver was about to put something in the mailbox on the wall by the front door when he saw Taz crawling out from underneath the porch. His name was Pete. Pete took a long look, complimented Taz with the old saying about a three-day axe fight, laughed, and handed him a small flat package—FedEx overnight. There was no return address, but the stamp and postal imprint were from Mexico.

Taz stood in front of the rattling air conditioner while he tore the envelope. The note was written on very fine dimpled stock. Her longhand looked a bit shaky.

> *Dear Taz,*
>
> *You probably don't want to talk to me. I know Boise didn't end well for either of us. The things you said that night were hard for me to accept, but you weren't wrong. I was reluctant to involve you, and now you have no reason and perhaps no desire to help, but I didn't know who else to call. If you do decide to contact me, despite everything, don't call on my old cell – Laney has the new number.*

Taz read the note over again. A raised embossment at the bottom right corner of the sheet caught his eye. It read *Ciudad de Reynosa* above a undistinguished shield. Just to add to the mystery.

Taz called Laney and got her message. She was probably still at the auction of an estate library she had mentioned. Taz had accepted an invitation to dinner from an old friend in Cape Charles who was going through a difficult divorce. When she returned the call, he was halfway back. He punched in the number Laney gave him as quickly as he could after he got home, relieved to hear Lucia's voice on the other end of the line. A guarded hello.

"Lucia, I just talked to Laney."

She whispered her reply. "Taz. You can't know how good it is to hear your voice. I only have a little time . . . maybe a minute. Did you mean what you said in Boise? About helping me?"

"I wouldn't have said it otherwise. What's going on?"

There was a noise at her end of the call. Silence for a few seconds, and then she continued. "I was trying to rustle up some funding for my panther project, on the Mexican side. Now things have gotten complicated. I can't say much more. I just need you to know that, and to do me one favor, and not ask any questions. Would you do that?"

"I can come down..."

She cut in. "No. You'd be in danger and there's nothing you can do down here. And I won't be anywhere you can find me, at least for the next week or so. What I need is for you to give our friend John a message from me. He needs to hear it word for word. I need him to get a guarantee from the people who count that if I do this last thing they want, that'll be it. I get to go back to my real work, with a permanent green light. And his word that he'll hold them to it."

There was another rumble at her end of the call. She hesitated for a moment; her tone changed ever so slightly. "What it is, is I need to find my panther and get her to someplace safe. There are men hunting her. They think she's some kind of threat. We're pretty sure she's somewhere in this stretch of the valley—near Reynosa, I mean. I've even asked the mayor for his help. He's willing, but he wants something for his trouble, so that's complicated too." The words, the cadence didn't sound like her. He realized she was dropping clues. Trying to do it in a way that someone overhearing the call wouldn't get.

Keep it about panthers. "Lucia, listen. If you've run into some kind of glitch with the survey, maybe I can help work it out. You know—talk to somebody in the wildlife department here?" She would know there was no such thing.

"I . . . I don't think that would necessarily help."

"I know this isn't a good time for you to talk—it's late, and you probably want to get to bed. But if there is anything I can do, let me know, okay?" Taz waited. He thought he heard the sound of a door closing.

"Thanks, Taz. Hearing your voice is good for me—really good. I'd like to talk more, but it's not easy. Just text me John's yes or no, okay? I'll get in touch as soon as I can." She hung up.

Taz started pacing. *She's in trouble*, that much was clear. But she couldn't talk about it. *Why not? What's she hiding? And who is she hiding it from?* She had told Laney that the panther project might take six weeks. *Is she really going to wallow in whatever mess she's in for that long?* Taz stopped there. She was afraid of the consequences if he showed up. For him, for her, or for both of them. Whatever the problem, it seemed related to her effort to get support for her panther project in Mexico. Maybe she was being threatened. There were probably plenty of people who were opposed to her conservation meddling. Ranchers, developers, local Mexican authorities.

One way or another, and despite Lucia's warning, Taz couldn't be any use unless he got down to the river and learned more about the situation. He needed a plausible reason to show up on the Lower Rio Grande. He decided it was time for that long-sought visit to see the spring birds there. He'd drive. That way his name wouldn't show up on any airline manifest. Just in case somebody got curious.

Taz needed at least a day to get ready get Old Faithful tuned for a road trip. And he wanted the answers to some questions that had been buzzing around his mind like angry bees since his first conversation with John White. Had the DEA put her at risk? And were they the same ones she was afraid of?

*

Taz punched the number for White's desk phone at seven, early enough that the call would go directly through to him.

"You sent her down there."

"Hold on a second, Taz, I need to switch phones." Taz heard some clicking and then a quick, "Yes?"

"John, she's in trouble. Are you even listening in?"

"Of course I am. But so are the Zetas."

"Fuck me, and while we're at it, fuck you too."

"Taz, you being angry won't get her out of this."

"Well maybe this will." He read White Lucia's message from the note he'd written for himself during their conversation.

"Are you planning to talk to her again?"

"I sure hope so, but I don't know when."

"She'll want to know my answer. Tell her I'll do everything I can."

Taz texted Lucia as soon as he was back in his car. He was sure Lucia had found a key to unlock whatever predicament she was in, and White's guarantee was it. Whoever White had to browbeat to get the commitment she needed—probably someone at DEA—was the one who could solve her problem. And if they could solve the problem, maybe that was because they had created it.

✦

Taz had the mechanics at Ferrara's give Old Faithful a thorough once-over. While they were working, he walked the six blocks over to Rainy Day. He drafted Laney for coffee, recounted his phone call with Lucia, and told her what he had decided to do. She looked away for a few seconds and then turned her gaze back to him. "Taz, I think you're right. But if you're thinking of doing something that's going to get you into the kind of trouble you got in with the Russians, you better call me first."

His second call was to Carl Pettin. Taz told him that he needed to go AWOL for a week or maybe even more. Like the pro he was, Carl assured him that he had gone over the Brazil plan and would see to the logistics.

Old Faithful had needed a tire rotation, an oil change, a new timing belt, and some brake adjustments. Taz paid the old man, who was doing accounts in his little shambles of an office, thanked the mechanics, gave each one a President Grant, and started driving. His plan was to overnight in Nashville, get up before dawn, make Memphis in the early morning, and then find his way to the Gulf coast.

The fastest way from Memphis to the Rio Grande would have been to take the interstate through Little Rock, then Texarkana, then Houston.

Taz didn't have much use for any of the three. A few extra hours on a less traveled route would give him time to consider his options. So, he headed south along what was now known as the Mississippi Blues Trail: Tunica, Clarksdale, Greenville. The towns with ramshackle roadhouses where heroes like Charlie Patton and Robert Johnson drank rotgut whisky and played bottleneck slide on the rough and tumble tunes that later became blues and rock standards: "Crossroads Blues," "Ramblin' on my Mind," "High Water Everywhere," "Walkin' Blues."

A few hours in, he was almost sorry. The cultural powers that be had managed to preserve a few of the old juke joints, but now, much of the trail was flanked by industrial cotton farms or, worse, closely mowed Kentucky bluegrass behind wrought-iron fences. Interpreted by well-designed historical markers that rarely if ever mentioned the background of rural poverty, racism, and lynching that ran like a river of blood just beneath the surface. Taz knew Louisiana and east Texas from his childhood, and the whiff of the blood river had stayed with him all his life.

Taz kept the pedal down, all the way to Lafayette and Lake Charles, where he finally felt at home. Unworldly gumbo in Lafayette. He spent the night in a cheap motel. His bed was rumpled, and his window refracted the neon signs out front.

He started before dawn the next morning. Took Route 87 down the Bolivar Peninsula and then hopped the ferry to Galveston. That allowed him to skirt the immense sprawl of oil facilities on Houston's south side, although he still didn't manage to entirely avoid the acrid stench of the refineries.

He imagined the refinery workers—their children, on their way to school, breathing ozone and volatile organic hydrocarbons all the way. Most people don't even know what the chemical names mean. But if your home is in Dickinson, by the ship canal, or in Alvin or, God forbid, in League City, you, your wife, the girl who charmed you in high school and now holds your love completely, your kids, the little guys and girls who bring you such joy—you're all breathing a chemical soup all day, every day, while you work, while you grill burgers out back, while your four-year-old plays on the swing, while you sleep.

Taz gripped the steering wheel, wiped his eyes. No matter, the tears kept streaming. Was it the petrochemical fumes? More likely his mood, a mix of sadness and rage. He kept driving, blindly, not even bothering to tune the radio. He left the petrochemical haze at seventy-five miles an hour and turned towards the coast. Through Bay City, Corpus Christi, Harlingen, and Port Isabel, on the way to the Rio Grande delta and the Mexican border.

Taz needed to find a place for the night. He figured he'd escape the inevitable flock of birders by heading upriver to McAllen. It took three tries to find a clean motel that still had rooms. He fell into bed just before midnight and dreamed about the dinner he had missed.

In the morning, just as the sun was sending its first light over the horizon, he pocketed an orange from the free basket at the motel desk and headed down the road to the Santa Ana Wildlife Refuge. The Gulf air was warm but not too muggy. Everyone with wings was coming up from the south, from ruby-throated hummingbirds to broad-winged hawks. Even though it was a little late, the refuge still harbored pulses of warblers, hawks, and shorebirds. Taz was bound to come across at least a few. And, if he was lucky, he might spot some locals: Altamira orioles, crested caracaras and Aplomado falcons, the most beautiful hawk of the Americas north of Panama.

In the afternoon, when he'd had his fill of birds, he pointed his mud-splattered truck back to the motel, intending to make a round of calls to find at least a little information that would help him locate Lucia. His birder's instinct told him to stop at the refuge's visitor center. There would be a spiral-bound notebook, or sometimes a leather-bound blank book, where you could find handwritten notes of the endemics, exotics, and sometimes just the regular locals that had been seen during the day. This one was leather, and very old. The most recent page was almost full. There were entries in pencil, in red, in a crabbed older person's cursive, and a child's block printing. Some were signed, some not. The young one, whose name was Anna, had seen a reddish egret, a green jay, a hooded warbler, and a wood stork. And there were some other standouts. Green heron, ivory-billed woodcreeper, yellow-headed parrot. Then he noticed it—at the bottom right corner, under the final bird list, someone had noted that a panther had been seen just upriver from the refuge, and that it was being sought for tagging. Asked anyone who had any information to call the refuge manager.

Taz found the refuge manager in his office in a trailer just behind the visitors' center. Lucia was apparently in the habit of calling in to check recent sightings. The manager hadn't seen her for weeks and didn't have her contact information. Taz imagined a host of scenarios—none of them pleasant. He was seven miles from the Mexican border, looking for the woman who had told him to stay out of her life in Boise and only hesitantly asked for his help from Reynosa. The same woman who had torched the ice palisade he had built for himself on the Island and then tried her best to hide half her life from him. Even now she was a mystery. Yet she was drawing him to her like a riptide draws the shore break to the deep. He had been doing just fine drifting with the longshore current, but now there was a voice urging him to ride the rip. To where the cold-water corals thrive, and bioluminescent creatures defy the imagination.

You know you're already on the way down. Pretty soon you'll be deep enough to be entranced by the cuttlefish and angel sharks. You'll shed the need for structure and order and, God knows, any sense of perspective at all. And when that happens, Taz, you know the consequences.

It was the risky course. He had tried it twice and wound up wet and shivering on this or that cold beach, flopping like a mackerel, gasping for breath, and trying desperately to reclaim his heart and his life.

Love lives in the depths of the heart, where you find the greatest risk. *So how do you feel about diving, Taz?*

CHAPTER TWENTY-THREE

Don't Have to Live Like a Refugee

HE GOT BACK TO HIS motel just after noon. His phone blinked. The lovely voice on the message asked him to return the call at his earliest convenience and left a Matamoros area code. When Taz connected, he was greeted by the taped voice of Ignacio Morela. Taz had first met Ignacio during one of his border visits for Interior. Ignacio had later been part of the Mexican negotiating team on the natural resource mapping agreement that Taz had struck with SEMARNAP, Mexico's environmental ministry.

"Taz, *mi amigo*. According to our excellent intelligence service, otherwise known as the State Department, you have for some days been domiciled in our less interesting sister city just across the river. But you didn't call. I'm officially hurt. Still, call me on my cell, and I'll arrange a time when we can get together." *So much for secrecy.*

Taz smiled. Ignacio was chief of staff to José Quintero, the governor of Tamaulipas. He had been an ally in the discussions of the mapping agreement. Intensely defending the interests of Mexico, but also seeing the bigger picture, the benefits that Mexico could gain from an agreement, with enough clarity to convince his perpetually anxious minister, who, as he told Taz later, "was not about to hang his ass out the window on just anybody's say-so."

When they finally connected, Ignacio once again reproved Taz for his negligence. Taz tried his best to give an honest explanation. "Ignacio, my friend. It was a last-minute decision. A whim—it's been a long time since I saw the spring birds down here. State didn't send me on this one. And even I know enough to stay out of Brownsville."

"An extremely disagreeable town, if you ask me."

"That's why I'm up in McAllen."

"Yes. Good choice. A nicer town altogether. Easier to find a decent place to stay."

"Ignacio, I'm happy to hear your voice again. But—"

"*Sí.* I didn't call just to inflate your self-esteem. I want to invite you to dinner with the mayor of Reynosa, Antonio Contreras. Tonight, at his house. I do hope you'll be available."

"I'm always at your service, Ignacio. I drove down from Virginia, so a trip to Reynosa should be a jaunt. Of course, I will come. What's the occasion?"

"The two-hundred-and-fifty-fifth anniversary of the founding of Reynosa. Our constituents view every anniversary as an opportunity for celebration—as long as we pay for it. So, it's not an intimate sit-down. Rather a backyard barbeque. Nonetheless, will you still grace us with your presence?"

Taz recalled that Lucia had said she was trying to raise money for her panther project on both sides of the border. If the funding she was looking for was on the Mexican side, the mayor's party might be a perfect place to pick up her trail. "I'd be honored."

"I almost forgot—you'll have two other countrymen there. Though I doubt if you'd know either of them. They're in quite a different line of work than ours."

Taz ate a late lunch at a local café and found a used car dealer in the midst of the Honda dealers on the east side of town. He convinced the dealer to rent him an old Dodge Dart with Mexican plates and left Old Faithful in the rental lot as collateral. Back at the motel, he ironed his only presentable shirt and brushed his linen jacket, considering his strategy for the evening.

He still had his SENTRI pass. Once he crossed the border, his only real challenge was to find the mayor's house up in the hills. After a few wrong turns, a very understanding woman with an infant in a stroller listened to his broken Spanish and gave him directions in perfect English. He arrived only an hour late. The noise and muffled music reached him when he was fifty yards from the gate. It looked like the crowd was still gathering. The center of gravity seemed to be behind a shoulder-height stucco wall. There was a doorway in the middle of the wall, under an arch lined with tile and with tall oaken doors thrown open. Well-dressed couples were making their way through to join the other celebrants.

The doorway led to a red-tiled back patio facing a large, well-manicured lawn. The courtyard was lit by torches and carefully placed ground lights. Taz estimated there might be somewhere around a hundred and fifty well-dressed party goers, talking in small groups at little round standing tables or milling around the two bars on either side of the courtyard. He had spotted a smaller, plain archway on the side or the wall nearest the house, a handsome hacienda-style affair in the same cream-colored stucco as the wall. He stepped through it and into the torchlight. After a quick survey of the crowd and some Brownian explorations, he located Ignacio, who ushered him through the milling guests and introduced him to Mayor Contreras and his wife, a slim, elegant woman just a few years older than Taz. She flashed a quick smile and turned to the side to greet an admirer.

The mayor might well have been handsome at one point, perhaps even fit, but he had put on a few pounds and a lot of worry lines since. The pounds showed in a slight but noticeable paunch, and oddly, in his fingers, which looked like crooked sausages. His black hair was shining with pomade, swept back, and parted perfectly. He clasped Taz's right hand in both of his, gave him a politician's smile. He smelled of sweet perfume, cigar, and sour armpits.

"Ignacio tells me that you are a friend, and a friend to Mexico. Also, an excellent negotiator. Who knows, maybe one day we will sit across the table from each other to negotiate something more important than a mere mapping agreement. I think you might not do as well in that circumstance." His eyes wandered over Taz's shoulder, but the voice was still aimed his way. "Meanwhile, I am of course happy to meet you, and I wish you the best while you are our guest." Holding Taz's fingers in his sweaty hands as he moved so smoothly from greeting to insult to kiss off. Taz reminded himself to wash before he touched the food.

Meanwhile, other guests were waiting expectantly for the mayor's attention. As Taz turned to rejoin the milling mass, Contreras had a quick word with Ignacio, then turned to greet the petitioners. The mayor's wife turned to focus on Taz. She wore an attractive light blue ball gown lined with gold brocade. He was idly guessing at her age—*early forties?* She apparently spent a lot of her spare time in the gym; she had the figure of a woman ten years younger. Her hair was gray with tones of silver and just a hint of blue. It was done in a loose coiffure that left her exceedingly smooth neck open to inspection. She had an aquiline nose, and, depending on where she was looking, the kind of smile that a hunter might put on while looking down the barrel of a rifle at a rare antelope.

She nodded towards her husband, smiled at Taz again, and extended her arm with a bent wrist, palm down. "Politics. His gift, and his curse." Taz held her hand gently between his thumb and index finger, brought it to his lips and brushed it with the lightest kiss. She left her hand in his for a moment, then raised it to adjust a stray lock of silver hair, looked at him sideways, and whispered in his ear, "*Veo que eres un verdadero romántico.*" Taz, buying time, smiled and gave a slight bow in her direction. He finally settled on a rough translation, "I see you are a true romantic."

Then she too was wooed by other guests—mostly upper-crust women who looked and dressed very well, but who would have given anything to have her elegance and beauty. Taz nodded her way as she turned to engage her admirers. He drifted in the direction of a bar set up by the inner wall of the courtyard. The mayor was about to give his official welcome. Four workmen brought the platform he would stand on, along with two speakers and a standing microphone. The mayor watched them set up with obvious pleasure when he was approached by a man, a few inches taller, who enfolded him in an assertive bear hug and gave him a lingering kiss on the cheek. The man wore a navy blazer over tan slacks and sported a leather Italian-style flat cap that revealed parts of a thin tonsure above his ears. Leaving his arm over the mayor's shoulder, the man began speaking directly into his ear. The mayor flinched, and the man's eyes blazed with anger for just a moment. He tucked what looked to be an envelope or a folded note into the mayor's breast pocket—with a thin smile. None of it looked all that friendly.

Taz continued wandering through the crowd, keeping his eye on the mayor and his guards, who looked troubled. Two of them scurried away, talking on their cellphones.

There was a minor disturbance near the courtyard entrance. Taz turned from the table where the drinks were being served, cast a glance in that direction. The crowd seemed drawn towards the heavy oaken doors, open to the night. The men nearer the entrance were craning to get a look at something, while their women looked sourly at their cocktail glasses. Someone or something was moving through the undulating crowd towards the center of the courtyard. At first, all Taz could see was an occasional flash of red amid the blue and gray suits. A small gap in the crowd opened and Taz had an impression of a slender but well-shaped woman winding her way through the throng. She must have been stunning, at least from the reaction.

Taz asked the bartender for a glass of white wine. He took a few steps towards the speaking platform to give the appearance of interest in what the mayor had to say. A small phalanx of other guests did the same. After a few deft shoulder fakes and sidesteps, he found himself standing a yard or so behind the mayor and Ignacio, standing together on the low platform. The mayor had turned momentarily away from the crowd. He reached into his breast pocket and drew the paper out, read it briefly, grimaced, swore, crumpled it, and threw it to the ground behind the platform.

Taz sipped his wine, scanned what he could see of the assembled guests. Now it seemed that the crowd was parting like the Red Sea to let the woman through. His first glimpse revealed little. She was wearing a hooded black satin cloak over a dark red dress. Downcast eyes behind wisps of black hair—perhaps she was shy, or introspective. She looked at the floor as she walked. A tress of black hair had fallen over her right eye. She occasionally raised a hand to put it back in place. Something about her gesture caught Taz's attention. Then a short, round man brushed by his side, struggling for a better view. Taz had been pick-pocketed before, and he looked down to make sure it hadn't just happened again. He spotted the crumbled white paper that the mayor had thrown to the floor. He picked it up, flattened and folded it, and put it in his jacket pocket.

An earnest young man who was trailing behind the mystery woman paused to have a word with one of the men in the crowd. The men and women nearby hesitated, then backed away just enough to allow an empty space in front of the speaking platform.

The mystery woman raised her head to look the mayor's way, at the same time brushing her hair out of her eyes once again. Ignacio leaned over to say something in the mayor's ear. The mayor turned in her direction. "*Mi favorita. Mi tesoro. Es muy bueno verte.*" He said it quietly, with the kind of ironic lilt a man might use when he has waited too long for the arrival of a dinner guest. Taz stood close enough to hear the words quite clearly. He surveyed the crowd, found the mayor's wife. She watched her husband with a steely gaze. The mayor stepped off the platform to greet his favorite, lifted her chin for a chaste kiss on the cheek as he drew the cloak off her bare shoulders to reveal a very shapely burgundy ball gown trimmed in dark blue. This time, Taz's view was unimpeded. He was looking directly at Lucia Turan.

She hadn't seen him. He backed quickly into the crowd. His thoughts were raw and turbulent, and he was ashamed of most of them. He headed back to the bar, asked the bartender for a margarita. The man reached for a mix. Taz, in credible if agitated Spanish, "Thank you, but I'd rather have you make one." Held out a twenty, his hand shaking. "*Ya sabes: jugo de lima, Cointreau, tequila—Patrón.*"

When the barman had finished salting the rim, Taz gulped it down, held out the glass and another twenty, his head still awash with reactions to what he had seen. The tequila merely increased their velocity. He stood in the shadows with his back to the courtyard wall as the festival whirled around him. He lost Lucia in the crowd, then saw her talking with Ignacio and a young woman who he supposed was his friend's companion. The tall man had shanghaied the mayor for yet another round of heated conversation. The mayor was saved by two constituents, who approached him wagging their fingers and talking loudly. The tall man turned angrily on his heel and started towards the door. He passed just behind Ignacio, staring briefly over his shoulder at Lucia.

The mayor's wife was in conversation with several women who were facing her in a circle, with their backs to the bar. He must have caught her eye. She looked his way over her friends' shoulders, spoke to the women for a few more minutes, then slipped through several knots of guests that separated her from the bar. The barman handed her a whisky on the rocks. Woodford Reserve. She took a healthy swallow, glanced quickly over her shoulder, stepped Taz's way.

"So, my romantic gringo. What brings you to our poor troubled country?" With a slightly sarcastic emphasis on the "poor, troubled" part.

He spoke deliberately so as clear his mind. "To watch the spring birds at Laguna Atascosa. Mostly your birds, by the way."

She brightened: "Oh, I know the place—my little wives' club traveled there last March . . . *para ver las grullas blancas.*"

"Whooping cranes. Your way sounds better. Nice adventure… the group you were just talking to?"

"*Sí—amigas de la universidad.*"

The workmen were dismantling the stage. Taz's senses were playing tricks on him—Lucia's voice fading in and out, her face sorrowful. *"Mi tesoro."*

The mayor had apparently given his talk. Taz hadn't heard a thing. He came back to the mayor's wife. *"Me parece que estás en otro lado."* Yes, another place. "Sorry—*perdóname.*" He refocused on her face. Waved his arm to encompass the crowd. "So, is this party for them, for you two, or for duty? I mean the politician's curse, where you pretend to enjoy people that you'd never be caught dead with in any other place?"

"You intrigue me. How is it that Ignacio knows you? He told my husband that you were a most strategic negotiator." She couldn't have looked more bored if she had been watching the third inning of a no-hitter. "I don't suppose you'd have a cigarette?"

He was looking for an escape route. Searched his pockets. "No light tonight. Very sorry. Couldn't even light a cigar if I had one."

"A cigar. Of course." With obvious distaste. "You're just like my husband."

"I don't know—perhaps not. Your husband isn't much of a diplomat. Really, he's not even a good politician." Her eyes flared. She slapped him, hard enough to draw the attention of those nearby, but not hard enough to wipe away Taz's sardonic smile.

"Are you always so impertinent?"

"Depends. Once in a while I'm sober."

"You don't think well of my husband."

"I hardly know him. I'll say this. He has good taste, or perhaps he's just lucky. Otherwise, he wouldn't be married to you." She smiled stiffly. "Still, I don't feel that he and I are much alike at all."

A long draw on a cigarette she had cadged from a well-dressed man who was leaving the party. "Oh, really? It seems to me that all men are alike. At least in their attitudes towards women."

"All men? I don't think so."

She was looking over her shoulder as her husband massaged Lucia's shoulder. She turned her face back to Taz. "No? Tell me more."

Taz thought for a minute. She raised her eyebrows and smiled, waiting. He returned the smile, tried his beginner's Spanish. *"Como se llama?* What should I call you? I mean, what is your given name?"

"Bianca."

"It's just that I think if we are to have a serious conversation, Bianca, we should know something about each other. My name is Taz. Taz Blackwell."

The crowd slowly thinned. Bianca kicked off her heels. Without them, she was about the same height as Taz. Maybe he had a half-inch advantage. She stepped towards him. Close enough that he could feel her breath on his neck, his chest.

"So, Mister Taz Blackwell, you still haven't explained how your attitude is any different than that of my husband. He subscribes to the 'women as property and playthings' theory. How about you, Señor Taz?"

That supercilious smile again. Taz considered for another moment. "I enjoy the company of women. There were none when I was young—I never knew my mother."

"I see." She was searching his eyes. "I'm still trying to understand the male point of view."

"Search away if you like. There is no such thing. We're all different. Sure, some of us are boorish, even cruel. But on a good day, we can be romantic, loyal, and even mildly entertaining, or so I'm told." He was confused. Struck by Bianca's presence, by her bearing. Her scent. All too aware that she was using him to get back at Mayor Pudgy Hands. He felt an undercurrent of pain and anger. He needed to talk to Lucia, to tell her, "If you're thinking I'm a fool, you'd be right."

Bianca moved closer to him, brushed his cheek with the back of her hand. "What I think is that you are a very unusual man." Her tongue flicked across her lower lip. Which was, of course, the moment that Lucia showed up at the bar to retrieve two glasses of white wine. While the bartender fetched a bottle of her favorite sauvignon blanc, she surveyed the scene around her. Taz saw the train wreck coming with more than the usual clarity, as if it were unfolding in slow motion.

Lucia scanned the core of the remaining crowd; perhaps a third had left once the food stopped being served. The courtiers—those who wouldn't depart until the mayor and his wife had retired, seventy-five or so—remained, talking in twos or threes. The bartender placed two glasses of wine on the starched white tablecloth well within her reach. She picked them up by the stems and showed every sign of returning to the party. Taz felt a cascade of relief flow over him. Then, for some inexplicable reason, she reversed course and turned toward him and Bianca. Lucia's eyes widened with shock. She struggled to hide her reaction, even as her cheeks flushed bright red. The glass in her left hand clipped the table, shattering on the slate floor. She bent to pick up the glass shards. The bartender put a kind hand on her wrist, made clear that he would take care of it. His colleague poured another.

Lucia slowly rose from her crouch. When she did, she looked like she had seen the edge of the world, the one where all the boats are pulled into the great nothingness that surrounds our little planet. It was with difficulty that she wrested her attention from Taz, who also couldn't tear his eyes away from her. She clasped her two wine glasses, swiveled, and walked unsteadily back to the dwindling center of the party.

Bianca had seen the whole exchange. "You know her."

"I do."

"She's stolen my husband." Who was just then dancing somewhat clumsily with two young women, waving for Lucia to join him, and smiling proudly at his subjects. Taz flinched. All of a sudden, he felt sober.

"I've only known her for a short time. But I don't think she's the kind of woman who would do that."

"Why?"

"She believes in love."

"And you?"

"Not really. Not anymore."

A brittle smile. "So. Maybe he's been looking for an escape route. And she fit the bill?"

"Bianca, I really can't answer. Certainly not for your husband. She and I only spent a very few days together. We ran into each other in a little fishing town on the Atlantic coast of Virginia."

"And was she good in bed? Did she have new moves? Tricks?"

"I wouldn't know. We never had sex."

Her eyebrows rose in disbelief: "You must be kidding. With a woman who looks like that? Are you gay?"

Taz found himself staring at the mayor, who appeared oblivious to anything but his sycophants' applause. He was guiding Lucia through the crowd with his hand on her elbow. She took an anxious look over her shoulder in Taz's direction. He watched for a second and then turned back to Bianca.

"Not as far as I know. And I've known myself for a long time."

The torch near them guttered out, leaving them in penumbral darkness.

Bianca smiled. Then, with the gentlest of touches, turned his cheek until she was looking directly into his eyes. She bent forward to touch his lips with hers. Hers were soft, sensual. She found his hand, guided it to her collar bone and then inside her dress and placed it on her breast. He felt her nipple draw itself up to his touch.

"The party's over. Mr. Mayor's going to spend the night in his penthouse with your friend." She snorted in her husband's direction. He and Lucia were pressing through the remaining guests towards the door of the hacienda. "Perhaps we should also depart. Why don't you lift a bottle of champagne from the ice." Taz hesitated. "Over there."

After all he had seen, Taz wasn't sure why not. He had come to rescue Lucia. She didn't look like a woman who needed rescuing. Or maybe he had just arrived too late. A night with the mayor's wife wouldn't improve things, but it could hardly make them worse.

CHAPTER TWENTY-FOUR

Undercover

TAZ AND BIANCA FINISHED THEIR drinks and headed towards the archway that separated the courtyard from the polished brick driveway. As Bianca graciously received the farewells being called her way, Taz noticed the young man who had escorted Lucia earlier standing in a small knot of similar young men, smoking, and talking in quiet tones. The young man turned to shake his hand, pressing a folded piece of paper into Taz's palm. Taz nodded and jammed it in the side pocket of his linen jacket. Bianca pointed towards a small white two-seater sports car, got in the driver's side, and patted the passenger seat.

Taz woke not long after dawn, Bianca still asleep with her arm across his chest. Her lips curved in a lovely smile. She was making small purring sounds. Only an ingrate would call it snoring. Taz swung his legs over the counterpane. He felt a gentle hand on his left arm. "*Quedate. Quedate en cama conmigo. Por favor.*" Bianca's morning voice, breathy and soft as sand. He turned back to her. She welcomed him in a way he could not later forget. When he next checked the clock, it was almost nine. The sheets were damp with their sweat, and he could still hear her voice, pleading and murmuring endearments in sibilant Spanish.

He gathered his clothes. He couldn't, at first, find his wallet. Checked his jacket and finally found the note the young man had given him in his right-side pocket. The handwriting was shaky, and there were spots on the paper where it had been wet.

> *Taz, we need to talk. Please? I can't stand leaving it like this. Nothing you saw was real. Nothing! I'll be at the Saturday market just off the zócalo. Will you come? Shit! I forgot—there's more than one. The one on Calle Zapata. By the mariachi corner. At noon? I'll try to stay around if you can't make it until later—I'll have a lot of shopping to do.*

The note made no sense. What he had seen seemed all too real. But he wasn't planning to start the next leg of his trip until the following morning in any case. He had some sense of the general direction to the zócalo. Bianca stretched in a most pleasing manner, all the while eyeing Taz.

"I have a lunch with the mayor. At twelve, at the municipal building. *Muy feo, lamentablemente.*" It wasn't entirely clear whether she was referring to the building or to her husband.

She walked over to where he was sitting—at one of those hotel room desks that were not designed to be used. Ever. She felt no need to hide her charms in a sheet the way the female leads always do in the movies. Wrapped her arms around his chest and traced a winding path from his collarbone to his shoulder and the nape of his neck. That she kissed, with amazing delicacy and then with real intensity.

"I still have an hour before I have to get ready. How do you propose to fill our time?" It had been a long night. Taz wondered whether he was up to another round. Her hands wandered over his chest, down towards his hips. There was really only one possible answer.

An hour later, after Bianca had dressed and given him one last deep kiss, he took a shower and began putting on his clothes. He was slipping his wallet into the back pocket of his pants when he felt the other note, the one that mayor had tossed from the platform. It had been a great night for written messages, apparently. He looked at this one, stained with dust from the courtyard patio. It was a single line in Spanish cursive, and at first it was hard to make out. When Taz worked it out, it read *3.5mm dolares depositados en el banco para el martes, si no!'* The amount of money and the "or else" captured his interest. The note was signed with a somewhat floral capital *C.*

He looked at his watch— eleven. Taz had no idea how far it would be to the Zócalo Zapata. He pocketed his keys and his passport. Turned out it was only about seven blocks.

He stepped into the square from the southeast corner just a little after noon. The Saturday market was clearly a major social event for Reynosa. Everyone was there—not just the kids playing soccer or the mothers with strollers, but the grandparents, the country cousins, newlyweds, and even a bride and groom having their portrait taken. All mixing, dancing, running around, laughing. Music from all sides, from every corner—norteño, ballads, rap. The life of the community. In one square, on one morning, for all to see. Taz loved it completely.

He listened and searched for the mariachi corner through the crowds, the voices, the laughter, and children's wailing. He finally heard the strains of horns over the general din. It took a while for him to get there, through the picnicking families, the jugglers, around the couple taking wedding photographs. There were three bands. Competing? Not really. More like enjoying each other, passing the cards, raising, and calling. The atmosphere of a good poker game among friends. The bands took turns. Measured their success by the audience response, like horn players in a Kansas City cutting contest in the days before bebop transformed jazz.

Taz stood in the shade of an old banyan tree. Watched the scene swirl around him, fascinated. Except for a few teenagers on skateboards, everyone was dressed in their Sunday best. Even with his cream-colored linen jacket, which the temperature ensured would be slung over his shoulder, Taz didn't feel overdressed.

He saw the two watchers before he saw her. They were following about ten yards behind her as she walked reluctantly out of the zócalo towards a park enfolded by two broad avenues. The avenues and the park were closed for the weekend market. She was dressed in blue jeans and a puffy-sleeved peasant's blouse. She occasionally looked over her shoulder, even turned to walk backwards once or twice, seemingly searching for something amidst the cacophony and the technicolor swirl.

The two burly men in ill-fitting suits continued to follow her at a respectful distance. Telltale bulges in front of their armpits. Earbuds, just like the Secret Service. Taz disliked them immediately. But he had only found her by following them, so maybe they had some utility after all. Lucia was visiting the food and flower booths along the west side of the avenue. She garnered waves and smiles as she strolled through. It appeared that she knew everybody, and that more than a few of the country people behind the little stands knew her.

It was only a week until *Día de los Muertos*. In the northern interior, the poor kept the preconquest tradition of celebrating the holiday just before summer, even as the cities had moved it to the week of Halloween to keep pace with the US and Europe. Already there were parades, with the masks of death, the portraits of ancestors lifted high, the floats with skeletons, and the ghostly bands with their muted trumpets and strange drummers.

Lucia headed directly towards a procession circling the park between the two avenues in a counterclockwise direction. Just as the first cotillion of about a hundred revelers came between her and the minders, she ducked behind the outer rank of stalls to the median, then to the other side of the avenue, where the flower vendors and the spice merchants had booths. She lingered for a moment at a favorite flower stand. Taz followed, just a yard in front of the revelers. The back of the booth opened towards the open rear door of a good-sized Ford van of the kind that was used to transfer the precious flower and fruit cargo from the apple orchards and greenhouses above Saltillo, and the occasional load of pine nuts from the coastal forests just north of Acapulco. Taz watched as she chatted with the shopkeeper and examined the roses. He approached her from behind, holding his finger to his lips to quiet the proprietor, a small and somewhat round *mestiza* with a delightful smile. He leaned towards Lucia's shoulder.

"I like how you stranded your protection."

She straightened. Kept her eyes on the roses. "It's a little game I play."

"Do you know the flower lady well?"

Guardedly, Lucia said, "She's a friend."

"Why don't you ask her if we can use her van for a little talk."

Lucia leaned over the cut flowers and said a few words. The woman nodded, with a shy smile towards Taz.

They ducked quickly by the table, walked stooping to the back of the lean-to tent, slipped into the back of the van. Dropped the canvas backflap that prevented the fruit from toppling out over its long ride.

Lucia found a seat on the driver's-side wheel well. Her back was to the van's side wall. Taz sat directly across from her. He waited, not knowing what to expect, nor what to say. In the shadow world, she bent forward and reached for his hand. Her voice sounded almost ragged.

"Taz, I know what you must be thinking."

He jerked his arm back. "Please, Lucia. Do you really think so? Because I don't think you do."

"Taz, don't you see? This isn't anything I wanted. Oh God, everything is so screwed up." She held her head in her hands, stifled a sob.

He winced in the shadows. He wasn't buying it. "I guess I shouldn't be surprised. Lucia—is that even your real name? I'm not sure how to say this, but you're really good at being the woman you played last night. Movie stars would line up to date you. But I won't. I don't like lines."

She put her hand softly over his lips, regaining her composure. "Taz, don't. Don't pull yourself away. None of what you saw last night was real."

He gently pushed her hand away. "It looked pretty real to me. But you know, it's okay. You don't owe me anything. We barely know each other. Just a few moments in Spring, right? I have no claim on you at all."

She tried again. Reached and caressed his lips and his cheek with the soft palm of her left hand. "Oh, Taz. There's so much you don't understand. First, you do have a claim on me. You've had it since our first words that day on your stoop. Second, what you saw last night was an illusion—a complete illusion. Taz, I'm not dating the mayor, I'm investigating him."

"Investigating him? You really expect me to believe that? Who for?"

"The DEA." Taz recalled his meeting with White. But White hadn't told him how DEA had decided to use her talents. He pulled in his breath, whistled. "You're not kidding, are you. Just imagine. Lucia Turan, who still believes in the tooth fairy, now starring in a cloak and dagger movie." His voice bitter, even to him.

"It's no movie, Taz," an edge to her voice. "And maybe I'm a better actor than you think."

"So, your story is that this was all make-believe? I really don't know what to say. Except is this who you are? A shapeshifter? Or just a dangerously good-looking woman who enjoys making fools of men. Were you ever really attracted to me? Or did you fake that too?"

A flash of anger. "How would you even know? You've spent more time in bed with Bianca than you have with me."

"I don't recall ever being invited to your bed. And as far as last night goes, it looked like you were otherwise occupied."

A quick, sad chuckle. "Not by choice. And according to at least two of my friends, you didn't seem all that put out. What's she like in bed? Bianca. She hates me."

"I can only say that she feels unloved in her marriage, and I saw an opportunity to share some of the pain the mayor caused me. Not that Bianca doesn't have her charms. She's actually quite a lovely woman. I ended up liking her."

"Well, you needn't go on and on about it."

"Really? What about your squeeze, the mayor with the pudgy hands?"

"A sacrifice to get what we need."

"I guess that's how you translate *camping alone*. How do you do it?"

She flinched, clenched her fingers into fists. "Okay, a major sacrifice. I didn't expect to have to carry the illusion this far. The only reason I can is that he means nothing to me. Actually, I despise him. I have a lot of migraines. He's so self-absorbed he hardly notices. And I'm not his only mistress. Not by a long shot."

In the shadows, Taz winced, recalling the words she had asked him to repeat to White, about needing a guarantee that they'd be satisfied *"if she did this one last thing."* Held his breath. "I'm in the dark. Help me out."

"The DEA people want to get a better take on the chain of corruption between the border states and Mexico City. Starting with the cartels and running through the mayor, the military, and the bureaucracy."

"Jesus! I can't believe they would ask that of you. The cartel's government network would be hard to penetrate, even for a pro. But you're a wildlife biologist. Unless that was just a cover, too. How were you supposed to do it?"

"Just by listening to the mayor and his staff. The only cover was the part about raising money for my panther research. That's how I was supposed to gain their confidence."

"Looks to me like you were a success."

"Don't—please. It's bad enough already."

Taz retreated into his thoughts.

"Taz, are you still there?"

"Sure. But let me know, am I a step in the grand design? Or just the local fool?"

"That's not fair."

"I guess not. Maybe it doesn't make a difference. You're not the only one who was caught that morning. Sure—I was coming out of a fool's paradise. Hopes and dreams and all that. I was Don Quixote. Except my windmill was impregnable."

"Dana?"

"Who else?"

"Laney told me a little—not the gory details."

"I do love Laney, from the bottom of my heart. She tried hard to smooth the way for Dana and me. I finally came to the realization that I was aiming at an unreachable target. At the end, Laney agreed."

"That's all in the past. This is now. You can reach me, Taz—you already have. And I'm not impregnable." A kiss as close to his lips as she could manage.

He hated it, but he was softening as inevitably as a scoop of ice cream. "What about your minders? Shouldn't you head back soon?"

"I'm all right for a little while more. The bodyguards are actually okay. I talk to them now and again. Their mission is to protect me, and to watch where I go and with whom. But for the last three days there's been a third watcher. One I could feel, never locate. My DEA contact sent me an encrypted message this morning. They've intercepted some cell phone traffic. The narcos —the Zetas, probably —they know there's someone here they need to find and silence. They don't know who it is, though, so I have at least a little time."

"Days? Or hours?" Lucia shook her head. Taz considered for a while. "And what did your . . . handler say you should do if you think you're in danger?"

"Just sit tight and wait to hear from them."

Taz's voice sounded more like a hiss. "Now there's a plan. Fucking DEA assholes. You might as well give yourself a death sentence. When we get out of this—"

"We? Are you sure? You're not in danger yet. You don't need—"

"Lucia. I didn't come down here to see the sights. I came to get you out. I have an idea, maybe a route out. But it won't be easy. Are you game?"

"I have to be, don't I?"

"Have you ever seen the boiling pools at Cuatro Ciénegas? Thermal pools out in the desert. Like the ones in Yellowstone. I think we should go sightseeing."

"Taz. We can't even get out of the city. When I go back to get my things, they'll have me right where they want me."

"Have you got your passport and your cell?" Lucia nodded, squeezed his hand. "So, we don't go back at all. We wait right here until your friend closes up. Until dark. We get her to drive us to my rental car. I left Old Faithful with the refuge manager at Laguna Atascosa.

"I'm parked on the west side of the city. Far away from any of the major roads. The car is pretty beat up and anonymous. A full tank of gas. We go for a drive. Meanwhile, give me your cell phone." He shut it down and removed the SIM card.

Lucia made her way to the canvas backflap, lifted it a few inches, said something to her vendor friend in Spanish. She turned to Taz. "Maria will help. It will take about forty-five minutes for her to close."

She returned to sit next to him. "Taz, I had no right to drag you into this. It's just you were the one person I knew I could count on. And I told myself it would be okay because you wouldn't be crazy enough to risk getting yourself killed pulling me out of a jam. And now look at us!" Shaking, she finally let her stress show.

Taz brought her in closer. "Hey, hey. I'm here . . . we're together. It's going to be alright. You'll see. It'll be at least an hour until your friend is packed up. You should try to get some sleep. You're going to need it." She rested her head on his shoulder. Sighed. He stroked her hair, using his fingers like a comb. It was only a few minutes before her breathing slowed to an even pace, like waves lapping the shore of the lake he fished when he was ten.

Lucia slept through the packing and the twenty-minute drive to the west side of town. The van stopped and Taz lifted the canvas backflap. Starlight. They were just by his rental car, far enough on the periphery of town that the ground light was considerably diminished. She said goodbye to her friend with many heartfelt endearments.

*

Taz sat behind the steering wheel, relieved to hear the engine cough and rumble. He headed south on Calle El Magro, which, if he was right, would lead to the western exit from town. A less imposing road than Route 40 south to Monterrey, Route 97 south along the coast or, God forbid, the direct six-lane highway north to the border station and then to McAllen. The minute the Zetas noticed that she was gone and figured out what was up, they would have gunmen on every one of those routes.

Instead, he headed up Route 2, a two-lane highway that parallels the Rio Grande to Nuevo Laredo. One problem; Nuevo Laredo was under the control of the Zetas. Taz wanted to avoid that scene at all costs. So, when they reached the southern end of the Falcon Reservoir, he turned onto the country road heading west to Sabinas Hidalgo. If they needed to, they could gas up there. Highway 85, the main route between Nuevo Laredo and Monterrey, passed by the east side of town.

As it turned out, the Dart got better mileage than Taz had any right to expect. When they passed the wretched little town, they were still half full. He found the turn which put them on Route 30, towards Monclova.

They pulled in for gas and hot coffee at a dusty little station about ten kilometers north of Monclova. It was already dark, and in the following thirty seconds Lucia's easy fluency in Spanish saved their lives. They had used the filthy bathroom to wash up. Taz went first, then walked around front, bought a couple of Cokes, two jugs of water, and a bag of peanuts. While Lucia was in the bathroom, she heard two men chatting outside. She didn't catch it all, but enough to send chills up her spine: *"¿Crees que son la pareja que el asesino estaba buscando?"*

She walked out as if nothing at all was the matter. One of the men said a few more words in Spanish, directed at her. She turned on her Spanglish. "Sorry—*no habla.* I only speak English." The two men exchanged glances. She walked calmly, hopped in, turned to Taz. "Let's get out of here right now."

Taz revved the engine, headed north on the narrow two-lane road towards San Buenaventura. After about two miles he braked hard, skidded to the right and turned onto a dirt road that went up over a hill and down the other side into a shallow canyon created by a recent flash flood. He turned off the engine.

"So, what's the story?"

"Two men were talking outside the bathroom. One of them asked the other whether he thought we were the couple the hit man had been looking for."

Taz jumped out of the cab, reached behind the seat, and grabbed his flashlight. Knelt, then rolled to his back and pushed himself under the rear axle. "Taz, what are you doing? Don't you think you're dirty enough already?"

The device was taped under the rear wheel well. Taz pulled it off and put it on the hood. Lucia looked at it: "What is that?"

"The pinger they're using to track us. We're only about fifteen miles from Cuatro Ciénegas. The turn to Torreón is about three miles before the park. We have to convince them that we've turned south there to follow Route 30 to Torreón."

"Taz. Remember the trucks by the side of the road? Just back a half mile or so? They were all headed west. What's their likely destination?"

"Torreón. Has to be. There's no other city until you get to Durango, and that's another hundred and fifty miles."

"Give me the pinger and take us back there." Something in her voice. He made the U-turn without a second thought. They passed the three trucks. The last one had the engine running while the driver relieved himself behind the trailer. Taz slowed, took them another fifty yards, and stopped.

"Okay. Stay here and cut the engine. I'll only be a minute."

Taz watched in fascination as she crossed the road and began chatting up the driver, who was just about to climb back into his cab. She propped herself on the truck with one hand while she leaned over and adjusted a shoe. Far enough over, Taz figured, so the truck driver could get a really good view. A few more words, as he made some adjustments in the cab. A quick motion to the back of the cab as the truck lurched into the lowest gear. She waved goodbye gaily as he pulled out.

Once the truck was out of sight, Lucia ran back to their car. Opened the door and swung into the passenger seat with a big grin.

"So where is he headed?"

"Torreón. With the pinger. I wedged it between the exhaust pipe and the cab. I told him you were a loser in the sack, that I needed a real man, and the quicker he got to Torreón, the sooner he and I could be together."

"Thanks so much for the *loser* part. It makes me feel so much better."

"Just a little payback, that's all."

"For what? May I ask?"

"How about for Bianca's personality change at lunch, or for her beyond-contented smile? Like all her constant tension had been washed out by a king tide. She positively smirked at me, as if she had just won a game show where I came in second."

"You just might have saved our hides. It's two hundred and seventy miles to Torreón. By the time they find the truck, we'll be over the border. By the way, what did you show him?"

She pouted. "More than I'm going to show you, if you don't get us out of this stinking desert by tomorrow morning."

"Go ahead and play rough. We're only about fifteen miles from Cuatro Ciénegas. We can sleep there. It's two hundred and twenty miles to the border. If we get up just at sunrise, we can make it by two. What do you say?"

She took the wheel on the way to Cuatro Ciénegas. Taz opened the window, letting in cool night air. The road was a barely paved one lane.

"Let's not leave any wheel prints outside the paved right-of-way, especially right after the turn."

"You must think I'm some kind of city girl." She cut the lights and drove by starlight and the slight blue illumination left by the setting crescent moon.

As soon as Taz detected the scent of sulfur, he motioned her to pull off the road and into a little wash behind some mesquite bushes and two acacias. He got a painter's tarp out of the trunk, spread it on a patch of softer sand where at least their heads could be above their feet. Then an old woolen blanket at the foot of the tarp, and a rolled-up towel at the top. He lay on his back, left a space on his right side.

Lucia slid in next to him and pulled the woolen blanket up so that only their faces showed in the starlight. They watched the Milky Way stretch across the sky from horizon to horizon.

Lucia had crossed her arms above her heart and made herself busy snuggling into his side. For a moment, she reminded Taz of a penitent in prayer. Pulling herself up on her left arm, she rested her cheek in the palm of her hand.

"Taz, why don't you let anyone into your life? Is it that you can't? Whenever I ask you about yourself there's always something to do, something more important to talk about. Is it always going to be this way between us? Or will you let me in? Even a little bit?"

She sniffled and started to turn away. Taz stopped her with a gentle hand on her shoulder. "I do want you to know me. It's just—"

"Just what?"

"Well, I'm not very good at explaining myself. I never know where to start. I always end up with a jumble."

"Try, Taz. Okay?"

"Okay." He clasped his hands under his head, his eyes on the constellations, particularly Scorpio and its red giant, Antares. "Like tonight. I'm the man lying next to you, listening to you breathe, looking at the stars, feeling the little desert breeze, listening to the burrowing owl off to the left and the little desert mouse scrambling just over by that cactus." He held his breath for a few moments, bent his whole being towards listening.

"And I'm all these feelings that are washing through me—joy, awe, the heightened awareness from being scared earlier, the happiness of being by your side." She reached a finger out, let it glide over his shoulder.

"But I guess I'm also this basket of memories, right? Gratitude for the friends who've passed through my life. Regrets for the things I've done badly, for the people I've hurt." The gliding finger was replaced by a warm hand that slid down his arm to his hand, threading fingers through his.

"I get sad sometimes, and I'm not always sure where it comes from. I have a hot temper."

Sleepily. "I couldn't help but notice."

"But I've also been lucky—a lot. I have a friend in Boquillas—maybe you'll meet her—who used to say, '*Suerte sigue el gaviero.*' Luck follows the lookout—right? Your Spanish is better than mine."

"*Sí.*"

"You don't have to rub it in."

"*Lo siento.*"

She snuggled into his ribs like a mouse burrowing into the softness of rotting cactus. She had made him smile.

"I love music. Bach's fugues, Count Basie's blues. And let's not forget the Grateful Dead, the best rock 'n' roll band ever."

Taz listened as the regularity of Lucia's breathing slowed and deepened. She sighed and burrowed even closer. Later, he heard her murmuring.

Waking from a dream, maybe. Taz leaned close. She seemed to be repeating the same phrase. "I knew. Don't ask me how, Granma. I just knew."

❧

In the predawn mist, Lucia slipped out to relieve herself and spotted a coyote. She followed its tracks for a few hundred yards, until they petered out near the main road. Now back, shaking Taz's arm, her voice was soft, restrained, intense, telling him he had to wake up. He lifted himself onto an elbow, rubbing his eyes with this free hand.

"Taz! The Zetas came this way. I found tracks out on the side of the road. One of them must have gotten out to pee. I recognized the boot track. There's a nail in the right heel. Whoever it was left the same track outside your truck back in Reynosa, probably when they put the pinger in."

"Are you sure?"

She shook her head, smiling. "Taz. I tracked my first cougar when I was fourteen."

"Shouldn't we—"

"No. That's what I want to tell you. The only tracks that turn into the dirt road are ours. They must have missed them in the dark. Their tire tracks are on the main road. Looks like they were in a hurry. They burned rubber when they got going again."

"Which way?"

"The ruse worked, Taz. They're heading to Torreon."

The sun was only minutes from climbing over the horizon. Taz staggered out from underneath the tarp, shook his head, and gave her a high-five. Started picking his way through the mesquite and the cholla cactus towards the first pool. The cool of the morning snuck through his shirt. Lucia followed, shivering. When they got close enough to get a good view, she gasped. The pool was about two hundred feet wide, with a white calcite ring for a perimeter. The water was a bright azure blue. It was boiling. Neither of them could see to the bottom.

"A miniature Yellowstone!"

Once they had soaked in the view, Taz started the car and backtracked to the fork where the north road turns towards Boquillas. Their discussion centered on the lonesome coyote. Lucia said he had undoubtedly been nosing around them in the night.

"Think of it this way, Lucia. We're rolled up in our tarp. He probably decided we were the biggest, worst-smelling enchilada he'd ever found."

Their subsequent effort to pin the aromatic blame on one another resulted in any number of bad jokes, the real joke being on the two of them; there was no place to take a shower until they got to the Rio Grande and Big Bend. Until then, they rubbed themselves with wild sage, which was of some help.

Taz turned west out of El Magro, then north on the first serious dirt road to the right. The idea that it might be helpful to have road signs had apparently never occurred to the local authorities. On the upside, the morning had begun to warm the desert frost, and they were bathed in sunlight again. They cranked their windows open. Lucia turned on the radio, tuned to a news show. She translated snatches here and there.

"The Mexican government is very upset with the new US administration for screwing around with NAFTA. Meanwhile, the *federales* have arrested some guy named Cárdenas, suspected of being an upcoming drug lord." Taz paused with that thought for a few minutes while Lucia continued her sporadic narration. There was only one logical inference, and he didn't like it much at all.

She finally gave up on the news. "So, Mr. Blackwell. Would you like to tell me why we're here, in the middle of the Chihuahuan desert? In an old shaky sedan with only a quart of water between us? And the gas gauge just above a quarter? And, equally important, where we're going? And, even more important than that, when you're finally going to let me drive? And I don't mean just for fifteen minutes."

Taz let the truck roll gradually to a stop on the side of the road. "You okay to drive now?" Once she had taken the wheel and felt the clutch, she looked Taz in the eye and arched her eyebrows, Lucia was not one to let unanswered questions lie.

"As far as why we're here. It occurred to me that once they discovered you were gone, they'd be looking for you on all the obvious ways out of Reynosa. All the major highways, and the airport and the train station as well. But maybe not on a road that winds and wavers up the Rio Grande directly towards their home base. We're talking about Los Zetas. But Nuevo Laredo is also an important target for the Sinaloa and Gulf Cartels—thus the mass murders and executions of the last five years."

"No way we wanted to come within fifty miles of that hellhole, so I put us on a bunch of country roads that even the *federales* have forgotten about. We'll skirt the southern side of the Maderas del Carmen and get back home through Big Bend."

"Great. We're going to get lost, turned around, and worse. We'll be out here until we die of thirst!" Her exasperated expression made it clear that she didn't believe a word of what she said.

"Don't worry about a thing, Ms. Damsel-in-Distress. You're with *el gaviero*—remember? The navigator. At least that's what the locals used to call me when I was a crazy twenty-year-old searching this desert for Gambel's quail and lucifer hummingbirds. Not to mention elf owls and black-capped vireos."

"*Gaviero*? Don't you mean '*navegador*?'"

Taz smiled ruefully. "I didn't choose the name. Sometimes '*el gaviero loco*.' I know it's more like a lookout on a sailing ship than a navigator."

"For God's sake, don't let the truth get in your way, Mister Pathfinder. The *gaviero* is the one who climbs to the crow's nest on the top of the foremast to watch for what's ahead and help the captain chart the course."

"If we could just silence the peanut gallery for a minute. What I'm trying to say, I've birded all over this high country. I used to bring candy and jerky for the kids in all the little towns. Their parents did their best to help me. They were good at remembering even the most remote locations where they had seen the kinds of birds I was seeking. That's how I got to know my way around. So, you can think of this as a long, not very successful birding trip."

Taz switched on the radio. They sat listening to some co-ed banter over a background of canned laughter. He was just about to find another channel when a news bulletin broke in, accompanied by what sounded like a police radio transmission. Lucia wedged herself forward, gathering as much as she could through the static. Her eyes betrayed her sense of alarm as she stared at the radio.

"Taz, this is about us! . . . We're armed and dangerous. No, it's you. You robbed a bank in Reynosa. And kidnapped me! Gave out our names . . . patriots in Chihuahua should be aware, report any suspicious behavior, any gringos on the roads . . . wait . . . we're likely on back roads southwest of the Sierra del Carmen. Oh, and we betrayed the most feared cartel in Tamaulipas—the Zetas."

Taz braked, hit the shoulder of the road, and stopped in a cloud of dust. He ran around the front of the truck, opened her door, pulled her out. "Just stand there. I'm looking for something." She stood stock-still as he walked around her.

"What kind of something?"

"We got rid of the pinger. How do they know where we are? Something you always have with you, something that can hold an RFID microchip." He continued his survey until he found himself staring at a silver chain down her neck. The chain held a large turquoise pendant set in silver. "You're not wearing the raven."

"For God's sake, Taz, this isn't the time to go through that." He continued staring at the pendant, which he was now cradling in his right hand. He tightened his grip to a fist, yanked, broke the necklace, and pulled it off her neck. She gasped. "How can you—" She sputtered as he pulled out his jack-knife and pried the turquoise from the setting. Dropped the microchip into his hand.

"This is how. Where did you get the necklace? Did somebody give it to you?"

"Fuck. Of course. Contreras."

"That fits." He put the chip in his pocket. "Get in the driver's side. We're going to have to split up. We're going to drop me off in El Milagro. You'll have to drive alone to Boquillas."

"What are you going to do by yourself? What am I going to do?"

He tore off the corner of a quickly yellowing *Reforma,* wrote two names, an address, and a telephone number. "You can stay here. A woman I know—a friend—it's her house —Consuela Gutierrez." He reached in his pockets and pulled out a wad of pesos. "Stay with her until I join you."

She grabbed his hand, searched his eyes. Fiercely. "And you? What about you?"

"I'll get to Boquillas by a different route. I'm going to take a little trip into the mountains. I'll take the chip with me."

She looked away for a few moments. "So, you'll have them tracking you, instead of me. That's what it is, isn't it? You're going to shuffle me off to sit around with one of your old girlfriends where I can watch TV while they hunt you? What if I just tell you no?"

"We don't have a choice. The pinger was how the DEA was tracking me. I imagine the young man who was shadowing you at the mayor's party put it on. It's gone, so they can't be sure where the car is. The smart chip is how the Zetas were keeping tabs on you. When they see it's in the mountains, they'll figure we're headed for a different crossing point—maybe over by Amistad. That's almost a hundred miles away. Meanwhile, you'll be safe with Consuela. I'll ditch the chip and make my way to you as soon as I can. It'll probably be a few days, maybe a week, but then we'll be across the border and out of the reach of their Mexican partners."

He grabbed his rucksack, got out of the truck, slammed the door, and waved her off. She put it in gear, staring at him through the open passenger window. "Just so you know—I hate this. You better take care of yourself." Then she rolled slowly away, picking up speed until she was leaving a cloud of dust in her wake.

Clara and Juanita were home. Two of his favorite birding partners, and honorary aunts, they welcomed him with endearments and open arms. Clara's grandchildren were in the backyard, playing soccer with a tattered volleyball. Juanita didn't say a word. She just started feeding him, like the old days. The two were sisters, and both avid birders. They became friends with Taz as they spent days together on the table land on top of the Sierra, looking for crissal thrashers, elf owls, and Rivoli's hummingbirds. Years and years back. They drank mescal and coffee and reminisced. It wasn't until they were finished with dessert that Taz told them what had brought him back to their door.

Talking quietly together, they came up with a course of action. Taz thought it just might work. In the morning, they would take Taz to their cousin's house in Las Casas, a tiny village high in the mountains. Their cousin would take him to the La Linda bridge, down river from Boquillas, where he could safely cross the river.

Except that he had no interest in crossing the border where the only people to meet him would be migration officers or DEA agents. He was going to walk, wade, if necessary, swim the eighteen miles upstream through the canyon between La Linda and Boquillas. It would be a grueling trip, but as long as he could carry enough water, Taz felt reasonably confident that he could make it. It almost worked.

❦

La policía found Taz seven miles upriver from the long-closed La Linda Bridge. An hour earlier, he had seen the glint of binoculars along the northern bank of the river. *La Migra* —the border patrol. It wasn't exactly a surprise that their first move was to call their Mexican counterparts. When he heard the helicopter overhead, he knew the jig was up. A man in uniform stood in the door of the cargo bay, gesticulating in his direction, and shouting in Spanish through a bullhorn. His words were lost in the sound of the rotors echoing off the walls of the Sierra del Carmen. The pilot lifted off, circled, and put down in a cloud of dust. Four fully armed soldiers hopped out and ran towards him. Taz put his hands in the air.

The first two grabbed his upper arms, hustled him to the copter. A third put the manacles on. The fourth raised his rifle and clobbered him in the cheek with the butt. They dragged him the rest of the way, dumped him unceremoniously in the helicopter's well.

Taz awoke on a damp cement floor. A small room that he supposed was a cell, except for the table and chair. He dragged himself to the chair and sat at the table, head in his hands. Some time elapsed. He felt in vain for his watch. After a time, the door rattled and opened with a loud creak. A soldier—maybe an officer—entered and threw blank notepaper and a pen on the table. "Write your confession. It will go easier."

Taz began writing. When the officer returned several hours later, he had written all he intended to—*Tengo sed. Necesito agua*—as many times as it took to cover the page. The officer cuffed him on the back of the head. "Well, maybe not so easy after all." Motioned to the open door behind him. Two burly soldiers came in and dragged Taz a short distance down the hall to another room where the light was slightly better. That's when the beatings started. At first, they strapped him in a hardback chair. They took their time, drinking beer in between blows. Then they hung him from a chain by his wrists so they could have better access to his ribs, back and feet.

They dragged him back to the cell as the sun was going down. The pain made it impossible to sleep, at least for the first few hours. When he woke in the morning, his lips had cracked, and his tongue felt like sandpaper. His head ached and his eyes were rheumy and clotted. There was no water to wash with. Two soldiers came in, grabbed him under the arms, and dragged him out of his cell, down the hall past three broken incandescent lights, and into a window-lit office. An officer sat behind the only table. He looked bored, finally raising his head, and staring at Taz. "Perhaps you would enjoy a drink." Poured two glasses of water. Taz snatched the first, greedily gulping. His hand was shaking, but the water tasted good. He kept drinking until the officer pointed to the second cup. Taz finished that one too.

"Where is the woman, Mister Blackwell? The one you kidnapped in Reynosa?"

Taz had difficulty focusing. There was no telling whose side the officer was on. The narcos? The *federales*? The DEA? *Maybe he's just a cop who listened to the radio.* Did it matter? He was probably dead one way or another. He looked the officer over with all the concentration he could muster and started talking. He hadn't kidnapped anyone. He didn't know where the woman was. She was just a whore he had picked up for a little fun. They had parted ways in El Magro. When he was finished, the officer slowly stood, with his hands on his desk. "In a day or perhaps two, you will tell us where to find her, Mister Blackwell. If not, you will have a very long week."

The soldiers dragged him back to his cell.

A note had been slipped under the metal door. "*Soy Federico Gutiérrez, sobrino de su amiga Consuela. Búscame en el patio del cárcel.*" Federico turned out to be a good-looking boy about seventeen who had been jailed for a bar fight, had a weekend pass, and was leaving that night for Boquillas. Consuela had asked him to look for the *yanqui,* hoping against hope that the police had arrested him, rather than just leaving his dead body by the side of the road. Having found him, Federico was only too willing to take a note to his cousin.

Morning, two days later. The beatings had become almost pro forma. Taz could still stand, and when necessary, walk. Two soldiers came in and walked him down the hall to the office where he had been questioned. Another officer looked him over and sighed. He picked up the telephone and two soldiers different soldiers came in, escorted Taz down a long flight of stairs, which he negotiated with no little difficulty, and led him to a waiting flatbed truck with a flap covering the back. Blindfolded him for the four hours it took to cover the sixty-five miles around the southern end of the Sierra to Boquillas.

They dropped him off at the bus station on the south side of Boquillas. It was only about a half mile from there to Consuela's place. He shouldered his tattered rucksack and started limping.

After about forty minutes, he stepped stiffly up Consuela's porch steps. She had added a wicker loveseat and attached it to the porch ceiling with chains. Nobody home. He let himself in to visit the washroom. He dropped his rucksack and recovered a Bohemia from the refrigerator, popped the top, and stumbled back out to sit on the swing in the late afternoon heat. Went to sleep holding tight to the half-empty bottle, with his head resting on the right-side chain. That's where they found him.

He heard their laughter and playful chatter first. Then some back-and-forth in a lower tone. It sounded like Lucia asking a question and Consuela giving a hesitant answer. Then they were on the steps.

Consuela saw him first and gasped: "*¡Dios mío!*"

Lucia leapt the last step towards him. "You're here! You're here. I . . . I thought maybe . . . Taz, Taz. You're here!" Now laughing and crying at the same time, cupping his face in her hands, reaching for Consuela's hand, kissing him tenderly, on the lips, forehead, chin, cheeks, ears. She pulled away just far enough to give him a searching look. After what he had seen in the bathroom mirror, he wasn't surprised by her startled expression. She touched them one by one—the purpling bruise that ran from beneath his eye to his jaw, the bandage on his right hand, the torn cloth and bloody scrape on his right shoulder. She didn't say a word. She unbuttoned his thin cotton shirt, tossed it over her shoulder. Turned his shoulder just enough to get a look at his back. Gasped.

Her eyes wide, she looked at Consuela. "Where's your medicine cabinet?"

Consuela examined him as well, running her fingers lightly over his wounds. "Taz, Taz. You haven't changed at all." She kissed him gently on the cheek. Lucia came back with a red case, a stack of bandages, and some rolls of adhesive tape. She stopped briefly in the open space between the hall and the kitchen, continued, and tended to Taz as if she hadn't seen a thing.

Consuela stepped back towards the kitchen, watching them with a sad smile. She caught Lucia's attention. "Taz must be hungry. Bring him into the kitchen and let's see what we can find."

After they finished the homemade *pozole* Consuela had found in the refrigerator, the three of them sat at the kitchen table drinking beer and discussing their options. They decided that Taz and Lucia should leave for the border early in the morning. The faster the better, before the hunters on both sides realized they were in Boquillas. Consuela would already be at work – she was a nurse at a local clinic. They said their farewells just before midnight. It was clear that Lucia and Consuela had genuinely enjoyed each other's company.

Boquillas del Carmen stood on a little bluff about forty feet above the Rio Grande. It couldn't have had more than a couple hundred residents. Taz recollected a sunny afternoon years past, also in April, drinking Pacíficos with Interior's solicitor and the superintendent of the Big Bend National Park at a round iron table in the courtyard of a small taverna, sharing the same perfect view of the Rio Grande. The courtyard was newly swept, and the red tile was sparkling. They were looking down at children from both sides playing together in the shallow riffles.

In those days, most of the women made their family's living doing laundry for the park guests from the US side. Now the taverna was boarded up, and the fringe of the village on the riverbank appeared to be almost empty. When the incoming administration had elected to close a border they knew very little about, the impacts reached even the most remote communities. The Mexican villagers no longer had income, the park guests no longer got their laundry done, and the riverbanks were empty.

Taz parked behind the taverna. "We have to ditch the car and walk across. Have your passport ready. And any ID you have from DEA."

It was almost noon, and the ground was starting to heat. Taz was sweating as they stumbled down the riverbank. He surveyed the river to find the best way across. He was on the lookout for park rangers. Saw only one. Meanwhile, ICE—*La Migra*, as the Mexicans called it—was everywhere. There were at least seven of them. Taz put his foot in the water on the shallowest ledge he could find. One of them yelled, "Halt! ¡*Regresa aquí!* If you take another step, you will be shot!"

To Lucia, he said, "Stay directly behind me, no matter what. I'm going to step back." Taz stretched his leg behind him, his toes feeling for a foothold. Lucia's hand was against his back. He surveyed the northern bank. It was mid-morning, and the sun had bleached the desert and was even now flashing in the river's ripples. After a moment, he located the Border Patrol agent who had shouted the command. He had a rifle at his shoulder.

Taz looked at him directly, held up his passport. Shouted loud enough to echo off the cliffs of the Sierra del Carmen, just behind them on the Mexican side of the river. "We're US citizens. Take a look through those fancy binoculars and read our passports!"

He heard the unmistakable buzz and zing of a bullet passing his ear, then the crack as it took a shard off a large rock behind them. Only then, the sound of the shot itself, echoing off the Sierra Del Carmen. Three park rangers emerged from the cabin, stood together a little off to the side of the Border Patrol group.

Taz tried again, waving his passport, and addressing all of them. "My name is Taz Blackwell, and this is Doctor Lucia Turan. We both work for the Intelligence and Research bureau of the fucking State Department. If you want to check, you can call Assistant Secretary John White." Then he stared directly at the gunman. Maybe he could shake him up. He shouted as loudly as he could. "You're a lousy shot, asshole. But if you're really dying to put your ass in a sling, go ahead, take another one. Otherwise, find us the park superintendent." Corporal Macho hurriedly checked his scope, fumbled to adjust a small knob on its side.

Taz steadied himself. He had just enough time to wonder whether hurling an insult had been his best strategy before he felt a hammer blow and staggered to his right. A loud crack echoed off the cliffs behind them. He went numb for a moment, and then there was a burning sensation as if someone was holding a welding torch above his left hip. He slapped his hand to his side and felt blood seeping through his fingers. His knees went weak. Lucia grabbed his arm and put it over her shoulder. She stumbled on a wet rock and went down on her knee under the extra weight. Taz's feet slipped out from underneath him, and he felt the water through the back of his shirt.

Lucia pulled a kerchief out of her pocket and pressed it to his wound, bent over him to cover his body with hers. Turned to glare over her shoulder, yelling for help and letting loose a string of curses. At which point one of the park rangers stepped in and pushed the barrel of Macho's rifle down until the muzzle was in the dirt. There was a quick scuffle until the other two rangers ran over and a second agent stepped in. He looked like he might be in charge. He yelled at the other ICE agents. "Hold your fire! Let them over."

Lucia did her best to pull Taz up. He had finally gotten to his knees when a fourth park ranger waded over to them and helped Lucia get him to a standing position. The three of them made their awkward way to the mudbank on the US side, and then slowly climbed the little slope towards the Park Service cabin. Lucia laid Taz on his back on the bare wooden deck. The ranger ran inside for the first-aid kit. Lucia ripped off Taz's shirt and wiped the blood off the skin around the wound.

"Taz, listen to me. I know it hurts like hell, but I'm pretty sure it's just a flesh wound."

Dizzy, he finally lifted his head and focused on her. "Good news, I guess."

Lucia was rummaging in the kit bag. She looked at him, shook her head and smiled. "Well, here's the bad news. The only antiseptic they have is iodine." She wiped the wound with a moist cloth. Taz watched as she poured the contents of the small brown bottle right into the wound. The pain was so intense that he practically levitated. The burning sensation gradually subsided and he was finally able to lever himself into a sitting position. Lucia put a bandage the size of a bar of soap on the wound and circled his torso with adhesive tape.

A Jeep came barreling down the road to the cabin, shrieked to a stop, and another ranger jumped out, running their way. From a distance Taz thought he recognized him as the superintendent, Brian Rand: he ran Bryce Canyon when Taz worked for Secretary Talbot. Taz greeted him with a weak wave. "Right on time, Brian."

Rand was still a few yards away: "Good to see you too. We heard you might be coming through." Then he saw the bandage. "What the hell's been going on? Are you okay?"

"Other than the fact that those assholes decided I'd be good target practice." Pointing at the ICE agents. Rand scanned the scene, eyes wide. Taz grabbed his wrist. "Can you check and see if any of your people got the last ten minutes on camera?"

Rand turned and asked one of his rangers a quick question. Introduced himself to Lucia. The ranger reappeared, nodded at Rand, and smiled at Taz. Rand turned back to Taz. "They got it all."

That was the answer he was hoping for. He grasped Lucia's hands, pulled himself up with a grimace, and began walking awkwardly but purposefully towards a half dozen Migra agents who were milling around a white Ford Expedition with four rows of seats, La Migra's version of a paddy wagon. Lucia held him by the elbow to make sure he didn't fall a second time.

"Who's your senior agent?" One he hadn't noticed before stepped forward. "Your name?" Lucia was still holding his arm, glaring at the agents. Taz grimaced and put his hand to the bandage. "And what about Mr. Trigger-Happy?" He turned and faced Macho. Looked him over, as if he was determined to remember every acne scar. Macho was in no mood to apologize. He was still glaring, now at both of them.

Taz turned back to the leader of the group. Loud enough for everyone to hear: "You can tell this piece of shit to enjoy his job hunt. I'm going to make sure he never puts on a federal uniform again."

Macho muttered, finally couldn't contain himself, and charged towards Taz. He had to be restrained by two of his colleagues. Lucia moved to stand between them, bristling. Once they had him secure with his arms behind his back, Taz walked over. "Fuckwads like you never learn, do they? Even now, you don't get it. Well, let me put it in a way even a lifetime dumb shit might comprehend. I'm going to scald your ass so hard you won't be able to sit to take a shit for at least six months. Got it?"

Taz started to walk away. Turned back to the senior agent. "Superintendent Rand knew I might be coming this way. Maybe your people did too? Were you instructed to stake out this spot today?" The leader nodded. "Who gave the instruction? And who's their boss? And theirs?"

Lucia noted all three names.

Taz didn't feel the need to go to the very top of the chain of command. He put his arm on Lucia's shoulder, asked Brian if he could arrange to get them at least as far as Alpine.

CHAPTER TWENTY-FIVE

Alpine

THEY LEFT BIG BEND AT eight the next morning and were in Alpine by half past twelve. The ranger dropped them off at the Holland Hotel on what passed for Alpine's Main Street.

Alpine is the prettiest town in West Texas. It nestles on a little plateau between the Davis mountains and the Chisos Range. The Holland was a traditional hotel built in the 1920s. It had gone downhill, as such structures do, but it had recently been purchased and lovingly restored by a California hedge-fund manager. It was an open rectangle, in the old Mexican style. The middle of the courtyard was tiled and graced by a lovely fountain that threw a spray at least twenty feet high. These days, the staff served an excellent dinner and breakfast in a quaint side room off the main living area.

Once they had showered, the two of them strolled around town, admiring the old courthouse, the tidy homes with their cactus gardens. Poked their heads into a women's clothing store, Taz lingered for just a moment and then caught up to Lucia in front of the liquor store down the street. Thank the Lord Brewster County wasn't dry. Taz found two bottles of sauvignon blanc from California and added a corkscrew.

Lucia grabbed his hand and headed them towards a small shady park.

They sat on a bench across from their hotel, sipping from the shared bottle and watching the sun recede. Lucia pulled his hand onto her lap, turned his way, sought his lips with hers. It started as a polite kiss, a city park kiss, but quickly became more intense, as if they had both been waiting for it too long. She lifted herself off the bench and swayed in the direction of their hotel.

For the moment, Taz was mesmerized, following her as if in a trance. He turned to her under the Holland's balcony, sought her hands. "Are you sure this is what you want?"

She pulled him to her until their lips were almost touching. "What I want . . . is for you to come upstairs and stop being such a gentleman."

Later, he tried to remember what they had felt, what they had done with each other, but the images were too vivid and too blurry. Her gentle touch as she unbuttoned his shirt and caressed his chest, taking care not to touch the bandage. Laughter when she opened her little store-wrapped present—a silly red negligée. The beauty of her breasts as he drew down her shoulder straps. The taste of salt as he brushed his lips around and over them and felt her nipples harden. A startled giggle when he reached under her ribs, tossed her on the bed and began pulling her panties down over her legs. The hint of musk as he licked his way up her inner thighs. How she reached for his arms to pull him further, placing his hands on her hips, smooth and strong. The soft sound she made as he gripped her there and used his leverage the way she wanted. The tension almost unbearable until that electric moment when her eyes widened with surprise and lightning surged through him and she bit his neck, clawing at his shoulder blades with a thin little wail. Side by side, wondering, hearts pounding, glistening with sweat.

After their breathing slowed and the quiet settled in them, she turned on her side and raised herself on her elbow, looked at him with soft eyes. "Taz, this is so crazy. I mean all of it. We should both be suffering PTSD—maybe we are already."

"An unusually pleasant version, I'd say."

She snuggled closer. Gave his nose a gentle push with her forefinger. "I mean really, Taz. What we did just now . . . the things I felt . . . that's never happened to me before." Her soft eyes rested on his.

He stroked her cheek while trying to hold back a grin. "Me either."

She pulled her head back and glared. "Don't you dare tease me about this." She rolled to her side with her back to him.

He caressed her shoulder. "Lucia, this is new for me too. I've never been with a woman who lit me up the way you do. Not just tonight. Yesterday. This morning. All the time." She sighed and he wrapped her in his arms, feeling her breath. They stayed that way a long time.

Later, just as Taz faded into sleep, Lucia pulled off her covers. "I'm going to get some air." She rolled out of bed and slipped on her negligée. Taz waited a few minutes and wandered to the window overlooking the fountain, lit with moon silver. Lucia, arms held out, twirling in the spray with a radiant smile.

CHAPTER TWENTY-SIX

Different Paths

BRIAN HAD ARRANGED A CAR to take them from Alpine to Midland, the urban hub of the Permian Basin oil country. To be precise, the Midland International Airport and Spaceport.

In the oil crash of the late '80s, with oil prices plummeting and the airport losing money and airlines by the week, the city fathers had accepted an offer from a coalition of unhinged financiers and hopeful engineering companies to have the airport recognized as a potential launching site for tourist expeditions to Mars. Or, for that matter, to Arcturus, which was equally likely. So now the airport hosted Southwest Airlines, Armadillo Air Services, and Outer Space Incorporated.

Lucia had cadged the last seat on the morning Southwest flight to BWI, and Taz was scheduled to take Armadillo's once-a-day flight to pick up his truck in McAllen. Lucia's flight would leave first. The airport boasted only one bar, a seedy place with a sour smell, so they just walked and talked.

"INR will want a detailed report," Taz observed.

"I wish it was just them. I'll be reporting to every three-letter agency in the government—the FBI, the CIA, the DEA, you name it."

"So, you're going to be Miss Popularity for a while."

"I guess. I'm not looking forward to it. Particularly not DEA."

"Why not? They'll be toasting you for outing Cárdenas."

"I don't want their praise. I'm done with them. Well, with it all, but especially with the DEA. I really am a wildlife biologist. I really do study panthers. And, believe me, I really do want to find my way back to all that as soon as I can."

"Lucia, can I ask you a question?"

"Sure."

"What did you have to do to get me out of that La Linda shithole? And how did you even know I was there?"

"Your friend Consuela. She has quite a network, and not just in Boquillas. She made a lot of calls. I only made two."

"To whom?"

"First, to my contact point at DEA. And you know what he said? In this bored-beyond-description monotone, 'Thanks for the information. We'll make sure it gets reported through the appropriate channels.' I ended up screaming at him and hanging up. Then I called John. I told him what happened. He was furious, said he was going to call the head of the El Paso DEA office. He said if they didn't fire the agent-in-charge of our operation his next call would be to the administrator. Sounded like he was ready to rip him a new one."

"So, the guy caught hell—either that, or White had some information that would embarrass the asshole . . . I forget his name."

"Nice try. I never told you his name."

"*Touché.*"

"Romero. Felix Romero." Taz filed the name in his mental Rolodex. He'd take care of Romero later.

"It was Romero who told me the intelligence I was getting wasn't any good. First my assignment was to get to know the mayor's chief of staff. Then that wasn't enough. I had to play to the mayor. He had a reputation for hitting on anything feminine in sight. I told Romero that I wasn't interested in cozying up to the man. He threatened to block my permit. That would have made it near impossible for me to finish my survey and gutted our effort to protect the panthers. Then he dropped one other pearl—said if I wouldn't do what he wanted I'd be useless, and he wouldn't be able to guarantee my safety." Taz's fingernails dug into his palms. "But there was one thing the bastard was right about." Her anger subsided; her voice was tinged with bitterness, and regret. "You know when a woman can uncover a man's real secrets? Early in the morning, while the son of a bitch she let fuck her the night before is still asleep."

Taz turned to stare at the window as a plane nosed up to the gate ramp. He forced himself to cool down before replying. "Those assholes would throw Goldilocks to the wolves. But you're safe now. Your cover is blown, and you're no longer in a position to get DEA the intel they want. We can deal with them later."

It was time to move the conversation to less dangerous ground. "So. There's another question that's still bothering me. How does a wildlife biologist go from field research in the Rio Grande Valley to an undercover assignment for US intelligence in Mexico?"

She smiled, seemingly enjoying the humor of what she was about to tell him. "You make it sound like it was some kind of promotion! But it's easier than you think. One of White's deputies knows me through a mutual friend. He decided that I had the perfect cover for a listening assignment in Reynosa. Actually, I think he was right."

"I hate to admit it, but it does make a kind perverse sense. All the same, would you do me one favor?"

She lowered her head and gave him a searching gaze accompanied by that devastating crooked smile. "You rescued me. You can ask for pretty much anything you like."

"Okay. Please tell me you won't let the intelligence boys use you for bait again."

"What makes you think I was just bait?" Her eyes blazed with indignation.

"Because at the beginning, you were. But White told me you surprised him, the DEA, and the Zetas too. You were bringing in valuable intelligence about the Zetas' network inside the government, stuff they never thought you'd get. That was your problem. They saw how effective you could be. But what the DEA really wanted was to get rid of a cartel lieutenant—one who was actually loyal to the boss and not to them. So, they used you to expose Cárdenas. He headed their operations in Reynosa. They knew if you got close to sensitive information about the Zeta's financing, he'd have to come out of the woodwork to try to stop you."

"But Taz, that's not all. I haven't told them everything yet. There's some stuff White wouldn't have known when you talked, because I didn't know it then, either."

Taz reached for her arm to turn her towards him. "Tell me."

"I don't know if it means anything, but there's this guy. They all call him Mr. Money, and they're afraid of him, or at least *very* respectful. He was at the reception the night you . . . you found me." She pulled her arm away. "I heard him talking to Contreras. He had some connection to the Colombian cartels. He was working Contreras pretty hard. Something about helping the Zetas launder their extra cash. When Contreras asked how, he just told him not to worry, it was all legit. Something about a timber import business, if I heard him right." Taz smiled, shaking his head. "Taz, are you alright?"

"I'm just trying to get used to the idea that I lucked into an amateur colleague who's better at this game than most pros." Her smile widened. "One more favor. When you tell White about the Mr. Money, swear him to secrecy. And don't tell Romero. I have a feeling he already knows. And if I'm right, it will be better for you if you don't."

"Oh. If I don't know, you mean. You have a short fuse when it comes to bullies, don't you? Even if they're on your team."

Taz recalled the note that Contreras had thrown away. It was almost too convenient. The day before the DEA outed Cardenas, his replacement parachuted in from Colombia and offered to launder the Zetas' money. "Don't be so sure about whose team they're on. Particularly ICE and the DEA. I'll find my own way to tell them. If they're ever fool enough to do this again—to put someone I care for in danger—they'll find one person who's definitely not on their team, and they'll regret it."

"So, you do still care for me. I mean, at least a little bit."

"Do I really have to tell you?"

"Well then, what are we going to do? Because at Quatro Ciénegas, lying next to you under the tarp, under the stars, I was in heaven. Last night too, by the fountain. This wasn't part of the plan, you know? Taz, I'm in deep, and it scares me a little."

He folded her in his arms, his chest to her back, kissed the nape of her neck. "At least we're in the same boat."

Lucia pulled away. "I have to go to the girls' room. I'll pick up a magazine for the plane." He watched her graceful walk as he made her way through the sparse groups of people waiting for their flights. A few families, mostly women and children. Businessmen in jackets and cowboy hats, oil workers in hard hats. She drew more than a few glances. He smiled.

As they approached her gate, she turned to face him, put her hands on his chest. He held her cheeks between his palms and kissed her open mouth. Travelers running for their gates streamed by. The kiss lasted. Taz pulled back first. "So, after you debrief every agency in town, what's your next secret destination? Will you at least leave some breadcrumbs?"

She stepped back, hands still on his shoulders, and smiled into his eyes. "News flash—I won't be that hard to find. I caught up on my messages this morning. The University of California has asked me to help them ground-truth their most recent cougar population estimates for the area around Mount Lassen. That means a stay over in Alturas with my grandmother. Then to a friend's wedding in Davis. And then I'll be back on your coast. I have a short-term assignment at the Eastern Shore campus of the University of Maryland. Would you believe it? They're going to make me an adjunct professor. It's not forever, but it'll give me a temporary home while I figure out a more permanent base to do my research. And they've got a new chancellor who says he's going to boost their science programs. He's apparently a real go-getter. Maybe you know him? Carter . . . Carter Swindell."

"If I remember right, he's a big player in Maryland politics. New on the scene. An ally to the Republican's conservative wing. Rich as Croesus from some import-export business. Ambitious, too. He knows how to get his name in the papers."

But it was time to consider more important things. Lucia was going to be only an hour away from the Island, at least for a few months. Taz pulled her hands down and held them at hip height. "Since you're going to be so close, maybe I could cadge an occasional date?"

She grinned. "Yes. Now—*and* then. After I get back from California, I'm a free woman, at least until the fall semester. With the exception of some writing and a couple of research projects, that is. I'll call you."

"You can reach me at the Pony Pines."

"You're just teasing me. And—" An announcement over the PA with her flight number. She broke off to look at the flight screen. "Damn! Did you really think you were going to get away with it again? You let me go on and on about myself and you're standing there like a smiling sphinx. So?"

"I have to get Old Faithful back to the Island. I'll head out to South Padre and then follow the migrants up the coast. Then back to Brazil, with the team from Boise. I can help Carl finish the preparations from the road. Our in-country itinerary isn't set yet. As of now, we're planning to fly sometime next week. Jessica Lansman's staff will know how to reach me."

"First Mexico, now Brazil. Out of the frying pan and into the fire." He tilted his head. "Okay, bad pun. Really bad. Sorry." Southwest was already boarding the B line. She had to go. One last kiss. She handed him a brown paper bag. "Open it." He pulled out a book, a compilation of children's fairy tales. He held it, looking confused. Lucia was grinning. "Remedial reading. Goldilocks wasn't the one with the wolves. That was Little Red Riding Hood. And the one with the tiger? The fiercest cat of all? That would be me." She turned, blew him a kiss, and gave her ticket to the agent.

❧

At five o-clock in the afternoon four days later, Taz turned into his little shell driveway. He took a shower, changed, pulled a suit off the rack, and drove to DC. He was in his room at the Tabard Inn just before midnight and was sitting in John White's office at nine in the morning the next day.

"My staff told me you survived, and now I know they weren't lying.

Jessica will be relieved. I don't think she liked the idea of fighting the Amazon fires by herself. Congratulations."

"No thanks to your friends at DEA."

"I don't seem have so many of those, after I went over their heads to get you out of jail."

"I owe you."

"Don't forget it. But I'm giving you a pass. You sprang Lucia from the corner those idiots put her in."

"What's going on over there, John?"

"Someone's playing both sides of the field. We haven't figured out if they're up here in the Springfield office or down in the Intelligence division in El Paso. I'd drag them over the coals until they give up the culprit, but the secretary doesn't want me to ruffle too many feathers. We have to work with them."

Taz picked a glass cube paperweight off White's desk, turned it over in his hand. "Maybe I could help sort that out. It wouldn't have to come back to you."

White gave him a wan smile. "We never had this conversation."

Taz placed the cube carefully back on the desk and gave White a mock salute on the way out.

*

Later that morning, Taz called Ignacio Morela. "Taz! You're alive! Thank the saints. Your little escapade with Bianca Contreras stirred up a hornet's nest down here. You may have even gotten yourself on the Zetas' target list. That's a list you really don't want to be on, Taz."

"You're not kidding. Is Bianca alright?"

"I think so. She's gone to Mexico City to see her family—a very rich, very powerful family. And she's filed for divorce. A bitter pill for the mayor—losing his wife and a mistress in one weekend. I thought you would want to know. I know you hold him in high regard."

"Well, at least he has his work."

"Not for long."

"Aahhh . . . speaking of which, I have a few issues to discuss with you."

"This connection is a little fuzzy. Give me five minutes and I'll call you back."

Once they had a more secure connection, Ignacio shared what he knew. Outing Cárdenas had left the Zetas in turmoil. Suspicion had fallen on the other lieutenants, and two of them had already disappeared. The mayor's limousine had been reduced to ashes by a car bomb. Fortunately for him, he hadn't been in it. Unfortunately, his chauffer had. The mayor had left for parts unknown.

"But Taz, something else surfaced during all the turmoil."

"Let me guess. Cell traffic between the Zetas and the DEA."

"Well of course, we all expected that. Something more intriguing. Listen closely. Cárdenas wasn't just a lieutenant; he was the Zetas' treasurer. He was laundering their profits through two banks in Mexico City and one in Venezuela. All three accounts were closed the day after he was blown. Now the money is being routed through three accounts in the Caymans."

"Who controls the accounts?"

"We don't know yet. Given the type of account that's being used, we consider that it must be a private individual. Not a Mexican. We monitor all the cartel bankers. So maybe someone on the US side. There's one other possibility. We've known for a while that two of the big South American cartels have been competing to form an alliance with the Zetas."

"*Medellin?*"

That's just one of their bases these days. They're operating in Ecuador, Peru, and Brazil as well. We can't investigate any of it through Mexico City—*el Secretario de Hacienda*—because the investigation would be leaked to the cartels. Perhaps we could get some help from your side? But not from DEA, for the same reason. It occurred to me that if anybody would know how to bring the right US agencies in, it would be you. Can you help?"

"Ignacio, *mi amigo,* I think you may be overestimating my reach. But I'll do what I can. Are you the right contact on your side?"

"Sí. Buena suerte, Taz."

✦

Taz was back on the Island just before dinner. Laney and Richard were down in Cape Charles playing bridge with a male couple they knew who ran a gallery there. Taz tried calling Lucia, knowing it was a long shot. Left her a message. Hoped her briefings had gone well. Was she still in Washington? Or maybe already in California. Was the wedding the first thing, or her grandmother Tillie? Either way, he hoped . . . He stopped talking. A recorded voice asked if he wanted to edit the message, send it as is, or delete it. He scrubbed it, cursing himself for being such a drudge. All the things he wanted to say, and he came up with what—twaddle.

He walked out the front door, climbed into Old Faithful's cab, drove to the Chincoteague Inn to talk to Diane about clams casino and something to wash them down with.

Taz wandered back just before midnight. Scrabbled in his cabinet for a cigar and found an Arturo Fuente—one of those little ones with the Connecticut wrapper. A warm night, dry. A glass of rye to chase the beers he had drunk with Diane—it had been slow at the Inn. He walked as steadily as if he were sober, down the dock, to his very own wooden Adirondack chair and the slow burbling of the channel. The glow of the short cigar, the mildly bitter taste of the wrapper and the rich, dark odor of the smoke. His set his cellphone on the flat top of a dock piling. It cawed the minute he sat. He scrambled to get it, but it was too late. Her recorded voice, from too far away.

"Taz. Hope you're safe. I'm going over to Lassen, probably won't be able to call for a while. I miss you." Taz took another belt of rye and punched in her number.

"Hey, you, I have to tell you something. Alpine is now my official favorite town. And room eleven in the Holland. Definitely my favorite number. That, and a divine sylph in the fountain, better than a trifecta at Churchill Downs. I'm out of here soon. Next time I call you I'll be speaking Portuguese."

✦

He started the morning of the following day with a Bloody Mary and a dive off his dock into the channel. Eventually, he drove over to Rainy Day to see if Laney wanted coffee.

They sat on the café's front patio, watching the summer traffic come off the new bridge. Most of the cars went straight down Maddox—only a few turned into town. Another reason to miss the old iron drawbridge that came in on the street that intersected Main just at Rainy Day's corner.

"You're really going again in two days?"

"I'm afraid so."

"Right, but you know the question I'm going to ask you when you show back up?" Taz merely raised his eyebrows. She turned her eyes to him, totally deadpan. "What did you say your name was?"

"It's only two weeks, for God's sake."

"And what about Lucia?"

"Have you talked to her?"

"Not since she left. But she did come by late last week. While you were still in the Carolinas. I swear, Taz, she was walking on air. It made me happy to see her like that, like she was before all this Mexico business. I asked her about that, but all she would tell me is that you had pulled her out of a really bad situation, that trying to find local funding for her panther work had ended up with her crosswise with a border cartel. And I thought I was kidding when I scolded you about leaving her down there with the alligators. Jesus, what would have happened if you hadn't gone?"

"She can be pretty crafty when she needs to be, you know that." He had sworn he would never lie to Laney, but if he told her anything more, he'd have to tell her everything, and that wouldn't be good for either of them.

"Yes. She told me how relieved you both were to get back on our side of the border. She was telling me about Alpine. Oh, and the hotel, how sweet it was, after everything that went down. Then the front door banged open and guess who charges in? Suzanne!"

"Oh Jesus, tell me it went well."

"Except for the fact that I never got to hear the juicy part of Lucia's story, you mean. But I was so glad to see my little one. She'd been away at that camp—the one I can never remember the name of—where she's a counselor. She's turning into a woman, you know? I almost started to cry."

"How did Lucia take it?"

"I was kind of amazed. I guess it could have been awkward, but Lucia handled it like she was choreographing a ballet." Laney flashed her brightest smile, tried for a version of Lucia's voice. "Taz has told me so much about you!" Then back to her own. "What a great big sister she was, how smart. That you had told her it was Suzanne's quick action that saved Moyer when he fell through the Landmark deck. How much you enjoyed being her almost-uncle. Now she understood why you said she always had such a smile about her. Then she asked a few simple questions about Suzanne's life—the kind you ask when you actually want to get to know someone, when you want them to know you care about who they are. There was a thunderstorm. I made us lunch while we waited for the rain to stop. The storm took a good two hours to move out to sea. Meanwhile, the three of us are sitting around the living room drinking wine—don't give me that look—it's not Suzanne's first time, and you know it. And we're telling our stories and eventually, we're telling tales about you."

Taz shook his head slowly. "My worst nightmare."

Laney laughed. "You've got that right—let's see. First Suzanne, about how you slathered her and Moyer with marsh mud so they could chase their mother around the garden. How you taught her to strip and clean an Evinrude engine when she was twelve. The time you took them to Ocean City after they confessed neither of them had ever been on a rollercoaster. Oh, and how she learned her first five cuss words from one single blue streak you let out after you hammered your thumb instead of a roof nail. Then Lucia—what a crustacean you were when you two first met, how you pretended to hate poetry just to get under her skin. How really, truly atrocious your Spanish is . . . did you really thank a *sopaipilla* vendor for cooking a wonderful slug?"

"Pretty sure I said *baking*. But, hey! It sounds like a total funfest. How about you?"

"Oh, you *really* don't want to know. But that's not the point."

"Of course not."

"Anyway, after Suzanne left, Lucia pours us both another glass and says, in a kind of astonished voice, 'She loves him like a father. He adopted them, didn't he?' What could I say? I said, 'Yes, every way but legally.' And that the adoption went two ways. That's kind of where we left it. She had to drive back up to Baltimore for a doctor's appointment—woman stuff."

"I guess it's none of my business, but was everything okay? She wasn't having problems, was she?"

"If she was, she didn't tell me. She called a couple of days later, just before she left for California. She was more subdued. Maybe she was just thinking about the trip. Wanted to know more about what you would be doing in Brazil. Didn't you tell her anything? I told her what little I know . . . that didn't seem to ease her mind. She said she talked to a mutual friend of yours and all he would tell her was that she shouldn't worry because you were *too important to waste on the fire line.* What the hell does that mean, Taz?"

"The two of you. A couple of nursemaids. I'm just going to look at their wildland firefighting capability and see what they need. They want a loan from the World Bank, but they must show the Bank's senior environmental staff a realistic plan first."

"And that's where you come in?"

"Sure. You know how good I am at planning."

Laney snorted her last sip of coffee, worked to regain her composure. "All in all, a good visit, really. She was more like the Lucia I remember from when we were first getting to know each other. The phone call later, she seemed far away at times. I put that down to everything being up in the air. She was leaving, you hadn't come back yet. There was one thing I wondered about, though. We were talking about the friends she was going to see in California and the wedding she was going to. She asked me a question, and I didn't know how to take it. I wouldn't remember but she seemed really torn up about it. I won't get it exact. 'Laney, have you ever been in a situation where you knew you were going to fail someone who means the world to you?' I wanted to ask more, but then I don't know her friends, and what would be the point?"

CHAPTER TWENTY-SEVEN

Brazil on Fire

TAZ CAUGHT UP WITH HIS team just as they were joining the boarding line at the end of the concourse. Arthur, always on the lookout, handed him his ticket. Taz stuffed it in his pocket, shouldered his rucksack, headed to the back of the economy queue. He pulled out a paperback novel—*Maqroll,* by the wonderful Colombian, Alvaro Mutis. After a few minutes, Arthur stepped carefully back towards him, working his way over a couple of supine would-be passengers and through the crowd.

"Taz. Your ticket is business class." Taz looked at it, then back at Arthur, his irritation evident.

"I didn't even travel business class when I was the DAS."

Arthur smiled. "I know. Everybody who's had your job since hates you for it."

"Shit, Arthur, it wasn't nobility. If I had traveled business, it would have come out of my team's budget. I wanted to spend that money to get where I was really going, and I don't mean to which airport." Arthur nodded, smiled, and pointed to the business entrance. Taz shouldered his backpack.

They had him seated next to Jessica, on the window. He said his apologies, sidled by her. She looked relieved. "You made it. I was beginning to wonder."

"I had to drive over from the Island. Two and half hours on the Beltway."

Jessica shuddered. "Well, I'm glad you're here." He took that in stride. "I'm going to ask you to be the deputy head of delegation. With what we have planned with Everton, the trip might take as much as ten days. I probably won't be able to stay the whole time."

"I'm not a regular anymore. That could be an issue. Is Arthur the keeper of the itinerary? I should talk to him."

"Everybody knows you, even at the consulate, and they'll take your direction. We can deal with the paperwork later. That's the good news. The bad news is that we've only got an hour in Belém, and we have to change planes, so no time for tambaqui, I'm afraid."

"You know, I'm tired of that stuff anyway. Give me a good Philly cheesesteak anytime." No laugh. Jessica looked tired, the job wearing on her. Just like his had worn on him.

He was curious where Sylvia was but decided not to ask. They both did their best to get some sleep. The descent towards Belém – early morning, sleepy passengers. Their stewardess offering orange juice and coffee. Taz asked, "Any chance I could get a reasonable facsimile of a Bloody Mary?"

Yes, with an extra mini bottle of vodka on the side. Jessica gave him a sideways look. "Join me?"

"I don't like tomato juice," Jessica replied.

"So let me order you a mimosa." She looked uncertain. "I make a good one with grapefruit juice instead of orange. I'll check to see what they have."

She looked dubious. "Okay, but just this once."

Taz merely smiled.

Everton met them at the airport in Brasilia. He offered Jessica some time to freshen up at the hotel. She hurriedly finished registering, then ran to the elevators.

He turned to Taz. "Lunch?"

Everton favored a restaurant about a mile south of the ministries, a place that specialized in food from Minas Gerais, the mountain province just north of Rio that was his homeplace. Without so much as a casual inquiry to Taz, he ordered the squash soup, which came in a hollowed-out gourd and tasted both nutty and sweet. Taz thought it deserved a praise song, like they have in Mali. Then dessert. Taz demurred.

Everton said, "Don't worry. You will be taken care of." He motioned to the waiter, who came back with two elegant shot glasses on a teak tray. Pulled a bottle from under his arm, worked the cork out, and carefully poured each of them a glass.

Everton explained, "Cachaça, but not the kind you're used to."

Taz took one sip and agreed immediately. This cachaça had a rainbow of flavors, from *interesting* to *I think I've just seen God.* As good as an old cognac, but almost opposite in the way it hit your palate. Instead of the well-knit range of flavors that you get, say, from an old Martel, the cachaça exploded in your mouth, sending shards of flavor in every direction. Startling, but the longer you savored it, the more pleasing it became.

Everton took a sip. "I see your hand in the most recent composition of the delegation."

"I hope the new team meets with your approval."

"Of course. You know us so well. We weren't very interested in redundant lessons from NASA. I particularly look forward to meeting your fire managers. My interest is this. If this first visit is successful, can we convert it from a one-shot review to an ongoing relationship? That would benefit us more."

"I don't see why not. But we'd each have to put in some kind of budget marker to make it work."

"I've already cleared mine with the Finance Ministry."

"Everton, you're so predictable. Always a step ahead."

"But in some way, Taz, you're ahead of me." He smiled. "You're out of government and, to all appearances, happily retired. And yet, you still guide them when you desire to, and when they need you to. How is that?"

Taz figured it was better not to respond to that one at all. They sat for a while, happily sipping cachaça.

Everton's day was far from finished. He had to rejoin his staff to review the cable traffic from Europe. Taz stood for a true Brazilian handshake. Everton took his right hand in his, and used his left to turn Taz's shoulder, gave him a kiss on the cheek.

CHAPTER TWENTY-EIGHT

Bombeiros

THE NEXT MORNING, EVERTON TOOK Jessica aside to offer modest adjustments to their in-country itinerary. He had arranged to introduce her to the environment minister, the leading conservationist in the Parliament, and a number of other very senior and influential officials. Her team would be on their own, but only for two days. He would arrange for Jessica to join them at their first stop in the state of *Pará,* on the edge of the Amazon. Jessica agreed, gracefully.

An hour after the two of them left, Taz found himself sitting in the hotel lobby, holding his cellphone in his lap while he deleted one crap message after another. He tried Lucia for the second time that morning. Started to leave a second message, then cut the call. The first would have to do.

He raised his eyes and saw Lucky Jarrell strolling in his direction. Lucky was the Boise team's senior hotshot and smokejumper. They were headed to the headquarters of the *Grupo Bombeiros Militar, Área Especial L, Shis Qi 11 Conjunto 11—Lago Sul.* Everton had written the address down on a small note pad. Thank God their taxi driver knew what it meant. Taz sure had no idea.

The bombeiros' capital district brigade was housed in a building a few miles beyond the southwest edge of the city. The building bore a remarkable resemblance to the Girdletree Volunteer Fire Company station on the road from Chincoteague to Snow Hill. The Girdletree boys had a four-rolling-door firehouse of which they were justifiably proud. The bombeiros didn't have to worry about rolling doors. They didn't have any fire trucks. Two vans, well equipped, in a triple bay garage with old wooden barn-style doors. Inside was all business, though—ranks of rakes, shovels, axes, torch kits, heavy canvas protective suits. One phone—a landline with a rotary connection. Brazil, in its vastness, had basically skipped the switchboard and landline era, and gone directly to cell towers. The switch had apparently happened after the bombeiros had proudly installed their very first telephone.

As Taz paid their cab fare, a sturdy man in a tan short-sleeve shirt and khakis came out to greet them. His shirt bore the epaulettes of a commandant. Taz shook his hand. Mutual pleasantries in Portuguese, for the commandant, and English, for Taz. The commandant guided him into the station and offered coffee. Knowing the attention that Brazilians lavish on such things, Taz smiled as he extended his hand for the cup. They drank for a while in silence.

Mercifully, just as they were finishing their coffee, Everton arrived with a translator from Itamaraty. They chatted amiably for a while. Jessica was still meeting with the minister and planned to join them later. The conversation limped along, with Everton asking the commandant to describe the group's operations and the translator following the questions and answers in somewhat awkward English. Providence finally intervened as the lone phone began jangling loudly enough to be heard at the ranch next door. The commandant answered, eyed his troops, clenched his fist with his forefinger up and twirled his hand for the team to move. The commandant pointed Taz and Everton to the first van. Lucky and four of the bombeiros climbed in behind them. Eight more jumped in the second van. They had driven about twenty minutes when they spotted the smoke from a grass fire; the front, at least two hundred yards wide, had already burned several acres of rolling grassland. It was being blown in the direction of a small group of ranch houses.

The bombeiros from the second van leapt into action, using mattocks, hoes, forest adzes and McLeod tools to dig wide trenches on two sides of the fire. Once the trenches were sufficiently long, half the group turned to setting backfires. Then they'd rejoin the trenchers for the next round.

Lucky and the four bombeiros leapt out the back and ran to the second van to get tools. Taz watched for half a minute as Everton made sounds intended to reach his ear. Growing up in the Brazos country, he had seen his share of grass fires, and he admired how the bombeiros were attacking this one. Finally, unable to sit another second, he opened the van door, grabbed the last McLeod tool, and joined the line—Everton shouting objections. The tool was like a hard, heavy three-tine steel rake with an adze-hoe on the back side. The teeth bit into the clay, and the hoe stripped the grass cover. The work was sweaty but satisfying.

After about an hour and a half, the fire started to die out for lack of fuel. But a breeze picked up, coming now from the north. As one of its last gasps, it sent a small fire spout up about twenty feet from Taz, flinging flaming sod as it twirled. A burning root ball scraped Taz's cheek on its way by. Finally, the commandant signaled that they had done enough. Smiles all around. A couple of the bombeiros slapped Lucky on the back and shook Taz's hand appreciatively. One of them turned to say something to one of their companions, a young man with an engaging smile and curly black hair. He reached into the van's glove compartment, pulled out a flat pint bottle of cachaça. He poured a splash on a dirty bandana and used that to swab Taz's burn. Taz stopped himself from leaping right out of the van, and the lightning bolt of pain gradually subsided. The young man winked at him, held the bottle up for his colleagues to see and nodded at Taz, smiling. Then he offered it to Taz, and after Taz had taken a very satisfying drink, he shared it all around.

The bombeiros delivered them to the airport. Everton had been driven separately. He greeted them at the entryway of a hangar used by the military. He shook Taz's hand, looked at his cheek with a knowing smile.

Then he had a word with the senior bombeiro. It appeared that he was asking a question. The bombeiro laughed and gave a short reply. Everton motioned Taz over to a small ersatz office, poured them each a cup of coffee. He sat on the side of a bare aluminum desk.

"Taz, I must remonstrate with you, on behalf of both our governments. Am I correct? The fires you are meant to put out are the diplomatic kind. For my sake and yours, will you please refrain from engaging with the real kind?" Then he smiled and clapped Taz on the shoulder. "And now that I have fulfilled my instructions and given you the required warning, I can also tell you that the commandant expressed his admiration and gratitude for your help."

*

The next day, a thirty-seat jet chartered by the Brazilian government carried them an hour north to Redenção, a city of about a hundred thousand on the Rio Gurguéia just east of the Kayapo Indigenous Reserve. Jessica was there ahead, waiting for them on the apron. A sixteen-seat turboprop was to take them from there.

While they were changing planes, Taz checked his cell, which showed a single Wi-Fi bar. He tried Lucia's number anyway, heard her voice, but it was just her message obscured by static. He pocketed the cellphone with a muttered curse. He, Lucky, and Jessica were headed towards the heart of the Amazon. It would be at least two days until he could try again.

From Redenção, they flew a western course over the 426 million acre Kayapo Reserve, then crossed the mighty Xingu river, the largest of the Amazon's clearwater tributaries, and finally to Jacareacanga, a small community that boasted one of the few airports on the middle stretch of the Tapajós. Everton had suggested spending the night there–he wanted to give Jessica a true taste of the Amazon. He had arranged for her to meet the leaders of the Munduruku Women's' Association, who were engaged in a struggle to limit illegal gold mining in the nearby indigenous reserves. The struggle had resulted in violence, including a recent attack on the Women's'

Center by a gang of drunken miners. Meanwhile, Lucky would travel seventeen hundred miles northwest to Boa Vista, where he was supposed to meet another brigade of bombeiros who were already working on the year's Roraima fire. As the pilot took them down for a first look at the runway, Taz scanned the broad white sand beaches between the town and the river. There were several loose rows of colorful canvasses on tent-poles, with mothers washing clothes and children swimming and standing on the submerged sandbars on the river's edge. The pilot landed their plane on a red clay airstrip and pulled up in the neighborhood of a long thatched-roof hut that apparently did double service as a terminal. After a short wait, Taz spotted the dust of an approaching Jeep. The pilot had a word with the driver, and they were motioned onboard. They spun through a wide belt of trees, mostly *babaçu*, which resembled a very tall palm, and *pau brasil*, the Brazil-nut tree after which the country was named, emerging seemingly randomly from the brush below. Taz guessed the area had been selectively logged and then left to itself to regenerate.

They were to stay at a little inn just off the red clay road into town. The inn served a rough churrasco. They ate in a large open courtyard by a small fire. Finished their meal and avoided what looked like a way-too-sweet dessert. Taz accepted the bottle of cachaça offered by the innkeeper, which was on the firewater side, but still drinkable. Tropical night comes fast. Chorus frogs started their chants. They sat around a little campfire under the stars. After a bit, the pilot said goodnight and headed to his room in the inn to get a little shuteye.

Jessica and Taz had taken one look at the available rooms and decided they'd be better off sleeping outside. The innkeeper rigged two hammocks near the fire. There were already too many stars to count.

Taz heard a pop and a crackle, but not from the direction of the fire. It was the restaurant's sound system. A dusky, heartbroken voice reached their ears from the direction of the bar. Without becoming louder, it gradually gathered strength, until it enveloped them.

Jessica reached to touch his elbow. "Really. How is it possible to go twenty-nine years and not hear that voice?"

"It's Maria Bethânia, one of the leaders of the musical rebellion against the former dictatorship—what they call *Tropicalismo.* Kind of a national icon."

"And here I had you cast as a Willie Nelson kind of guy."

"He's okay, but in a pinch, I'll take Uncle Jerry every time."

"Garcia? The Grateful Dead, right? Maybe you're an anarchist?"

"Basically." He smiled. "Is that what got you arrested?" She'd been reading his FBI file.

"Listening to the Dead? No. Some friends and I helped organize an anti-apartheid demonstration in front of the South African Embassy in DC. They sent out a bunch of Special Branch thugs to bust us up. One of them started after the girl next to me and we got in a little scuffle. I got lucky and broke his nose. He had diplomatic immunity, and I didn't."

"So how in the world did you get a security clearance high enough that you could do the work you did at State?"

"I make it a point never to lie to the FBI. I told them everything. If they're any good, they know the answers before they ask the questions anyway. We hadn't done anything illegal. And by then, the Mandela government was in, and the domestic climate here had changed as well."

The talk slowed. Jessica slipped into sleep. Taz was about to do the same when his cell began buzzing in his pocket. He slipped out of his hammock and took a few steps around the fire to avoid waking her. Laney's voice on the other end. "Taz, is this you? There's a lot of static."

"I'll move around a little and see if that improves it." He took a couple of steps towards the inn and her voice came through more clearly. "That's better."

"You said you'd call. Don't tell me you've been too busy."

"Well, I got to help fight a good-sized grass fire, but mostly I've just been out of cellphone range. I'm having trouble believing I can get a signal where I am now. So, what's up?"

"Where *are* you now?"

"On the Tapajos River, the most westerly of the southern tributaries of the lower Amazon. It's just a feeder stream—where we are, the opposite bank is only two miles across."

"A river as wide as Assateague Bay. Wow."

"And surrounded by rainforest on every side. You should see it sometime."

"How's the swimming?"

"Great! If you don't mind fifteen-foot crocs and schools of piranhas."

"Sure, I'll put it on my bucket list. Right after the second circle of Hell. But you have a good time. By the way, I heard from Lucia."

"And?"

"She had a great visit with her grandmother—Tillie? She really loves that woman, and she finished her work at Lassen, so she was headed to La-La Land for the wedding. Sounded pretty excited." After a little more conversation, they hung up, both vastly relieved. When Taz returned to his hammock, Jessica was murmuring and turning her head from side to side. It must have been quite a dream. Finally, a quiet in her feelings, or whatever she was processing. For a moment, she actually looked peaceful.

Later, as they were both waking up to the dawn light, "Taz, I've decided to ask Sylvia to join us for the next leg. She'll make the trip a little more complicated. I trust that won't pose a problem for you."

"Never in life. I enjoy Sylvia."

"Perhaps a little too much. I've seen the way you look at her."

"Take my pulse. Am I still alive?" She snorted. "Anyway, Sylvia isn't the least bit interested in me. She's in love with you. I figured that out by the time we left Andrews." Jessica's worry lines faded. "As to how I look at her, you and I would probably agree that the female gender is just more attractive than us awkward boys."

Jessica smiled. "I bet you use that line on all the girls." He laughed and put the little tin coffeepot on the fire. He reached for his whisky flask and poured some into her coffee cup, then his.

"While we wait for the coffee."

She took a long sip. "Seriously, you don't have a problem?" Another long sip.

"Actually, I have many problems. It's just that you and Sylvia aren't among them." She laughed hard enough to spit out half a cup of good whiskey.

CHAPTER TWENTY-NINE

Fado in Iquitos

TAZ SAT AT THE BAR of an open-air restaurant on the bank of *La Laguna Quistacocha,* a kind of enclosed bay off *El Rio Amazonas,* on the east side of Iquitos, the largest city in the Peruvian Amazon. It was a floating bar, anchored by rusty chains to the bulwark fronting a muddy lot on the riverbank. Taz could feel the current underneath his table. He had become a regular in the three day's he'd spent in the city.

Jessica had been required back in Washington and Lucky was already in Roraima.

Alone again, Taz waited for his third pisco sour, Peru's national drink, one hundred miles from the Brazilian border, a hundred and fifty from the equator, and six hundred from where he was supposed to be. Night in Iquitos. The moist air was still cooling down from a steamy afternoon. It had drizzled most of the day. When the music went quiet, he could hear the rivulets from the tin roof as they hit the water.

Things were not going as planned. He had been in Brazil for almost five days and in the western Amazon for three. A gigantic wildfire complex was blazing only two watersheds to the south, on the border of the Javari Indigenous Reserve, in the headwaters of the Ipixuna. Taz's assignment was to help the boys from the Boise Interagency Fire Center coordinate efforts with their Brazilian counterparts. Now, instead of hitting the fire line, he was stuck here trying to shake off his loneliness in the oldest city in the Peruvian Amazon.

The plan had been for the Boise firefighting team to pick him up on the way to Cruzeiro do Sul, the closest city to the Reserve, but the smoke from a whole different set of fires in Roraima had grounded the boys for two days. There were no roads into or out of Iquitos. He would have to wait until they showed. It was all like some loser's trifecta, and the joke was on him.

As Everton had reminded him, his terms of reference definitely didn't include firefighting. His instructions were to stay out of the way, watch the teams work together, and assess the overall response. He grimaced, imagining sitting on the sideline with a scorecard and a stopwatch. Everton had arranged for a Lockheed C-130 Hercules to be staged at the Iquitos airport to airdrop water and fire retardant when the ground crews were in a position to tell them where it would do the most good. He had asked Taz to take a look at the plane and interview the crew. Everton wanted to know how they would compare to their counterparts in the States. None of that was even in prospect while he sat in Iquitos twiddling his thumbs.

The only others at the restaurant's bar were three bored prostitutes five stools down at the far end, by the kitchen door. Most of the locals had taken tables and were busy tucking into unidentifiable cuts of grilled meat or local fish, some grilled, some smoked in banana leaves. Several families, and a few tables of single men drinking cheap *cerveza*, cheaper *pisco*, leering at the hookers. Taz was content to have his back to the whole thing while he meditated deep into the cloudy remains of his pisco. He became dimly aware of a brief hubbub some way behind his left shoulder, near the bar's plank entrance. He took a brief scan of the bar mirror. His gaze settled on the opaque reflection of a dark-haired woman wearing a loose-fitting maroon blouse and low-slung black denims. She was in her mid-to-late thirties and had a pleasant, if distant, smile, which she rested momentarily on three undeserving fools who were declaring their love from the table nearest the door. She looked to be about five-seven. Her hair hung in loose ringlets well below her collarbones, leading the eye easily down a very dangerous road.

Taz continued watching in the mirror as the woman eventually tired of the trio's boisterous adulation and made her way to the bar, followed by a sturdy-looking man who had long ago forgotten how to smile. She settled onto a stool two down from his, ordered a scotch on the rocks. The man moved to the end of the bar by the prostitutes, keeping a careful eye on the room.

Taz motioned to the barman, ordered a high-end cachaça neat, and kept his eyes on the mirror. He sipped the cachaça slowly and with appreciation. It wasn't the refined style of São Paulo, but it wasn't firewater either.

A voice like a cool breeze found his ear. The only words he recognized for sure were "*voce*" and "*Americano*." *Voce* came out, liltingly, as *vochay*, "*Voce ser o americano*." Taz was somewhat surprised to hear her speak Portuguese rather than Spanish, but perhaps she was from Brazil. He turned to her mostly out of politeness. Before he could it put it all together, she tilted her head to the side and smiled his way. "So. what brings you to Iquitos?"

He showed his surprise. "I'm sorry—your English is much better than my Portuguese. I came just to visit this beautiful bar. And you? I take it you're not a local either."

She scoffed. "Such an impertinent answer. But perhaps my question was of the same character. I'm here for work, and yes, I too am a visitor." A jaded smile. Taz adjusted his guess at her age—she had four or five years on him, and she seemed a decade wearier.

"A much more honest answer than mine. Really, I'm here to meet a team of wildfire managers from the States. We're supposed to fly to Cruzeiro do Sul to see if there's anything we can do to help the bombeiros fight the wildfires in the Javari reserve. Just now, my team is stuck in Boa Vista because of the fires in Roraima."

Her eyes widened. "So, you're a firefighter?"

"No. But I know some good ones, and I brought them down to see what we could do together."

"You're with the US government."

"Well, I used to be. Now I just help them on occasion."

She took another sip of scotch. "You don't enjoy being known, do you? You like to hide."

"Let's just say that early on, I learned that it wasn't necessarily good to be the object of attention. In any case, I don't think I'm hiding."

She shifted to the stool next to his. Motioned to the bartender for another scotch. He lifted a Dewar's off the shelf. Taz looked him in the eye. "Not the Dewar's. How about that Ballantine's 17 right next door?" She gave him an inquiring look.

"This one's on me."

"Generous, but still impertinent." She took an appreciative sip, closing her eyes for a moment, then looked at him very carefully, as if drinking him in. "So, you're headed to a wildfire, but you're not a firefighter." She placed her glass back on the bar, giving it a gentle half-turn. "And yet you have a taste for smoke." She lifted her glass to him. "And a burn scar on your cheek." She gently brushed the tips of two fingers across it. "You're homesick, but you don't want to admit it. You're here to assist Brazil, but you're on your own." A nod to his right hand as he raised the drink to his lips. "You play guitar, and maybe sing, but you stopped some time ago. What else do you hold back?"

"I'm a cross-dresser. I pose for photographs as Marie Antoinette."

She snorted at least half a shot of scotch, took a breath, gave an extended and very charming giggle, her eyes tearing as she coughed.

"You're missing someone. Right now. As we talk."

"What makes you think that?"

"Let me see... Maybe because you looked morose until I caught your attention. Also, you've been drinking like a fish."

Taz eyed the three empty glasses lined up on the bar in front of him. "I am missing someone. Someone I'd like to spend more time with. So far, we've been apart more than we've been together."

"So ardent. I like that. Common among some of our men and nearly ubiquitous among our women. Not so much in your country, I think. Yet you stand out. You are so American."

"I didn't mean to be so obvious." He would have been irritated but her voice had grown soft and even more pleasant. "Are there really so few of us?"

"Not at all. There are plenty of tourists, waiting in queues for the paddleboats to take them to the luxury lodges on the Amazon. And Lord knows there are more than enough oil workers. But you don't seem to fit either category. Naturally, a person wonders."

Taz was struck by the dismissive tone with which she disposed of his countrymen, and simultaneously by the perceptiveness of her questions. He turned her way and did his best to absorb her before the conversation ended, when she got tired of trading pleasantries. Her eyes were not quite symmetrical, but they were achingly beautiful. The smile that showed when she was surprised was warm and inviting. When she looked down or became pensive, she projected a powerful melancholy. Taz watched and waited.

The table of oil workers who had greeted her with such enthusiasm was now focused on a pair of young waitresses, shouting their appreciation. Which Taz thought must be endlessly endearing.

She considered her drink for a few minutes. "I find myself wondering. What is he doing here? The one that doesn't fit in?" Reeling him back to the conversation.

"And if I asked you the same question?"

"Oh, that's easy. I'm finishing my career. Here in the outback, as my Australian friends like to say."

"Aren't you kind of jumping the gun? Most people wait to retire until they're at least thirty-five."

That got him a bleak smile. "How gracious of you. I'm forty-two. And my voice has traveled a few too many miles, according to my manager. As you can see, I've been left to ply my trade in the most remote areas he could find on the map."

"You're a singer, from the timbre of your voice."

"Like you, I used to be, yes."

"Jazz? Surely not *bossa nova*." Her voice was closer to jazz than rock, and too earthy for the most delicate of all the offshoots of samba.

"No."

"Then what?" Brazil boasted any number of choices, from *forró*, the country music of the *sertão*, all the way to samba and punk. She didn't fit any of them.

"I sing fado."

"I had the impression fado was Portuguese."

"You would have been right. But my label told me to take a little vacation from the studio and sent me here to 'open a new market.'" She used air quotes. "Turns out I'm expendable. As a consequence, I'm here in God-knows-where, trying to cultivate a new audience for a musical form that belongs in a museum."

"I haven't heard much fado, but what I've heard I liked. Romantic, and then despondent. And the high guitar is wonderful, particularly when it's paired with a voice as dusky as yours."

"*Dusky*—I like that word."

Taz took a longer look at her. She was really quite striking. A graceful neck, especially when she tilted her head back to look at him, eyes live with skepticism. Prominent collarbones when she laughed or when she bent towards him.

"You do play guitar, yes? I noticed your fingernails. Are you good?"

"People tell me so, but I'm sure I'm not in the same league as your partners. I'm just an amateur. I like working tunes out by ear."

"Well, that's how we all start, isn't it?"

"I don't know. How did you start?"

"I was just a girl. I liked Madonna, and later, the punk bands—the Clash, Joan Jett, Chrissie Hynde. My mother insisted that my voice was too good to waste on 'that kind of music.' I fought against it for a while, but then she made me listen to some fado, and I became addicted. The style did fit my voice. It's been quite a journey— 'a long, strange trip,' as your Grateful Dead would say."

Taz must have shown his surprise.

"What? You think because I'm Portuguese I don't know anything about your music? No! It's you Americans who don't explore the music of the rest of the world! Well, also the Brazilians, I'm afraid. You both have so many styles of your own that you're musically arrogant. And insular."

"Guilty as charged. But how in the world do you know about the Grateful Dead? We thought they were an American secret, a rock and roll band that played country music and jammed like jazzmen, anarchist heirs of the black Memphis jug bands of the thirties."

"Okay, Mister Grateful Dead fan, what you don't know about your band is a lot. They played some of their best music on their last European tour. I saw them at the old music hall in Lisbon. Most of us knew them solely by reputation. What we knew were the stories—about the acid tests, the Deadheads, the space jams, all that. It was as if they were history—not a live band. But how they played! They took us totally by surprise. We all fell in love with Jerry Garcia, the cuddle-bear who adorns every melody with ornaments and triplets worthy of Mozart. They played a collage of the American music we grew up on—the blues, country, rockabilly, jazz. To me, they were the ultimate American band."

Taz took that in, still admiring her elegant wrist as she held her scotch just a little way from her lips while she looked at him.

"Do you always check women out this way?"

"Have I made you uncomfortable? I apologize."

"Don't. I took it as a compliment. And I haven't had many compliments on this trip."

"The table by the door certainly liked your entrance."

"A bunch of stupid *rusticos*. How do you say? *Boors*."

"Enough to give men a bad name. Not that we need much help."

She gave a yip that he decided was another version of a laugh. "Now you've given me the hiccups."

"I'd like to hear you sing."

Her eyes flashed. "Really?"

"Really." He had ordered another caipirinha for himself, and a second Scotch for her.

She took one more sip and wrote on a little notepad that she had pulled from her clutch. Handed him the paper. "I'm singing tomorrow night at Música. A club off the Plaza de Armas where they specialize in cocktails that are supposedly aphrodisiac, because they come from weird flowers and plants, somewhere in the Amazon. It's not exactly La Scala. But the people are okay, and money is, well, money."

"If I'm still here, I will definitely show up."

"We start at nine. Give them this note at the door." Touched his hand gently. "Nice talking to you." Then she was gone.

Taz was intrigued. He was also dead set on finding a way to Cruzeiro do Sul—in the morning, if possible. He would likely miss her show, which was too bad, because he really wanted to hear her sing.

CHAPTER THIRTY

Javari Calling

THE NEXT MORNING, AFTER A few hours of sleep, sweat, and unsettled dreams, Taz found his way to the Iquitos airport and bought a ticket on the only flight of the day to Cruzeiro do Sul. An hour later, he stood on the tarmac staring blankly at the kitbag at his feet and holding his airline breakfast in his hands—a hunk of *pao de queijo* and the obligatory plastic cup of orange juice with the tinfoil top. The meager breakfast had been served to the half-dozen passengers before takeoff, on plates of brown cardboard. Now takeoff was no longer in the cards—engine trouble.

His cell phone started cawing. It was the call he had been waiting for—Lucky, his lead firefighter. The Boise team had finally been cleared to fly. They had also heard from the bombeiros. The two teams were planning to fly directly to Cruzeiro do Sul, where they would have more immediate access to the fire, which was now threatening the southern border of the *Vale do Javari*. Should they swing by Iquitos to pick Taz up?

He thought for a second. They would be burning extra fuel to make the stop. Refueling would run them into sunset and cost them at least a day. "Time is definitely not with us. Get to Cruzeiro do Sul as fast as you can. Hook up with the bombeiros. Just leave me a message at the airport as to where you're headed, and I'll find a way to join you."

Shit! He could clear the team for Cruzeiro do Sul, but he had no way to get there himself. Much less to the Javari reserve. He walked over to the private air terminal to see if anyone was headed that way. Mostly he was met with laughter. One wag, a fat man who looked like he had spent too much of his ill-gotten gains on rich food and skinny whores, leered at him. "American. You're from the USA, right? The land where cars are king. Why don't you drive?"

Taz eyed him levelly. "And where are you headed?"

The fat man replied dismissively. "Porto Velho. Why does it matter?"

"Why don't you run? It would do you a world of good." Laughter all around, at least among those who understood English. The fat man quickly busied himself rearranging his briefcase.

Taz was still cursing when he got back to the floating hostel. It was lunchtime, but he didn't feel at all like eating. He dialed Lucia. She picked up on his third try. "It's so good to hear your voice. Sorry you had to leave so many messages. Until two days ago I was in the foothills out of Susanville—no reception."

"Just tell me you're okay."

"I'm okay."

"Where are you now? The connection is shockingly good."

"I'm still in Davis. Actually, I'm combing confetti out of my hair."

"Sure sorry to miss *that*. How was the wedding?"

"I told you it was my old girlfriend Liz, didn't I? The one who was going sweep the world by storm? The one we all thought would be president someday."

"I think so."

"Well, I was wrong. She gave it up. The man she married . . . anyway, it was a great wedding, you know . . . lots of dancing, lots of crying. I cried along with everybody else."

"Isn't that the law? Everybody cries at weddings."

"I wasn't crying for joy, Taz. I was crying for Liz!"

"Why?"

"She's given it all up. All her ambitions, all her dreams. Kevin—that's his name—he's a corporation guy, lots of money, too much power. He doesn't want her to work. He's already spun a web around her, and now he's going to keep her in a jail cell made of velvet and diamonds. I wanted to say something to her but, really, she was too far gone. So, I just stood there and applauded with everybody else. And now I hate myself for it."

"It hit you pretty hard."

"No kidding. I don't know . . . well, yes, I do. My work is important to me, Taz. I'm good—really good—at what I do. At least at the science and conservation part. I only got tangled up in the Mexican mess because I needed financial support for my conservation work. Then I saw how corrupt Reynosa was and what the crime and drugs were doing to the people, and I got angry. Righteously angry, like you do sometimes. I decided I needed to do something about it, and suddenly, I was in this other world— the world of politics, corruption, money, and power. That's your world, Taz, not mine. You're good at it . . . at fighting alongside underdogs and making twisted things come out right. And now you've become a big force in my life. I just need a little space to find some balance."

"Okay. I think I get it. But I'm not Kevin, and you're not Liz. And you're stronger than you think you are. Your dreams are part of the reason I'm attracted to you. You must know that."

"I guess. But that doesn't make it any easier."

"I know you well enough to know you're going to do what you have to do. But I think you owe me a face-to-face conversation before you decide what that is. Don't you? Meanwhile, I've got to find my team and head down to the fire. I'll leave you a message when I get back in cell range."

"Okay Taz. It's going to be a while before I get back to the Island. I'm going to take a couple of weeks to look at some research opportunities out here in California."

They said their goodbyes and Taz headed to the bar, ordered the same high-end cachaça that he had been served the night before. He was wondering about Lucia's mood. He watched the mirror, recalling their conversation word for word until he finally tired of it.

The cachaça went down with ease. Its flavors reminded him of his back and forth with the mysterious fado singer the night before. He hadn't even asked her name—nor given her his. He took another slug and let his mind wander to other things.

He was about to order some bar food when that unforgettable voice reached his ear. "Still trying to drink away your sorrows? I can tell you—it's not possible." She was standing to his left, her right hand on the back of his stool.

He patted the empty stool next to his. "Please." She smiled and sat, pulled herself closer to the bar. He did his best to help. She turned to him.

"I spent the morning doing vocal exercises. You?"

"Morning from hell. I canvassed the private airport to see if anyone was headed to Cruzeiro do Sul, down by the Javari reserve. One asshole suggested I drive."

"Yes. You said something about Cruzeiro yesterday. Why in the world would you want to go *there*?" He told her the condensed version of the story. She thought for a while, chewing on her thumbnail. "Perhaps I should take you."

Taz was incredulous. "I don't think the Cruzeiro airport can accommodate private jets."

"How do you get by, being so dense? We're not village-hopping in the Amazon on jets, for the love of God. They've got me in a Cessna Skyhawk—a four-seater."

"Sorry. I had no idea."

"I'm singing in Porto Velho tomorrow night. I can gas up in Cruzeiro and then hop through Rio Branco. Yes, or no? We'll have to rebalance the plane."

"Yes. But only because I enjoy your company. I hear it's an easy drive."

She yipped again. "Jesus." Smiling with her eyes: "If you give me the hiccups one more time, I'm going to slap you."

CHAPTER THIRTY-ONE

Carolina Flies

TAZ SPENT THE AFTERNOON SORTING out his gear, packing only what he would need. He alerted the woman at the desk that he would be checking out in the morning. She was very sorry he was leaving. Taz was a good tipper. He stored his extra bag and considered what to do until eight, when his mystery woman's concert was supposed to start.

After several tries that were interrupted by the sporadic Wi-Fi service, he reached the Música Club's website. The evening's bill was to be headlined by Carolina Souza, *the renowned fado singer from Lisbon.* Taz pronounced it to himself the Brazilian way, with a long *e* in Carolina and the *ou* in Souza like the *oo* in cool. Rolling her name on his tongue made him smile.

He wandered around town for most of the afternoon, admiring the new hexagonal cathedral, walking the rough plank boardwalks of the slums where the sewage flowed just under his feet. Towards the end, when the sun was on the merciful verge of dropping behind the forest horizon, he made his way to the harbor, where a couple of river steamers were loading freight and passengers for the ride downriver to Manaus. Amid the tangle of broken warehouses and rusted cranes, there were down-at-heel cafés and one seedy bar just off the wharf. Taz chose the nearest of the cafés. Ordered an espresso and a Brazilian pilsner—Antarctica.

He was drinking alone at an outside table under a tattered awning. Watching the wharf rats; in Rotterdam, they would be called *dokwerker*—stevedores—and they would have a union and be paid a living wage. Here, they made pennies on the dollar and barely scraped enough to feed their families. They formed a loose line and passed their loads hand to hand. For the bigger items, they used a cart. For the largest, a block and tackle to hoist them onboard. The block and tackle looked for all the world like it had been looted from a Spanish galleon.

Taz sat mesmerized, until he made the mistake of glancing at his watch. He was already late for Carolina's show. The plaza was almost a mile away. He headed inside to see if someone could call him a cab. The regulars just smirked when he asked. Finally, he waved a twenty-dollar bill and resorted to broken Spanish to ask if anyone would drive him. Three hands went up. Taz pointed to the one who looked the most sober.

The ride was exciting in oh-so-many ways. The car was a rust bucket—a 1970s Oldsmobile 88 convertible. The floor had holes big enough that you could see the road between your feet. The driver had apparently gotten his license from a forger. He enjoyed careening through red lights and driving on sidewalks to pass cars that were dawdling in the main lane. Amazingly, they did arrive at their destination. The driver held out his hand. Taz handed him the twenty. The driver pocketed it, held out his hand again. Taz pulled out his wallet and offered him a wad of bills he had changed in Belém—mostly ten-*soles*. The driver smiled and wished him well.

Most of the buildings on the other side of the street were boarded up, but his side seemed to be quite busy. Women in short skirts and low-cut tops lingered in small groups under flickering streetlights. Cars cruised by with open windows. Occasionally, one of the women would smile at her friends and get in.

There was a neon sign at the other end of the block. The remaining neon spelled a barely decipherable word, Música. The *u* was missing, and the *a* was hanging on by a wire. He made his way up the street, tried to avoid any of the available diseases, pushed open the old wooden door, and climbed the stairs to the paying entrance. Handed a girl the note. She

turned to her manager, who was sitting on a comfortable back stair. He
motioned in the direction of an attractive waitress in a very short skirt.
She crooked her finger in Taz's direction. Led him to a door that opened
onto the main room of the club. Pointed to a round table for two in the
third row off the stage. Carolina was between songs. Her guitarist was
taking up the slack, tossing off high riffs and melodies that seemed to float
somewhere above the range of normal music.

The waitress offered him a panatela. He politely declined. He was
sipping his pisco and glancing around the room when Carolina returned
to the stage, wearing a maroon dress with a white jacket, open in front,
easy on her shoulders. She looked elegant and smart.

She had put her hair up, which only accented her eyes and her smile.
Taz decided the word for the smile was *effervescent.* The stage was lit with
spotlights from the balcony, which left the dining tables in darkness. And
that was just where Taz wanted to be.

His game plan worked for a few songs, but at the set's finale, a swiveling
strobe light gave her a stuttering view of the audience. That must have
been when she saw him.

The lights went up ever so slightly for the break. And then she was
at his table, watching him. "You came! I didn't think you would, not for
a second." Taz smiled. "Well, don't be so self-satisfied, Mister Grateful
Deadhead! You're late."

"I know. A day late and a dollar short, as we say in Texas. I was down
at the wharf, watching them load the paddle wheelers."

She rolled her eyes. "That must have been fascinating."

"You sing like an angel."

"You shouldn't feel that you have to compliment me."

"I don't. What I feel is—when I'm looking at you—that I have to tell
the truth. And, Carolina, the truth is, you sing like an angel."

Her eyes were moist. "You know my name, and I don't know yours.
That's not right."

"Taz. Taz Blackwell."

He pulled out her chair, turned to the waitress, who was watching from a railing a few feet away. Asked in a whisper for a bottle of champagne. "Something good."

"Well, Mr. Taz Blackwell, now I know your name, but nothing else. We've got a half hour before the last set. So?"

"I could ask the same question."

"Oh, no you don't. Coming in second doesn't give you any rights at all."

"You're tough."

"When I need to be. First, how is your love, the lucky one you call 'the heart of my heart'?"

"I'm pretty sure she just told me goodbye. At least for a while. I just need to accept it."

She raised an eyebrow. "Don't be too sure. We women say things sometimes. . . when we're not sure about the way forward in love, or when our hearts are too full, or when our own desire frightens us. But you men are in a difficulty even more severe. You're afraid of the very uncertainty that we embrace. And when you don't know what to say, you don't say anything at all. But I know she means a great deal to you. I'm sure you'll find a way—and then you'll know the right thing to say." She placed her palm on the left side of his chest, as if to feel the pulse. "Because it's there in your heart. Still, it might be better to let go for now—to give her the space she needs." She brushed his hand with her fingers, soft eyes on his. "And for you, too, some openings may appear."

With perfect timing, the waitress brought an ice bucket and the bubbly, a Moet rosé. She giggled. "You're both charming and rich, is that it?"

"I robbed a bank—a big one."

She yipped. Covered her mouth with her hand and glared his way. "How do you make me do this? I can't go back to the stage with the fucking hiccups!" Put her hand to her heart and took a deep breath. Two. Her eyes softened. "I've got to do a last set. Stay, I'll sing to you."

Taz absorbed that one. Told the waitress to keep the champagne on ice. He made it clear he'd open it when the time came.

There was a short break while the technicians shifted the microphones and adjusted the monitors. Carolina came on stage briefly, looked his way, smiled, and stuck out her tongue. Very quickly. Nobody seemed to notice. Taz wasn't sure he had seen it himself.

A few minutes of darkness. Then a spotlight on the center of the stage, and a sidelight on the guitarist, who was seated on a chair slightly to the side and behind the mike.

At which point she stepped into the light. *Radiant*. She had changed into a dark blue sequined dress that seemed custom-designed to display her figure, which didn't actually need a lot of help. The dress was cut low in front, and very low in back. Her shoulders were bare.

She waited until the loose table conversations dwindled and went quiet. Then she motioned to her guitarist, who began picking a beautiful melody, with the kind of crooked arpeggios fado players favor.

Carolina's voice, ascending, descending, trembling with emotion, stoked by love, infused with saudade. Dusky in the low register, crystal clear in the high. She explored every color from scarlet to blue to black. Taz could only catch some of the words—his Portuguese—to the extent it existed at all, was quite primitive. Still, he thought he caught some of the song's essence. It was about love, the pains of love.

All the women in the crowd, and a number of men, stood for the applause that followed. Taz clapped and, under his breath, to no one in particular, said "have mercy," the traditional jazz compliment for an intense solo. Carolina turned her back and seemed to be deep in conversation with her bass player, then with her guitarist.

When she turned back around, she was looking directly at him. Her accompanists started a tune that he didn't recognize. It didn't sound like a typical fado. For good reason—it was the melody of a Joni Mitchell tune. He didn't recognize it until she got to the bridge. *"I could drink a case of you, and still be on my feet."* Later, he couldn't remember what came before, or what came after.

She sang two sambas for her finale. The audience sang along. Then they gave her a standing ovation. Taz stood with all of them and applauded for a long, long time. He sat to tear the foil on the champagne, check the ice in the bucket, and remove the cork.

"The pop of a champagne cork is one of my favorite things in life." She was standing just to his left, looking at the chair across the small round table. "May I?"

Taz patted the chair and smiled, held the cork tight and twisted the bottle ever so slightly. Just enough to start the inexorable push of the cork as it sought to escape the pressure from the ever-releasing bubbles.

He offered a toast. "To the most charming of all fado singers."

She took a long sip. "It's fabulous."

"Anything else would have been beneath you."

"Stop. You really don't have to—what's the phrase? *Butter me up,* Taz. I'm already there. And, as long as it won't tie you up in guilt, I'd prefer not to be alone tonight."

He wrapped a napkin around the neck of the nearly full bottle and drew it from the ice, doing his best to conceal his emotional turmoil. Nodded and motioned for her to lead the way. "Glad to wait if you want to change."

"I think I'll change back at the flat, if it's all the same to you." He paid the tab, left a high-end tip. Offered his arm to help her. They left the theater in silence. Taz scanned the street, but the sordid spectacle he had seen before the show seemed to have disappeared. They walked a couple of blocks into a slightly more presentable neighborhood, and then up two flights of ornate stairs to her flat. Taz realized he may have had one too many drinks, but there was no repairing that now.

She unlocked the heavy mahogany door. Flicked on the light, decided better. Instead she lit a lamp in the large room off the kitchen. Taz didn't know whether to think of it as a parlor, a music room, or a den. It didn't matter. The minimal décor was perfect—a concert poster on one wall, an abstract painting on the opposite, and a rough-woven Quechua throw rug on the floor.

She had disappeared into what he assumed was a bedroom. Her voice clear: "The glasses are in the little rolling cabinet next to the stereo." Which was not hard to locate. He found two flutes—they looked like pilsner glasses, but so what? The flat was clearly a high-end rental, and the beer flutes would do the job.

He was pouring when he felt her presence. He hadn't heard her at all. She stood just this side of the threshold of the candlelit room behind her. That was enough. But that was not by any means all. She was wearing a diaphanous rose-colored robe, almost a kimono, tied by a light blue belt. If anything, she was more stunning than he had imagined. He brought the champagne glasses, gave her one, kissed her lightly on the cheek, trained his eyes on hers and lifted his glass in a toast. They spoke the words at the same time, each in their own language. *"Saúde,"* and, "To you."

Afterwards, as he fanned her while they were lying on their backs side by side, she told him that she hadn't been with a man in the eighteen months since her husband died. "Carlito was a wonderful man, Taz. You would have liked him. I loved him just as you love Lucia—what did you call her—'the heart of your heart.' I'm sure she is wonderful as well, or she wouldn't have a man like you head over heels."

Even through the fires ahead, the memory of that long night made him smile. The sheer joy of it. Her hesitancy at their first touch, then her glow, her surprised laughter, and her sighs as they made love. At the same time, the sense that the breaths they exchanged were suffused by absent partners, which made the hours bittersweet. As they returned to earth the second time, they stayed entangled in each other's arms, watching each other's eyes, and smiling, until they finally rolled onto their backs. Then Carolina turned away and wept, and Taz knew it was for Carlito, because he was thinking of Lucia, wondering where she was now, how she was feeling, why she allowed herself to be frightened by love's risk. Carolina turned back and reached to lay her hand on his shoulder. Finally, Taz let the darkness and Carolina's steady breathing settle over him.

He drifted to a light sleep, then returned to the surface of awareness as he felt her hand moving gently over his chest and down his side to his hip. They continued to explore the desire that somehow embodied their sorrows until Carolina cried out and the approaching dawn brought them back to earth. Taz dressed while Carolina watched sleepily, opened and closed the door as softly as he could, and made his way back to his own room to get his bags and check out.

*

Carolina was already at the airport hangar when he arrived. She was wearing a simple white top and khaki pants. She stepped his way, kissed his cheek for a long, slow moment, and then pointed to the scale. There was some miscellaneous baggage there already. He added his backpack to the pile. The ritual was familiar from his days with the bush pilots in the Alaskan north.

He stepped on the scale, winced just a little, and then put his bag on to weigh that as well. She attached a cream-colored tag that specified the bag as weighing twenty kilos. That was to make the pilot's job easier when he had to balance the load. Taz figured the pilot must be running late. Carolina decided it was time to load.

"Why don't you take the pile to the left of the scale, and pack it in the back on the left side." She started on the right-side pile. When they were done, she just said, "Thanks. If you have to visit the bathroom, this would be a time."

Taz reckoned he had never experienced a morning-after remotely like this. Carolina motioned him to the copilot's seat, made sure he understood the fairly complex seat and shoulder belt arrangement. Then, as he looked on in ever-growing fascination, she climbed into the pilot's seat. Dusted her dashboard, flicked a few switches, found her air control channel. Told him where to find the headphones, donned her own.

She flicked a few more switches. It was a single-engine plane. The propeller started slowly, becoming a blur as she taxied out of the hangar and onto the tarmac. Then, looking at the windsocks, which were alarmingly limp, she spoke into her mic.

"There's no wind direction. Let's flip a coin." Taz should have been unnerved. Instead, he felt a growing confidence. Carolina was talking back and forth, probably with an air controller. He went silent until they lifted off. They took off to the east, circled to the north, and then, as they gained altitude, turned south towards Cruzeiro do Sul.

In the immediate area surrounding Iquitos, maybe fifteen miles in any direction, the forest was badly cut up. In some places by soybean fields, in others by burning. Patches of forest remained, sometimes big ones, rectangular sections as much as a mile or two on the long sides. Taz had learned from Everton that this pattern was the result of a decree that required landholders to keep twenty-five percent of their property in standing forest. Unfortunately, despite the effort to conserve them, these residual tracts, cut off from the main forest, would act as islands, gradually losing biodiversity until they became nearly as impoverished as the fields around them.

Just as the depressing reality of the ongoing destruction of the world's greatest forest was setting in, they left the development zone. Soon they were flying over unobstructed forest as far as Taz could see. Occasionally, he caught the sharp glint of the sun, reflected by water. They were over part of the *varzea*, the flooded forest favored by tambaqui, caymans, and giant otters. The northern reaches of the Vale do Javari.

They had been flying for an hour and a half, more or less. It took another hour to reach the radio perimeter of the Cruzeiro tower. Carolina had already started the obligatory conversation with ground control. When that ended, she reached towards him and touched his cheek, very gently, with the back of her right hand. Smiled.

They touched down and rolled to a stop in front of the little Quonset hut that served as a hangar. Carolina jumped down, motioned to Taz to help her pull the gas cart over, and began refilling her tanks. Once she had the hose fixed to the tank, Taz shouldered his kit bag and stood to the side, admiring her extreme efficiency as she completed refueling and ran through her inspection checklist.

When she was finished, she turned towards him, walked over, and put both her hands in his. He looked her over, head to toe. "I thought it took angels to sing fado. I've ridden with a lot of bush pilots in the Arctic, and none of them are angels. It didn't occur to me that a bush pilot might sing fado better than an angel."

Carolina blushed, momentarily at a loss for words. "Stop, Taz. You're going to make me cry."

"So, where are you headed after Cruzeiro?"

"To Minas Gerais, down to Belo Horizonte, and then back to São Paulo."

Taz dropped his bag, pulled Carolina in closer. "When do you get back to São Paulo?"

"I've only got one gig, for two nights. I have to be there on the fifth. My plane to Lisbon leaves three days later." Taz's day had just brightened considerably. It must have shown. "Don't tell me!"

"My flight to DC is scheduled for the ninth. I have to spend a couple of days at the consulate debriefing and drafting a cable for the home office. Unless I'm caught at the fire, we should overlap by at least that long."

She caressed the back of his neck. Gradually pulled him towards her and oh so gently kissed his lips. "Taz, every day I will imagine our time together in São Paulo. Please don't let the fire keep you."

CHAPTER THIRTY-TWO

The Wisdom of Socrates

THE TERMINAL OF CRUZEIRO DO Sul's airport was a rusted steel Quonset hut far too large for its usual everyday traffic. Jessica and Everton had flown in to meet Taz and the team. State's dispatchers had routed Sylvia through Leticia. The four of them were standing in a little group, drinking strong Brazilian coffee, waiting for Lucky.

The sound of buzzing cells. The first call was for Jessica. She listened for a second, furrowed her brow, and turned away to talk in private.

Within seconds, Everton had pulled his phone from his vest pocket and begun reviewing a text. He looked directly at Taz, smiled, and rolled his eyes as if he were an actor in a Yiddish theater.

Jessica returned, visibly crestfallen. She was being called back for an urgent consultation with the secretary. Taz guessed it was the developing refugee crisis in the Horn of Africa. But there were a dozen other issues that could have required her attention. Sylvia had just arrived the night before. Jessica straightened up, looked at the other three. "Call from the boss. Have to go." Jessica kissed Sylvia on the cheek.

Everton took her arm to tell her how much he had appreciated her visit. He regretted the unfortunate interruption of their discussions, but he also understood. After all, she had global responsibilities. They would see each other in Nairobi in less than a month. She smiled through her tears. Everton knew full well the tears weren't for him. He offered to take Jessica to Brasilia so she could catch a plane to DC. Taz watched the pantomime with real admiration. Everton turned to him and Sylvia. With the utmost courtesy and concern: "I'm afraid that I, too, must depart. It appears I am needed in Brasilia." He and Jessica walked across the tarmac and boarded a private jet. An officer from some very well-dressed branch of the Brazilian military escorted them.

Taz and Sylvia stood looking at each other. Her eyebrows went up. He laughed. She was in shock. He brushed a strand of hair out of her eyes. "I've got to wait up for Lucky. If you'd like to share a couple of caipirinhas, I imagine I'd enjoy my wait a good deal more."

"Well, why not?"

There was no bar in the dusty little terminal. Taz slipped outside and waved in the direction of one of the hacks idling by their cars in the morning heat. After some prodding in a bizarre combination of English and Portuguese, the cabbie dropped them off at a little ochre clapboard house just on the north bank of the Juruá.

Behind the house, the river was wide and muddy. Taz and Sylvia ducked in through the door frame—there was no door—and found themselves in a spacious room lit by two small windows, with an old wood and brass bar on the right side. Taz had a floating sensation, realized they were on a houseboat. It was well secured to the bank, but he still enjoyed the motion, as Bruce Hornsby or Jerry Garcia would sing it, of the "Black Muddy River."

The bartender was a slender woman, maybe in her forties. He caught her gaze and asked for two caipirinhas. Very gently, she pointed him towards an acceptable table.

It was only three in the afternoon. They had just finished their second round when Taz's phone buzzed. Lucky had just touched down, and he had brought one of the bombeiros with him.

Taz queried their hostess in the best pidgin Portuguese he could muster, and obtained, after several tries, the name of the place.

The two of them arrived a half hour later. Lucky, tall, a trifle scraggly, but unusually presentable: a blue work shirt with the sleeves rolled up, and khakis, looking none the worse for wear.

The bombeiro ducked through the door frame just behind him. Sylvia drew in her breath. He was half a head taller than Lucky, lanky as a college basketball player, with curly hair and a smile that would light up a wine cellar.

Taz motioned them over. By then, there were a few other customers scattered around the room. Taz got up to greet them. Lucky gave him a Wyoming hug—quick, with a back slap. The bombeiro looked Taz over and offered a warm handshake. No show of strength. Taz ordered another round of caipirinhas. They toasted before anything at all was said.

Lucky. "Glad to see you two. Meet my friend Socrates." Sylvia couldn't take her eyes off him.

For that matter, neither could Taz. "So, are you named after the Greek philosopher? Or after your father?"

Socrates' smile became wider and warmer. "You know my father?"

"I've never met him. But I have watched tapes of his playing days, and you look a lot like him. That was the team with Zico and Rivellino, as I remember. Poetry in motion."

Socrates leaned back in his chair and offered half a toast to Taz, who raised the other half. Sylvia and Lucky were nonplussed by the whole exchange. Taz looked at Lucky. "He didn't tell you? Your new friend's father was one of the great heroes of Brazilian soccer—an attacking midfielder who ended with—what, sixty caps? And two World Cups."

Socrates said, "I didn't think yanquis paid attention to any game that could be played without helmets and shoulder pads." Sylvia and Lucky were trying hard not laugh.

"I was too light to be able to play our kind of football." Taz, an inch short of six feet, weighed in at just above one hundred and ninety pounds. The discord between his words and this fact spurred more laughter. "So, I played your kind. In college. Not well, by your standards. But enough to learn a little of the game. And destroy my knees."

"I should look at them at some point."

"So, are you a doctor, too?"

"Like father, like son."

Lucky exclaimed, "You didn't tell me that! I thought we were friends."

"We are. But I couldn't tell you everything in three conversations. It would have been so boring."

After he retired from international play and finished his stellar career with Corinthians and Santos, two of Brazil's most famous clubs, Socrates' father had returned to his medical vocation, and ended up tending to the poor and the indigenous in the region around Leticia—Amazonas—and scattered ranchers and dirt farmers who couldn't travel to a city just for an annual checkup. He became a local legend, particularly among the Guarani, whose tallest chief could, if he stood on tiptoe, barely lay a hand on his shoulder.

Socrates turned to Taz. "Where did you play?"

"High school, then two years for Stanford."

"Stanford is a great university."

"But not exactly a soccer power, at least in my day. San José State used to beat us like a drum. Anyway, that's when I did in my knees."

"Yes, Americans think soccer is not a contact sport. But we know differently." A lazy wink at Taz, with just enough left over to share with Sylvia, now relaxed into her chair, but still intently following the conversation.

Taz couldn't entirely suppress his curiosity. "So, they say your father smoked four packs a day, even when he was playing at his peak."

"I'm afraid it's true. He was something of a medical miracle. And that's not all he smoked."

Time for Taz's eyebrows to go up.

"Not just marijuana. Also, more esoteric medicines. He became close friends with a local Kanamari shaman."

Taz thought they'd better order some food. Socrates talked to the woman who ran the place. She brought them four bowls of a cream-colored broth surrounding small mountains of the firmest, whitest fish Taz had ever tasted.

Except that it wasn't fish. It had the texture of just-boiled shrimp. Taz realized it was a caiman, caught by hook or net and wrestled, probably by a local boy, just for a little pocket money.

"This is at least as good as the best lobster stew in Maine."

"A high compliment."

Taz couldn't remember, later, which one of them had thrown out the challenge. But soon, they were comparing notes on great seafood soups and, more importantly, on great experiences associated with procuring the ingredients for great seafood soups.

Sylvia had grown up on the central California coast. She remembered the days when, if you knew what you were doing, you could skin-dive for fresh abalone. In order to prevent overexploitation and, as Sylvia pointed out, to make the contest just a little more even, the state prohibited abalone divers from using scuba gear. So, you held your breath and took a screwdriver to pry the muscle off whatever rock it had stuck itself to. You had to move fast—and the suckers were stuck hard, so it took serious leverage. If you came away with an abalone, you brought it back to a friend's house, cut the muscle out of the shell, and then pounded the muscle steak with a mallet until, sufficiently softened and sliced Spanish-ham thin, it was miraculously transformed into one of the great seafood tastes of all time.

Socrates looked at her with new interest. "So, Ms. Sylvia, how long can you hold your breath underwater?"

She flashed him a sweet smile: "Long enough to bring up dinner when I needed to. . . okay, a little less than two minutes." She blushed. Socrates went back to his lazy smile.

Taz played in with a story about how shad avoid polluted rivers to spawn in clean ones, how good their roe is, how tasty the fish, how their bones crisscross, making them almost impossible to filet, and how the locals plank them—cook them on hot wood.

Lucky was from the Bitterroot Valley in Montana. The only fish on the menu was brown trout. But, by God, that was pretty damn good, especially fried for breakfast. Shellfish, though? Not so much. He recalled the day that Northwest Air first flew oysters into Billings. All on ice, of course. The funny thing was, when most folks in Billings heard the word oyster, they thought of the Rocky Mountain kind.

They spent a good part of the afternoon exploring these and other critical topics: alligator wrestling, catching suckers by hand, noodling catfish, bow-hunting for howler monkeys—well, that was only Socrates.

Lucky had to leave to be present at the first meeting of the Boise team and the local bombeiros. They were to train together for a day and then helicopter into the fire line. Socrates sat up, looked at Taz, then at Sylvia, then back. Suggested that they spend the open day exploring the forest outside Porto Velho. Looking at Taz, he said, "I think there's someone you should meet."

That sounded a lot better than hanging around a cinderblock airport terminal waiting for his cell phone to ring. Sylvia was ready to do anything at all, as long as it involved Socrates. Better if he wasn't required to be fully clothed.

CHAPTER THIRTY-THREE

Sylvia Learns to Love Helicopters

EARLY MORNING. HEAT. TAZ'S PILLOW was soaked. The window unit rattled and wheezed under the strain. His cell buzzed and he put the phone to his ear. Within seconds, the phone was slick with sweat. Everton's voice came through softly but clearly.

"Taz, I've been taken off fire duty, at least for now. I apologize, my friend. I've been directed to take charge of a negotiation with our neighbor to the south regarding joint management of the *Cataratas do Iguaçu*." The world's biggest waterfall system. The falls divided the Upper Iguaçu from the Lower, and thereby defined the boundary between Brazil and its prickly southern neighbor.

"I understand. But let me ask a favor. Can I use your name when I need introductions to some of your provincial colleagues?"

"Certainly. I believe they'll do their best to be helpful. But I have new information that may bear on your plans. Our satellite data shows the Javari fire is rapidly moving to the northwest towards the Peruvian border. That is one of the areas I talked to you about when were together in Sao Paulo. We're mobilizing another group of bombeiros to join you, but it will take four or five days to get them into place. Some of them will be from an operational unit of the army's elite force. My government has asked that you not proceed to the new fire zone without your full complement."

"But what about the existing fire?"

"Wind conditions have been helpful, and we believe that older part of the fire is largely burnt out. Starving for lack of fuel, as they say. The governor has mobilized several brigades of ranchers and *macheitaros* to suppress the remaining fires, but they aren't trained or equipped for the expanding fire front—that will have to wait for you."

An hour later, Taz found Sylvia in the lobby of their little residential hotel. Over coffee he told her, briefly, what Everton had told him. "They've told me to wait here for the boys and a second contingent of bombeiros. Even if we get into the fire in the next couple of days, I'll be lucky to leave for Sao Paulo before the end of the week. You?"

"I don't know, I'll check. Jessica's office made the arrangements."

They agreed to meet for lunch. Taz had found a little café that served good fish and steak. Taz arrived first, ordered two caipirinhas. He was reading the biography of Alexander Humboldt, the great natural scientist who pioneered the early exploration of the Amazon basin. Sylvia showed up wearing a light summer dress that set her off rather well.

"So, I have the same problem. Flight from Belém on the twelfth." It was the seventh of April. "And since State bought it, I can't change it."

"Well, we could swelter here, or maybe we should do some exploring."

"Oh God. Jessica will kill me."

"How about if I guarantee you that I'll be a complete gentleman?"

"You can keep that pledge?"

"Well, I'm not saying it will be easy."

Smiling. "Good. I hate to think that I'm past attracting men's attention."

Taz knew full well who she had in mind, and it wasn't him. "Not to worry."

Just as they were finishing their soup, Socrates ducked his head through the open door. Sylvia smiled and, working under the table, pulled her top down to expose just a little more cleavage.

Socrates was delighted to hear that they were going to stay a few days. He had a few ideas about what they might do. "It's strange, Lucky also had to leave. Apparently, there are severe fires in northern California, up near Mount Shasta. Seems early in the year for that, don't you think?" Taz nodded, relieved that Lucia was at the other end of the state.

"I don't suppose you'd like to see the medical clinic where my father worked? I've arranged to drop by to see what supplies they need."

"How do we get there?"

"Helicopter. I've already chartered it. It's only a hundred and sixty miles, so about an hour and a half."

Sylvia asked, "What's it like there?"

"Extraordinarily beautiful. Unbroken forest and free-flowing rivers just out of the high Andes."

Sylvia exclaimed, "Count me in . . . yes!" Taz smiled and nodded in Socrates's direction.

"Good. The helicopter leaves in two hours. Be at the airport, but not the terminal side. Across the tarmac where they have the private plane hangars."

Taz was the first one to the hangar. Sylvia came lugging an oversize roller suitcase. Taz couldn't help himself. He took one look and laughed. Sylvia scowled, and he walked over to help.

"Well, I didn't know I was going to a fucking frontier town."

"And not only that. With a fucking frontier copter company. They'll weigh everything, including you and me. If we're overweight, we're not going. We've got an hour and a half. Let's go to town and see if we can find you a pack."

When they returned to the airport, Sylvia was wearing sneakers and sporting a new canvas backpack. They ditched the suitcase in the helicopter hangar. Socrates looked on with a kind of casual attentiveness.

CHAPTER THIRTY-FOUR

Loggers and Jaguars

THE MEDICAL CLINIC WAS AS far from the hospital in Taz's imagination as it could possibly be—a series of cabanas and some larger thatched-roof buildings high on a thirty-foot bluff above the south bank of the Purus. The river here had lots of eddies and occasional riffles and rapids. Muddy too, except where small tributaries from either side contributed the acidic blackwater that, seven hundred miles north, justified the name of the great Rio Negro, which comes from similar rocky soils in the Venezuelan highlands and joins the Amazon just upriver from Manaus.

Socrates introduced them to the medical superintendent, a doctor from Belo Horizonte named Joao Rocha. He had dedicated his life to helping the remaining Amazon tribes resist the diseases they would never have encountered were it not for their Portuguese overlords. They made the rounds. It didn't take too long. There were only about thirty patients, most recovering from typical tropical infirmities: parasites, dengue, malaria. A few, including three lepers, had more exotic complaints. All seemed happy to be there.

As they were leaving, the superintendent got a call on his cell. He rounded towards Socrates and spoke in low, hurried tones. Socrates motioned for Taz to join them.

"There's some trouble between the Txai and the illegal loggers who operate in the Hi-Merimā Reserve. We need to get out there as soon as possible."

Taz asked, "How far is it?"

"About two hundred miles."

"So, you'll be taking the helicopter."

"We must. I'm taking Joao. He knows the local dialect better than I do. You could join us."

"And Sylvia? We can't leave her here by herself."

"Okay, but you'll have to be the hand holder."

Taz gave Sylvia the gist of the discussion. Rocha thought it might be dangerous and offered to arrange a flight to Cruzeiro for both of them with one of the hospital's regular resupply planes. She gave Taz a dispirited look.

"You're not going back, are you." Taz shook his head. "That means Socrates needs help. Well, I'll find a way to help too."

So, they ducked the dust, the air blast, and the whirring blades. Threw their gear into the back, climbed into the cab. The pilot motioned for Sylvia to sit right side, second row. Taz climbed into the left-side seat. Socrates rode shotgun.

They flew over continuous forest to the Xapuri upriver from Rio Branco, then to the Rio Madre de Dios—the River of the Mother of God. Then finally to the juncture of the Madre de Dios and the Acre at Boco do Acre, a little river town with fewer than a thousand inhabitants.

An old Toyota Land Cruiser was waiting for them there. It looked like it had been on the losing side of a firefight someplace in the African bush. They took a logging road into the indigenous reserve. The reserve had been surveyed and demarcated but, as was all too common in Brazil, not protected. They passed several muddy tracks where large trees had been dragged to the trucks. The only village along the road appeared to have been abandoned for some time. They passed two disused logging camps. What was left of the dirt track disappeared at the third. They decided that Rocha should return with the driver and give the authorities their location, in case of trouble. Then they headed south on foot, a four-hour walk.

When they got to the next village, everything seemed in order, except there was nobody there. Taz stuck his finger into the ashes of the communal cooking fire. It was still warm. "They haven't been gone long. At most, a few hours."

Socrates said, "The next village is three hours away. Or, you two could stay here, and we'll pick you up on the way back."

Taz: "I think it's better if we go with you."

Socrates turned and strode back into the forest. They walked for about an hour along a winding path through an understory of ferns, trying to avoid tripping on the roots of tangled vines and strangler figs. Then through an area where the water came up to their calves, and finally to a small river. They scrambled along the bank, and after a few minutes found a place to cross. Two hours later, they forded a second, broader stream. Fortunately, it was shallow, with a sand and pebble bed, and led to a series of little waterfalls. They descended to the lower level of the falls on the opposite bank. There they found the smoking ruins of the next village.

Taz counted six huts, all burned to the ground, ashes still smoldering. Then he heard what sounded like sniffling. He walked around the village perimeter until he found a little trail into the bush. Not far down the trail, a small boy sat on his haunches, quietly crying. He looked fearfully at Taz when he reached for his hand. Taz tried to reassure him. "Everything's going to be all right." He knew enough not to try and pick him up. The poor kid was already terrified. Taz held the boy's hand gently and encouraged him back to the village. Socrates and Sylvia were waiting there. Sylvia immediately gathered the little boy in her arms and began making cooing noises.

Socrates gathered them together. "The only other village I know is about a four-hour walk, or, if we can find a boat, two hours downriver. That must be where they've gone. Sylvia, would you be willing to bring the child? He'll trust you, and his parents might be there." Sylvia nodded.

After some searching, they found a dugout hidden in the trees a few hundred yards downriver, where the floodwaters obscured the bank.

There were two rough paddles hidden just above the landing place. They clambered in and floated out into the stream.

Socrates took the stern, Taz the bow. Sylvia and the boy sat in the middle. The little one had climbed into her lap before they had gone a mile. They arrived maybe ninety minutes later at a makeshift dock, hearing voices on the bank above. As they mounted the low bank, they saw the women of the village running from hut to hut, hurriedly packing. The men were in several groups, trying and stringing their bows, and dipping their arrows in what Taz assumed was curare. An old man with an elaborate headdress made from leather and macaw feathers leaned on a long staff and observed the scene. He looked towards Socrates and Taz and spoke in rough Portuguese.

"They are afraid. They will make war. I'm sorry to greet you in such a way."

Socrates walked to where the old man was standing, put his knuckle to his forehead, introduced himself and humbly asked the old man's name. "I am Salvador Chindoy." The man smiled as he surveyed his unexpected visitors. Socrates spoke to him, first in Portuguese, then in Guarani. He gestured to Taz, who introduced himself, copying Socrates' gesture of respect. "I am Taz Blackwell."

Socrates explained that they'd come a long way, had seen the empty villages, and that they hoped they could help. The old man spoke to him at some length, again in Guarani.

Socrates turned to Taz and Sylvia. "It seems that when the loggers burned the last village, they kidnapped a twelve-year-old girl. The men have been insulted, and they're determined to get her back."

Taz recalled his conversation with Everton at Tia's. "The loggers will be armed. There must be something we can do to prevent a slaughter."

Socrates was pulling a SAT phone out of his pack. "I'm going to call FUNAI and see if they have anyone who can get here fast. The Indigenous agency in Acre . . . they have a station there." He walked to the edge of the bluff so he could speak freely.

Meanwhile, Sylvia had joined the women and was helping to load various leaf-wrapped packages on the kind of sledges that could be pulled by a woman with a head strap. Taz and Socrates watched for a while. She was pretty handy. The Txai women were affectionate, touching her hair while casting occasional anxious glances at their men.

Socrates returned, frowning. "They say there's nothing they can do, and the local militias will line up with the loggers. We'll have to try and stop the men ourselves."

Salvador said, "If you try to stop them now, they will kill you with the arrows they carry to kill the loggers."

Taz thought for a moment and turned to Socrates. "There is someone who could help if we can reach him. Can you help me find a number for the Environment Ministry in Brasilia? Tell them I need to talk to the minister."

Socrates took a step back. "You know our minister?"

He did. The minister's name was José Lutzenberger. Taz had negotiated a bilateral cooperation agreement with him earlier in both their careers, when Lutzenberger's title was still *Secretario Especial del Medio Ambiente*. Socrates looked his way. There was no time for explanations. He just nodded.

"Well, they do have a presence in the region, at least. Better make the call." He dredged in his pack and pulled out a SAT phone. It took him a couple of minutes to make the connection and work his way through a series of operators, and then he handed it to Taz. A moment later, José's voice came on the phone:

"Taz. My friend. It's been . . . what? Four years. To what do I owe the honor?"

"José, I'm not sure this is the kind of honor you deserve." He told him about the problem in as few words as possible.

"Let me get my chief of staff in here and we'll see what we can do." Taz thanked him. All they could do now was wait for his return call.

Meanwhile, the men had finished preparing their weapons and had started to dance, in a circle, facing along the perimeter, each warrior with a hand on the back of the warrior in front. Their chant was blood curdling.

They'd be up against guns. Socrates said, "I better talk to Salvador. Maybe I can persuade him to stop them."

Just then, the SAT phone buzzed. It was Minister Lutzenberger's chief of staff, Braulio Teixara. "Mr. Blackwell, the secretary asked me to call you and let you know that we are prepared to dispatch a team of five enforcement agents at dawn tomorrow."

"That will be very helpful. You have my gratitude. Will they be armed?"

"They will."

"Please give the minister my warmest thanks. I won't forget your kindness." Plural, intending Lutzenberger, but also wanting to convey his gratitude to Teixara.

The men were getting ready to leave. In less than two hours, the sun would go down. Dusk in the tropics is a matter of a very few minutes. Socrates spoke to the old man to see if there was any way they could be convinced to wait until morning. He shook his head. "What must be, must be."

Taz asked, "Where are the IBAMA special forces?"

"They're back in Porto Velho. Only an hour away by helicopter."

"Our friends in Brasilia say they'll be here in the morning."

"The men will run all night if they have to so they can attack before dawn. Morning might be too late."

The old man continued to watch them.

Taz pointed in the direction the men had taken. "Still, if Jose's enforcement team can get here early tomorrow, the main thing is to make sure the clash doesn't happen before they arrive. Do we have any idea where the loggers are?"

"Let's see if Salvador will tell us. Shamans often surprise you." Socrates spoke with the medicine man in Guarani for almost a minute then turned to Taz. "As of two days ago, the loggers were at a makeshift river camp about twelve miles downstream. It would take the warriors at least six hours to reach the camp on foot."

Taz said to Socrates, "Let's take the dugout."

"Good. As long as there are no barriers on the river, we should be able to get there in less than half the time it will take the men."

Fortunately, it wasn't cloudy. At first the dark seemed almost total, but then the rising moon gave the river's surface a soft illumination. It was off full, but not by much. By the second hour, they had silver light to paddle by, enough to cast a clear shadow. Taz took the bow, kneeling on the bare wood of the hull. Socrates settled in the stern, where most of the steering would be done.

They passed through some riffles, then a quiet pool that stretched for more than a mile. In the quiet, Taz whispered, "When we get there, announce me with as much formality as you can muster. I'm going to try and bluff them."

"What's your title? I forget."

"Hell of a herald you'd make."

"Okay, okay."

"I am Eustace Blackwell, The United States State Department deputy secretary for Environment and Development. We need to make it sound as official as possible."

"You know, Taz, these loggers are country boys. Tough. 'Rough and tumble,' as you Americans say. They'll be hard to bluff."

"Do you have a pistol?"

"Of course."

"Okay, keep it close. Just in case things get hinky. Somebody's paying for the logs they take out. A company or a broker. That's who we need to bluff."

They heard only the burbling of the river and the occasional call of a night bird, sounds that were part of a much larger silence. Soon enough, they saw the light of a campfire not far downstream, on the west side of the river. The bluffs were only six feet above the river. They pulled the dugout onto the bank about a hundred yards above the camp. Walked slowly down the riverbank until they were right below the campfire. They could hear men talking. Taz pulled himself up just enough to peek over the bank. There were four of them, passing a bottle of cachaça around the fire. The girl was sitting cross-legged a little bit away. Her hands were tied behind her back.

As they had planned, Socrates was the first to interrupt the loggers' campfire. He appeared in the firelight as a figure from Giacometti. *Or,* Taz thought, *an NBA point guard.* Taz followed close behind. The men looked up, befuddled. The nearest spilled his coffee as he was turning towards them. He struggled to get up, sputtered and asked Socrates a question in Portuguese. His tone was vaguely threatening. Socrates laughed, took a step closer, using body language to make clear he meant no trouble. Meanwhile, Taz walked over to the girl and shushed her gently when she started to whimper. Used his pocketknife to cut her bonds. Took her by the hand and started back towards the dugout.

Now two of the remaining poachers were struggling to stand. Taz had a sense of their uncertainty, their predicament, caught between the desire to fight and the urge to flee. The nearest one was shouting at Taz in slurred Portuguese. Socrates kept talking to them. The remaining two looked edgy but made no move. Taz put his hand on the girl's shoulder and paused, to avoid riling the situation further.

He heard Socrates speak his name. Socrates was using his height to his advantage. Got close, smiled down on the two angry loggers. The tallest barely came up to his chin. At long last, a fifth man emerged from a tent on the other side, away from the fire. The tent's front flap was adorned with some kind of company seal. The man's ratted tan shirt had the same seal on the left-side pocket.

Taz fixed his attention on him. He continued watching him while he walked towards the fire and put the girl's small hand in Socrates's very large one. The logger who had yelled at Taz muttered under his breath. The two hatchet men reached for their pistols, slowly and uncertainly.

Taz walked around the fire to stand toe to toe with the man he took to be the logging boss.

"¿Dirigente, sim?"

"*Sim, eu estoy.*"

Socrates set the trap. In loud enough Portuguese for everyone to hear, he told the *dirigente* that they had not yet committed a serious crime, but if they hurt the girl, or took any action against their friends from upriver, the IBAMA special forces would kill them all at first light. Then he told the dirigente who Taz was. It sounded even more official in Portuguese than in English.

Taz turned to the dirigente. "I want to speak to the man who pays you. Give me his name and put him on your cell phone." Socrates translated.

The dirigente stuttered and looked wildly around, as if the very thought of calling his boss filled him with fear. *Good,* Taz thought. Socrates said a few more words. The dirigente nodded, gave Socrates some numbers. Socrates punched them in, waited a few seconds, and started talking. "Taz, he speaks *inglês.*"

Yes, Taz thought, *I bet he does.* He reached for the phone. "Who am I talking to?" The connection was not great, but he thought he heard the name "Gabriel de Souza." He put his hand over the mike. To Socrates. "What's the name of the company?"

"Fontana Timber."

Taz had already had one run-in with Fontana, at a conference of the Convention on International Trade in Endangered Species. The meeting had been held in Harare, Zimbabwe. The European Union wanted a declaration that mahogany was endangered, which would essentially have ended legal international trade in the species. The Brazilian delegation opposed the listing on the grounds that while mahogany might be commercially endangered in other countries it was not in Brazil. Fontana had led the business coalition effort to block the listing. The EU motion was headed for failure. Taz had talked to the head of the Brazilian delegation and gotten agreement to list the species as threatened, which wouldn't prohibit commercial trade but would at least require proof of legal harvest and a CITES export permit. The EU was ready to accept the deal when Brazil's team received new instructions, turned on a dime and walked away from their agreement. The rumors at the time were that someone high up in the Brazilian Ministry of Justice had been bribed to engineer the result. Everton had told Taz later that the effort to find out who was involved had been conducted in the traditional Brazilian manner, with little in the way of diligence and an overabundance of relaxation.

"Well, Gabriel, you're Fontana's top man here, is that right?" They'd have their most senior VP where the best commercial timber could be taken out, and the border of Peru and Brazil fit the bill perfectly.

"Gabriel, my name is Eustace Blackwell. The deputy assistant secretary for Environment and Development at the US State Department . . . Are you still there, Gabriel?" On hearing a mumbled yes, Taz went on. "Gabriel, I'd appreciate it if you'd do me a favor. I'd like you to call your CEO—it's Frank Chapman, isn't it? —well, I'd like you to call Frank, and tell him that one of your illegal logging crews has kidnapped an twelve-year-old girl from the Txai Indigenous Reserve. Tell him they also burned two Txai villages to the ground."

Gabriel de Souza had regained his breath. "That's not possible. We would never do that. We have very good relations—"

Taz cut him off. "Drop it, Gabriel. I'm standing in your men's logging camp. I've got the girl, and I'm taking her back to her village. If anybody interferes, I'll be making more calls in the morning. In the meantime, tell Frank that this whole operation stops tonight. If it doesn't, I will have him testifying under oath before a congressional committee within two weeks. After that, we will revoke all his import permits and bill him for all the illegal mahogany he's ever imported into the United States. Gabriel— tell him now. And tell your logging boss to pack his stuff up and head downriver. Do you understand?"

Gabriel choked out the words. "*Sim, compreendo.*"

Taz handed the phone to the dirigente. The diregente listened for a moment, rang off. Turned to the men around the fire and issued instructions in a somewhat strangled voice. They started dismantling the tents.

To Socrates, Taz said, "Tell him we'll need to borrow one of their motor skiffs. And let's take their firearms." There were two skiffs tied up just downriver from the camp. They selected the skiff with the driest bottom. Socrates sat the girl on the middle bench and gave her a blanket he had taken from one of the tents.

Meanwhile, the pace of dismantling the camp seemed to have slowed. Socrates barked an order to the assembled loggers. They returned to work with a new intensity.

Taz pushed them off once the motor started coughing and Socrates was safely ensconced with his hand on the tiller. They motored slowly upstream. Kept to the side of the river, away from the center current. Still, it took three hours.

Once his breathing had slowed down sufficiently to allow him to utter a complete sentence, Taz called back to Socrates. "So, what did you tell them?"

"That if they took more than an hour to clear out, they'd all be killed by poison arrows."

"That'd definitely do it." Taz laughed, for the first time that day. They continued paddling upriver as the moon came out from behind the clouds. They reached the village just after midnight and crept into their tents to sleep.

*

Taz woke up early enough to watch as the warriors returned to the village in the morning, desolate and empty handed. They were clearly startled to see the girl who had been kidnapped sitting in the middle of a circle of women and girls, regaling them with stories about her captivity. She had apparently bit one of the loggers so hard she drew blood. Sylvia told Taz later that she was named *Kauwané*—hawk-eagle.

Socrates and Sylvia were just getting up. They emerged sequentially from Sylvia's tent. Came to sit at the campfire and sip hot coffee. Socrates crouched on his toes, like a football player stretching his lower back. Considered the situation with great gravity. Sylvia held her cup with both hands, somewhat impishly. Between sips, she radiated a quiet happiness.

Once their astonishment had subsided, the men began eating from the wooden bowls the women gave them. Sylvia brought Taz a bowl, then sat with her back to one of the timbers supporting the long house, looking for all the world as if she had been born there.

Later in the morning, Salvador appeared, this time with a different feathered crown made from leather and the blue feathers of a military macaw. He made a beeline for Socrates. They spoke for a while. Socrates motioned towards Taz, said a few more words.

Salvador approached Taz. "*Obrigado.* Thank you, *Senhor* Blackwell. It appears you have helped us avoid what must be." His English was soft but clear, with a Brazilian lilt.

Taz smiled and put his knuckle to his forehead in acknowledgment of Salvador's manifest seniority. Salvador put his left hand on Taz's right shoulder. His touch was gentle but powerful; Taz could feel a wave of energy coursing through his body.

Salvador seemed to be considering something—a choice—and then turned once more to Taz.

"You are free tomorrow, yes?"

"Yes."

"I would like to take you into the forest with me."

"I would be honored. But what of my companions?"

"It is better if they stay. The village will treat them well."

"What should I bring?"

"A water bottle and a cloth to sleep on. We leave at dawn."

*

Taz woke at first light, maybe thirty minutes before dawn, hearing more birdcalls than he could process. Songs, cackles, rattles, whistles, and random cries. He brushed his teeth, put his toothbrush and some meds in his pack, threw in a water bottle, a conga, and a weathered paperback copy of the Heart Sutra. He emerged from his tent and joined Salvador at the fire. There was a coffeepot sitting on last night's embers. Salvador lifted it off and poured the coffee into two old and dented tin cups.

They sat for a while, sipping hot coffee, and listening to the quiet burble of the river. Finally, Salvador turned to Taz. "Mr. Blackwell, I am *Xama. A feiticeiro. Un brujo, en espanhol.* Many are afraid of me. But you do not seem afraid."

"No." Taz had a strong feeling that he should listen—not talk.

"Taz. That is a name you chose for yourself, yes? May I call you by that name?"

Taz did his best to keep his composure. "Of course."

"I think there is a side to you that you don't show. Perhaps a side that you yourself are only partially aware of." Taz took this in. "You are not

Txai, nor are you a shaman. So, I cannot promise you success. And yet, it appears you have the owl's sight. I watched as your eyes saw how to prevent the battle our men would have brought upon the loggers. And you were right, our men are brave, but they would have perished. When we reach the deep forest, you will have an opportunity to see your life from a different angle, as you Americans put it. But what your people call intellect will not help. You must be willing to trust. Do you have the courage to do that, Taz?"

Taz was beginning to see where Salvador was headed. "I think so, but I also know there are powers beyond what I understand. I'd be more confident if I knew you would be there to guide me."

"Some are foolhardy. You are not. That is good. I will indeed be there."

Taz smiled at the fire. *This is going to be interesting.* Salvador stood and slipped silently into the forest. When he reappeared a few minutes later, he carried what looked like an orchid. Motioned wordlessly. Taz shouldered his rucksack, grabbed the plastic water bottle, and looked at his companions.

"Salvador and I are going to take a little walk." They looked at each other.

Socrates said, "I think we'll stay by the river. Watch the camp."

Salvador turned on his heels. Taz stepped around the fire and followed.

They were on a path, a very subtle one that appeared and disappeared, working its way around towering mahoganies and even larger kapoks wrapped with strangler vines and orchids of kinds he'd never seen. There were some swampy areas where he wished he were barefoot like Salvador. They crossed four or five streams, slept two nights alongside the trail, and forded one river above a fall that would have crushed and broken even the largest dugout canoe.

They found themselves far upstream of their takeout, looking at the vertical face of an escarpment that was at least three hundred feet high. Without the slightest pause, Salvador started climbing up an open chimney, with his back to one sidewall and his feet and hands working his way up the opposing side, a technique best suited for someone with Salvador's build— short with unusually good arm strength. Taz, tall and lean, had learned a reasonable version from a dear friend who was a far better climber than he would ever be. He watched Salvador ascend and did his best to keep up.

The top of the escarpment was vastly different from the forest below. It was a plain, sparsely covered with grasses, small bushes, and occasional groups of flowers the like of which Taz had never seen. There were small tarns scattered here and there, and expanses of exposed rock, mostly granite. An upright stone at least fifteen feet in height stood on the far side of the largest tarn. Salvador headed straight for it. When Taz huffed up behind him, Salvador put his forefinger to his lips, pointed at the ground. A path of footprints. Circling the stone. Big footprints. Very big. A very big cat.

Salvador murmured, "A ghost trail. Generations of jaguars have walked here, always using the footprints of the ancestors. Always rubbing their shoulders and backs on the rock and leaving strands of fur behind."

Taz touched the rock, came away with a small shock of hair. He smelled it, put it back. Licked his thumb to glue it where it belonged. Salvador smiled. There was a small hill behind the rock, maybe forty feet tall. A path led up through a rocky promontory to a flat grass patch on top, surrounded by flowers of the same family as the one Salvador had brought back to the village earlier.

Salvador said, "Let's gather some wood." They went to opposite sides, looking first where the bushes and trees had dropped old branches. Came back with their arms full. Salvador started to build a fire. Motioned to Taz to get water from a stream running just downhill. Taz noticed a large piece of wood that would serve as a rough bowl. Took it to the stream and brought back fresh water.

Salvador pointed to a small plain of good-sized river-washed rocks, most at least two feet long and a foot and a half wide. Motioned for Taz to pile them where he was standing. Meanwhile, Salvador cut some of the larger dried branches to sharpen their digging end, started to dig a shallow pit. When he finished digging, he began breaking branches and placing the sticks carefully into the pit.

Salvador twirled a stick on a flatwood, blew on the burning grass in the center to get it to flame. The wood caught within minutes. It was getting dark. They sat and watched the fire for some time. Stars began appearing, one by one. First the evening star, then the Southern Cross, then, on the northern horizon, Scorpio with its great red giant, Antares. Eventually, Taz thought he saw the edge of the Milky Way and, separately, the Magellanic Cloud, a distant, glowing vapor. Just to the left of the cloud there was a long isosceles triangle whose brightest star was just overhead. Taz learned later that it was called Ocitan.

While Taz was stargazing, Salvador had found some long green branches that he bent and tied together to make the frame of a circular hut. Covered the frame with large leaves—two feet or more across and three feet long. Taz had no idea where he had found them.

Salvador wanted the largest round rocks placed on top of the coals, which were now glowing bright red. Each rock weighed thirty pounds or more. Taz placed four at the corners of the fire, and four more in the center. Salvador nodded, pulled out a long pipe, packing it with a mix of the tobacco the locals called *mapacho* and several herbs Taz didn't recognize. He surmised they must have been leaves of a plant known to the Txai as 'yagé.' Salvador gently shoved a thin stick into the coals and lit the mix. Offered the pipe to Taz. He took a long pull. It tasted like a strong cigar, and like sage.

Next, Salvador fished in his fiber bag, and pulled out an old wooden bowl. He filled it with a dark liquid from a leather flask he wore around his neck. He took a sip and offered the bowl to Taz. Motioned for him to drink up.

Taz took a sip. It tasted like coal tar mixed with cheap wine. He almost gagged, held back. Salvador smiled, motioned for him to finish the bowl. He did.

He waited. Nothing. The stars still overhead. The fire dying down, the coals heating the rocks. That was all. A few sounds—the call of a macaw, fluttering of wings near the edge of the cliff.

Then he felt the first rumble. He turned away from the fire, crawled into the darkness, and retched with every sinew he had. Lava was coming out of his mouth, burning all the way. Again. And again.

Finally, he settled down enough to feel thirsty. Crawled unsteadily back to the fire, lifted his water bottle, and took a long, long swig.

Salvador smiled again, offered him a different flask. *Aguardiente, fire cachaça,* the aquavit of the poor. Cheap aguardiente tastes like harsh moonshine. Taz gargled with it. It helped him forget the bilious taste of the vomit.

Taz craned his neck until the night sky was all he could see. The stars were spinning. The Magellanic Cloud had changed shape. The ground under him began tilting until it suddenly rose up to meet him and he found himself on his side. He struggled to right himself. Salvador went in and out of focus. Meanwhile, a strange sound was magnetizing his attention. It resembled a didgeridoo, alongside a strange, plucked instrument that Taz couldn't identify. The two were playing a hollow melody in a pentatonic scale.

Taz looked up again. The stars were in place like never before. He lay back and watched, fascinated. That was when he heard the low growl that sounded also like a moan. The sound jarred him out of his reverie. He levered himself up on his elbow and scanned the camp. Nothing. Another scan. Still nothing. Except for two eyes creeping around the rocks, glowing green and occasionally red when reflecting the light of the fire.

The fire jumped for just a minute, casting its light in all directions. A jaguar stepped softly, silently, between a nurse log and one of the large rocks that surrounded the meadow. A big cat—Taz, wide-eyed now— estimated it at six feet long, at least, and more than three feet high at the shoulder. It would have weighed in at more than two hundred pounds. Despite its size, something about the way it moved told Taz it was female. The cat took three steps towards the fire, now more a pile of glowing embers, stretched, and settled down on its belly, posing like the Sphinx.

There was a raspy sound as the jaguar breathed and purred. Taz looked around for Salvador. The old man had vanished. Taz had a moment of panic and then remembered a story Lucia had told him about the Pit River Indians of Northern California. They believed there were two kinds of animal spirits. *Daamagomis* are tricksters—not necessarily mean, but unpredictable. *Dinihowis* are friendly, protectors, strength-givers. Taz felt a growing warmth. Maybe, just maybe, his jaguar was a dinihowi—a very big, very fierce dinihowi.

I'm dreaming, Tax repeated to himself. He recalled being a boy of twelve, walking along the banks of the Brazos, looking for turtles and catfish. A stream of dirt and small rocks rained down from high on the bank. He looked up and saw a cougar looking right back at him. His uncle, a rancher, had told him that if confronted by a cougar, you don't run. You want to stand tall, look big, even menacing.

But this jaguar, this dinihowi, seemed almost indifferent to his presence. So, Taz remained stone still and waited. The jaguar snorted and settled back into her Sphinx posture. Taz found himself in the sandy ravine again. This time, there was a girl on the other bank. She beckoned to him. It was Lucia.

Taz rolled slowly to his knees and, carefully, hand by hand and knee by knee, crawled towards the beast. The purring continued. Taz moved close enough to smell the creature's breath. He was shoulder to shoulder with the biggest cat he'd ever imagined. He slowly reached out a hand, gently scratched the soft tissue under its chin. The jaguar stretched her neck to ask for more. Taz complied, gradually lengthening his strokes. Then the cat rolled slowly over on her back, like a housecat looking for a belly rub.

Taz cautiously repositioned himself, scratched the cat's belly, paying special attention to the sensitive area just between the rear leg and the abdomen. When he found the right place, the cat's right leg began to twitch and stretch at regular intervals.

After what was probably only half a minute, but seemed like an hour, the cat gave a quick snort, squirmed once, seemingly to scratch its back, and then rolled onto its belly and resumed its pose, keeping a wary eye on him.

Tired, so tired. Taz lay his cheek on the cat's paw and went to sleep. That was where Salvador found him, just before dawn. Taz woke to the sensation of the old man's warm hand on his shoulder, only then realizing his cheek was resting on a pillow made from a bed of ferns.

He got up to piss. Groggy at first, and then, as differences in light and shadow became clearer, he felt as if he was somehow empty. That all his customary thoughts, fears and anxieties had been swept clean with nothing left behind except an excruciating awareness of everything around him. Salvador had placed the leaf frame like a tent over the fire pit. The coals were still hot, the rocks still glowing a faint red. He tapped Taz gently on the shoulder, motioned for him to come in.

The old man took some herbs from a leather bag on his belt and tossed them onto the stones. The tent was immediately suffused with the smell of burning leaves, and something like marijuana. The leaf frame proved to be a good insulator. Taz started to sweat.

Salvador put his hand into a bowl by his side, and sprinkled water on the rocks. Clouds of steam filled the tent. Salvador reached into a pouch and withdrew some small leaves. These also went into the fire, producing a sweet aroma. Taz felt uncomfortably hot, but Salvador motioned for him to stay seated. Sweat poured from the crown of his head. The salt made his eyes burn.

After some time, Salvador got up, leaning on a rough-cut cane. Taz held still, breathing slowly and regularly. Salvador crossed behind him, ducked his head, sidled out of the tent opening, and stepped into the cool predawn light. Taz sat for a few more minutes, then followed. Salvador was back on the other side of the little dirt basin where they had slept, bent, and slowly walking around the cold campfire, holding a loose bundle of leaves in his right hand, using it to smooth the dirt as he walked. He watched Taz for a moment, placed the leaves on the ground, and trotted over to join him. They stood together as the sun began to rise. Then Salvador motioned him to sit. Passed the long pipe.

Taz took a long draw, savoring the herbal aroma, then looked in Salvador's eyes and smiled. "You keep a very clean campfire." He offered the pipe.

Salvador smoked contentedly, nodded at the blackened fire pit, turned back to Taz. Gave him a sly smile. "Spirit animals don't leave tracks." He thought for a moment, seemingly choosing his words with care. "It is as I said to Socrates. You are a strange one, Taz. You are cousin to the owl, yet the jaguar is your *espírito animais*—your spirit guard."

"I didn't think it was possible for people like me . . . to have such a tie."

"It is true. The men of your world are *aveotó*—men without bows. Many have lost their way. Still, your ancestors arose from the soil, as did ours."

"Yes. But what does it mean? What do I do?"

"You will know. When the time comes, your jaguar will be there. Until then, let life flow as it should. For now, we should go back to your friends before they begin to worry."

They walked the four hours back in silence, listening to the birds. Found their way to the river, slid down the steep bank to the ford. Taz saw a patch of scarlet upriver on the opposite bank. As they got closer, it became clear that the wash of scarlet was a flock of green-winged macaws, maybe two dozen, pecking salt out of the clay that was exposed on the bank. Taz and Salvador stayed downriver so as not to disturb them.

Back at the village, life had returned to normal. The men were gardening or tending to their weapons, the women mending or weaving baskets and watching the children. Socrates saw the two of them coming, spoke a few Guarani words to Salvador, took out the SAT phone, and arranged for the pickup. An hour later, a military helicopter arrived. They made their goodbyes. Sylvia had a hug for each of her woman friends. Taz looked for Salvador, but he had disappeared.

Just as Taz was about to climb into the helicopter, Salvador reappeared, walking slowly towards them, unbothered by the dust blowing from the rotors. Socrates, who was behind Taz, touched him on the shoulder, smiled, and nodded towards Salvador. Taz turned, ducked under the rotors, holding onto his cap, and stepped out of the dust to shake Salvador's hand.

Salvador motioned to tell Taz to hold up. Then he stepped forward and, with both hands, touched Taz on the shoulders and on the chest. Taz felt again the surge of energy that emanated from the old man. Salvador reached into a little pouch and pulled out a dark rawhide loop about the length of a necklace. He hung it around Taz's neck, then turned it so that its pendant would be centered next to Taz's heart. The pendant was a jaguar claw, wedged ever so carefully into a beaten gold cap. Taz held it to his heart for a long time and couldn't stop smiling. Salvador was smiling too.

Socrates instructed the pilot to head for Cruzeiro do Sul, where Taz planned to meet a military rig in time to join the bombeiros and the Boise boys at the fire line. He and Sylvia were going to be picked up by the helicopter that had taken them to the hospital, and then flown Porto Velho, where she could get a quick flight to Brasilia and home.

✤

The Cruzeiro do Sul that Taz had transited only days before had disappeared in the smoke from the giant fire in the Javari Reserve fifty miles to the north. Taz stood alone on the tarmac. There didn't seem to be a tower—or if there was, he couldn't make it out in the haze. He was in front of the Quonset hut that served as the small plane hangar. It was the first time since he left Iquitos that he'd seen even one Wi-Fi bar on his cell. He called Lucia. "Hi. You've reached me, but I'm not here, or there, depending on where I was, that is. Leave a number and I'll call back when I can."

He was just about to jam the damn cell back in his pocket when it started cawing. "Taz, are you there? I didn't see your number in time. I was so worried when I couldn't reach you. I thought you didn't want to talk to me anymore. I mean after what I said the last time."

"Hey, hey. Slow down. It's okay. You didn't say anything to hurt me. I just got that you needed some space."

"But then I thought maybe something's happened to him—maybe he got hurt. I didn't know."

"Lucia, I'm fine—really."

"Where are you?"

"In Cruzeiro do Sul, on the Juruá near the Peruvian border. We're going to take a look at the fire tomorrow. We have to see if we have got what it takes to deal with it."

"You make it sound like it's a backyard bonfire. That's sure not what

I'm seeing on the news. And who is *we*?"

"The Boise boys and their bombeiro friends, and any help we can rustle up locally."

"I thought tomorrow was the day you'd be coming out of the fire—not going into it. And I had to call John White's office even to get that much."

"A lot has changed in the last few days. Lucia, this is bigger than any fire my team has ever seen—and they've seen a lot. They're calling it a *fire complex* now. The oldest burn—the one that started on the patchwork ranchlands just south to the reserve—that one is burning itself out. But the fire's leading edge—the most intense part—is moving northwest towards the Peruvian border. They're even less prepared for what's coming than the Brazilians. If we don't slow it up until we get some rain, it won't stop until it hits the Andes. Brasilia told us we couldn't go in until they worked out an agreement for how to handle the legal issues if it ends up burning on both sides of the border. It took them until yesterday. In the meantime, we ran across some illegal loggers who were threatening the local Txai villagers. We decided to see what we could do to straighten things out. It took us a few days."

"You mean *you* decided. Like always." She sounded stressed.

"Before you read me the riot act, I had an accomplice. Someone I dearly hope you'll meet one day."

"So, it was two of you against how many? Would you like me to call the hospital and reserve you a permanent room?"

"Remind me . . . which one of us volunteered to go down to Mexico and spy on the cartels? Because panther tracking was starting to get boring?"

"What does that matter?"

"Just trying to put things in perspective."

She hooted. "How would you know? You have absolutely no idea what you put people through. Every time I think I've got a handle on you—on how I could handle *being* with you—you plunge into some new kind of trouble. You're like that line Dylan sings when he's stuck in Mobile. You're the guy who lit a fire on Main Street and shot it full of holes."

"Then what?"

"I don't know how to love a man like you. Maybe I can't afford to.

You're an adventure addict, Taz. You know what your friend Tom told me? He put his finger on it. He said, 'Most folks, they're just driving through life with the windows closed and the air conditioner on. Your friend Taz isn't like that. He's like a hound dog in a pickup truck going seventy miles an hour, and he's got his head right out the window to feel the wind in his face, 'cause that's when he feels alive.'"

"Tom's a serial exaggerator, and you know it."

"Taz, he was giving me a heads up, that's all. And, just so you know, I thought it was a pretty damn good description."

He heard tires on gravel, turned his head and saw a pair of headlights jumping on the rough road a hundred yards away and closing fast. "Look— there's a truck coming—I think they're coming for me. The fire boys got in today. We're headed out tomorrow. I'll call you when the smoke clears and we get back out."

"You mean if you're still around to make the call? I'd like that. I really would." Taz wasn't completely sure she meant it. The call went dead.

CHAPTER THIRTY-FIVE

Fighting Fire with Cachaça

TAZ WATCHED THE APPROACHING HEADLIGHTS, planting himself directly in their beam. The sound of brakes forcefully applied. The pickup stopped just a few yards past where he stood. The driver came around to introduce himself. His name was Luca Correia.

"*Senhor* Blackwell? I'm supposed to pick you up and take you to a café on the waterfront in Da Cobal. I must tell you that area is very doubtful, particularly after dark." Dusk was lengthening its shadow. "The police still show up on occasion, but they don't own it."

"But that's where my companions are?"

"Yes. With our bombeiros," Luca said with a sense of pride.

"Then I'll be okay. Just drop me off and give me your cell number. That way we can get in touch with you if we need to."

Luca complied, grudgingly, taking Taz on a winding route through city streets which gradually narrowed and led through a kind of shantytown maze to the waterfront, where all the buildings, including the houses, warehouses, restaurants, and cafés were on stilts to protect against the annual floods. The Café-Bar Juruá was loud and well lit. Taz recognized the music as forró, the classic country music of the arid Brazilian northeast—the sertão.

Taz opened the creaky front door and stepped into a dimly lit foyer with weathered, wood-planking walls. On the right side, caught in the light from a half-open curtain leading to the barroom, there was a black-and-white photograph of a barren landscape, charred and burned. Facing the photographer, a rancher, smiling.

Taz pushed his way through the curtain. The bar was raucous and crowded. There were about a dozen round tables to his left. Most of them were taken by men or by couples scurrying to and from the dance floor. Patrons stood two deep at the bar. Taz spotted his fire crew and the bombeiros drinking together with their backs to the bar. A good sign.

Toby Kress, the youngest of the Boise crew, saw him first. "Hey guys, there's Taz! Boss, good to see you." The boys surrounded him to shake hands and say hello.

Lucky clapped him on the shoulder. "You made it! I'll ask you how later." Pointed to the most senior bombeiro. "Taz, this Luiz Ferraro, the chief of the bombeiros in all of Acre."

Taz clasped his hand. "I'm honored." The bombeiros saluted in the informal Brazilian manner. Taz made sure to shake their hands as well. Luiz put his arm around Taz's shoulder.

Luiz said a few words in Portuguese, loud enough to be heard over the din. Taz looked at Toby, who understood Portuguese. "What did he just say?"

"He said you were an important leader from the States who has come to help put out the forest fires. He laid it on a bit about how high up you are."

"Oh boy. That's all I need. Now I'm a number one target for anyone who has a grudge against the US. Listen, Toby, translate this for me, at the top of your voice, okay?" Taz motioned for the bartender. *"Senhor,* I'd like to buy a round of cachaça for my friends." The bartender used his finger to count the bombeiros and the Boise boys, who, by the look of them, had been drinking for some time. Taz looked him in the eye, said, "No, not just for the fire crews. For all my friends at the bar who are going to support us during the days we fight the fire."

As Toby finished his translation the crowd cheered. Many smiles and *obrigados* directed to Taz. The bartender looked momentarily stunned, and then began bringing out bottles of cachaça, four at a time. He made five trips and then started filling glasses. Luiz's arm was still draped over Taz's shoulder. He smiled a deep, happy smile and squeezed.

CHAPTER THIRTY-SIX

Fighting Fire with Fire

THE HANGOVERS WERE VICIOUS. AT least for Taz. Despite their agony, the crew made it to the helicopter hangar by six in the morning. They had arranged to be ferried by helicopter the forty miles to the fire's leading edge.

The bombeiros had brought their ground-clearing and firefighting tools. The Boise boys brought clearing tools of their own, as well as satellite phones, binoculars, and digital cameras that could transmit images in real time. The bombeiros had Wi-Fi phones too, but their range was limited, and their frequencies didn't match the frequencies used by the water tankers that would soon be flying in from Porto Velho and Iquitos.

Despite the glitches, they made significant progress on that first day. Their sector was one of three on the fire's southern edge. Army units worked the others—large agricultural areas outside the fire where crops and buildings needed protection. They lacked training but had the advantage of greater numbers. The bombeiros' fire, which they called *nosso fogo*, burned in the patchwork region at the edge of the real forest. Working from satellite photos and Google Maps, they decided that their priority was to protect two small villages and a large *fazenda*—the Brazilian version of a hacienda—situated just east of the Juruá. The helicopters landed in an open field less than a kilometer from the villages, each of which was home to a couple of hundred loggers and small farmers.

The bombeiros assessed the situation and began trenching and lighting backfires near several strips of forest downwind from the fire in order to channel it away from the villages. Taz and Lucky walked the length of the fire line; the Boise crew and the bombeiros were already working smoothly together. Lucky had raised the Porto Velho control tower on his satellite phone and handed it to Luiz, who explained the situation, and then handed the phone to Ray Williams, who gave the controllers the coordinates of the fires. Within twenty minutes, two water tankers appeared on the horizon. To Taz, they looked to be a C-130 and a Lockheed Orion. They weren't going to be able to drop enough water. Still, the dump would protect the villages; it was a start.

The tankers dropped their first loads on the fire front closest to the villages, then turned back to Porto Velho to get more foam and water. After two more round trips, the deputy of the bombeiros gave Luiz a thumbs-up, which Taz took to mean that the local threat was under control.

Luiz left six of his crew to stay with his deputy, motioned with his right hand to imitate a helicopter rotor, and they walked back to the clearing where the helicopters had landed. Their two helicopters had been replaced by an early-model Chinook. That baby could hold forty-two Marines with all their gear. Luiz sat up in the copilot's seat, told the pilot to head for the fazenda. Taz climbed into the back and sat against the side with the bombeiros. The helicopter rumbled, roared, and lifted off.

After a time that was longer than it seemed, the Chinook slowed and started its descent towards a green field not far from the fazenda's main buildings. A heavy pall of smoke seemed to stretch over the entire region. They landed in a soybean field. A gigantic soybean field.

A fancy-model Jeep roared up a dirt road in their direction, leaving a dust cloud in its wake. It skidded to a stop just yards from them. Taz tossed the water from his plastic bottle into his eyes to clear the dust from his vision. A man exited the Jeep and waddled towards the crew and their helicopter.

To call him portly would be too kind. He immediately started yelling.

Taz grabbed Toby by the elbow and asked him to translate.

"Well, he's upset that we landed in his soybean field. Also, that we are so late in attending to his *fazenda*. That we favored the workers' villages for no good reason. That he, too, had a right to the protection of the government. When he got to his taxes, I'm afraid I tuned out."

"Well, that only shows your basic good sense. Thanks, Toby."

The fat man still yelling at Luiz, pointed his finger threateningly. Taz motioned to Toby, who said only two words, "Glad to." Taz interposed himself between the fat man and Luiz. Motioned for Toby to join him. Then, with Toby translating, Taz stared directly at Porky. "Only a hopelessly stupid man would insult the leader of the team which has come to save his *fazenda.*"

The man grew red in the face: "And who the hell are you to instruct me, Feora da Lozano, the owner of ten thousand hectares—in fact, of all the land all around you, as far you can see?"

"My name is Taz Blackwell. I work for the US government. I am here to assist your bombeiros in fighting the wildland fires that have broken out all around the periphery of the Amazon. Mostly because of the carelessness of ranchers like you."

As Toby continued to translate, the fat man spit in the dust and directed a malevolent look in Taz's direction. "The forest is our only asset. If we don't make it productive, the only people who will benefit will be rubber-tappers. And," he fairly choked on the word. "*Índios.*"

Taz looked him over like he was inspecting a lame horse at auction. "That is a problem, isn't it? We'd like to help. Really, we would. It's possible we could save your *rancho elegante.* The problem is, your bombeiros' instructions are to work with me, and my instructions are to direct my attention to settlements rather than to individual fazendas. So, there it is. The fires are approaching from the south and the west. Maybe you will be able to tell by the smoke. We'll see you the next time we pass through, I hope."

The man went pale. Luiz covered his mouth with his hand in an only marginally successful effort to suppress a laugh. Finally, the man pulled himself together. "No, no, no. I can't lose everything I've worked for. I will reward you handsomely for anything you can do to stop the fire from reaching my land." *A bribe to do our job.*

"Thank you, but we can't accept your money just for doing our job. However, our colleagues, your bombeiros, lack the new communications equipment necessary to talk with their airplanes—the ones that drop the water and the fire-killing foam. Perhaps you would be willing to contribute to a fund to help in that regard?"

"Yes, of course. Generously!"

CHAPTER THIRTY-SEVEN

Fighting Fire with Water

BLOCKING THE FIRE WAS TRICKY and more difficult than they expected. The flames approached the fazenda from two directions, feeding on the dry soil and the stubble from fallow fields.

Lucky found Taz on the fire line. He and his partner, a young man named Paulo, had just finished digging a trench not far from the leading edge of the fire. "What in the hell are you doing there? You're supposed to be overseeing the whole thing!"

Taz just smiled and kept digging and scraping. He was enjoying working shoulder to shoulder with the bombeiros, and he wasn't at all concerned about coming out as sooty and dirty as they were.

Someone was yelling from maybe thirty yards down the fire line, flames visible through thick smoke. The fire had leapt the backfire trench and lit up a stand of *huacrapona* and oil palms. It had already reached the tops of at least three of the trees.

Taz shouldered his McLeod, motioned to Paulo, and ran down the fire line. By then, Luiz had already called in his troops, and two or three had revved up their Stihls to drop the burning trees before the flames could leap from their crowns to their neighbors. Taz watched as a wing of bombeiros trenched a new fire line at the edge of the trees to clear the scrub and dry grass that would otherwise fuel the wildfire. He and Paulo had turned to join them when a burning crown of palm fronds and bundled oil fruits landed on his shoulder and knocked him to the ground.

Feeling the flames, Taz rolled and smothered his burning shirt, choking on smoke and dust. He could hear screaming a few yards to his left and crawled blindly in that direction until he heard what sounded like a sob, and then touched cloth and flesh. Paulo had been speared clean through the abdomen by a burning branch from one of the toppled trees. If Taz pulled the branch, the boy would bleed out. He pulled his canteen off his belt and doused the boy's wound. Paulo could only wheeze. Taz held the canteen to his mouth and the boy drank greedily. Taz heard only shouting, burning and the whistling sound of falling branches. The nearest bombeiros ran to them. Paulo coughed up blood. One of the bombeiros knelt at his side while another poured the contents of his canteen on Taz's back and shoulder.

The man kneeling by Paulo was crying and cursing at the top of his lungs. Luiz ran over, looked at the boy's body, now lifeless, and made the sign of the cross. Luiz shouted a command and two of the bombeiros pulled Taz upright, arranged their shoulders under his arms and began half walking, half carrying him to the trucks. Lucky ran up, dug a tube of cream out of his pocket and applied it liberally to Taz's shoulder. Taz felt blood running down his cheek. One of the palm branches had apparently scraped his forehead and face. Lucky told two of the bombeiros to get the boss into the helicopter. Taz had already been loaded through the side door when Lucky climbed in through the hatch and checked Taz's forehead and cheek even as another bombeiro was just beginning to bandage them.

"Okay, hotshot, they're going to bring in the big boy." The words were coming in and out of focus through a fog of buzzing and ringing noises. "Luiz and his deputy have figured out where they think they should dump the load. Do you want to take a look?"

"You agree with them?"

"I do."

"Well then, it's done."

Lucky said something to the pilot, turned to lever himself out the copter's bay door. He reached back to give Taz a gentle fist bump to the knee. "Listen, Cap. You were good out there." Then he climbed back out to talk to Luiz and join the remaining bombeiros. The cream had started to ease the initial pain of Taz's burn. All that did was to make him aware of the ache in his shoulder and the searing pain in his ribs. Somebody needed to check for breaks, but he couldn't find the words to make that clear in Portuguese.

The big boy. When he was still in Iquitos a week back, Taz had gotten authority to requisition a Martin Mars Flying Tanker that the DEA had been using to spray coca fields in Colombia. The DEA resisted mightily, but John White had outlined the situation to the secretary of state and Taz prevailed. That baby would be carrying a payload of seventy-two hundred gallons of water or flame retardant. Enough, Lucky said, to drench four acres. Taz had his fingers crossed.

A rusty Land Rover swept to a stop under the rotors, scattering dust in all directions. Luiz ran over to the side door, saluted Taz. Touched his shoulder with utmost tenderness, smiling. Lucky told him the state of things. Luiz scratched the back of his neck.

"Can you tell me the cost for all this?"

When he was forced to give up the Mars, the DEA director had insisted that State should pay DEA back in full. This one deal would eat a big chunk of John White's discretionary budget, which covered more than the department's environmental work. Human Rights, INR, global health. Taz struggled to remember the amounts involved. He gave an approximate figure to Luiz.

"Taz—I'm sorry. You've done so much. But even with that, we don't have the money. We will have to compensate IBAMA for the fuel and operating costs, and we can't."

Taz ran through his instructions, at least the ones he could remember. Luiz gave him a total cost in cruzeiros. Taz did a quick calculation. "We'll pay the cost."

"On top of what you've already done? Just to save an arrogant rancher's *fazenda?*"

"No. To make a point." *And if we succeed, maybe we can convince the White House to tell the SOBs at DEA to eat the cost.* "But wait, you've given me a thought." Taz pointed to the Land Rover that Luiz had commandeered from the Amazonas State police. "Let's pay another visit to our rancher friend." Luiz smiled and climbed into the driver's seat. Lucky put his arm around Taz's waist and helped him limp over. Luiz turned the key, the engine rumbled to life, and they swung around on the dirt track towards the fazenda.

Even though—or perhaps because—the bombeiros had been so successful at setting backfires, the smoke immediately around the fazenda was thick and acrid. The closest backfire was sending flames high enough to be seen clearly on the eastern horizon.

They knocked on the oversize mahogany door and were let in by a teenage boy in a school uniform. He pointed to the study with a disgusted look. Taz and Luiz made their way through a kind of parlor and then through the study door. The fat man was on two phones, yelling into each in turn. According to Luiz's account later, one call was to IBAMA and the other was to the governor of Acre.

The fat man shouted the loudest into the right-hand phone. It appeared he had been cut off. Finally, he put the other phone down as well, turned to them with a snarl. "None of you are any help. The governor I got elected says there's nothing he can do. How feeble can you be? And IBAMA hates me. Luiz, they say I'm ruining the forest! Fuck them! *Fuck you all!*"

Taz motioned to Luiz to translate, looking levelly at the fat man. "Unlike your governor, there's something we can do. In fact, the plane that can stop your fire is sitting on the tarmac at Porto Velho, ready to take off. But we can't get it here without your help."

Luiz explained the situation. Taz watched the fat man relax the moment he realized it was just about money. In the end, he contributed nine million *reais*—about three hundred thousand dollars—to the bombeiros' firefighting fund. Luiz told Taz that would cover six flights from Porto Velho, fifty thousand gallons of fire retardant, and four years' salary for him and his entire crew. They only needed four flights from Porto Velho and twenty-five thousand gallons of retardant to take care of the fire.

Luiz smiled and said, "Our own early-response plane." He patted Taz's hand.

CHAPTER THIRTY-EIGHT

Nosso Chefe

MIDMORNING. TAZ BOARDED THE EMBRAER jet to Campo Grande, the capital of Mato Grasso state, for his connection to São Paulo. He had said his farewells the night before, in a dive bar on the bank of the Madeira. After watching and waiting as he thanked each one of the Boise boys, the bombeiros gave a collective cheer. The Boise crew responded in kind. Then they left to get some well-deserved sleep.

The bombeiros surrounded Taz. First, Luiz presented him with a gold pin in the form of a crossed pick and shovel. One by one, the bombeiros came over to put a hand on his good shoulder. Then they all gave a cheer. During the cheer, Fernando, the most senior of the crew, reached to the table behind them and came up with a clean shot glass and an ancient bottle of cachaça. He motioned for Taz to drink. Taz threw it down and was assaulted by a rainbow of flavors. The bombeiros shouted a word that sounded like *chefe*. More cheers. Later, Luiz told him the word meant *chief*.

"But you are the chief."

"No. I am their *comandante*. I tell them what to do, and when. But you are now their *herói*—their hero." Fernando pressed the bottle into Taz's hand.

Luiz said, "That's for you."

Taz looked around at the circle of smiling faces, made a drinking motion. Pointed around the circle. At first hesitantly, then with more confidence, they held out their glasses. He transferred the bottle to his good left hand, poured a shot for each until all were full. "This is for Paulo." They raised their glasses and drank the last shots together. Smiles and tears all around. Then a ragged shout, "*Nosso chefe.*" Then laughs, and backslaps. Our chief.

*

The plane landed in São Paulo at seven in the evening. Taz was in his hotel room by eight. With some difficulty he unpacked his pack, put most of his clothes out in the hotel laundry bag. Took a long look at himself in the bathroom mirror. His hair was a mess, and there was a ragged scab covering the wound at his hairline where the burning branch had scored him. He had a long red welt on his cheek, and his chin was covered by an ungovernable stubble. There was a bruise on his right collarbone that extended from his shoulder halfway up his neck. It was blue, turning green, and it was surrounded by a scarlet halo that looked like a second-degree sunburn. He threw up his hands, headed downstairs to the bar.

Someone at the State Operations Center must have given the consulate special instructions. They had put him up at the Hotel Emiliano, a five-star in the middle of Jardins, São Paulo's most fashionable district. The bar was an elegant, old-fashioned affair. Mahogany, brass rails, rosewood veneer. The details were perfect, as were the martinis. Taz was on his second when he began to think about who to call. First, that is.

He hadn't talked to anyone in the States since his call with Lucia a week back. He had no idea what might have transpired on the Island since he left. Pondering the question required a third martini. Finally, he called Laney. It was ten o'clock in São Paulo, seven o'clock on Chincoteague. She had just closed the bookstore. He reached her at home.

"Well, Jesus Christ. We thought you had gone native. Richard is convinced you're in some cave wearing a loincloth and smoking ayahuasca."

"You don't smoke ayahuasca. You drink it."

"Whatever. The point is, you've been on radio silence a long time. And not a good time, either."

"Why? What's going on?"

"The Nazis are back. Deputy Chief Whipple arrested a whole bunch of them for disorderly conduct and disturbing the peace. Now they want revenge. Richard had to call the police to get two of them out of the bookstore. They were shouting White Power slogans. One of them confronted Dana two days ago in the parking lot of the grocery store. Said he'd be back. So how is Brazil?"

"Not nearly as exciting as the Island, I guess."

"When you clam up, there's always a reason. What's going on?"

"I spent most of the week with the Boise boys and the bombeiros. Fighting wildfires in Acre, on the western fringe of the Amazon. Soaking rich ranchers for money to fund poor firefighters. Drinking way too many caipirinhas. Now I'm in São Paulo for meetings with the consulate and hoping they can get me on a plane home sometime in the next few days. Meanwhile, I'm going to listen to as much music as I can find time for. That's what you do in Brazil." All true, even though, it could be argued, his account skirted important facts. Best he could do until he could talk to Lucia face to face.

"So, when do you stop lollygagging and come home?"

"Come on, Laney. As soon as I finish debriefing every American or Brazilian official in São Paulo who wants to understand the wildland fire challenge. Meanwhile, I'd really like to talk to Lucia. I've left three messages already."

"You won't be able to reach her for a few days. She's still in California."

"Still hanging with her Davis crowd?"

"I don't think so. She's scheduled visits two universities where there might be research opportunities. I think she's trying to get a sense of her priorities."

"Based on our last conversation, I'd say she has her priorities pretty clear."

"You don't sound too happy about that."

He figured he'd save the details for their next coffee. "No, I'm fine.

Actually no— I'm not. After what happened in Mexico, it took both of us a while to get our feet back on the ground. And I thought Alpine . . . well, maybe I thought it meant more than it did. But she's been getting farther away every day since. Could be that's just the way it is."

"Don't go there, Taz. She's got a whole bunch of choices on her plate. She'll work her way through them. And now at least she's starting to sound like the real Lucia." Taz thanked Laney and eyed his martini. Tried to read his e-mail, but his cell phone was too small, and his vision was blurry. He couldn't make out the characters, the strange script that appeared every time he punched up a message. He finally turned the thing off.

"Maybe a strong coffee would help?"

Her voice. The one he had thought he might not hear again. Dusky, sweet, at first modulated for conversation and then a breathy whisper in his ear.

It took all his discipline to prevent himself from whirling around. He motioned to the bartender. "A double espresso, please. And a martini for my friend." The bartender smiled and hurried down the bar towards the coffee machines. Taz kept eyes on the mirror behind the bar. "There are eleven million lost souls in this city. How in the world did you find me? It's supposed to be a state secret—my location, I mean."

"Oh, I'm sure. That's why I had to practically pry it out of the consulate. It took one phone call."

"Guess our security isn't quite as tight as I thought." He watched her smile in the mirror.

"Okay, Mr. Hard-Ass Diplomat. No 'Carolina, it's good to hear your voice?' No 'delighted to see you?' Well, of course not, since you can't actually *see* me, because you haven't bothered to turn your stool around. You know, Taz, they spin. They really do. You ought to try it sometime."

He finally did. Slowly, to get the full effect. Carolina wore pleated black pants and a maroon blouse with puffy sleeves. The top buttons of the blouse were undone, just enough to give a hint of the pleasures that could be found under the silk.

He was still on the stool, now facing her. She drew in a sharp breath.

"What's happened to you?" She touched the scab on his hairline with such delicacy that he wasn't sure he felt it at all. Then she kissed the welt under his eye.

Taz stepped off his stool, stood just a few inches from her. Looked down into her eyes. Traced the line of her collarbone with his first two fingers. Drew her towards him, very gently. "Probably don't look like much. Just a normal shift, you know. . . on the fire line. What the bombeiros do every day, all year round. I meant to clean up. I just needed one drink first. You see how that went. I apologize. Not at my best, I know. Sorry. Really."

Carolina cupped his cheek with her hand. "You really are a handful, aren't you? Do you actually do anything the way normal people do?" She used her hand to guide him until his mouth was only an inch from hers. Lips gently on his. He kissed her with what strength he had left. She responded to every little shift of his lips, his jaw, his tongue. Pulled back and looked in his eyes.

"You better come up to my room." She put her arm around his waist and guided him to the elevators.

CHAPTER THIRTY-NINE

Everton's Proposal

TAZ WOKE TO THE SMELL of strong coffee and the sun streaming through the picture window. He was lying on a futon mattress on the floor. He pushed himself up far enough that he could lean on his right elbow, with his hand supporting his chin. His shoulder felt like it had been hit by a sledgehammer.

He surveyed what he could see of Carolina's suite. She was on the other side of a marble kitchen counter, with her back to him, making stovetop espresso. She waited until the upper chamber of the pot was half full and the stream of dark coffee had slowed to a trickle. Then she took the pot off the burner, before the first flecks of foam made their appearance. Sweeter that way.

She turned, saw him, and smiled. "So, sleepyhead. I wasn't sure you were ever going to get up." She brought over two small cups of espresso, sat on the edge of the mattress. Held out his coffee so that he could hold the handle with his free hand. She wore a dark green kimono fringed with gold. They sipped espresso. She put her cup on the rug just by the mattress, reached for his, and placed it next to hers.

She touched his shoulder, gently so as not to aggravate his technicolor bruise. With equal delicacy, she pushed him down on his back and, with her other hand, untied the belt on her kimono. Started kissing him just above his hip. Moved ever so slowly up to his ribcage, to his nipple, and then to his neck, where she could almost, but not quite, touch his lips with hers. Lay her head there, lifting it now and then to brush her lips across random places on his chest.

Taz's breathing turned ragged. He put his hands under her arms, brought her up just a few inches more. She began rocking slowly, transporting both of them. Afterward, she lay her head back on his chest. "I'm singing tonight. Will you come?"

"You couldn't keep me away with a shotgun."

Carolina giggled. "I have to do my vocal exercises now and then rehearse in the afternoon."

"Of course. I need to spend some time at the consulate and then meet with my friends from the Environment Ministry and Itamaraty. What time is your show?"

"Nine, at the Club Fasano Baretto. Just up the hill in the hotel of the same name."

Later, after he had showered and headed out to meet with Everton, he asked the concierge about the club. "It's the most exclusive nightclub in the whole city. Very small, very expensive. They only showcase the best music, usually jazz." The concierge suggested other nightclubs down the hill, uncertain that Taz was the kind of person who would be comfortable in Club Fasano's rarefied atmosphere.

Taz checked in with the consulate first. The deputy chief of mission was also somewhat perplexed by his appearance, at least judging by his initial reaction. Taz explained a little of the circumstances, which seemed, oddly, to reassure him.

Everton had invited him to lunch at a men's club often used as a remote office by senior officials from Itamaraty. Their wine had been served, and he didn't take long to get to the point.

"Taz. Your work in Acre has had quite an impact. Your combined team with our bombeiros proved more effective than the effort the army put together with twice as many people. Everyone in Brasilia thinks the cooperative project was a success." Taz nodded in appreciation. A waiter stepped over to offer brandy and cigars. Everton sniffed a cigar and nodded to the waiter who took two snifters and placed them on the table. "But as you of all people know, success has its own consequences. For instance, your array of injuries, which I'm sure you received as the result of your entirely unnecessary escapade on the fire line." That ironic smile—Everton's negotiating signature.

Here we go. "No good deed goes unpunished," as his favorite boss, Interior Secretary Talbot, used to say. "Everton. You can't be in that situation and not want to help. Your bombeiros are courageous and, better than that, effective. I was honored to get to know them."

"Yes. And they know it. They now speak of you as *nosso gaucho*—our cowboy. You've become a story in the press." Everton smiled, lit a cigar, offered one to Taz. Taz felt reasonably sure that a woman whose voice was her career would not be a fan of secondhand cigar smoke. He declined, not without regret.

"Taz, word of the events in Acre has reached President Carvalho, who had decided—and already announced yesterday, at a UNESCO ministerial—that he will soon launch an initiative to reduce deforestation in the Amazon. Of course, we have nothing but an outline of what he's thinking—he didn't preview the speech with anyone, not even his own chief of staff. But he desperately wants the initiative to succeed—it will make his name on the global stage.

"The governor of Acre recognizes the opportunity, and he wants to champion the president's initiative. He's a progressive, of the same party as President Carvalho. And he's a straight shooter. I think, if you were willing to work with him, we could get such an initiative off the ground. What do you say, Taz?"

Taz said nothing for quite a while. Then, "I don't know, Everton. I have to think it over. I have some personal business to attend to at home. Once I see how that goes, I'll be able to give you an answer."

"I'd much rather have the answer now, but we do have *some* time. It will take a few months to forge the domestic political alliances we will need to take such an initiative. It's bound to be opposed by the ranchers, land-grabbers, and by the agri-business lobby."

"Okay. I'm pretty sure I'll have the answers to both questions by then."

"Both questions?"

"Right. Mine, and yours."

CHAPTER FORTY

I Dream of Fire

THE CONVERSATION WITH EVERTON HAD gone longer than expected. Taz got back to his hotel a little after seven. He showered. Brushed his hair and shaved. Tried his best to trim the ragged parts of the scab at his hairline. There's nothing like a Swiss Army knife with good, sharp scissors.

He put on the button-down Oxford that he'd bought at the hotel gift shop and his linen jacket, which they had taken out for cleaning, then headed down to the bar for some proper premedication. The caipirinhas went down easy, as always. At eight thirty, Taz was ready for his trek up the hill.

The club was as advertised. Once he had gotten his hand stamped and sidled carefully past the bouncer, he was greeted by a very attractive young woman in black pants, tux shirt and bow tie. "May I find you a table, sir?"

"Is it still possible to find one with a good view of the stage?"

A look of recognition. Blushing. "Pardon me. You must be Carolina's American friend, yes?"

"Yes."

"We have a table waiting for you." She led him into the room from the back, steered him to a two-person table next to the soundman's table, with its abundant cables and low lights. All on a platform with an unobstructed view of the stage.

He stood and reached over the low siding to introduce himself to the soundman. Gabriel Foreigra, from Belo Horizonte, greeted Taz warmly. He was hoping to do sound for musicians in the States at some point. But just now he had to get back to work balancing the sound for Carolina's opening set.

Taz motioned to the young woman who had seated him, asked if the show had an intermission, which it did. He handed her another fifty-dollar bill, requested an ice water and a double martini. Suggested that she might like to bring a bottle of the club's best champagne to the table just before the break.

"Thank you so much, Mr. Taz. I will."

The martini arrived just as he liked it. Not the Botanist, but Bombay Saphire, straight up in a frosty glass, with a lemon twist and just a hint of vermouth. He sipped it appreciatively.

The house lights dimmed. A spotlight picked out a bare wooden chair on the left side of the stage. A well-dressed man carrying a Portuguese guitar the size of a large mandolin circled the chair and sat down. He started playing a silvery melody.

A second spotlight illuminated a standing microphone at the center of the stage. Carolina arrived in the light, swaying gently to the guitar. She was wearing a spangly dark blue jacket cut short over white bell bottoms, which came up to her midriff. No blouse. The jacket was open just enough to excite the attention without being explicit. Her eyes were closed, her eyelids darkened by blue eye shadow. She held a hand microphone gently, listening thoughtfully to the guitar. Waited for the tune to come around. Then, in a low voice, she began to sing a love song by Caetano Veloso. "*Você é linda.*" Most of the twenty or so tables and all the women in the room began to sing along.

Carolina's set was a mix of fado and Brazilian love songs. It was clear that fado was a new style to most of the audience, but within a couple of songs, they were captured. Carolina's voice, and the music, dripped with longing, sex, and saudade. She was tapping the dark side of the Brazilian happy-go-lucky persona. She ended the first set with a samba by Gal Costa. Gentle but bright. The kind of song that made you think of spring.

Taz motioned to the young woman, who brought a bottle of Billecart Blanc de Noirs, already on ice in a silver bucket. He gazed at the neighboring tables. A few older jazz lovers. Some foursomes, talking closely among themselves. One man sitting alone at a table close to the stage, wearing one of those raffia porkpie hats you find in the better men's magazines. Taz watched as he spoke to a waiter, an old man, judging by his crooked stance. He couldn't see his face. Other tables set for four with two obviously successful men, inevitably accompanied by attractive younger women. Not necessarily arm candy, but it was all too clear who was paying the bills, and why.

A different server came to sweep away Taz's water glass and place a new glass on the table. Taz gazed briefly in his direction as he left, wondering at the unnecessary service. The waiter could have been the same older man. He had a wandering eye. Taz took a sip of the water and felt a quick sting on his upper lip. There was a crack in the lip of the glass. He touched a finger to it. Blood. Only a drop, though. He put his napkin to his lip twice, and the second time showed nothing.

Then she was there, standing beside his chair. "Are you hurt?" She touched her finger to his lip where he had placed the napkin.

"Just a little nick. Chipped glass."

He pulled the empty chair away from the table. She smiled, gliding in, gracefully. "Finished checking out the comfort women?"

"I was just looking for someone as beautiful as you. I failed." She snorted and giggled. Then the hiccups started. She glared, gave him a gentle slap across the cheek. But not so gentle that it didn't catch the attention of more than a few of the people at nearby tables.

As they turned away to hide their interest, Taz rubbed his cheek and smiled. "You really do know how to make an entrance."

"Oh, Taz. Always trying to fly above life's melancholy." Stroking his cheek and looking at him with a sad smile. Shaking her head, slowly.

He twisted and pulled the cork on the Billecart, ever so gently. Poured them each a generous flute. The *mousse,* as they say, was fine and flavorful.

"I think you could stop my hiccups, if you wanted to."

Taz pushed back his chair, stepped around the table, and leaned over her, bringing his mouth to hers. He kissed her for what seemed like a blissful eternity. The sensitivity of his nick only heightened the delicacy of the first brush of their lips and intensified the deepening passion of the kiss. She finally broke away.

"I'm a singer, in case you didn't know. We have to breathe." Taz nodded. "Occasionally." She closed her eyes and pursed her lips. A second kiss, longer and even more delightful.

"Taz, my plans have changed. I've been invited to sing at one of the best clubs in Porto Alegre, way down south. A week-long engagement, Taz! Even my asshole producer will be impressed."

Taz loved the triumph in her eyes. They finished the champagne, toasted with their empty glasses. She got up to prepare for the next set. Nuzzled his good shoulder, kissed his neck. "But I have to leave at an ungodly hour tomorrow morning. Taz, we may not see each other again." She cupped his cheek with a gentle hand. Her eyes were tearing up as she stood and walked carefully backstage. As she passed through the tables, the man who was sitting by himself followed her with obvious interest. Taz had an uneasy feeling that he had seen him before. When she had disappeared behind the curtain, the man looked briefly over his shoulder in his direction. His stare was cold.

After several minutes of shadow, the spotlights were turned back on. The guitar intro, this time shimmering towards something like happiness. Then Carolina, resplendent in a golden sequined dress with a plunging neckline and a back that was barely there at all. It hugged her body at every appropriate spot.

She sang a few more fados, then a couple of sambas that the audience sang along to, sounding for all the world like a chorus. Slightly ragged, but beautiful, nonetheless.

She wandered to the back of the stage, turned, and approached the microphone again, steadied it with one hand, looked out at the crowd.

Spoke for a minute in Portuguese. A number of the women, and even some of the men, turned their attention in Taz's direction.

Carolina's voice turned to a whisper, magnified by the sound system. She looked directly at Taz. Blew a kiss. "Don't worry, Taz. I only told them that we had a special guest in our midst, one who helped their bombeiros fight the wildfires in the western Amazon. And that you don't like to be the center of attention. Well, sorry. But I wrote this song in the week since we first met. Whether you want it or not, it's for you." Her guitarist began fingering arpeggios in a minor key.

I dream of fire
Where you used to lay your head
This cruel desire
Is all that's left here in my bed

Please don't believe me
When I say, 'I will never miss you'
All that it means is that
I really need to kiss you.

I dream of fire
It's all that I've got left to warm my bed
My heart is tired
Filled with so many words left unsaid.

Please don't believe
when I say
'I will never miss you'
All that it means is that
I really want to kiss you ...

And awaken
from this dream."

The room blurred and for a few minutes Taz saw nothing but the tablecloth. Some gentle hands brushed his arm as the audience streamed out. He looked up and got a glimpse of the man in the porkpie hat as he left his table and turned to follow the crowd towards the exit. He gave Taz a quick, cold stare and then smirked in a particularly dislikable way. Taz felt dizzy, as if he were somewhere at sea.

When he finally looked up again, the stage was empty.

CHAPTER FORTY-ONE

An Angel Falls from the Sky

TAZ WOKE WITH A START. He was trying to shake off a dream. Something was very wrong. *Dark. Rain. A familiar woman running away on a dirt path. Lightning.* Again, she was gone. Gone where? His head was splitting, his sheets were dripping with sweat. He had the chills so bad that he was shaking. The plane they had booked for him was to take off just before noon. He wrenched himself out of bed, staggered to the sink and washed his face and hands, which trembled as he packed his duffel and called the desk to check out.

He was still feeling woozy when the taxi dropped him off at the airport. Disoriented, he stumbled at the curb. He kept a white-knuckle grip on the escalator's rubber handrail for every second of its agonizingly slow ascent through the crowded concourse. Amid the bustle, travelers stood in groups, watching the hanging news screens, and talking with each other in hushed tones. The airport TVs were tuned to the Brazilian affiliate of CNN. It was showing footage of a small plane that had crashed and burned early in the morning in the Atlantic Forest south of São Paulo, on the route to Porto Alegre. No survivors.

Taz knew. He knew. It was no accident. Someone had meant to kill him and had taken Carolina's life instead. He found the nearest men's room, reeled to the first sink, and retched again and again until he emptied his soul. He turned on the faucet, realized he was hanging on to it to keep himself upright. Did his best to clean his mouth, spitting out bile and guzzling from the faucet. He was shivering uncontrollably and breaking into a fever sweat at the same time. He staggered out and tried to locate his gate. Now the whole concourse spun as he stood, stunned, at the center of the carnival ride. The lights blindingly bright, and an overpowering din made it impossible to think. He could feel his balance slipping, struggled to right himself, spun to his left, and crumpled to the hard, smooth, cool tile floor.

❧

His eyes opened briefly. Everything around him gray-green, hard metal. An overwhelming rumble. Nearly impossible to hear anything. On a low cot in the cargo hold of what looked like a military transport plane. Two men, one with a white face mask. The one without, shouting at the top of his lungs, "If it's dengue, I'm getting out of here." Taz rolled to his side and threw up. His mouth tasted sour, and the smell of the vomit made him gag. The men faded away.

Cold. Taz shivered, crossed his arms with his hands in his armpits. Violent shivers and sweats. His cot was damp and the sheet he was under was wet and cold. He tried to call the medic. Nobody answered. He rolled off the cot thinking he might land somewhere dry. Hit the metal deck with a thud. His shoulder wet with his own vomit. Overwhelming pain. He passed out.

A bump and a nauseating sideways twist. Silence as the engines whirred to a halt. Scrape of metal on metal as the rear ramp was lowered. Two pairs of boots running up the ramp. A muffled male voice, "What the hell? Help me get him up. Who's the medic on board?"

The female partner said, "Let's see . . . Lieutenant Bascom."

"He'll be lucky to be a private after I file my report."

"Looks like dengue."

"It could just as easily be zika or chikungunya. They're hard to tell apart. Let's get him to the ICU."

"I'll call and tell them he's coming."

Taz felt himself being wheeled to the rear of the plane and down the ramp to the tarmac. Chills again. He drifted off.

The rumble of engines and a kind of rough vibration, like driving across a cattle guard. The room, or whatever, swayed. Still sweating and tossing. A male nurse sitting, watching, occasionally talking to what looked like a tape recorder.

Then it was still. Every joint in his body ached. He tried to open his eyes. They were crusted and what he could see was blurred. A man in uniform, another one in a white jacket over a blue hospital shirt. They were talking in quiet tones. He wanted something to drink, tried to move his hand, to wave or something. Nothing happened. He tried blinking. They didn't notice, turned away. He could feel himself fade until only a shadow remained.

A bee sting on his arm just underneath the inside of his elbow. He turned his head, saw an adhesive bandage. He started ripping it off to make the stinging stop. Loud beeping and shouting voices. Cursing. Someone holding his arm at the wrist, hard. Another needle pushing into him, worming around to find a vein. He squinted at the pain, let go as it eased. Then a kind of blessed blue behind his eyelids. Fading again.

✿

"Good morning, Mister Blackwell!" The voice was sunny and maternal. Its source, a woman in white, was peering down at him from what seemed to be a great height. "Time to wake, I'm afraid. The doctors will be here to see you soon." She opened the curtains over his window.

Taz squinted at her through the blinding white. From the sound of her voice, she was standing at the foot of his bed. "Are you comfortable? I've brought you some water, there on your bedside table." He looked to his side, but the scene was in shadow. He felt the starch in her jacket as she brushed past him to place the plastic bottle in his hand. "You must be quite the important one, Mister Blackwell. It's not just Doctor Stuart this time. He's bringing a colleague, a very senior colleague." Taz took a long drink. Offered a weak thank you. His voice sounded like a rusty pipe. The nurse asked a series of ritual questions to check his mental competence. Birthdate? Today's date? Address? Where are you? He flubbed the date and had no idea where he was. The Naval Hospital in Portsmouth, she told him. The nurse said a few words as she passed out the door, and the two doctors stepped in.

The first introduced himself as Doctor Stuart. His voice made Taz think they were old friends. How was Taz feeling? Did he know how long he'd been here? Four long days, and longer nights. Alternately delirious and nearly comatose. A temperature of 104 degrees that had finally come down to 99.5, thank God. He couldn't eat, so they had to feed him intravenously. Good, because they were able to give him antivirals and plasma at the same time. When he wasn't ripping out his tubing, that is. Still, he was progressing nicely.

Doctor Stuart's colleague, older and more businesslike, wore dress whites with epaulettes that indicated high rank. He also had the intense eyes of an experienced physician, which he was now using to examine Taz's face, while at the same time palpating the soft area under his jaw and behind his ears. He stepped back, looking thoughtful. "Mister Blackwell, I'm Doctor Bentham, director of forensic medicine in Navy Surgeon General's Office. Your case was referred to my superiors by the State Department. Actually, by the undersecretary for global affairs."

"Forensic medicine?" Taz had more questions, but those two words were all he could cough out.

"Yes. My team is called in cases in which there is suspicion that the illness may have unnatural causes, or be caused by external agents, such as poisons or toxins." Taz was becoming steadily more alert. "My specialty is forensic toxicology."

"How does that involve me? The nurse said I had dengue. Or was that a hallucination too?"

"No, you definitely have dengue. And my colleagues at State tell me that you were on department business on the western margin of the

Amazon, so that makes sense. However, I can assure you that you didn't get it from a mosquito. That's the good news."

What's he getting at? Taz looked him over. "So… what's the bad news?"

"The bad news comes from my examination of your bloodwork. Someone intentionally gave you dengue, Mister Blackwell. You were poisoned."

Taz took a little what to let that sink in. "I . . . I don't understand. How—"

"I'll make it short. Dengue is caused by one or more of four antigenically distinct serotypes that we number DENV 1-4. Most cases show a mix, and most dengues act like a severe flu, though a very dangerous flu. Your blood only shows one serotype, the one that happens to cause the most severe cases. It won't mean anything to you, but it's a nonstructural viral protein we call NS-1. There have been reports—only a few, mind you—that a soluble form of NS1, if introduced to the bloodstream, can cause dengue of an extremely severe kind. We are reasonably certain that this is what happened in your case. I've consulted NCIS, our criminal investigators, but since it's clear that the actual incident occurred in Brazil, they're going to let it be dealt with by the competent national authority there."

"You're right, Doc. That is bad news."

"Yes and no. Once we identified the culprit, so to speak, we were able to fashion a more specific antiviral to deal with it. And if I do say so myself, you're progressing nicely."

◢

Progressing nicely? Taz remained feverish and achy three days later, when Laney brought him back to the Island. The terrible ache in his joints, the reason dengue used to be called breakbone fever, had eased considerably, but he was still too weak to do much but stay in bed and stare out the window. What he later recalled of those days, in addition to Laney's tough love and salty commentary regarding his reckless mode of life, was the sound of Lucia's voice and the feeling of her hands, which he recalled as being ever so slightly cool on his forehead or his cheek, or when she swabbed his cracked lips. And the smell of her—like grapefruit and fresh-cut flowers. The fog in his head had cleared. Still, he found the occasional nap unusually inviting.

"Taz. Are you there?" Laney asked

"I was dreaming."

"You were asking for Lucia again. I'm beginning to think you don't love me."

"Sorry. Blame it on the fever. Where is she?"

"She came back as soon as she heard. She was here with you for the first three days, reading to you, feeding you, holding your hand. But now her semester up in Salisbury has started. Yesterday, she told me she had been called back to the campus for a special meeting. Apparently, the new chancellor wants to address the staff. There's something weird going on there, Taz. No matter. She'll be back tomorrow."

"Before then, there's something I need to tell you."

"I know. Carolina. You've been repeating her name in your fever dreams."

Taz covered his eyes with his hands. Who would want to hurt him so badly that they would be willing to kill an innocent woman to do it? They obviously thought he would still be travelling as her passenger. He had plenty of enemies, to be sure. But none of the ones he could think of had a Brazilian connection. And if they wanted him dead, they—the Zetas, the Russian mob—could have taken care of that little task well before now.

Whoever did it had to be in Brazil or have interests in Brazil. Not the rancher—he may not have enjoyed Taz's style, but ultimately, he got what he wanted. Not De Souza, surely. The man just wasn't high enough in anybody's pecking order to order a hit. Frank Chapman–had to be. Except Taz had met Chapman during the CITES mahogany fight, and he wasn't the type to murder his adversaries. Who then? That's where Taz hit the stone wall.

Laney yanked him from his mental fog. "You're blaming yourself for everything. 'My fault, all of it. She's dead because of me.' Then, how badly you needed to be with Lucia, to tell her."

"Did she hear it all?"

"Enough."

"Is she alright?"

"There were tears. We were both struck by how heartbroken you are."

"Oh, Laney. I don't even know where to start. I'm not sure it could get any worse." It could. It always can.

*

He managed six hours of sleep and troubled dreams that night. In the morning he asked Laney to give him a ride to his cottage to pick up Old Faithful, sort his mail, and start moving his stuff back in. It had been five days since he left the hospital in Portsmouth.

"You sure you're up to this?"

"Much as I like poaching from you, yes. I need to get back to work. Jessica will want a briefing and I'll need to write a report for Interior on the fire work with the Brazilians. And that's a good thing, because I'm going to have a mountain of bills. Not to speak of the zillions of unreturned messages from my fan club."

She smiled. "I guess I better say yes then. At least you're starting to sound like the crustacean we've all come to know and love."

He wasn't wrong about the briefings; three messages from Jessica's office and an invitation to coffee with the Interior secretary. There was one question he needed the answer to before he responded to any of them. He stood on his stoop, sorting his bills, and retrieved his cell phone from the truck. He punched in the required numbers.

"Everton."

"*Meu amigo.* I was expecting your call."

"The small plane crash in the Atlantic Forest."

"You hadn't heard? Yes, it was Carolina. I'm so very sorry, Taz. I was told how ill you've been, and I was concerned not to aggravate your condition."

"Do we know what happened?"

"The TV is saying it was pilot error."

"Not possible. I flew with her. She was as good as an Alaska bush pilot, and just as careful."

"Yes. We've interviewed some local small-holders who all say they heard a single-engine plane, then saw it explode in flight. Our intelligence people—the SNI—think she was brought down by some kind of bomb."

Taz unlocked the front door, dropped his bag on the porch floor, walked dazedly across the living room, sat at the little kitchen table, looking out the window at the fig tree by the shed, and let the tears roll down his cheeks.

CHAPTER FORTY-TWO

Finding the Way Back

DUSK. GRAY, COLD RAIN. TAZ ate the last of the crab chowder that Laney had brought him the night before. He found a half-full bottle of Beam in the back of his kitchen cabinet. Felt nothing but gratitude as he swallowed the first shot, then another. It was possible he passed out. He couldn't be sure.

It didn't matter. He tossed and turned, nodded off, woke up sweating. Reached for his jaguar claw. Not there. Must have lost it somewhere between Sao Paulo and the hospital. He tried to go back to sleep, but his mind roiled with nightmarish visions. Carolina's Piper Cub breaking up in a blaze over the Atlantic Forest. Paulo's screams as he tore the flaming branches off his legs. The flames in the trees as he was dragged out of the fire and carried to the helicopter. The tower at Cruzeiro do Sul, lost in the smoke. Then, as the terror faded, Salvador, crouching at the fire, preparing the ayahuasca. The jaguar's bright green eyes, as he cautiously circled the smoldering ashes of their campfire. Salvador, locking eyes with him and smiling, *"Spirit animals don't leave tracks."* The bombeiros in a circle around him, laughing and knocking down their cachaça. Carolina, singing fado meant for him. Carolina, teaching him so gently that fire isn't the end of the story.

He woke just before sunrise, shivering violently under the sheets. Turned on the hot water, soaked a washcloth, and scrubbed his face and neck. Wet his shaving brush and went to work, looking at his mirror image. He didn't find much to like. His thoughts came back to Carolina. *Why did you have to bring her into it?* Her beauty, her voice, the songs of sadness and longing that riveted the crowds in Iquitos and Sao Paulo. *And now she's gone, Taz. Because of you.* After what seemed an interminable time, he turned away from the mirror, made himself a pot of strong black coffee and, sipping it, considered how he might find out who ordered her killing, and what he would do when he did.

*

By late afternoon, the rain had slowed to cool drizzle. Taz had spent the morning bicycling awkwardly around the island, soaking up the scent of wet pine and new-mown grass on Ridge Road, the dark vegetable odor of the fowling gut and the marshes, and the cool salt breeze on the beach road. On his return, he took the plastic cover off the herb garden and let his peppers soak. He had already put the knives through the first two stages of the sharpening process. First the coarse stone, 1,000 grit, to reestablish the edge. Then the medium stone, about 8,000 grit, for erasing the fine scratches left by the coarse stone, and to take off the burr. Then the natural quarry stone, for polishing. The stones were mined from just a few quarries, the only ones that produced the quality that could polish a razor, a sword, or a fine Japanese knife.

He was just finishing his little petty knife on a strop in the kitchen when he heard a soft knock on his door. Lucia, sheltering herself from the runoff under the hood of her slicker. She gave a tentative smile as he opened the door.

"Let's get you out of the rain, at least." He took her coat and sat her at the little kitchen table. "Would you like something to warm you up?"

She shook her head. "Maybe just a cup of coffee." He stepped to the stove and lit a match to the burner under the little copper pot that held his morning brew. She waited for him to sit back down, touched his forehead with her fingertips. "You're still feverish. What are you even doing up?" Gripped his shirt collar so she could bring his lips closer to hers. She had been crying.

Taz did his best to smile. "How about we make it an Irish coffee?"

"We better. I don't know how much Laney told you."

"She said you'd been by my side every day. That you care more about me than I do."

She touched his cheek with her fingers. "Taz. You're such a mess."

"I know. I'm sorry for it. And I know being sorry doesn't make any difference at all." She was watching him with those somber, deep-set eyes that could presage a storm or project an impossible sadness. Or, in different circumstances, dance with delight.

Lucia pulled his lips closer to hers. Taz tasted saltwater—her tears mixing with his. "I'm not talking about Carolina, Taz. I'm talking about you."

"Lucia, have I ruined it for us?"

She gripped his hand, digging her nails into his palm, glared at him. "Do you really think I'm that shallow? That when I said I care for you, I meant when you're nice to me, when you shower me with rose petals? Now you're just pissing me off."

Confused, he got up to pour the coffee. Heavy cream, double shot of Jameson in each. The rain and wind were picking up again. He sat back down and passed her cup.

"Did Laney tell you that every day we watched you sweat and ache left us with more questions? Taz, there are so many things I want to ask you." Taz raised his eyebrows. "Your new scar above your left eyebrow, the burn marks on your shoulder and back, and that nasty-looking gouge on your cheek, for instance." She kissed his cheek and his shoulder, lightly, tenderly. "I thought they sent you there to 'observe and assess the potential for future cooperation.'"

"Where did you learn those words? I've never heard you speak bureaucratic."

"I spoke with John White."

"About me?"

"Oh, Taz. I had to find out what happened to you somehow! And, these days, it's almost as if he likes you. An emotional leap for him, I know. When I first talked to him—while you were still in Brazil—all he knew was that you had been dropped at the fire line. But he knew you wouldn't stay on the sidelines, and he was worried about you too. So, when you came back all feverish and broken up, I went to see him. We talked for almost half an hour before he got called out to attend to some emergency. There were a couple of documents on his desk, and the top one was a cable from the embassy in Brazil. There was no way I was leaving that office without reading it."

Taz stayed quiet, tried to absorb the inflections of Lucia's voice, wondering what was in the cable. "It included the notes from your debriefing in Sao Paulo." Taz rolled his eyes. "Not just about the fire. Trust me, that wasn't the most interesting part, not by a long shot. There was a letter from the environment minister about how you broke up the logging ring—you and that doctor with the Greek name." He couldn't take his eyes off hers. Hers were fierce. "They want to give you some fucking medal! And you know what, Taz? I want to slap you!" A tear rolled down her cheek. "But I can't, because . . . because you're so busted up . . . and because I love you, okay?" She stiffened and glowered. "But Taz, I can't do it—can't go on—if you keep trying to get yourself killed. You have to at least try to take care of yourself. And not just for me. People care about you."

"Why? I fuck up every time I turn around. And now I'm supposed to sit in that yoga pose where you pat yourself on the back for all eternity? Just like all the other self-inflated idiots whose greatest love is the affair they have with themselves?"

Lucia cut in. "I'm not talking about when you turn aside compliments or run away from gratitude. People hurt when you close them out, Taz. When you take crazy risks like you did on the fire, everybody thinks you're being courageous. But it's not bravery, is it? You're a gambling addict. Except you don't gamble with money . . . that wouldn't be exciting enough."

"You know it's not like that."

"Oh, but it is. Laney sees it too. You just don't care, do you. What happens to you. Or about the pain. Whether you'll ever get to see your friends again. You're just like your damn knives—your life is just something you want to keep sharp. That's it, right?"

Taz downed the rest of his coffee, struggled out of his chair, took two cocktail glasses from the dish drainer, began polishing them with a hand towel.

"Taz?"

He stood staring at the late afternoon sky through bleary eyes. Turned back to Lucia. "Have you ever heard of a snake ball?" She shook her head, puzzled. "We're talking about maybe two dozen snakes, mostly males trying to mate with one or two females. They do it in the spring in the branches of trees. And sometimes they fall, you know? And maybe they fall into a river beneath the tree. And then, if they're cottonmouths, bad things happen."

"Well, there was a kid I knew—Nathaniel Bowman—when I was fifteen. He died. It was my fault." Lucia stood and slipped her arms under his, hugged him until her breasts pressed against his back. After a time, she disengaged, stepped back, and reached for his hand. "You'd better come with me."

Something in her eyes, a warm, soft regard, melted him like the spring melts the ice dams on Alaskan rivers during breakup. She led him to the couch, sat next to him, knee to knee, looking into his eyes. He ran the fingers of both hands from his forehead and through his hair. It occurred to him that he had never shared the story before, not with anyone.

"After my mother died, I went a little wild. Not right away, but later. I didn't really fit in to any of the groups at school. I played varsity soccer, but I was only in middle school and the jocks resented me for crashing their party. I was getting *As*, but I was too country for the college-prep crowd. By the time I was fifteen, I was getting in fights at school. Mostly with older kids who thought it would be fun to push my friends around, and the ones who liked picking on the weaklings at the bottom of the food chain. My father reacted like a lot of dads—with a leather belt. Didn't help. There was a girl I liked. She played on the girls' soccer team, and she had spirit.

One day during break, I saw the varsity quarterback pushing her down the hall towards me with one hand gripping her shoulder and the other in her hair. He had this loud voice and was saying 'This is what happens to bitches who insult me.' His friends were all laughing and shouting. He pushed her close enough that I could see it was no game. He was hurting her. He yelled at me to get out of the way, and I snapped. I cold cocked him and dragged him to an open locker and shoved his head in. I was doing my best to punch his lights out while his football buddies were trying to pull me away. If the gym teacher hadn't stopped me, I would have killed him. As it was, I got my first taste of jail."

"But you were only what—fifteen?"

"Sixteen. But there's more. I got a reputation and I kind of enjoyed it. Maybe too much. Pretty soon I had my own sidekick, a bright young kid who started to ask me about things he wanted to know, to have me take him hiking, to teach him how to box, that kind of thing. His name was Nathaniel Bowman. He was twelve then. One ranch hand who had spent a few years in Baltimore called him 'Natty Bo' and it stuck.

"Natty loved exploring together—*playing naturalist*, he called it. One spring day we came to a place where we had to cross a river—a small one, only about fifteen feet, but still carrying a good spring current. There was a gravel ford only a few hundred yards downstream, but I decided it would be more fun to skip across on some big flat river-washed stones up where we were. I went first. I made it, but it was trickier than I thought. Natty was already tensing for his first leap. I shouted at him to walk downstream, that I'd meet him at the ford. He wasn't having it. He leapt to the first stone, then to the second. That was when I saw the cottonmouth. Its head was above water. I yelled for him to stay where he was. Then he saw the snake too. And three more. He looked stricken, yelled, 'Taz, what do I do?' He turned towards me, his foot slipped, and he fell in on his back. Suddenly, there were snakes everywhere. Natty kept yelling, 'Taz, I'm scared.' I waded in to get to him. He was covered in them. There must have been a dozen just on his legs and back, biting him, biting each other, anything they could get their fangs to. I was scraping them off as quickly as I could, but they kept coming faster than I could pull them."

"My God, Taz, my God."

"This skinny twelve-year-old with his arms around my neck, crying and doing his best to shake the snakes off. I carried him out, but by then he was shivering and telling me how cold he felt. Lucia, his house was a quarter of a mile away. He was dead before I walked two hundred yards, so I stumbled on until I fell on his mother's porch, still holding him. She told me that she pulled three snakes off my back before she realized I was holding her son in my arms."

"You got bitten too." Taz nodded, shivering just like young Natty. She stroked his hair, tried to find some way to comfort him. They ended with her arms around his shoulders and her head cradled in the crook of his neck.

Later, Taz found some kindling and built a fire in his old cast-iron stove. They watched it, absorbing the warmth and sipping red wine.

Her head on his shoulder. "Taz, you did everything you could."

"No. What I should have done was die instead of him." Lucia winced and shook her head, tears in her eyes. "That's the way the folks in town saw it. Including my father. Natty's mom was the only person in the county who stood by me. I packed my bag and went to live with my aunt in Dallas. My father died that summer. My first year in college started the next fall. I did my best not to look back. Ever."

*

The cottage had cooled with the sunset's afterglow. Taz and Lucia sat at the kitchen table drinking red wine. She reached over and gently stroked his cheek.

"The scars aren't the only wounds you picked up in Brazil, are they? You look sad. Almost hollowed out. Like something you saw or felt was just too much to take. That's not like you, Taz. What happened?"

Here we go. Well, it had to happen sometime.

Taz thought for a second. "One of our bombeiros died on the fire line. I guess that's what made me think of Natty. He was my partner, a young man who'd just married and had a long, happy life ahead of him. Except he didn't. The whole thing happened so fast. Some of the other bombeiros were trying to down a flaming tree before it caught the whole forest edge on fire. The tree fell before we thought it would—on his back. I tried to pull the flaming branches off him, but they were so tangled I couldn't."

"That's how you got the burns."

Taz nodded. "He was my front-line partner, Lucia, and I couldn't save him."

"Oh, Taz. I'm so sorry." She reached across the table and stroked his hand. He motioned towards the front porch. They took their glasses to the porch and sat together on the wicker loveseat.

"There's something else. Lucia, I got a woman killed."

She squeezed her eyes shut, as if she knew what was coming. "Carolina. She was with you in your fever dreams. But what makes you think it was something you did?"

"Her plane didn't crash. It was blown up. I don't think she had an enemy in the world. But I did."

She wiped her eyes with the back of her hand. "Oh my God, Taz."

"Lucia, it was my fault. If we had never met, she would still be alive, singing."

"She was a singer."

"Fado, the tragic music of Portugal."

"I've heard a little. I imagine she was good."

"She wasn't sure anymore. She felt she had passed her prime. Imagine— at forty-two. Worried that she had lost some of her high notes. Her label had shipped her to Brazil for what she figured was her last tour. 'Finishing my career in the outback,' she called it."

"Taz, I need to know what it was… what was it that led you to become so fond of her?"

"I was drinking in a seedy riverside bar in Iquitos. I guess I kind of stood out. An *Americano* with a bunch of empty caipirinha glasses in front of him."

"You don't have to tell me. You were probably just trying to drink away that awful call—the one when I had the panic attack. What a fool I was,

Taz. I would have run the other direction too if I were you."

"This isn't on you. Really. You just had a little case of the hesitation blues, is all. Maybe I was feeling a little lonely, or sorry for myself. Anyway, she comes in and chooses a stool not far down the bar. We ended up having an interesting conversation—the kind where you're just trying to find out who the other person is. It was uncanny. She knew right away that I was missing someone. I tried my best to describe you. She told me how lucky I was, not that I needed to be told. She mentioned that she was singing at a club in town the next night, but I was supposed to leave for Cruzeiro that morning. I'm pretty sure neither of us thought we would ever see the other one again." He poured them both another glass of wine. "My plane never got off the ground—engine trouble. So, I did end up at the concert."

"Did you sleep with her?"

"We shared a drink afterward. Her husband, Carlito, had died exactly eighteen months before. She had been totally in love with him. Said my description of you reminded her of how much she had lost. She didn't want to be alone." Lucia looked down at her lap for a second, then back to him.

"That was the week I spent on the fire line. Then to Sao Paulo for the debriefing you saw. State had me put up in a nice hotel. It turned out she was singing in a club just a few blocks away and staying in the same hotel. I ended up in her room for the night. The next night I went to the concert. That was the last time I saw her."

"You miss her."

"Yes, but not in the way you think. It's more that I'm sad she's not in the world anymore. She was world-weary, really. I know that. And yet there she was, still trying to impart some beauty to rustic crowds in ramshackle bars and theaters in the headwaters of the Amazon."

After a few moments, Lucia stood and reached for his hands and pulled him up to face her. Her eyes, searching his, were wet with tears.

"Taz, I have to tell you something. After that call when you were going into the fire, I kept thinking back to the words I flung at you under that damn fish at the Pony Pines—about you being afraid to love. I realized it was me—I was the one who was afraid. And when you came back from

Brazil all broken and I realized I could have lost you—then I knew what real fear was—that I might have to live my life without you. I never want to feel that way again, Taz." Her hands gripped his as if she was pulling him into a lifeboat. She gave him a tender kiss, led him to the bed.

CHAPTER FORTY-THREE

Academic Discipline

PROFESSOR LUCIA TURAN'S RETURN TO academe was not going as expected. In one sense, that was hardly a surprise. She was more comfortable wandering mountains and riverbanks looking for big cats than she was in the classroom. Still, she had looked forward to the collegiality of the campus and its day-to-day exchange of ideas. Now, a setting that should have been reasonably convivial felt like a prison where the inmates were united only by their fear of the warden. Laney had been dead on when she told Taz that "Something hinky is going on over there." As one of Lucia's friends—an English professor—put it, folks were "keeping their heads down."

"Jesus. It's like going to school in a fucking morgue." She and Taz were drinking beers on the dock. "It has something to do with the new chancellor of the university system. He's been making the rounds of the university campuses. He's telling everybody he's going to shake things up, so we can 'take our work to the next level, whatever the hell that means. Okay, some shaking is definitely needed. But he's pitting the leaders of the faculty and the administration against each other, and my friends say he's sprinkling the whole university system with hand-picked acolytes who will be loyal to him and only him." Taz looked sideways and smiled. He knew just how well that would wash with Lucia.

"Let's start at the beginning. What's his name? Oh right, Carter something. You mentioned him in Midland."

"Carter Swindell. He's a high roller, apparently. Started out rich and made another fortune in the import-export business. Politically ambitious, too—at least some of my colleagues think so. He lives in a Potomac mansion, just up the river from DC. You can't get much swankier than that. He's going to be here tomorrow—they've told the faculty to be available starting after lunch, and they're throwing some kind of welcome reception at five. Want to come?"

I'd rather go in for a root canal. "I can't. The boys want to play a little music down at Rainy Day. It'll be the first time in months, and I have to shake the rust off somehow."

"That's a good excuse, I guess. Something tells me you wouldn't have wanted to, anyway."

He heard her disappointment. "Any chance you could swing by after? We're starting at seven, so we'll probably be done by nine. I could take you out for a late dinner or whip up a little something here."

"That sounds nice. I'll call you when I hit the causeway."

*

It was almost ten. They had played almost three hours and were putting away their instruments when Taz heard a faint buzz from the porch. Realized after a moment that it was probably his cell. He had, for once, remembered to put the thing on silent before they started playing. He closed his guitar and headed back to the porch to find it. He found it on the bookshelf where he had been leafing through a used copy of Wade Davis's marvelous book detailing the explorations in the Amazon undertaken by Richard Evans Schultes, perhaps the greatest botanist since Spruce. He grabbed the book and his cell, waved the book at Richard as a way of saying he'd pay him tomorrow, and headed out to his truck.

He hung up his windbreaker and felt the weight of the cell, remembered that he should check his messages. The most recent was from Lucia: "Taz. I can't . . . can't get there tonight. I'm not really in shape to drive." A sniffle. Her voice had that hoarse, broken quality that comes with a crying jag. "Don't worry . . . it's probably just the wine. Let's . . . let's talk in the morning, okay?" He sat on the bed and punched in her number. Got her message line.

Taz stared at his cell, took the windbreaker off the hook, and headed out to start Old Faithful. An hour later, he was knocking on the door of her flat just blocks from the university. No answer. He listened, knocked again. "Go away! Whatever it is, it can wait."

Taz knocked once more, called her name. The door opened a crack. Then, as their eyes made contact, she opened it wide and stood waiting for him with red eyes and an expression so forlorn that he pulled her into his arms even before he closed the door. He searched her eyes while he brushed a few loose locks of hair back over her ear.

"Shhh, sweetheart, it's going to be okay. Whatever it is. Look at me." Smiling, holding her cheeks gently between his palms. "Really. Let's sit, okay?" Guiding her to her little futon couch.

Taz poured two glasses of white wine, put them on the little coffee table. He pulled a chair close to her and waited while her breathing calmed. Eventually, he reached and gently brushed her cheek with his knuckles. "If you don't want to talk just now, I understand."

"It's not that. I want to tell you, but I don't know how. It's so awful, Taz."

"Let's just start at the beginning. Just tell me about your day. You had your classes—"

"Only two out of three. They hauled us out at two-thirty, so he— Chancellor Swindell—could speak to the faculty. So, there's about thirty-five of us, sitting in the little auditorium, and he comes on the stage. Handheld microphone, laser pointer, very corporate looking. He made me think of the priest in *Robin Hood* —tonsure, cherubic looking—pink cheeks, beady eyes, close to the bridge of his nose, little glasses that he peered over, a smirk instead of a smile. He gave this little pep talk, but by the end it felt more like he was threatening us than cheering us on."

Lucia's voice had changed from uncertainty to rage. "First it was 'I'm here to take you to a new level,' and then it was 'If you're not with me, get with the program. If you don't you will be weeded out.'"

"He wasn't exactly pitching for your affection, I get that. But some executives who come on tough—"

"It's more than that. He was reading from some briefing notes, and he started picking on people. You know Henry Barnes, the dean of the English Department—the one you met at that first faculty party?" Taz nodded, moved her wine glass closer to her, took a sip of his. "He's only a few months from retirement, and everybody knows he's lost a step, but his students and colleagues love him, and he still has a lot to teach. Taz, Swindell showed everyone a slide of Henry nodding off at his desk. He started ridiculing him. Called him 'Sleepy.' Then he pointed to Rosemary Coughlin and showed a slide of her holding her partner Amy's hand. He looks at her, and goes, 'You're a professor of theology, and this is the example you show to your students?' Then he pulled up a slide of Terry Robbins speaking at a student demonstration, 'You need to start understanding that you're here to educate the students, not brainwash them.' Then . . . then . . ." Her voice sounded uncertain again. "Then he pointed to me and looked around the room. I'll never forget his words, that sneering voice. 'And then we have Lucia Turan, our *star* wildlife science professor. She just joined our ranks this semester, and she's already made quite a name for herself. You're all jealous of her, and you should be. She gets to spend months on the Rio Grande *researching* panthers. Whenever and however she wants to, apparently. She could use her celebrity to the benefit of the university and you, her colleagues, if she so chose. But her research, to which the university gives its unstinting support, comes first—of course. Maybe you wonder what that research consists of—I sure did. Here it is.' And he shows a slide of a party we held after we tagged our first panther. It's me, holding a margarita, wearing a big sombrero, and dancing with Matt, my teaching assistant."

Taz smiled, then tried hard to suppress a laugh. "I *have* to see that slide. I know how you dance. The men in the audience were probably drooling."

"Taz, it wasn't funny, and nobody laughed. Then he talked about how dancers need to 'choose their partners carefully.' Said 'A bad partner can slow you down, throw you off balance. But a good partner can make all the difference in the rating the judges give you.' He was staring at me the whole time, Taz. I didn't know what to do."

"What did you do?"

"I was gathering my stuff to walk out. But then he ended the talk and said he expected to see us all at the reception. I jumped out of my chair and practically ran up the steps and outside."

"You want my reading? He's already decided about the folks he ridiculed. They're as good as gone. But you, sounds like he wants something from you. He was threatening you and building you up at the same time. The question is why?"

"Why?" Her tone was bitter. "I'll tell you why. I found out at the reception when he pulled me aside. And he's doing his best to loom over me—he's not as tall as you—and he puts on this oh so sincere smile and does the old standard 'Let me give you some advice.' He calls me Doctor Turan, so I think it's going to be more of what he said in front of everybody. But no, here's what he said. 'You ought to spend more time up here instead of on that little swamp island you're so fond of.'

"And here's the kicker: 'As for that nobody you're wasting your time on,' that would be you, in case you're in any doubt, he said, 'I don't imagine he's told you, but his romantic relationships don't seem to end well, particularly for the women involved. Maybe you should ask him about that.' And then I realized he's got me in a spot where no-one can see us, and he grabs me and comes in for a lip-lock. I was all set to slug him, but in that setting it didn't seem like such a good idea, so I just gave him a hard push and told him to leave me alone. He laughed and smirked, looked at me with these weird close-set eyes and this perverted smile, like I'm some slut he just picked up in a bar, and he says, 'So, you were willing to fuck every politician in Reynosa to save one or two panthers, but you're going to play the vestal virgin with me?' Then he finally got to the punchline, 'You don't get it. I can make your career . . . or break it.' Taz, how would he know anything about what happened down there? Enough to shame me? And Lord he's good at that. I am ashamed—again. If he spreads that story around, I'll have to quit. I just wouldn't be able to face my colleagues again." She closed her eyes and shook her head.

Taz leaned forward. "You're not the one who should be ashamed. He should." He sought her hand and led her to the bed. They sat together for a while. He ran his fingers through her hair. She sought refuge, burrowing under his arm as if to bury herself in him. She finally rested her head on his shoulder. He wrapped his arm around her back and gently pressed her head to his neck with his left hand. She softened and sniffled. Her breathing became slower and more regular. He bent his head to kiss her.

"It's going to be okay. Your colleagues know who you are. They respect you, and now they've seen him—seen how petty and vindictive he is. And he can't afford to embarrass you again in public because he would have to reveal the source of his information. Whatever role he's playing, going public would uncover it."

Lucia nodded sleepily and snuggled closer. Taz unbuttoned her blouse and gently pulled it off her shoulders. He lay her on her back, stood and pulled her skirt down over her bare feet. Found a blanket in the closet and pulled it over her. He brushed his lips over her cheek. She was sound asleep. He sat with back against the headboard and put together a few more pieces of the jigsaw puzzle he'd been working on since Brazil. Just now there were too many pieces and not nearly enough pattern.

CHAPTER FORTY-FOUR

The Secretary's Verdict

TAZ RUBBED HIS EYES, SMELLED burnt coffee. He buried his face in Lucia's pillow. It was cool—only her scent remained. She had left early to have breakfast with some faculty colleagues who were equally appalled by the chancellor's talk. She had also left the gas burner on under the pot. Now what had once been a couple of cups of hot caffeine-laced cowboy coffee was instead a smoking pile of carbon flakes stuck fast to the tin lining of a very hot copper pot.

Taz smiled. Spotted the slip of yellow paper Lucia had left on the counter.

Thanks for letting me dampen your shoulder last night. Do me a favor and don't kill anybody. And take care of yourself! I'll see you tonight.

He rinsed out the French press and made a fresh cup, sat at the counter, and sipped slowly, thinking.

What was going on with Lucia's new chancellor? At one level, it was obvious. Lucia was a beautiful single woman whose career was, whether she liked it or not, dependent on his approval. That fact alone would make her vulnerable to his attentions, at least in his eyes, and a desirable conquest as well. She was also a hot commodity for the university. Her presence turned a barely above average natural resources school into a sought-after destination for other young scientists, particularly women. At the same time, her reputation for independence equaled her acclaim as a field scientist. She needed taming. Defiance of his authority on her part could infect her colleagues. And if Chancellor Swindell was contemplating using her prestige to raise the university's public profile he would need her assistance, willing or not.

And why would he know anything about Reynosa? He wants to put her on exhibit. He'd want to know everything he could about her, and especially her work on the river. And maybe he had figured out a way to check the DEA cover story. He would have put someone to work doing a little digging. How else would he have turned up the video from her team's party? Or maybe the video came first. Someone brought it to his attention, instigated his interest. But who would have given it to him, and what did they stand to gain?

Taz recalled watching her, soft and gentle in her sleep. He had reached across his chest and twirled her hair with a delicate touch, dread seeping into his heart. Perhaps if he had sensed the threat to Carolina. Was it there the whole time they were together? *How was I so oblivious?* If Lucia was in danger, he needed to ask the questions he should have asked for Carolina, and he had better find some answers quickly.

And then there was the part about how Taz's loves not ending well. Had Swindell been digging into his life as well? Was he referring to his divorce? To the bust up with Dana? Or Carolina. Someone ordered Carolina's killing. Why? She had a bodyguard with her in Iquitos. In the neighborhood they had her playing in, that was a perfectly reasonable precaution, and he didn't fly with them to *Cruzeiro,* so he was probably local. She had never mentioned any enemies, any spurned lovers. She struck him as weary, maybe sad—not fearful. Either her weariness was really a kind of quiet stoicism, an acceptance of what fate had in store, or she just hadn't known that someone wanted to hurt her. Or maybe harming her wasn't the point. Rather just a means to an end.

Her manager had given up on her, and there wasn't any money at stake, at least as far as Taz could see. Her parents were gone, and so was Carlito. Who else would be hurt by her death? There was only one answer, and even though it had already occurred to Taz, he didn't like it. It was something Taz had done. Carolina was just a stand-in. That was the only way it made sense.

✦

Taz was idly watching his cellphone, thinking of someone he wanted to call, but couldn't remember who. His little trip down his broken neural circuit was interrupted when the thing began buzzing—the jolt its way of telling him he had a message. Undersecretary Lansman's office.

Nobody he knew. "She needs you here tomorrow afternoon." Her assistant would call with the time in the morning.

The abrupt demand irritated him. He was tempted to tell her little duckling that he had a little too much on his plate to scurry over to DC for a show and tell. Or have Laney tell them he had unfortunately perished and would not be available any time in the foreseeable future. One key problem—he was in hock, and he'd be staying there until he got what he hoped was going to be a seriously heavy check from State.

He pulled a Bohemia out of the fridge—he was out of Pacifico. He sat on the stoop, drinking the ice-cold beer and cooling himself down. It occurred to him that a quick trip to DC might give him an opportunity to have a face-to-face talk with his friends at the DEA. Besides, he might as well face the music. Jessica had only waited this long because, despite all appearance to the contrary, she had the requisite ounce of compassion to withhold his punishment until his health returned, so he would at least have the strength to take it. Even so, he needed to ready himself for the kind of indictment that Jessica could deliver so effectively. He had spent twice the money allocated for the mission, exceeding his instructions to such an extent that it wasn't clear that he'd even read them.

If he was going to receive a dressing-down, he didn't see any point in dressing up. The suit was out, and so was the tie. He drove in his khakis and T-shirt and took along a clean but well-worn button-down shirt and his off-white linen jacket. He got in at nine, stayed at the Tabard and enjoyed a Sazerac with the young bartender.

Taz arrived outside Undersecretary Lansman's office suite exactly at five, in the hope, surely forlorn, that punctuality would ease the coming interview.

"Jesus, Taz. You could have dressed! Just out of respect."

"I figured if I was going to be raked over the coals at least I wouldn't burn my only good suit."

"Raked over the coals? Taz—have you been taking your meds? I briefed the secretary on your mission, but now she wants to hear it from the horse's mouth."

Right before she gives me the axe.

Secretary Redmond was waiting for them. "Jessica, coffee for you, right?" And "How about you, Mister Blackwell—would you be thirsty?" Taz nodded. "What will you have?" She regarded him with an ironic smile.

Taz had noticed a small refrigerator tucked away in an alcove to the side of her desk. There was a marble-topped bar just above it. "I wouldn't turn down a glass of wine, but anything you have will do nicely."

"You don't stand on ceremony, I see."

"No ma'am. Your undersecretary tells me that's not my strong point."

"She's right." Secretary Redmond brought a bottle out and began pouring. "White okay? It's still early." He smiled in what he hoped was an encouraging manner. "It's been a long day. I think I'll join you." He rose to help her carry the drinks. She returned the smile. "How kind. Thank you."

The secretary placed Taz's wine on the coffee table and sat opposite them. She had a certain nobility of countenance that reminded Taz of Edward Curtiss's photographic portraits of the women of the Nez Perce. Black hair cut in the Prince Valiant style and a weathered face with high cheekbones, tight cheeks, a straight nose, strong chin, and dark eyes that could fix a target at fifty paces. She raised her glass in a toast, smiled, and gazed at each of them in turn. "Job completed. Now tell me what we've learned."

Taz looked at her. This woman had spent the last four years as the governor of Oregon. She wouldn't want to hear the usual bureaucratic report, and he sure wasn't about to bullshit her. He started with the bombeiros.

"They are up against the most severe wildfire problem on the planet, and they have about as much equipment as our volunteer fire departments. But they're tough and smart. They know how to fight a wildfire just as well as we do. And they have a satellite system that can monitor for outbreaks. What they don't have is money and the communications and logistical network to get the right teams and equipment to a fire hundreds of miles from the nearest town—on the periphery of the Amazon."

She shifted her gaze to Jessica, then back his way. "I was told you were going to help them secure a World Bank loan. That would take care of their immediate capital needs, yes?"

Oh boy, here it comes.

"Yes Ma'am. We had made a start before the team left. I think the chances are good that with a little work we can still help them get it."

"But you're not sure. And you've been too ill to follow up. Unfortunate. Still, I can see why it might have been hard to find the time to worry about the bank—especially if you had decided it was more important for you to add yourself—one person—to the fire line."

He gazed down at his wine glass for a moment. Didn't pick it up. There was no point in trotting out the reasons he had for what he'd done, that cooperation had to start on the ground, that real trust can only be built in the crisis, in dealing with the common danger. He raised his head, so his eyes were on hers. "I'm afraid I allowed myself to be distracted, yes."

"And is that where the scars come from?"

"Well, the physical ones, in any case."

She took a long, satisfying sip. "Yes. An adventure such as yours would take a lot out of you, I imagine." Turned toward Jessica. "Would you like to tell him, or shall I?" Jessica grinned and pointed back at her.

Great, what fun. Can yo just fire me now so I can get back to the Tabard and nurse a few Sazeracs?

"Mister Blackwell. Taz. The loan was approved two days ago. Valentina Belin—I gather you know her? I didn't, until she called me to tell me about it, but I must say she's quite impressive. She said it was our approach that swayed the Brazilians, and that the Brazilians' enthusiasm and the practicality of their revised proposal were crucial to the bank's decision. And she told me that you had proved that the two teams—yours and the bombeiros—could work together extremely effectively, and that she was confident the two governments would do just as well. Her way of telling me to make sure your next little project gets the funding you'll need, I suspect. In fact, she and the bank leadership were so impressed by the joint effort that they matched the loan with a grant of equal size. All while you were recuperating." Secretary Redmond nodded to him.

"She also said you're something of a hero in Acre Province now, which won't do our relationship with Brazil any harm. The Brazilian foreign minister called me yesterday to express his deepest gratitude." She put her glass down. "Perhaps you'd like to enlighten me regarding *our* approach? I assume she was referring to your diplomacy?"

Taz thought for a few moments. "On that account, I think the credit goes to Jessica. She was the one who dealt with the upper echelons and convinced them that we were really there to help and not to take over the Amazon, which has always been the anxiety of the paranoids in their defense ministry."

Secretary Redmond turned a friendly gaze to Jessica. "She is indeed one of our best. Still, Mr. Blackwell, I imagine you had some input as well." Jessica nodded vigorously.

He thought again. "The Brazilians are a little like us. Proud, patriotic. The difference is their approach is a little lighter than ours. More musical, more humorous, and ironic. It wasn't going to do to go down there and tell them, you know, how to do it, or even how *we* do it. The only way was to work with them, to let them see how our system works, especially the parts they don't have, the communications and protocols. I mean, they're just as good on the ground as we are. So . . . trust. That was the most important thing."

"And that's why you joined the fire line." She closed her eyes and nodded. She looked at him with a smile. "Now tell me about the scars."

CHAPTER FORTY-FIVE

The Ghosts from the Border

THE SECRETARY WAS REQUIRED AT a White House dinner for the Czech prime minister. Jessica had plans for the evening. Taz said his goodbyes and headed back to the Tabard, not a little confused and vastly relieved. He had a light dinner and shared some stories with his friend behind the bar while sipping a Sazerac. Later, lying wide awake in bed, he turned his thoughts to how to approach DEA. Taz began where the whole tangled mess started—with Felix Romero. That was the name Lucia gave him in the Midland Airport. Somehow the Mexico pieces all led back to him. Sort of like the way the Brazilian pieces linked to de Souza. Romero had put Lucia on the firing line so he could find out what he wanted to know about Mayor Contreras' connections.

At seven-thirty in the morning, Taz called John White, who was becoming less of a DEA fan by the day. He knew White would be in his office, preparing for the daily deputy secretary's morning meeting with the assistant secretaries, where State's top-level team tabled their progress reports and got the day's guidance from on-high. White told him Romero had been promoted after the Cardenas bust. He had accepted a transfer to DEA's headquarters. He was now happily ensconced in a fourth-floor office at the Justice Department, on detail to DOJ as an assistant to the director of what's known in acronym-land as OCDETF—the Organized Crime Drug Enforcement Task Force.

With White's information in hand, Taz drilled deeper. No criminal record. Married with two children, ages seventeen and twenty. Address in Willowsford Estates, a recently developed community in Loudoun County where the median house price approached two million. Pretty fancy digs for a drug cop. He was a premier member of the exclusive Belmont Country Club, which required a $75,000 entrance fee. Season tickets to the Redskins.

It was hard to believe he'd be able to wrest enough time from wallowing in luxury to take care of his new job, but he apparently did find his way to the office, on occasion. His work record was a little less perfect than his private life. There were no awards in his file, but there was evidence of a couple of untoward incidents, one of which involved a sexual-harassment complaint. The other was more interesting—it had been taken under review by the inspector general of the Justice Department and reported in *Politico*. *Watchdog report slams DEA money-laundering operations.* It appeared that DEA had failed to report to Treasury millions of dollars seized during drug interdictions, and that the missing cash had instead been used in money-laundering efforts involving the cartels south of the border. The DEA's defense was that letting money walk was preferable to letting drugs or weapons fall into the wrong hands.

Taz kept drilling. With the help of a senior INR staffer he had known since his days as State's environment negotiator, he checked Romero's security clearance. High enough for a middle-ranked bureaucrat at OCDETF, but well below the clearance that allowed Taz to receive compartmented intelligence at State. As well as to comb DEA's classified personnel file. Taz decided to go fishing.

Fishing was not on Taz's list of favorite activities. He loved his time on Chincoteague Bay, digging for clams and lining for crab. He knew his friends on the Island had always thought his indifference to fishing was just a little odd, but he wasn't about to enlighten them. They'd be laughing about it until the end of time.

The truth? When he was nine, his uncle in Louisiana decided it was time for him to learn to fish. Even then, Taz wasn't sure he liked watching a fish squirm on the hook at the end of his fishing line, but he did enjoy the mornings when he would follow his uncle to the levee and eat ham sandwiches while he watched him set up.

One morning, Unc rousted him early to go to a special fishing place. Taz noticed that he wasn't bringing their rods. Soon enough, he understood why. They set up on a mudbank at the edge of a flooded cedar swamp. Pretty soon his uncle jumped in the water, clothes on, rolled up his right sleeve, plunged his arm under the surface and started poking around under the bank. After about a minute, he grimaced, shouted "Alright!" and brought up his arm with a catfish extending tail-first a good two and a half feet off his wrist. His hand was plunged deep in the fish's mouth. At that point, Unc motioned for Taz to join him in the dark brown water. Taz learned how to noodle catfish that day. He got one—a small guy, maybe a foot long—on his first try. On his third try he learned that noodling could be a two-way sport. He brought up a thirty pounder, and the question was whether they would be frying the fish tonight or would the fish be digesting his arm tomorrow. Unc had forgotten to mention that part—that catfish have teeth like a crosscut saw, and they like to spin on your arm to make you drop them. The really big ones will even drag you underwater with them. Maybe you come back to the surface, maybe no. It all depends on whether your free hand can reach your fishing knife.

*

Checking Romero out was surprisingly easy. At lunch hour on sunny days, Justice emptied out into a courtyard and then to Pennsylvania Avenue in pursuit of the latest midday cuisine, at restaurants where the assembled bureaucrats hold down sidewalk tables to see and be seen. According to White, when Romero wanted to impress someone, he'd reserve a table at the Capitol Grille, one of the most expensive steakhouses in the district, and a convenient stroll from Justice. He left the office at 1 p.m., day after day, always exiting the gigantic gray stone edifice on the 9th Street side. A friend of Taz's from Justice's Land and Waters Office had seen Romero guide a svelte young thing to the Grille—twice in the past week. So, this morning, Taz waited, and when they passed by, he trailed discretely behind them. The outside tables were full. He waited while they went in and then followed suit. The place was crowded. The couple were at the bar, waiting for their table.

Taz ordered a whisky and stood at a high table just behind them. Romero wore a custom-tailored Italian suit, cinched at the waist—a delicate proposition for a man in his fifties who was turning to fat. His companion was considerably younger and dressed a little too provocatively for an attorney—*legal secretary, perhaps?* She looked at Romero with adoration as he told her what were undoubtedly inspiring tales of derring-do, smiling and groping as he talked. Occasionally nuzzling her ear. Taz couldn't catch much over the din, but he did hear the one thing he needed—her first name. MaryAnn. Romero's wife was named Celia.

A young female greeter found them at the bar and led them to a table. Perfectly, from Taz's perspective, it was a table for four. He watched as they put in their drink orders. MaryAnn reached across the table to massage Romero's hands with her thumbs. There ensued a deeply meaningful conversation, her eyes pleading, his smiling condescendingly as he shook his head. A few minutes later the waiter returned with an ice bucket and a bottle of expensive Chablis. Once the wine was poured, Romero nervously scanned the room and toasted her. She replied in kind, with a charming giggle, and the romantic toast was downed.

Taz strolled amiably over to their table, raised his arms in a happy greeting and chortled like a long-lost friend: "Felix, I am so delighted to see you. It's been too long." He pulled out one of the empty chairs and dropped himself into it, full of good cheer. The older couple at the next table looked on with curiosity. Romero began to get up, gave a tentative smile. Taz placed a gentle hand on his shoulder and sat him back down, then turned to MaryAnn with another good-humored chuckle. "And you must be Celia. I've been *so* looking forward to meeting you." Loud enough to attract the attention of the table on their other side. The color rose in MaryAnn's cheeks. Romero was struggling to rise again.

"I'm afraid there's been—"

Taz cut him off with a jovial sputter, turned his eyes to the blushing young woman. He almost felt sorry for her. "But what a *barbarian* I am. I'm so sorry—I should have introduced myself. I'm Taz Blackwell, the man your friend Felix here tried to have killed on the Mexican border only a month ago."

MaryAnn looked like she was staring down the barrel of a rifle. Romero slapped his hand on the table and shot out of his chair like a rocket. Taz stared into his eyes and spoke slowly, his voice low. "Sit back down. Unless you want me to keep going." Romero glared, sitting slowly. Taz smiled at MaryAnn, raised his voice. "MaryAnn, don't be scared—it's just an old joke between friends." He scanned the nearby tables. "Sorry folks. That came out a little loud—it really has been a long time." He grabbed Romero's full water glass, tossed the contents into the ice bucket, lifted the wine bottle, and refilled the glass. Took a long sip, turned to Romero, and said, "Let's talk."

MaryAnn looked pleadingly at Taz. "I think I should go to the powder room."

Taz placed his hand gently on hers. "Of course." Looked into her eyes. She was innocent of anything except misplaced adoration. "I'm sorry if I embarrassed you. You look like a nice young woman." Nodded in the direction of Romero. "But honestly, you can do better."

He fixed Romero with his gaze. "You have a choice to make, Felix. You can tell me—now—how your connection to the Zetas works. Or—"

"Or nothing. I have nothing to say to you." His face twisted in elemental fury.

"You might want to think that over. If you don't tell me the straight story, with all the details, there are two packets of information that will find their way out into the big wide world. Packet One will have the full story of your extramarital affairs, including the apartment you keep for your little dalliances. Packet Two will include your banking information and show your mile-long dirty money trail, including the income you've received for working with the Zetas. In case you think I'm bluffing, here's the number for your account in the First Cayman Bank." Taz reached in his suit pocket and pulled out his cellphone. Flipped past the photograph he had taken of the two at the bar, and finally found the number. Showed it to Romero, whose fury morphed into nausea, his eyes losing their intensity as he pulled at his dampening collar. Taz slipped the phone back in his pocket, flicking the mic switch with his thumb on the way.

*

An hour and a half later, Taz walked north out of the Penn Quarter, considering what he had learned. Whatever play DEA had been running in Reynosa, Romero sure hadn't been quarterbacking it. He was just a cog in a very complex machine. Taz had sweated him, politely but clearly threatening his career and his marriage. Romero had coughed up as much as he was going to. He had been acting on instructions, which weren't coming from upstairs at DEA. He had been contacted by someone outside. Someone who made sure Romero never learned his identity. Whoever it was salted the instructions with a trickle of real intelligence good enough to convince the DEA higher-ups that Romero was one of their rising assets. That struck Taz. Valuable tidbits about the Zetas could only come from someone with ties to them or one of their competitors—the Sinaloa Cartel, or maybe the Jaliscos.

Romero's cooperation had been worth a lot of money—enough to fund a new and much more satisfying lifestyle. Maybe he tried to get out at some point, and they put the fear of God into him. After that, if he betrayed even a smidgen of doubt about the requests coming over the transom, he would feel a threat far worse than any Taz could visit on him. If he knew what was good for him, if he didn't want to die in pain, he would be on a burner phone right now telling his contact about his interview. If he didn't, and the one who was running the whole shebang found out, Romero was a dead man. Either way, Taz's questions would bring up the bottom-dweller—the one Taz was noodling for—and do it fast.

✒

Taz wandered up 21st Street, enjoying the warm dusk, not to any place in particular. He dimly recalled a little bistro near Dupont Circle and thought he might head over that way. After he settled at a little table for two by the inside of the entry wall, he asked for a carafe of *vin rouge* and a *steak au poivre with pommes frites.* The wine was some kind of merlot blend, and the meat was a grilled flat-iron steak, chewy but tasty. His waiter came to refill his glass and assure himself that Taz was satisfied. Taz thanked him and asked for a black coffee. He lingered over the steaming cup for a while trying to connect dots.

Brazil. Gabriel de Souza, Fontana's VP. The man in charge of the illegal logging in the Txai reserve. Everton's assessment of a coordinated effort to open the Indigenous reserves on the western margin of the Amazon to illegal logging. Did Fontana have a role in the larger scheme?

Taz's recollection of his first encounter with Fontana had led him to believe that de Souza reported to Frank Chapman. But John White had checked, and Chapman had left the company six months before the Acre incident. And there was no hint of illegal proceeds on Fontana's books. Where were the profits going?

Sao Paulo. Carolina seducing the audience, singing to him. The lone man at the table. Something about Lucia's description of her chancellor brought him to mind—how odd he looked in the light blue porkpie hat. How he had watched Carolina as she sang. The close-set eyes when he looked Taz's way with that smirk.

And then, further back in time and less distinctly, Mexico. The man who was bending the mayor's ear. The slightly unfocused look of his eyes behind the half-lens reading glasses. The shiny dome above his thin halo of dark hair. The bulbous cheeks. The self-satisfied little smile that fit Lucia's description of her amorous chancellor to a T.

Mexico. The obvious tension between the mayor and the Zetas. The mayor's decision to evade the Tamaulipas' governor's anti-corruption drive.

To show his fealty to the Zetas?

The money man. Who was he? Lucia had said something about laundering money through an import company. Ignacio's suspicion that someone from outside was now acting as a treasurer for the cartel— substituting for Cardenas and moving millions at a time through as yet unknown banks.

DEA's decision to take control of Lucia's intelligence gathering assignment. Their insistence that she cozy up to the mayor. DEA's effort to assassinate him and Lucia at the border—to protect what? —their informers in the cartels? Or their cooperation with them.

Carter Swindell's knowledge of Lucia's work in Reynosa. Which he could only have learned from one of two sources: the Zetas, or the DEA.

Unless he was working with both of them.

When Taz looked up, the busboys were clearing tables and it was ten forty-five. It was a three-and-a-half-hour drive to the Island. Good that he had reserved an extra night at the inn.

CHAPTER FORTY-SIX

Pandora's Box

TAZ LEFT JUST AHEAD OF rush hour and pulled into his little shell driveway at nine in the morning. Another cool day, this time gray, with a hint of rain on the horizon. The postman had overstuffed his mailbox with junk mail. Some of it had fallen to the cement stoop below. He ignored the little pile of shiny envelopes, some with cellophane windows, some without, a couple of newsprint flyers, and a yellow bill from ANEC, the Eastern Shore's utility co-op. He unlocked the front door and started a pot of coffee. The coffeemaker was still perking when his cellphone cawed. Laney's number.

"Coffee time?"

"For sure. And bring some Irish, okay?" Taz could hear the stress.

"I'm on the way." He turned off the burner and headed out.

They sat outside, watching the traffic come off the bridge. Taz doctored her cappuccino, waited for her to take a few sips.

"So?"

"Just a normal, run of the mill morning. Until some asshole tried to run me off the road." Taz spit out a mouthful of coffee, trained his eyes on hers. "I was on the Atlantic Road, coming back from a Matthews run."

Matthews Market, nine miles down Route 13, catered to a Latin and Black clientele—mostly folks who worked in the chicken factories. They had a great selection of chiles, fresh and dried, and the only serious butchers on the Eastern Shore. They'd cut you a top round fresh, skirt steaks for *carne asada,* or a four-bone ribeye you could trim and slice at home. The owners were friendly, and if you were a regular, they'd call you when they had top quality tenderloin.

"This guy comes up next to me and gives me a look, then jerks his steering wheel and whacks my front fender. I skidded to the shoulder, but he did it again. I ended up doing a one-eighty on the dirt patch at the roadside of the old Wright's driveway."

"Jesus, Laney. You okay?"

"Just a little shaken up." Her hand trembled as she held the cup. "Why would anybody do that?"

"I don't know. What kind of car was it? Did you get the license plate?"

"An old Lincoln. Pretty beat up. Maryland tags. Oh, and it had been repainted some kind of rust color . . . rough, with no shine. That's all I got. Pretty hard to read a license plate when you're sliding and spinning."

"You did pretty well is what I think. No surprise you were a little distracted."

"Shit. I'm more worked up now than I was then."

"Have you told the police?"

"If it was here on the island I would have. Richard's in Baltimore. I'm going to wait to tell him when he gets home tonight, and he'll be on them like a cheap suit of clothes . . . you know how he gets. But with the Accomack Sheriff's Department? I don't think we have enough to go on—they'd probably write me off as a hysterical housewife."

"No one in their right mind would think of you as a hysterical anything and you know it."

"Slight exaggeration. But the son of a bitch did get me riled up."

"Right. If you see the car again, give me a call, okay? I mean, *before* you kill him." Finally, he got a laugh out of her, half-hearted, but better than none at all.

They walked back to the store hand in hand. Halfway there, he stopped, turned her his way and hugged her while she cried. Sniffling, "You . . . you always know what I need."

On the way home, Taz stopped off at Church Street Supply to pick up a couple of drill bits and some fresh sandpaper. The disorderly pile of mail was still waiting. He found a cold *Pacifico* in the fridge and went out to sit on the stoop and sort through the clutter.

A small square envelope caught his eye. It was almost buried in the flyers and bills. Off-white. Vellum. Embossed, but Taz couldn't see it well enough to make out the title. He opened it with the dull side of a garden knife, plucked out a similarly embossed card. The message had been typed with what looked like an antique typewriter.

You interfered with one of my businesses. One that I value highly. In return, I took something you value highly. If you continue to meddle, I will take everything you hold dear. I trust you will agree that's fair.

Taz had never read anything so supercilious and brutal.

So, there was a link. Romero's missing drug banker and Carolina's killer were still out there. In fact, they were the same person, and that person had just done his best to kill Laney. If he had found Laney, Lucia was in danger too. Taz didn't have much time. Worse, he had three balls in the air, and he wasn't that good a juggler.

The initial investigation of the mahogany piracy in the western Amazon had bogged down irretrievably, which wasn't really surprising, since it was being pursued by the military police in Amazonas Province, who were better known for their harassment of conservation activists and human rights workers than for their anemic investigatory capabilities.

Taz had gotten all he was going to get out of Romero, short of torture. He had outlined the financial arrangement as far as he knew it, and whether he intended it or not, what he told Taz confirmed Ignacio's suspicion that Cardenas had been replaced by an outside financier with a link to the Colombian cartels. The signature on the note might mean something, or it might be intended to mislead. Either way, Taz was no closer to putting a name on the new moneyman.

His gut told him there was some connection between the man who wrote his little greeting card and Lucia's trouble at the university. But what? He had to find out, and he would need help. He wrote up a little list: *Eliza Clarke, Jack Donley, John White, Everton Martins, Ignacio Morela.*

Taz left messages for Eliza and Jack. He didn't want to call Everton or Ignacio until he had talked to White, who was in Bogota for a narcotics conference. Ellie would pass along that Taz called.

Taz sat at his kitchen table, stewing, mulling over his uncertainties, feeling adrift, useless. Eventually, he got his bike out of the shed and wheeled down towards the marina and the southern tip of the island. A cool breeze in his face, coming from the south, cirrus clouds up high— maybe ahead of a storm front? He hadn't bothered with a weather forecast for days. He rode into the marina to see who was in. A couple of smaller trawlers, *Miss U Sippi* and *Get the Blues,* three gleaming charter boats, a couple of the bigger tour boats floating uneasily on their gray pontoons. The water dark, with a little oil sheen collecting near the outboards. Smell of salt and gasoline. The marina suddenly in shadow—Taz looked up to see a raft of cumulus clouds moving slowly from the west.

"Blackwell!" A bellow, more than a sweet hello. Charlie Sanborn, the captain of *Get the Blues,* looking scuffed up as usual, crouching just in back of the open wheelhouse.

"What's up, chief? I didn't see you in there."

"Cause you weren't looking. Feelin' up to snuff?"

"That depends."

"I got some warp line fouled on the winch. I could use an extra hand."

Taz leaned his bike against a piling, stepped down to the pier and over the gunwale onto the deck. The boat stank of dead fish. They stood side by side, eyeing the line. It had twisted itself into a triple kink—not yet a bird's nest, but plenty bad enough. Taz stepped around the winch into the pilot's cabin, found a ten-inch fishing knife with a scaler on the top of the blade. He came out and held it for Charlie to see.

"Very funny. That rope is worth three hundred dollars—think I won the lottery?"

"So, unspool it and take apart the winch."

"Tell me something I don't know. Gonna unspool it but I need an extra hand."

"Crew quit?"

"Had a date, believe it or not."

"Not smelling like this he didn't."

"Right—just press down on the damn line. At least a foot from the winch, no matter how hard it bites, or you won't be playing any more guitar."

"I didn't know you cared. Anyway, Jerry Garcia cut off a finger and still played, and Django Reinhardt played with just two."

"You as good as them?"

"Not with seven fingers on both hands."

"Okay." A sound like a washing machine crunching gravel as Charlie started the winch. Taz pressed down, felt the line tighten hard, pressed harder with everything he had, and then snatched his hand up and off. The line snapped back into place; kinks gone.

Charlie chocked the winch and bent to examine the line. "Good." Then he stepped back, looked at Taz. "There was a guy around yesterday." Taz waited. "Never seen him before. He sure weren't no fisherman. Asking about who owned the boats—fool questions nobody would answer. Finally wanted to know if you had a boat here."

Taz felt a chill ripple down his spine. "Did you show him the skiff?" He had bought a used Carolina skiff when he first came to the island. He'd never used it much, and finally, when he started travelling for work again, he gave it to the Kiwanis Club as a teaching boat for their work with disadvantaged teens. It was still at his slip.

"Nah. I spat out a lot of words and didn't tell him a thing. Sorta like some come-heres do."

Taz didn't see any reason to take the last comment personally. "Look, Charlie. If you see Raymond come over to take the kids out, tell him to check the boat like he would if he just got it back from the shop. Especially the engine. And he should keep his gas canisters at home for now, okay?"

Charlie leaned back against the outrigger, crossed his arms, arched his eyebrow. "Okay, Taz. Thanks for the hand. Maybe it's better if you watch your back for a while."

When he got back to the cottage, Taz found the lava soap under the sink and scrubbed until he got the winch grease off his hands. When he was finished, he pulled another Pacifico from the refrigerator and strolled out to the dock, trying to get his thoughts in order. Took a long, cool swallow, watched the condensation trickle down the bottle.

He noticed that a couple of the lag bolts that held the benches to the pilings were rusted through. Then he must have nodded off. He awoke—it might have been five minutes or an hour, he couldn't tell. He had the strangest impression that he was warming from the inside, as if he had been infused with light and energy. He smiled, thinking of how he had awakened by the campfire in the Brazilian forest, his cheek nestled on the bed of ferns that he imagined had been a jaguar's paw. He let the impression settle for a while and then finished the beer and walked back into the cottage. His cell phone was cawing from the kitchen table. He jumped to get it.

Eliza answered. "Taz. I think I've got something. At least part of the puzzle. Our friend Mr. Swindell isn't just Maryland's most ambitious political neophyte, he's a bigger political donor than we thought. He makes his donations through a whole stack of charities and PACs, which is why we didn't find him right away. He gives to the national Republicans, but also at the state level. To the governor, before and during the campaign. Which definitely smoothed his way to becoming the chairman of the university executive committee. That, and he's also been supplementing the salary of the university president. It was $250,000 a year, which you might figure was enough. Swindell doubled it with a single contribution."

"Any idea where he's getting the money?"

"He's on a couple of corporate boards, but even if they pay the going rate, it wouldn't put him on easy street. Here's what would. His father is the founder of Darien Investors, a Wall Street hedge fund. One of the more successful ones."

"Eliza, this is the reason you're my favorite reporter."

"Oh, stick it, Taz. Just doing my job."

He wandered out to the shed, picked up a crescent wrench, a short sledgehammer, and a couple of new carriage bolts and nuts. The crescent wrench gave him just enough leverage to back out the rusty nuts, and he sledgehammered the rusted bolts back through the pilings far enough so he could use the wrench to wrestle them out. It was heavy work, but that was what he needed. He kept at it until his shirt was wet with sweat and his wrists were aching from torquing the wrench. He put away the tools and sat heavily back at his kitchen table. Thinking, or trying to.

The fatigue wasn't just momentary. Taz had a deeper weariness that seemed to have settled on him over the weeks since his recovery. He had hit the wall. All the inquiries he had made had taken him to loose ends, crooked trails, missing links, unsolved questions. Even Eliza's news didn't change that. Meanwhile, he had apparently opened Pandora's box—and it was spilling out threats to the people he loved. He cradled a cold beer, grateful for the chill. Picked up his cell and punched in the number for Everton's office.

"*Meu Amigo.* I wish I had better news. However, we both know that the Amazonas police were never going to uncover the ringleaders in all of this. They did just what we thought they would. They brought in a half-dozen lowlifes, perhaps the ones who had done the burning, perhaps not, and they'll probably free them, if their families pay. The others? They're dead already. Case closed. I wish that it were different, Taz, I really do."

"I know, Everton. You've done everything you can. It's just, maybe, you know, maybe if we want a different result, we have to take a different path."

"A different path?"

"The intelligence agreement."

"Oh, indeed. You are *astuto*. How would you put it in English? *Canny.* Of course. I talked to your friend John White yesterday. A joint intelligence team will conduct a more serious investigation—that much I can assure you. The *Ministério da Justiça* will be infuriated, but if the request comes from your side, under the agreement, there will be nothing they can do about it. Brilliant, really. They'd never have to know."

"At least not until it's time for indictments."

"And at that point we can force their hand if need be. We have much work to be done quickly. We'd better get started."

He really is. He's my brother from another planet.

❧

Lucia was working late. He would tell her what he could—what she needed to know—right after she'd finished her first after-school sauvignon blanc and was eyeing whatever little plate he'd constructed as her late-evening palate pleaser. Neither of them exactly lived for three squares, so they did this a lot. He wanted to tell her everything, but he didn't yet have the final piece of the Mexico puzzle, and she had plenty to handle already.

The morning after she talked with Taz, Lucia had touched base with some of her colleagues, including senior faculty members at the central campus. There had been rumors over the last few months that the new chancellor of the University of Maryland had bought his sinecure with a series of extremely generous contributions to the governor's campaign war chest. One friend, a grad student in anthropology at the College Park campus, had proof in the form of a copy of a check, pulled out of the trash at the governor's campaign headquarters, where she was an unpaid intern.

Lucia showed Taz the copy of the check as they were finishing off a cassoulet he had made over the weekend. He had found some veal shanks at a farmer's market north of Salisbury and decided to use them the French way. It took him most of Saturday and every pot he had in the kitchen. It was worth the price to watch Lucia lick her fingers after dipping the heel of a hard crust baguette in what was left on her plate at the end of the meal.

He poured the last of the burgundy, took another look at the check. "That's a chunk of change. I imagine he got whatever he was paying for."

Later, while Lucia was working on the second of her three papers, he called Eliza Clarke to relay what she had learned. Eliza had heard rumors of the contributions, but she hadn't been able to turn up a source who would speak for the record. But she was a good reporter. Her colleagues maintained she should have gotten a Pulitzer for her coverage of the Tobytown mess two years back. Now she was tracking down Swindell's personal contribution records. Based on the public record and a few anonymous interviews, she had been building a profile of Swindell's actions since he'd been awarded the chairmanship of the university and asking various of his colleagues and rivals to fill in the gaps, and fill out the backstory of why he was chosen.

✦

Taz's phone rang late that morning. It was Lucia. Her last class had just ended. She had a message on her phone from somebody she'd never heard of.

"I called back and said hello, and he didn't even give me time to get the next syllable out. Totally rude. So, he has this ragged whisper of a voice and says, 'Where's Blackwell? I left a message for him at least an hour ago.' Who do you figure it was? And how did he even know I knew you? Made me a little jittery, you know? An hour and he was all ready to blow a gasket? I didn't know what he wanted, so I just told him I'd call you."

"Hold on." Taz found his messages. "It's okay. I'm just looking at the message. Sorry if he was rude, but it's nothing to worry about. His name is Jack Donley. I've worked with him before. He's always rude. But he's also a hell of an investigator—one of the best around. I gave him a call to see if he might help us figure out what's really up with Swindell."

Donley had been a political reporter with the *Baltimore Sun*, and he and Taz had collaborated on a couple of stories during the last presidential transition. The crooked paths one takes to become an ambassador, that kind of thing. Eliza had mentioned having drinks with him, in an off-hand way, a little tidbit that Taz had promptly forgotten, but she had briefed Jack on her work to uncover Swindell's connections, and Jack suddenly found himself very interested. Now he smelled blood in the water, and he wasn't keen on sitting around twiddling his thumbs until Taz called back. His money trace had turned up an unusual number of banks and an interesting list of corporate boards of which Swindell was a member. It was against his better judgement, but he was willing to give Lucia a copy, assuming she'd share it with Taz.

As they shared a bottle of Chablis on the dock that evening, it became clear that Lucia was not altogether mollified by Taz's explanation. "He made it sound like he was giving me the key to Fort Knox! Why would you work with somebody like that?"

"Believe it or not, he's worth the pain and suffering. He's a born investigator, just like you're a natural wildlife whisperer."

"I think I like that description. Yes, maybe I do. My dean, on the other hand, would never get it at all. He only speaks academize. So, Mr. Glib, what about you?"

"Isn't that for you to answer?"

"Is it now?" She sounded pensive. *"You* are a direction finder.'"

"To quote every woman I know, 'Men don't ask directions.'"

"To quote every woman *I* know: '...because they're too thick to know when they're lost. Not like that, you ninny—like a compass!"

"Ouch—where did you say you were sleeping tonight?"

"Who said anything about sleeping?"

CHAPTER FORTY-SEVEN

The Free Press.

THE NEXT MORNING DAWNED WARM and muggy and deteriorated hour by hour until mid-afternoon. An occasional breeze brought the odor of marsh mud and rotting eelgrass. Taz had spent the last hour and a half using a pair of rusty hedge clippers to head the hydrangeas on either side of the front door. He had worked up a good sweat—his shoulder was sore, and he was grumpily grateful that he didn't have to do this for a living. He strolled to the back of the house to hang the clippers in the shed, slipped into the kitchen by the side door, and pulled a beer from the refrigerator. Popped the top and sat with a sigh at the round table, his back to the living room and his eyes on his next pruning target, a tangled redbud in the backyard.

His cellphone rescued him from the next chore. It was Jack Donley. "Damn. This is the first time I've gotten through without having to listen to that damn message."

"Slow day."

"Not anymore. Guess who has three separate accounts in the Caymans?"

"You're kidding."

"No man, I'm definitely not. This guy leaves breadcrumbs everywhere—

kind of in a circle, with him in the center."

"Tell me."

He did. He had proof; wire transfers in and out, mostly at a level that wouldn't excite the regulators. But there was also a trail of cash deposits, amounts unknown.

"Any chance of a recording of a bank transaction? Or better yet, a security camera picture? Something tying him to the accounts other than just draft and phone records?"

"See what I can do."

Early afternoon. Another call. Eliza on the other end. "Taz, can you come up? My editor says she needs to talk to us—together."

"Does that strike you as a little funny?"

"It's the Swindell story. I need her support to keep working on it."

"But I'm not even a source on that one."

"She knows that, and she still wants to talk. Will you come?"

"Sure. When?"

"Right now."

He showered and still made it in an hour and fifteen minutes. A receptionist ushered him directly to the editor's office. Eliza was already there, sitting in a chair with her back to the window blinds and chewing furiously on a pencil. The executive editor of the *Times* was sitting on the other side of a small conference table, with her back to a giant corkboard festooned with news clips, photographs, graphs, and diagrams, in no particular order as far as Taz could see. She was a small woman with a severe haircut that barely reached her ears, and half-lens glasses, over which she peered at Taz with an owl-like curiosity. He reached over the table to shake her hand, a gesture she dismissed by pointing him to his chair on the corner of the table opposite Eliza.

Eliza shot him a weak smile and began to introduce him. "Millie, this is—"

"I know who he is, thanks." She pulled a red binder from the desk behind her and slid it on to the table. Started leafing through it, twirling and occasionally tapping the pen as she did. After a minute or so, she looked up and fixed her gaze on him. "Why is it, Mister Blackwell, that whenever we take on a politically troublesome story, I find you somewhere at the center of it? And why is it that the stories you find your way into— the Chinese mining company that wanted to exploit Tobytown, the Nazis who spray-painted your little tourist paradise, and now some cockeyed notion that our university's new chancellor is corrupt. How is it that they always raise libel issues for me? How is it that our publisher yells at me on the phone, and then gives me the third degree?"

"Your publisher—Gannett, yes? The media corporation?"

"Of course."

"Have they told you to call Eliza off Swindell?"

"That's not how they do it. And it's not how I do it. And you know it very well, Mr. Blackwell." She was irate. "All they care about is protecting us from libel charges. And, no, they haven't called yet. But I have a feeling they will."

"Aren't they the ones who picked up a Pulitzer for their coverage of that terrible fire in the Flathead National Forest seven years ago? The one where twelve smoke jumpers died because the director of the state wildfire management program left them stranded while he used the state's only tanker plane to put out a grass fire near a paper mill outside of Billings? A paper mill of which he was a major investor. The *Great Falls Tribune* broke that one, if I remember?"

Millie looked a bit uncertain but summoned up what was left of her arrogance. "And what does that have to do with me?"

"Your new president, the one Gannett installed as your publisher's rep after Ratner retired—what's her name?"

"Jenna Sandalls."

"Aahh, yes. I don't suppose you know how she got her start in the news business. Do you?"

"No, why would I?"

"You might want to find out before you talk with her again—and you should probably do that soon. And when you do, ask her if she ever figured out which end of the martini is up."

Millie was speechless. Taz stood. Something in the street caught his eye. He stepped over to look down. A man was crouching between two cars. As Taz watched, he stood and walked quickly away. Taz turned, reached across the table, patted Millie's hand, and left.

Five minutes later, Eliza caught him on his way out to the parking lot. She was fighting back tears. "What *was* that? Really, Taz, you've lost me, and now she's going to can my story. What in the world were you thinking?"

"Jenna Sandalls' first publishing gig was at the *Great Falls Tribune*. She was there when they researched and developed the fire story. Gannet promoted her after they won the Pulitzer."

"Oh my God." A smile crept through her tears. "And you know this how?"

"Didn't I ever tell you about my time working with the federal wildfire team in Boise?"

Eliza threw her arms around his neck and gave him a lingering kiss on the cheek. "This time, I'm buying the drinks."

"Sure, come on." He ushered her through the crowded lot to his truck.

"You'll have to bring me back to pick up mine later, you know." He nodded, drove them to the little canal-side grill he favored. They shared oysters on the half-shell and double martinis. When the waiter put her martini in front of her, she looked up at Taz. "Okay, I guess I have to bite. Which end of the martini *is* up?"

Taz threw down a serious gulp, sighed and gave Eliza a sly smile. "The bottom, of course." They talked, joked, and plotted for a couple of hours. It was time for Eliza to head home to walk the dog and for Taz to drive back to the Island. When they got to the parking lot behind the *News* office, there was only a scattering of cars. They were hard to identify in the dark of a new moon. Eliza pointed to a silver Fiat near the back entrance to the building. As Eliza opened her passenger door, Taz's mind clicked. The Fiat was the same car he had seen the man crouching near while looking out of Millie's office window. He rolled down his window as fast as he could.

"Eliza, stop! Get away from the door!" At first, she didn't register what he had said, kept looking to find her keys. Taz opened his door, jumped out, and grabbed her wrist.

"Do you have a remote starter?"

"Yes, but—"

"But nothing. Get back in the truck." He drove to the other end of the small parking lot where there was a row of U-Haul trucks and vans. Parked between two panel trucks. Doused the lights and turned off the engine. "Now. Start it with the remote." She pressed a button on the key fob. There was a blinding flash of light and a sound like a rank of cannons on steroids. When they could look again, the Fiat was a smoking pile of metal with small flames still sprouting from the tires.

Taz's ears buzzed. Eliza's mouth was moving, but he couldn't make out what she was saying. She was trying to open her door. He held her arm and shook his head. He waited for the buzzing to subside. Eliza trembled. He wrapped his arm around her shoulders as she began quietly sobbing.

"If somebody's out there, we want them to think the job is done." He rubbed her hand while they waited. After about ten minutes, a black sedan turned into the lot, cruised down the aisle past the smoking Fiat, slowed, then exited and was gone.

Taz looked at Eliza. "You have your cell?"

"I think so." she fumbled in her bag.

"Call Millie and tell her we need her to meet us at the Sandy Clam on the Deal Island Road in half an hour. Tell her it's urgent. Don't tell her anything else. And get her to give you Jenna Sandalls' number. I'll call her."

The Sandy Clam was an old-style Chesapeake raw bar that served good burgers, lousy chicken, decent whisky, draft beer, and day-fresh clams and oysters that had barely had time to spit out their grit. The two of them and Millie arrived about the same time. and found a table in the shadows of the back corner. Taz sat where he could keep his back to the wall and his eye on the door. When Millie started in on why the hell they had dragged her out of her apartment at this hour of the night, Taz cut her off.

"Something's happened and we have to figure out what to do about it. I'll tell you the rest when Jenna gets here. In the meantime, try to keep a lid on it, okay? And get us a bottle of wine." Alarmed, Millie looked at Eliza, who was still shaking. Millie shut up and waved angrily at the waiter.

The door swung open, and two couples swaggered in. Jenna came right behind them. She spied Taz as he rose, smiled tentatively, and ran her fingers through her hair. She was as he remembered—dressed simply and professionally, wavy brown hair cut short, blue eyes set deep, prominent nose, radiating a kind of unsettled energy that made her look thinner and fiercer than she was. He gave her a quick kiss on the cheek and turned her to the side so he could whisper in her ear. "I'm glad you could come." She looked a question at him. "I wish this was a social occasion. It's not. There's something we need to work on together, tonight. I may need your help with Millie. Can you do that?" She nodded and he took her to the table.

She sat. Taz poured her a glass of water. A waiter was passing by with a check for another table. Taz held up a hand to slow him. "We'll need that bottle of wine and four glasses."

The waiter, a young man with an attitude, said: "You can see I'm busy."

Taz looked at him in a way that backed him up a step: "And you can see I'm thirsty. That makes me unhappy. When I'm unhappy, I sometimes do things I later regret. Bring the wine."

That done, Taz looked each of them in the eye. His eyes rested on Jenna. He nodded toward Eliza. "This is Eliza Clarke, the News's best reporter." Eliza smiled hesitantly and reached for his hand. "She's supposed to be dead right now."

Eliza lifted her head, looked at Millie, then at Jenna, summoned her strength. "I would be, too, if Taz hadn't stopped me from getting in my car. There was a bomb."

Jenna reached across the table to put her hand on Eliza's wrist. "Are you sure? How did you know?"

"It was rigged to the ignition. After Taz got us out of danger, we used the remote to start the car . . . boom!" Raised her hands to mimic a mushroom cloud.

Taz said, "We can get to the details later. The point is whoever tried to kill her has to be convinced they were successful."

Millie replied, "But we have to report it to the police."

"Absolutely not. Right now, it's just a burnt car in a parking lot, a car nobody heard blow up and nobody saw, with nobody in it. And it has to stay that way until we figure out who did it." He turned to Eliza, then back to the others. "If they think she's still alive, they may try again."

Jenna looked Eliza's way. "Taz is right, but this could be hard on you for a little while—at least a few days. Is there anyone—family or friends—who you see so often that they will be alarmed not to hear from your for, say, a week?"

"A week, really? You mean aside from the whole newsroom? I don't think so. My parents are dead, and my sister and I haven't talked in years. I'm a reporter, you know? We don't hang around in groups."

"Stop it right now." Millie, strident, glaring at Taz. "I will not be a part of some shabby coverup—not now, not tomorrow . . ."

Jenna interrupted. "Let's listen to Taz's reasoning before we go off half-cocked. Let's assume this isn't part of some personal vendetta, that it has to do with Eliza's reporting. Are you live on anything other than the chancellor's path to glory?" Eliza shook her no. "So maybe Chancellor Swindell is tired of seeing his name in the press. Your stories haven't exactly been flattering."

"No. And based on what I've gotten in the last week, they're not likely to get any better."

Jenna leaned back in her chair. "But the chancellor? He has a name and a reputation to protect. Would he risk everything just to avoid a story he could probably make people forget before Thanksgiving?"

"Maybe not. But the rumor is he's putting together an exploratory committee to run for governor."

"That's what I heard just yesterday. How did you—?"

Taz jumped in. "Let's say a backer of his—someone who stands to gain if he's elected—let's say that person decided to take things into his own hands. Maybe he farmed out the job. He's just waiting to do his victory dance until he's sure."

"So how do we make him sure?" Jenna.

"I don't have anything foolproof, since we're not going to have a police report or a death certificate. But I think this is where you and Millie come in. Maybe Millie tells the newsroom staff that Eliza is taking some personal time. Puts a little squib in the paper saying Ms. Clarke is out on a leave of absence for family reasons, whatever. Bad guy sees the notice. He has to wonder what's up. So, he waits. At least now he knows why there was no police report. Maybe the paper just doesn't want to publicize the fact that their reporter was killed in the line of duty.

"Then a couple of days later, somebody starts a rumor that she had a car accident, that she died. Maybe circulate a hint that the paper will be looking for an additional investigative reporter. The guy's confused, but he's getting more comfortable. Swindell's not on the front page anymore. Whoever it is doesn't have any reason to think a follow-up is needed, and he doesn't want to risk going back to the scene of the crime, so to speak. So, he puts the whole thing on the back burner."

Eliza asked, "And then?"

"And then we get you in a safe place. We do everything we can to find whoever's behind this. Shine a bright light. Create enough trouble for him that he can't chance another hit." He looked at Jenna and Millie. "I'm sure there's some holes in it. Find them and poke them, we'll make some changes. But we've got to start before the first pressman shows up at the paper tomorrow morning." Then he squeezed Eliza's hand. "And you come with me, and we'll stash you on the island of your dreams."

CHAPTER FORTY-EIGHT

Follow the Money

ELIZA WAS SAFELY ENSCONCED IN a rental house on Piney Island belonging to Laney's close friend Charlene Davenport, who had conveniently exchanged the Island's mosquitoes for an *atelier* in Paris. Lucia had scheduled weekly office hours for her grad students in the late afternoon, which meant he wouldn't see her until the next afternoon, if then. Since her confrontation with Chancellor Swindell, she had become even more driven about her work, if such a thing was possible. Taz called Rainy Day, got Richard.

"Wait, I'll tell Laney you're on."

"Not so fast, my friend. I have an invitation for both of you."

"A *ménage?* I'm not interested."

"*Pas de ménage . . . plutôt pour manger! Un repas.*"

"You speak French like a Texan. It's hard to listen to."

"Well, that's about all I've got, so don't worry about it. You can mock all you want. I want to invite the two of you over for dinner—tonight. I need her moral support and both your brains. What do you say?"

"We didn't have anything planned. I'll check."

Richard parked their BMW on the shell drive behind Old Faithful an hour before sunset. A good time to sit on the dock with an icy martini, so Taz concocted three, in the style that Fiona had shown him in Boise; it seemed like months back, not weeks. Richard sipped appreciatively. Laney looked at Taz, alarmed. "You've been taking lessons! What else are you hiding from me?"

"You can't imagine how much easier my life would be if I could hide something from you—really almost anything."

Richard scoffed, "You're joking. The way I hear it, you'd be dead in a week."

"And you'd have to find yourself another chess patsy. Meanwhile, why don't you pour us all a refill and let me do my magic." He turned on the oven and warmed up the pizza he had brought from Famous in the afternoon. He pointed Richard towards the wine glasses.

Richard took a look at the pizza. "Honestly, you shouldn't have gone to so much trouble."

Laney, pouring the Chianti she had found in the cabinet. "Just drink your wine, husband."

After dinner, Taz put on a CD of Maria Bethania, Laney opened another bottle of chianti, Richard poured, and they talked into the night.

"It's like playing chess with you, Richard, and I'm losing. Whoever he is, he's one step ahead of me—he has been since the beginning. He knows more about me than I know about him, and he knows who to threaten to get to me. He's threatened Lucia and Laney, and I think he's behind the bomb that was meant to kill Eliza."

"Okay." Richard, leaning forward and eyeing Taz through his Clark Kent rims. "Tell me what you know and let's play this like you said—like a chess match. We're in the middle game. So, let's lay out the moves that got us here and maybe we can put together a strategy for the endgame."

"I'll try, but it's all tangled together. It's starts in Brazil."

A half hour later, when Taz got to the bomb, Richard moved his glasses to his forehead and rubbed his face with his hand. "It's the same guy. Gotta be. Swindell or his twin brother. You're the connector. You're the one who blew up his action in Brazil, you're the one who was supposed to wind up dead in Mexico, and you're the one who bollixed up whatever scheme he was running with the DEA in Reynosa. You're the one who's bonking the fly in his ointment at the university."

Laney snorted. "Not just a mixed metaphor, but a pornographic one. I'm going to cancel your talk at that damn conference."

"Enough from the peanut gallery. By now, he's probably figured out that you're one of Eliza's sources. The note, remember? You meddled then, and you're meddling now. Q.E.D."

"It all makes sense, in some depraved way. But we have nothing to link Swindell with Brazil."

"So, we find the connection. Checkmate."

Afterwards, Taz would recall hoping against hope that he and his comrades were at least following the right leads.

They were. Not that it mattered.

∮

Another gray morning. Taz was rinsing dishes before hauling his toolbox to Clark Street to do a few minor roof repairs for Mrs. Handley, a sweet lady in her sixties who volunteered at the museum. His cell phone cawed again. *Maybe Lucia?*

No such luck. John White's voice. He sounded unusually jaunty. "Taz. Don't say I never did anything for you. You were right about the Amazonas military police—they were bought and paid for. No matter. We're close to cracking this thing. Our friends in the SNI have figured out who was organizing the burn strategy, at least in Acre and Amazonas. I think you know him from a previous encounter—Gabriel de Souza?"

"I do. Although I only ever talked to him on the phone. He worked for Fontana. He was running the network that was stealing mahogany from the Javari Reserve. Were they able to get anything out of him?"

"You mean before they sailed him into the forest from fifteen thousand feet? Old habits die hard."

"Jesus. Did they really rub out our key witness? At least tell me they have him on tape."

"They do. But it's tough to make out his confession through the screams."

"Great. So, what do we do?"

"We keep listening."

"What good will that do? De Souza's dead."

"Not to the recently departed. To Fontana."

"Okay then. That does sound like progress."

✦

Jack had dug up some new bits of information which complimented what Eliza had already found. Swindell clearly enjoyed the perks of life as a corporate board member. He held seats on at least half a dozen boards. They were a diverse group—a land trust with holdings in a number of South American countries, an independent oil services company, and an importer specializing in clothing labelled *Made in the USA,* even though its products had been sewn by teenage Filipino girls in sweatshops in Saipan. In addition, he was the chairman and CEO of a modestly endowed hedge fund—Avenger Capital. He balanced the public image of his interests through participation on various NGO boards, including the Heritage Foundation and Conservation International. And last but maybe not least, Wildlife Action, an environmental PAC—meaning it could legally channel political contributions. Speaking quickly into her cell, Lucia ran through the list with Taz.

Swindell's approach was unusually cynical, but not exactly scandalous, and with no hint of illegality. Still, it might yield further clues.

Lucia was not satisfied. She was a panther tracker, and they were on a trail. She called just before lunch. "Taz, I have a hunch. I've got to go. If I find what I'm looking for, I'll call you back right away."

Taz washed his breakfast dishes, dumped a week of papers into the recycling bin. When he was finished, he took a walk out to the dock, trying to make sense out of the welter of conversations of the past few days. He watched a barge ply its way up the channel, got a solid whiff of the diesels. His cell cawed, Lucia, sounding very excited. "Taz, the fund—they're neck deep in a company that doesn't seem to do anything other than own other companies."

"A holding company?"

"Yes, Triple-V Holdings, LLC.'"

Triple-V's subsidiaries included two Mexican oil services companies and a wood products company—FTN Timber LLC. FTN's central business was logging and finishing mahogany. FTN—Fontana. The chairman and CEO of Triple-V—Carter V. Swindell.

CHAPTER FORTY-NINE

The Switcheroo.

THAT NIGHT WAS ONE OF Taz's longest. All they had was a jumble of tantalizing loose ends—not the coherent picture they needed. Lucia was in Salisbury for a university ceremony of some kind. In penance, she agreed to drive down early so they could spend the morning together. At some point, as they lingered over their coffees, he was going to have to tell her.

She pulled in behind Old Faithful just before nine. Taz took a deep breath, walked over to get her bag. He poured coffee. They sat, elbows on the table, gazing at each other. She saw it right away. "If the news is that bad, give it to me quick, okay? And don't sugarcoat it."

She reached into the cupboard and pulled out a bottle of Green Dot, poured a splash in Taz's cup and then in hers. Taz gave her a detailed assessment. She listened, giving the occasional nod. What it all amounted to was that they knew Swindell was guilty, but they weren't anywhere close to proving it in court. When he was finished, she motioned him to rise, stood, stepped around the table to him and put her hands on his shoulders, looking him in the eye and smiling.

"Taz, we're going to do this. Okay, you've reached the end of a path. But it's not the only path. You've been trying to reveal the truth by getting justice. But the legal path isn't there yet, if it will ever be. Maybe . . .

maybe we get justice by revealing the truth. Somehow having everybody know what we know. The result might not kill whoever's behind this, but it would burn them pretty good."

"Reveal the truth? How? Billboards? TV ads?"

"Maybe. I'm sure there are other ways. Come on."

"I don't know any other way. Us saying it doesn't make it true. Why would anyone believe us? Unless we get him to spill it himself. But how? What threat could we make that would force his hand? I just don't see it."

The caw of his cell startled him so much that he almost threw the thing against the wall. Then he was glad he hadn't. He cupped the phone, whispered to Lucia. "It's Jack. I have to talk to him. Maybe he has something." Lucia grimaced, stepped none too softly out to the porch.

What Jack had was a piece of information so unexpected that Taz sat to digest it. "As I remember from that stupid biography on the college's website, Swindell was born in Charlotte, North Carolina, right? His father was a tobacco heir?"

"I think so, yes?"

"Guess what you find in the birth records of Mecklenburg County for the month he was born?"

"His birth certificate?"

"That's the thing. It's not there. There is no Carter Swindell, or rather there wasn't until somebody's name got changed."

"I don't follow."

"When that little baby went home from the hospital, his name wasn't Carter. It was Sylvanious. No kidding. Sylvanious Van Swindl was the second son of Carter Van Swindl, Senior. The real Carter Van Swindl Junior was born three years before your boy. He was Sylvanious's older brother."

"But?"

"Carter died at the age of twenty-one. I don't know the circumstances. But six months later, when Sylvanious was eighteen, he changed his name. And guess what he changed it to—Carter V. Swindell. He dropped the *Van* along with his first name, changed the spelling of his last name, and became his brother."

"How in the world did you unravel that?"

"I love reading court records. And because I do, I've got more. Before he founded his hedge fund, Van Swindl Senior was the CEO of a reasonably successful Wall Street brokerage. Something went wrong, allegations of fraud and self-dealing. He resigned under a cloud and avoided prosecution, but not opprobrium. And thus, Carl V. Swindell's first shot at a resume is filed under the name Carter Swindell."

"He threw his father's family under the bus. How proud."

"Well, that's not all. After it was all done, little Sylvanious not only became his brother, but he also took his place as the future director of a twelve-billion-dollar hedge fund. Not bad for a day's work."

Taz pocketed the cell, walked out front, found Lucia staring pensively at the channel. He sat beside her, draped his arm over her shoulder, nuzzled her cheek.

She stiffened and shrugged him off. "Don't."

"No, Lucia. You were right in there. I was like a racehorse with blinders on. I was running on the legal track. Your path is a better one. Come back in. I'll pour us some more coffee."

Taz kept his eyes on hers and poured.

"You know how we're going to do it, don't you." Her eyes were bright now. She put down her cup and slapped her forehead. "You do!" She was bouncing up and down on her toes. "Put a little whisky in this and tell me."

"We create the circumstances which compel him to tell the truth."

"Don't tease me."

"I'm not. First, Carter Swindell's real name is Sylvanious Van Swindl. The man you know as Carter Swindell had an older brother—three years older—*he* was the real Carter Van Swindl. Our Carter was seventeen when the real Carter died. When he turned eighteen, he had his name changed. *Pfft*, no more Sylvanious. Then his father got in trouble in a very public way. The new Carter wasn't about to let himself get tainted. That would have derailed his plans. So, he dropped the Van Swindl, and became Carter V Swindell. Young, ambitious, all clean and new. And next in line to run his father's hedge fund."

"Doesn't that make him even less likely to talk? He's sure covered it up so far."

"Yes, he has. But no matter how cold-blooded he is, a change like that—it's so personal. To take his dead brother's name? A person can only sit on a volcano so long. If it were to come out, it might really shake him up."

"But he still wouldn't volunteer to turn himself in."

"Maybe it wouldn't be entirely voluntary. Maybe we give him a little help. Something to make him *want* to tell the truth. In a public setting."

"Truth serum? I didn't think that was a real thing."

"It might not be, but I've got something that I'm pretty sure will do the job, the same thing that helped Salvador open *my* eyes."

"Ayahuasca? But won't he end up just spouting some incomprehensible nonsense or just retail whatever vision comes from the drug?"

"It's a risk. But there's no mental content in the drug. It's just a door opener . . . you know what I mean? Whatever's behind the door is what comes out. It may be a deep-seated fear, it may be an unexpected revelation. But it's going to be true. "

CHAPTER FIFTY

Setting the Trap

IT TOOK TAZ A COUPLE of days. He had to call some friends. Finally, on the longest shot of all, he reached Charles Kills-Enemies, his mentor in building sweat-lodges so many years before. Charles was still in California.

"Taz, good to hear your voice. I was beginning to think you weren't going to call after all."

"And yet here I am. How many years?"

"Years don't matter. Never did. You need a little help; you know where to find me."

"I have a knotty problem to resolve. I'm hoping you might have a friend or two out here on the east coast. True friends."

"Mmmm. Let me think. Okay, two: David Truelove—New York, Algonquin; and Delbert Pitt, he's an Accomac—down near you, right?"

"How do I reach Pitt?"

"Here's how . . ."

They talked a little more, just catching up. Charles was in Carson City at a meeting with the Nevada Gaming Commission. The Paiutes wanted to open a casino to generate some cash for the tribe. The Las Vegas casino moguls were in no mood for more competition, Native American or not.

Charles was one of the spokesmen for the tribal corporation. Taz gave him some names at Interior, since Nevada would have to get a federal clearance from the Bureau of Indian Affairs as part of the permitting process. And so it was that Taz Blackwell came into possession of enough ayahuasca to light up a small truth ceremony.

After he got off a call with Eliza, he had the rudiments of a plan. He had talked to Laney, Richard, and Lucia.

Lucia had found the silver platter, the one on which they were going to serve their nemesis his little cup of karma. Chancellor Swindell was on the board of the Wild World Fund, an A-list conservation group, and they had just announced that he would be named Conservation Champion of the Year at their annual fundraising dinner. He intended to use the event as the public launch of his gubernatorial campaign committee. From what Lucia could gather, the university trustees were preparing a formal evening, with full glitz and glam. The production would begin with a reception at the old Newseum building on Pennsylvania Avenue only two days away. One of Lucia's best grad students had told her the administration was already looking for volunteer meet-and-greeters.

The four of them sat on Taz's dock that evening, watching the channel, sipping wine, and sorting out the details. Lucia was going to keep track of the reception planning and design their intervention. Laney volunteered to run the logistics. Taz would take point when the time came. Richard would smoke a joint as large as a caboose and provide oversight.

Laney said, "You mean the usual division of labor."

Taz got up to get another bottle. The conversation ended just after midnight.

The sun woke Taz a little after six. A high-pressure front from Appalachia had moved in overnight, and the sky was blue, the day cool, the horizon clear. Taz had coffee and a glass of grapefruit juice for breakfast. He spent the morning pruning his anarchic redbud until he tired and sat down with a cold one. He realized it had been some time since he last checked in with John White and put in a couple of calls. White was in the deputies' meeting and would be out for the rest of the day. Taz called

Arthur, thinking he might know of any new news out of Brazil. It seemed that Taz's friends at INR, led personally by his friend the assistant secretary, had been working with Brazilian intelligence to learn all they could about the criminal activities in Acre. And his favorite undersecretary had decided to lead the charge.

"Taz, Jessica has decided that following up your suspicions about Fontana Timber has become a top priority. She's on the phone with your pal Martins every day, sharing intelligence. The Brazilians have gathered a lot of information already. More incidents like the one you so rudely interrupted in Acre. It's been happening all over the western fringe of the Amazon—timber thefts, harassment of villages. It's complicated though—there isn't always a direct connection—maybe Fontana is working through local companies, or even a syndicate in Peru. They're still trying to pin it all down. It's frustrating—they can't trace it all to one bad actor, and they don't want to make any arrests until they know where the whole chain leads."

They didn't have the identity, but Taz was beginning to think maybe Lucia did. She called Taz as soon as she finished with her last class.

"I'm almost free tomorrow—well at least tomorrow morning. Would you be there if I came over?"

"Tomorrow? Why not tonight? Let's say just before sunset this evening. I'll rustle up some dinner. I'll be on the front stoop looking for you."

Taz was running on adrenalin, and adrenalin made him happy. *But when life looks like easy street, there is danger at your door.* He could hear Uncle Jerry's ever so slightly hoarse tenor singing the line, with the remaining five members of the Grateful Dead forming an unusually harmonic ensemble. As anyone who followed the band would put it, the Dead don't lie.

Taz's cell cawed. John White sounded distinctively unhappy.

"Taz. I gather Arthur filled you in on our progress. But there's something else. We have some friends in another agency who've been sampling some phone traffic. No need to go to into it. But there's one thing you have to know. We're picking up some cell traffic between your friend Swindell and two of his senior advisors and a criminal syndicate the FBI has been tracking in Baltimore. The syndicate takes orders from a Guatemalan. Most of them are from Central America. For what it's worth, they call themselves *La Cofrasia*—the Brotherhood. We don't have the content of the calls yet, just pings off the cell towers. But it's at least once a day, sometimes more.

"There's also one call we have content for because it was made on an internal university network. It originated from one of Swindell's people. We don't know who took the call yet, but what Swindell's assistant wanted to know was whether the *nosy professor* was being taken care of."

Taz couldn't stop fidgeting for the next hour. Images of Lucia on the back roads of Coahuila. The sound of Carolina's smoky voice. Echoes of her laughter. Had she even had a second to know death was on his way? Would Lucia? He imagined Carter Swindell's smirk as his henchmen hunted his loved ones. He walked out to the dock, tried to shake off the images. Stood there for a few minutes, watching the dredging barge down towards Wallops Island. Then he headed back into the cottage and called Laney again.

"Lucia's going to need a place to stay tomorrow night, after the reception, and I don't think she'd be safe here. Can you put her up for a couple of days?"

"She's always welcome here, you know that. But just her? What's going on?"

"I think she's in danger, and this is too obvious a hiding place."

"Not to state the obvious, but if she's not safe there neither are you."

"I guess I could be persuaded."

"Oh boy! A slumber party!"

⸙

He was nursing a beer and picking a Dock Boggs tune on his guitar when Lucia pulled up. She jumped out of the Jeep and ran to the rail, reached over, and kissed his forehead.

"You will *not* believe this. Taz—they've set the stage for us." She bounced on her toes again.

"What? Tell me."

She danced over and sat by him. "The university leadership—his minions—they've concocted the craziest damn show I've ever seen. They did a sort of run through for the future wait-staff of America this afternoon. Imagine, our little extravaganza will just be a play within the play." She gave him the basic outline. They sat quietly, watching the gulls chase after a small trawler coming up the channel. "And I think I know about a half dozen grad students who can help us stage it."

After a dinner of pan-seared ribeye and onions sweated with port, accompanied by the best Barolo in Taz's closet, they discussed the plan.

"Tell me again how all this is supposed to work tomorrow." Her head was on his shoulder as he idly twirled her hair. They leaned back together on the thin cushions of his little wicker love seat, looking out through the porch screens at the channel and the dark marshes still thick with the cries of the laughing gulls.

"If it's like every other high-dollar DC fundraiser, there'll be three hundred guests, more or less. All the big conservation and environmental donors. At the least the ones who aren't in Aspen or on safari. Some political types—his backers, the ones who are grooming him for the governor slot. Nothing you haven't seen before."

"Very funny. The biggest political meeting I've ever gone to was in the Modoc County Municipal Hall."

Well, there was Reynosa, but that wasn't exactly a meeting, and anyhow, it was long ago.

"There'll only be half the number of folks at that conference in Boise, and you *spoke* to them."

"I guess. You know how I feel about these things. I'd rather spend the time giving myself an enema."

Taz spat out his drink. After he stopped laughing and straightened up, he shook his head at her. "You've already done the hard work, Lucia. You've choreographed the whole extravaganza. Now you don't have to do anything but sit at a front table and look staggeringly beautiful."

"Sexist pig." She snorted and shook her head, shooting the kind of look a teacher gives a likable student who's just played a harmless prank.

"A smart one, though. He needs to be off balance for this to work. Seeing you will unsettle him. He won't expect you to be there."

"Why not?"

Taz considered before he responded. He sure as hell wasn't going to tell her that Swindell had assassins out there looking for her. "Well, it's not a university thing. "It's mostly a benefit for the Wild World Fund. And an award ceremony for the great Carter Swindell, which is what he'll be focused on. He won't be expecting his most challenging professor to show up."

Lucia caressed his neck with her fingers. "So, *monsieur director,* what do you want me to wear? How will you dress your ornament?"

"Come with me, *chérie,* and we'll pick out something." She put her arms around his neck. He stood. She wrapped her legs around his waist and over his hips. He slipped his hands down and under her bottom to hold her. She whispered dirty words in his ear. They half-walked, half-stumbled to the bed. She quoted her favorite line from that adventure movie, the one with Kathleen Turner and the bespectacled Arab mystic–*The Jewel of the Nile.* "Are we jogging?"

CHAPTER FIFTY-ONE

Auto-da-fé.

TAZ WOKE JUST BEFORE DAWN. There were a lot of possibilities and plenty of loose ends to coordinate. But he had already chalked up one success. Lucia would be out of harm's way while they were together. Tonight, she would be with him in the most public of public settings, and safe on that account. And now she wouldn't even need to go back to her apartment to dress. Just to make sure, Taz had three of her favorite formal dresses in his closet.

The crowd began to assemble just a little after seven. Older couples sporting custom-tailored tuxedos and ball gowns. Diamond rings with stones the size of bergy bits. A smattering of young singles, the men in business-bohemian suits, colorful shirts with English lapel points, loud ties, the women in cocktail dresses, looking as svelte as possible. A few scientists emanating auras of curiosity and intelligence. Political staff from Congress and the administration, looking to hook up over the canapes. A few members of the press, including two TV camera crews, and Eliza with a *Times* photographer. After she and Taz had talked it over with Jenna, they had all agreed that she'd be safer scrunched among hundreds of people under the bright lights of the reception than she would alone on the island.

Last of all, the politicians themselves, a number of representatives looking to burnish their conservation credentials, along with Maryland's junior senator and lieutenant governor.

Sleek young women in black cocktail dresses circulated through the crowd bearing drinks. Taz recognized some of Lucia's grad students. She had told him that half the PhD candidate class had been drafted for duty. They must have come from every department in the system, including cosmetology. All between twenty and thirty, two-thirds of them women. Hostesses and bartenders dressed like penguins for the greater glory, their smiles magnificent.

The lights were being adjusted in the main hall. Guests waited in twos and threes, gathered at standing tables on the lobby side of a blue velour curtain at least fifteen feet high and forty feet long. Free drinks and piped-in slow jazz amplified the discussion and kept complaints to a minimum.

Taz watched from the farthest corner, with his back to a window wall that faced a construction site across the street and reached to the vaulted ceiling sixty feet above. The work crews had left for the day. He chatted now and then with the woman in charge of the waitstaff, a professional party planner with blonde hair, heavy makeup, and the smile of a tiger shark.

She stopped every once in awhile to check the status of various tasks, sometimes walking to other parts of the room to solve problems or give instructions. When that happened, Taz would step away too and find his own party planner, a graduate student of Lucia's named Savanna Louis. Savanna's tux was not only shaped exceedingly well, it included a take-off on the Cary Grant style—her cummerbund was white and set off her aqualine features, her ebony skin and black piled coiffure. Taz might say a few words, and she might then step away to talk to one of the waitstaff. Or sometimes just for a giggle—they loved trading Lucia stories.

The organizers at the Wild World Fund had decided that there would be a brief pull-aside for the press before the evening began in earnest. One of Savanna's runners had found the location, in a large room off the side of the main dining area. Taz wandered over just in time to see the executive director of the Fund usher Swindell in to meet the waiting members of the press. He was flanked by a bright-eyed redhead whose quick steps and constant attention practically shouted *press secretary,* and by a beefy young man in a business suit who Taz concluded was his aide-de-camp. There were three cameras and several radio reporters with their microphones pointing in the direction of the little square, bound by duct tape, where Swindell was to stand. There were also ten or twelve print reporters, including Eliza. Taz stood behind the gaggle in a spot where he could have an unobstructed view. The bright camera lights ensured that Swindell couldn't see anything beyond the first row of faces.

Swindell was resplendent in his custom-fitted tuxedo with a navy-blue cummerbund and bow tie, both imprinted with an elaborate gold-swirl pattern. His bald head shone as if it had been polished, and his tonsure had been carefully trimmed to look as natural as possible. His radiant smile bespoke the jolly good cheer he clearly felt inside. Something about him reminded Taz of a bobble-head doll. His head seemed mismatched with the rest of him. His eyes were compressed by ample cheek fat, with dimples that left an almost cherubic impression and a small mouth set in a permanent smirk. Taz had the sense of a reasonably good-looking middle-class accountant who had been invaded by a slightly inebriated pig.

"I'm so glad you were all able to be here on such an auspicious night! As you know, I'm Carter Swindell." He grinned for the two TV cameras. "I'm here to help my favorite charity win the war for wildlife. There is still so much to save." The redhead stepped up to whisper in his ear, then looked out at the reporters with an endearing smile of her own. Swindell put a well-practiced hand on her shoulder. "I'm due on the platform, it seems, so I'll only have time for one or two questions." Arms went up. Swindell pointed to one of the TV reporters and smiled like he was his only friend. "C'mon, Jake, take your best shot!"

Jake, a towheaded kid barely out of college: "Chancellor Swindell, the rumor in political circles is that you're getting ready to run for governor. Would you care to comment?"

A laugh, cut short. "Governor? I haven't even given it a thought. To be frank, I have enough to do leading the state university system and

chairing wonderful charities like the one we will be supporting tonight."
The communications director stepped to the mic. "I really do have to drag
this poor man up on stage. I'm sure you—"

There was a sudden shout from the back of the small crowd. "Wait! Just
one more question!" Eliza had worked her way around the TV cameraman
to face Swindell. She smiled enticingly, holding a small spiral bound pad
in one hand and a pencil poised in the other.

"I'm Eliza Clarke, from the *Salisbury Times.*" Swindell took a step back.
His eyes darted to the woman in the pantsuit. "When you were eighteen,
you changed your name to that of your dead older brother just six months
after he died. Can you tell our readers why? Isn't it the case that your birth
name was actually Sylvanious Van Swindl?"

Swindell fixed her with a tight-lipped stare. "That's a patently ridiculous
question. Any response from me would only dignify it." It took just a
moment for his little grin to reassert itself. He shifted his gaze back to the
cameras. "Enough of this nonsense. This is why the press has such a bad
reputation. This night is about wildlife, not about me. Let's go enjoy the
evening together."

A musical fanfare brayed from speakers all around the hall. The press
scurried, taking down cameras and mics as the dark blue velour curtain
opened and was roped to the side. Taz slipped back behind the curtain. The
crowd began moving toward the formal reception area, where there were
twenty round dinner tables spaced somewhat closely in a double semi-circle
facing the speaking platform and set in white and silver. Each table seated
twelve, each with name plates and white cloth bags with a purple ribbon
for each guest. The guests shuffled, smiled, excused themselves, looked to
find their appointed tables. The whole scene played out in front of three
screens the size of airport plate glass windows. The screens showed the
totem animals most loved by the older conservation movement—tigers,
polar bears, and whales.

Lucia was seated at a front table to the right of the stage, talking easily
with several well-known university sponsors. She wore a dark red V-neck
jersey gown with spaghetti straps and a slit that reached just above her left

knee. It was cut low in front and lower in back. Taz and Savanna moved slowly forward and found a niche just behind the corner table farthest from the stage.

A slight blonde with a blue streak in her pixie-cut hair whispered in Savanna's ear. She smiled at Taz. "The package has been delivered." Wine servers strolled by on their way to the tables. They each purloined a glass as the trays moved past.

The last of the guests were seated, and some began examining their packages. The ones who did pulled out white mugs, wrapped in tissue paper, with Carter Swindell's profile in black and the motto *Take it to the Next Level* imprinted in his distinctive handwriting. Those who hadn't already opened theirs did so swiftly, and Taz watched as more than a few hid them under their chairs. The hubbub quieted as the wine and appetizers were served. The Fund's chair emeritus, an ageless beauty, stepped to the mike and made several announcements. She gave way and then, to the apparent surprise of all, the sitting governor of Maryland strode in from the wings, mounted the small speaking platform and introduced the guest of honor as a "Dear friend and, when time allows, the chancellor of the University of Maryland." The audience stood and applauded politely.

The pixie returned to whisper to Savanna. Swindell's special tea, commended to him as a relaxant for his voice and served with large dollops of honey and at least two ounces of brandy, had gone down without a second thought. Taz smiled and continued to scan the room.

Carter Swindell rose from the center front table, nodded to his tablemates, and, seemingly spontaneously, leapt to the platform to embrace the governor. The hug seemed to go on for a very long time. A dowager at the table immediately in front of Taz turned to her companion. "They must be very good friends, indeed. Will they be making out, do you suppose?" With that, the governor eased himself out of Swindell's grasp and politely waved his farewell.

❦

And now the show Taz has been waiting for: Swindell steps to the middle of the platform, raises his hands in the manner of a late show host, and waits until another round of applause, this time somewhat faint, washes over him. He motions to quiet the final sparse claps. Smiling, beaming. He touches his fingers to his ear to adjust his earbud, and pulls his wireless mike from his tuxedo lapel, holding it under his chin like a fresh flower. He shifts that gleaming smile around the room this way and that, acknowledging and thanking his most important guests by name, sometimes adding a sly inside remark to indicate how well he knows them. He introduces his father and mother, sitting at a first rank table just to the right side of the platform. The father is in his early seventies, in good shape, with a gray buzz cut and eyes that could cut a diamond. The mother is a fiftyish platinum blond with excessive curves and a look of tender vulnerability, at least when she gazes devotedly at her husband. Taz shifts his gaze back to Swindell. He's wondering why a man would want to take his dead older brother's identity. *Is it so much better than his own?*

Taz's eyes catch a hint of movement just in front of the speakers' stand. Trixie had sidled up to Lucia and, with a cupped hand, speaks into her ear for a few moments. Lucia turns from a conversation with her next-door neighbor to focus on Swindell. He starts, eyes wide, and actually takes an involuntary step back. He hiccups, gulps, and then hiccups again. The hiccups seem to shock him. His eyes are wide and his Adam's apple is bobbing. He swallows, perhaps trying to avoid the next paroxysm. It doesn't work. He shoots another look at Lucia, more malevolent than shocked, then takes in several deep breaths, shifting his wireless mike from hand to hand.

"Pardon me. I'm almost speechless—so honored by this commendation, by my wonderful friends—and . . . I must be doing something right. There's so many of you!" A chuckle to imitate humility. "I'm touched that you all wanted to be with me on this occasion." He lifts his eyes to the heavens. "To celebrate me—" He catches himself. "Celebrate *with* me, I mean. I salute you." The classic smirk, pacing on the platform like he's giving a TED talk. He misses a step, takes another and grimaces, bending slightly forward in the way a man does when he's having severe stomach pain. He gazes out at the crowd, smiles sadly, takes a little bow. The apology of a Southern gentleman. He waves half-heartedly and crabwalks to the side, finally taking refuge behind the curtain.

A murmuring begins among the guests. An elegant man with swept-back silver hair who Swindell had pointed out as a dear friend in his introductions rises from one of the front tables and follows Swindell behind the curtain. It quickly becomes plain that the wireless sound network is still on. Beyond the curtain, Swindell must be at least twenty feet from the podium mike, but those with good hearing are still picking up a sound like a cat hacking up a hairball, followed by pulses of liquid gurgling and a series of uninterpretable mutters. The murmuring in the hall turns into a hubbub as the guests try to drown out the sound of retching. The sound gradually quiets and the elegant man re-emerges, cupping his hands as a megaphone, and reassures the crowd that all is well— only a bit of indigestion. "Chancellor Swindell will be back with us shortly."

Taz catches a movement on the other side of the stage and sees Lucia looking back at him. She's the picture of elegance, with her hair fetchingly arranged, a loose lock hanging over her ear. She mouths the unmistakable phrase *"What the fuck?"* Then smiles as recognition dawns, puts her hand over her mouth and returns her focus to her companions.

Savanna puts her hand on Taz's shoulder. "What if he doesn't come back?"

"Are you kidding? For *this* award, in front of *this* crowd? Beamed on TV? He'd get off his deathbed for it."

Still, he sighs with relief when Swindell does finally step back to the platform, walking determinedly but with great delicacy, one might almost say precision. He summons up his patented smile for the crowd, upper lip stretched tight to the teeth, lower lip stretching the corners of his mouth towards his dimples.

"I do hope you'll excuse me—just a little stomach trouble. I feel better already." He unclasps the mike on his collar, holds it up to the light. Satisfied, he returns it to his lapel, fumbling a few times before he gets it to stick. Looks out again at the crowd. "Where was I? Oh yes, I was being honored. That's what this is about." He begins pacing again, fondling his earbud. Cocks his head to listen: "What I meant? No, that's what I meant. I meant about conservation, about wildlife, about our efforts . . . to save it. All of it. The planet. And we're doing a bang-up job. Leadership . . . that's what it's all about. And of course you! Not just our staff, or our leadership, no, no. That's not what I meant. You . . . all of you, our donors and sponsors, my friends—you're a big part of this. Still, we get criticized, don't we, and I say yes! There is much more to do. Take it to the next level, right? Take it to the next level!"

He slows, brings a purple silk handkerchief from his breast pocket, wipes the sweat dripping from his brow. "That's what I want to do—take it to the next level. I'm good at that. Better than most people. Face it, there are lots of business models out there . . . " The sound of muffled laughter comes from Taz's right somewhere near the rear. For just a second, Swindell focuses on that corner like a laser. His eyes widen; Taz can see the whites surrounding the pupils. They start darting from table to table. Then he begins moving again.

"Who's laughing? I hear you, okay? Maybe you don't agree with me? I know you're out there. Always have been. There are always people who snicker, you know?" Now he's shouting, pointing at one table or another. The crowd has gone silent—it's as if they're watching a desperate man on a ledge. Swindell puts a hand to his ear once more. His voice softens. "Yes, of course. I'm meant to be showing you some slides, our work, the successes your generosity has made possible." Looks out over the tables. "You! Computer jockey! The slides!" He turns to the side and speaks to his aide, who's standing on the left side of the stage. His words are loud enough for most of the guests to hear. "Find him and get this fixed." The aide scrambles down the side steps of the platform and begins walking along the wall towards the back of the room. The aisles are crowded with servers. Two of them move together, unintentionally obstructing the man's progress. The crowd looks anxiously at the three screens. Still tiger, polar bear, whale.

It's time. Taz takes two steps to the right, just behind the curtain, where a young man is sitting at a table that looks like a soundboard, typing on a laptop, nervously trying to manage the stage lighting and cue up the

PowerPoint show. In the corner behind the table, Taz sees a loose heap of lighting cords and equipment, and a pile of metal rods and planks that appear to be the scattered pieces of a dismantled scaffold. As he approaches, another of Lucia's PhD candidates trots up and pulls the young man's arm. "Randy, stop the slides. There's been a screw-up. There's a blown fuse or something. The big blue light is throwing sparks! We need your help, now." She tugs, he stumbles to his feet, and they leave, moving quickly away from Taz and the little console. Taz pulls a thumb drive out of his pocket, plugs it in to the laptop, and dials up the stereo power-point program that Dana's son, Moyer Jarvis, developed for the occasion.

On stage, the tiger screen goes black and is immediately replaced by a picture of a small village in a clearing, surrounded by tropical forest. The houses are small, clapboard, some with thatched rooves. In the foreground stands a couple, parents apparently, and their son. The men are wearing codpieces and the women grass skirts. Fingers are pointed from the crowd. Heads turn to see. Then, on the opposite side of the stage, the whale goes black. It's replaced by a wide patch of burnt vegetation and scarred stumps sticking out of the carbonized soil, with the remainders of houses still standing—some blackened stilts, a half a wall here or there. Three rough wood crosses have been planted where the family stood in the first picture. Gasps from the guests. Swindell turns to see, his back to the crowd, moving his head from one screen to the other so quickly that it gives the impression that it's spinning. Taz flips the sound switch from Swindell's earbud to the house speakers and speaks into a mike.

"The village on your left is a native village of the Txai people in the western Amazon. So is the village on your right, after it was burnt by an illegal logging crew working for Fontana, an American firm that imports and sells mahogany. And who owns the holding company that controls Fontana? This man." The center screen goes black and then flashes a head-on picture of Carter Swindell, who is now dead silent, open-mouthed, watching his own bloated image.

Murmurs, catcalls, hisses, a few shouts of "What is this?"

"We're being hacked!" "Shut it down!" "This is an insult!" Swindell roams the stage, shouting: "Who is doing this? Turn it off! Get them out!" Taz watches as Lucia excuses herself, rises slowly and starts making her way back in his direction. Taz moves away from the computer to intercept her. He has the mike, and the computer is on its own now.

The left screen goes black, and the village is replaced by a dusty, ravaged city, full of one- and two-story commercial buildings with rusty rebar festooning their upper floors. The buildings along the street show bullet holes from a recent machine gun strafing. Taz walks behind the catering tables, watching the screens through an opening off the side of the curtain.

"This is the city of Reynosa, Mexico, which has been taken over by the Zeta cartel." The right screen switches away from the burnt Txai village and instead shows an enormous pile of plastic bags in an over-lit room, stacked like sandbags and filled with white powder, with DEA agents standing proudly off to the side. "And this is heroin. The Zetas ship tons of this out of Reynosa and into the United States every month." The catcalls slow. The crowd quiets again, whispering. Swindell paces the stage relentlessly, muttering to himself. Finally, he whips off his glasses and looks into the stage lights. "You're out there, I know you are!" Back to the crowd: "I am not who they say I am!" His fists clenched against his face, he turns in a kind of thespian agony. The center screen goes black. Swindell whirls to see. A black-and-white picture of a man walking into a bank, carrying a briefcase. A sign by the door: *Cayman-Larbour Bank and Trust, Ltd.* Taz speaks into the mike.

"In order to sell heroin in the US, Mexican cartels have to launder a lot of money. Here's where they do it." The black-and-white still—one of the bank's security shots that Jack Donelly had turned up after their last conversation—shows a man with a briefcase approaching the door, until most of the viewers can make out his face—*Carter Swindell.*

Across the room, people are standing at the tables, turning to leave, casting astonished looks at the stage. A steady trickle find their way out past the curtain. Many of the tables show empty spaces. A few in the front still hold their full complement of horrified donors.

Suddenly a shout from Savanna: "Taz, incoming!" He looks to his left and sees Swindell's oversize aide running at full tilt towards the computer. He's still hearing voices yelling in the crowd, and Swindell's garbled shouting at the mike. He lowers his shoulder and blocks the aide, knocking him into the loose pile of stage equipment. With surprising alacrity, the man rolls, picks up an aluminum rod about three feet long, and charges Taz, swinging as he comes.

Taz stands his ground, catches the first blow on his left shoulder. The blow drives him to the side and he dives to the floor to avoid the next one. He lands on his right side and rolls to escape the aide's third try. His shoulder hurts like hell. When he looks up, the aide is standing at the laptop with the bar in one hand and his other hovering over the keyboard. Taz launches himself forward and tackles him behind the knees. The aide yells, falls backwards over Taz and hits the floor with a loud thump, still swinging the rebar. Taz rolls again. He hears a woman's voice yelling his name. *Lucia.* Suddenly a bright red cylinder clangs on the floor next to him—a five-pound fire extinguisher.

Taz get his hands on it and frantically tries to pull out the cotter pin when the aide swings the bar again, backhanded, connecting just below Taz's left ear. He rolls to his back and holds the extinguisher above his chest to protect himself. Another blow, this one glancing off the extinguisher and then his leg. He hears Swindell screaming the slogan he had insisted on when he became chair of the board. "For our mission, for wildlife, for the future."

Taz twists to get up, shoves the extinguisher in Lucia's direction. Lucia picks it up and points at the aide, but nothing happens. Taz yells "Pull the pin, pull the pin." A jet of freezing halon catches the man full in the face. He howls and crumples to the ground, desperately trying to rub the frostbite off his face. Taz wrenches his hands behind his back, yells "I need a cord." Savanna finds an electric cord in the pile of lighting equipment and throws it to Lucia, who kneels on the other side of the prone aide and ties his wrists together the way you rope a calf.

The man, croaking now, saying "Oh God, oh God" over and over. Swindell's amplified voice echoes through the hall. "I'm sorry! I'm not perfect. I do all I can, but—" Another gut-wrenching sob. Taz crawls to the computer table, pulls himself up until he can see the speaking platform.

Lucia and then Savanna move to his side, supporting him with their arms around his waist. Half the audience is standing. Those who are headed for the coatroom are pushing past the ones searching for their handbags or standing awestruck in little groups, gaping open-mouthed at the stage. A few gesticulate and shout, and at least two fights have started. Taz steps to the soundboard, scans it for a few seconds, and flips another switch. Now the sound is coming from Swindell's mike. It's not pretty. "Not me! That's not me!" Close to a sob. "You don't understand—it's complicated— nothing we do is easy—do any of you understand? We do what we must, we overcome huge obstacles."

Swindell, still pacing and pointing to the back of the hall. "You in the back—you know who you are. The ones who are scuttling out the door. Embarrassed? You should be! The ones snickering . . . always those people. The ones who laugh at you, laugh at me." Suddenly the two flanking screens go black and then come up again. One shows a picture of two boys, Swindell and his older brother, the other a gravestone with the real Carter Van Swindl's name on it. Taz is in no condition to narrate, but that hardly matters. Swindell is facing the screens, slowly gazing at one and then the other. His voice turns soft, as if he's cooing to an infant. He looks over his shoulder, sees the horrified eyes of two hundred of the most rich and powerful people in Washington staring at him. His eyes look like he's watching a four-alarm fire.

"Because I'm not good enough? Is that why you're laughing? Just like he did!" Swindell throws his arm back towards the screens. His voice turns bitter. "Always laughing when I tried—and Lord knows I tried—to be like him, to be as good as him." Then it's as if the front table has just shouted "Who?" in unison. "My brother! My brother! He haunts me, you know? Haunts me . . ." His voice descends into an indistinguishable muttering, then suddenly becomes more cheerful. "Nobody knows it, but he died." A smile, quickly suppressed. "A sad thing—a dreadful thing." More somberly. "But not altogether bad. No, definitely not. I learned so much from him, you know—" He chokes, and his voice is hoarse. "How to win, how to be a boy a father could be proud of." Swindell sways like he's being buffeted by a storm. Taz wonders how manages to stay upright. He straightens and his voice calms. "The man is heir to the boy, yes? Well, I inherited a lot from my brother, I can tell you that." He picks thoughtfully at his microphone. "No. I can't tell you, can I?" A high-pitched giggle. "But I did tell you. Get it?" Another giggle. He falls to his knees, facing his father, who is sitting at his front table with a face like granite. "I told them. I'm not perfect. Your fault as much as mine, Father. Your fault as much." Swindell turns back to crowd, pleading now. "I have regrets, okay? I have dreams, too. Had dreams. Here's my favorite. We're at a carnival, him and me. At one of those booths where you throw the ball and knock over an animal. I'm throwing and missing, again and again, and . . . ," turns again to stare at this father, "you were snickering. *Snickering!* Then you grabbed the ball from my hand and gave it to Carter, and he threw and knocked down a furry bear, and I was so proud. But when the man gave me the box, you know what was in it? A snake! A snake! So, I had to kill him." Gasps around the hall. "I had to! All of you out there . . . you would have done the same, wouldn't you? Wouldn't you?" Swindell's father sitting ramrod straight, eyes on his son, disdain in his eyes. "I killed him, Dad." Pleading. "I was tough! Like you taught Carter, like you taught me. Now I can do it. I can carry on. Your legacy! Then I couldn't, could I? 'Little Sylvie, the wimp.'"

The remaining sponsors are staring at the stage, astounded. Politicians scurry towards the nearest exits.

The tall silver-haired man at the front table rises hurriedly and helps his wife into her coat. He turns to Swindell. "Young man, you're embarrassing yourself. Get a grip on it." Turns his gaze to the father: "For God's sake get him off there."

Taz and Lucia stand next to each other, transfixed, holding their breath. She put her lips close to his ear. "Shouldn't we call a doctor?"

"Not yet. We don't have him. We will. Just give him a chance. And make sure the recorder is still on."

Swindell fixes his eyes back on the silver-haired man. He and his wife are stepping carefully around chairs, heading for the center door. "You . . . you! Embarrassing myself? You're the one who should be embarrassed. I'm worth millions! I have a profile. I get things done. Who are you? Huh? *Mister* Stafford? A nobody, that's all, another fucking accountant, doling out other peoples' money to the ones who do the work. Well, I'm the front line, okay? Front line! People who try to stop me—go ahead—ask *them*. Ask them!" Shouting, spitting into the mike. "It's almost ridiculous! *They* found out! Those stupid, thieving Indians, the ones in that grimy little jungle hovel." He whirls and pointed to the burnt village, how on automatic rotation and back on the screen, twelve feet long and eight feet high. "They had it coming. Trying to stop *me!*"

A young man, perhaps a foundation press assistant, steps to the platform and tries to take Swindell's arm, but he's moved on from declaration to something like rage. "You don't think I'm tough enough? You don't think I could do it?" He rips his arm out of the young man's grasp. "Don't! Just—don't." His voice breaks, then lowers. Again that pleading tone. "My brother didn't." Louder. "He thought I was a weakling. A punk! What if I tell you I know the leaders of the biggest cartels in Colombia and Mexico? Not just the Zetas—they're just a local gang, and Reynosa is a dump. Hell, for all I do for them, they should be kissing my hands!" He holds his hands up in the attitude of a martyr. "They couldn't ship a bag of ice over the border if I wasn't handling their money. What do you think now?" He shifts his attention back to his father. "Doesn't that mean I've proved myself? Father? *Isn't* that what it means? Haven't I? Haven't I?"

He begins to cry, doubles over, crumples to his side, sobs, straightens, and shakes like a bow that has just released an arrow, then goes flat as if the wind has been knocked out of him. Two of the graduate ushers step up to the platform and gather him as best they can, then help him off the platform. The remaining guests stand, talking in amazed tones. One young man with opera-quality lungs who is apparently three shots over the limit keeps yelling 'bravo, bravo,' and clapping. The rest of his table are giggling, some nervously, some laughing out loud. Swindell's mother has gone missing. His father just sits, looking straight ahead, his jaw set in a grim half-smile.

❦

The show is over, and Taz's spell has broken. The remaining folks in the lobby have headed for the front doors, oblivious to the little group in the corner, half behind the curtain. Taz to Savanna: "Is this the whole team?"

Savanna smiled. "Just about. I think Molly is still gathering some of the, you know, the items that need cleaning." Taz laughed, brought an envelope out of his pocket. Savanna seemed almost offended. "You don't have to, really, Taz. You know how miserable he was to our Lucia," she said, looking fondly at the professor and friend in question. "We volunteered."

"I know, and I love you for it." Looking eye to eye around the circle. "I just wanted to show my appreciation. You are a great team—the magnificent seven or better, the seven samurai. There are seven slips in here." He tucked the envelope into Savanna's hand. "Each one of them is good for a dinner for two at Watami." Washington's premier and most expensive sushi bar.

Taz and Lucia made their way out to Pennsylvania Avenue. A periodic flash of red light came from Seventh Street, around the corner of the building. They walked over to see. An ambulance, its back door open, as two attendants wheeled a gurney out from a side door. The person on the gurney, secured with heavy straps and sedated—Swindell.

They stood together, watching. Lucia reached for Taz's hand. The attendants loaded the gurney into the ambulance, which began slowly moving up Seventh Street.

Lucia turned to Taz: "Is he gone, do you think?"

"He's gone."

"It was hard to watch. We were all squirming."

"Surely you don't feel sorry for him?"

"No. But to watch someone melt like that in public—I don't know—it hit me harder than I thought it would. What happens now?"

"I suppose they'll have to take him somewhere. He sure can't come back to his office and pretend it never happened. Everyone knows who he is now, what he did."

"Won't he just hide for a while and then say he was drugged? That none of it means anything?"

"He might try. But it's going to be hard. The Brazilians are about to indict him for murder and illegal appropriation of indigenous property. And right after that hits, Justice is going to be seeking indictments here. They'll probably empanel a grand jury for all the money-laundering he's been doing for the Zetas. And on top of that, he's going to be running for his life. I don't expect the Zetas take it kindly when one of their bankers paints a bullseye on their backs."

"Is there someplace we can go for a drink?"

"Sure. I thought we might make it back to the Island, but I booked a room at the Tabard just in case. How about a nightcap?"

CHAPTER FIFTY-TWO

No Certain Highway

TAZ AND LUCIA SAT AT the Tabard's little bar and slowly savored their negronis. She had only one class the next day, late in the morning, an introductory wildlife conservation seminar that she could teach in her sleep. Two elbows on the rail, her chin resting on the cup formed by her palms, she regarded him.

"Taz, how long have we known each other?"

"Six months, give or take."

"Do you think, if we keep doing whatever it is we're doing, do you think it will always be like this?"

"Do you want to?"

"What?"

"Keep doing whatever it is we're doing."

"Yes!" A hesitant smile. Her lower lip was trembling. "No?" A tear. "I don't know, dammit! I don't know!" She buried her head in the hollow of his shoulder, sniffling. Finally, she whispered, "There's so much you don't know about me." She clasped her hands in her lap. "But it'll be better if you know the truth now rather than feeling suckered later." Blinking away tears. "Taz. I know Laney told you what happened when I was fourteen.

You've known for months, haven't you? And yet you never gave up on me, like the others—my *boyfriends*." A wan smile.

"And I'm not planning to anytime soon, unless you chase me away."

"But Taz, there's more. After everything happened, I closeted myself in my imagination for a couple of years. Alone in one room or another, reading and listening to old Patsy Cline records. Then I turned seventeen, and everything changed. I started to get interested in boys. But I couldn't follow through on my impulses. It was like I was going to infect them. I felt dirty and ashamed. I decided that my first year in college was going to be different, no matter what the cost. I threw myself at a good-looking boy from my poetry class. I pretended to enjoy the sex. He never knew.

"It all came to a head in my senior year. It was like I was living two different lives. Half the time I was out in the wilderness, dreaming of being a cowgirl scientist. The other half I was pining for the life my parents had before everything went south. Then I met someone who talked me into believing I could have it all. I pretended with him too, but I convinced myself it was worth it. He told me he loved me for my freedom when what he really wanted was to take it away. I never saw it coming. I found out later he was bragging to his friends about bringing me to heel. He neglected to tell me that his life plan was to have a wife he could parade in front of his business partners and then leave home with the kids . . . you know, the American dream. I was such a fool. When I told him I had ended a pregnancy and might not be able to get pregnant again, he decided to cut his losses. And I really was at loose ends for a while. I moved to New York to live with college friends who had an apartment in a tony area on the Upper West Side. They were running with a rich crowd—artists, actors, Wall Street executives, that kind of thing. I had no money, no job, and a load of student debt. There was no point in talking to my parents. Granma Tillie was way out West and far from rich herself. I did what I had to do to survive and pay the rent."

They sat side by side. After a few minutes, Lucia bent forward and turned her eyes his way. "Taz, none of that meant anything to me. But earlier this year, just before we met, the doctor told me that my chances of being a mother were slim to very slim. I reckoned that was my punishment.

And I thought, you know, that's okay, because I have my work, and maybe I don't need anything else. But now it breaks my heart, because . . . because I know you, and there's something between us, and, well, I met Dana's daughter Suzanne, and I realized how good you would be with kids. So, I have a question. What am I supposed to do? If you stick with me, you might never have that chance. With your own, I mean. And that means you'd be punished, too. It's not fair."

He gently caressed her lips with the tips of his first two fingers.

"Maybe you don't have to have the answer to that question just now. And when you do, maybe you won't have to face it alone. I mean unless that's the way you want it. As for me, I'm past the something-between-us stage. What I know right now is that when I wake up in the morning, you're the one I'm thinking about, and when I go to bed at night, you're the one I want to be with. Isn't that punishment enough?" She gave him a little laugh, then a sniffle and a gentle shove, her hands on his chest. Tears flowing.

*

Taz dropped Lucia off at her apartment just before ten-thirty, plenty of time to make her class. Despite the inevitable buzz on campus, she was determined to do her best to shed the drama of the past weeks. He kept the conversation light, not wanting to push her to re-engage until ready. He called Laney as he turned back onto Route 13.

"Still like coffee?"

"Is that really a question?"

"How about I come and grab you in about an hour?"

They sat on the coffee shop's little wooden deck. "Okay, Taz. Are you in love with Lucia?"

"Is *that* really a question?"

"Ha ha. You could do a little more to show it. She thinks you left your heart with Carolina."

"But we've been—"

"I know. She says the two of you have been talking—about all of it.

But *Mister Blackwell*—and I never thought I'd have to say these words to you—sometimes it takes more than talk. Hearing your man say he cares is great—but it's not the same as feeling it. Knowing it. Especially if he's been as far away as you've been."

"Maybe I have been holding back. I hurt her; I know. I didn't want to. I want her to know how special she is to me—in every way. I didn't want to assume . . . I mean I wasn't sure if she was ready, if maybe things were still a little fragile. And I sure don't want her thinking I take her for granted."

"She's not as fragile as you think, Taz. She was hurt, yes. But she's strong, and she really loves you. She just needs a little reassurance that you feel the same way."

He was processing her words when he was rudely interrupted by a shriek. It was speeding ahead of Eliza Clarke, who was running pell-mell up the sidewalk towards them. "Taz Blackwell, you miserable, half-cooked, dipwad of a person."

"A what?" Taz, smiling.

"Was that an insult or a haiku?" Laney, starting to laugh.

"It's not funny!" Glaring at Laney, then at Taz. "How could you not warn me!"

She looked at both of them. "Swindell staged a meltdown last night—at a high dollar DC fundraiser." Pointed to Taz's chest. "And he was part of it, somehow. He was there, but he didn't tell me. I was covering it, but I had to find out what was happening real-time just like the rest of the crowd. And who to get quotes from? Half the most quotable people were gone before I had my first question ready." Looking at Taz, "Couldn't have you told me *something?*"

Laney gave her the most sympathetic simmer-down look Taz had ever seen. "I think you'd better sit down."

Taz asked, "Coffee?"

Eliza nodded.

Laney put her hand on Eliza's. "I saw your article this morning. You're a damn good writer. You totally captured it—what happened—I could feel your surprise. Isn't that what's important?"

Taz gazed at Laney with gratitude, shifted back to Eliza. "And you asked the most important question, the one that sent him over the edge."

"Okay, okay. That was a good tip, but—"

"Plus, the real story is going to happen two days from now, and you're going to get the scoop."

"What? How?"

"The Brazilians are going to indict Swindell for murder. That should be worth a headline. I'll know more about the timing tonight."

"You know this how? Anyway, the *Times* will still catch it first. Don't they always?"

"With foreign news? Almost always. But their Brazil stringer is in Sao Paulo, and they won't be looking for this. I'll get it so you can cite unimpeachable sources."

"How the hell are you going to do that?"

Laney shook her head. "How long have you known Taz? By hook or by crook, like he always does." Then she turned and punched him in the shoulder. He winced, began rubbing.

*

Lucia called at five. Laney and Taz were sitting on the dock discussing the topic of vanity. "My Jeep and I are at Moe's—my catalytic converter is kaput."

"Nice alliteration."

"I don't need a remedial poetry class. I need a ride. I'm sitting out front watching the semis on Route 13. When are you coming to pick me up?"

"I don't know. There are a lot of taxis—and Uber. Your on-time record for pick-ups is really not so hot."

"Okay, Mister Quip. And what will you do with your sorry little self if I'm not here when you don't swing by?"

"You don't want to know. You ought to be considering what I intend to do to you when you do finally show up."

"Are you kidding? I've been dreaming about that all afternoon. I mean if you're still interested?"

"I'll be there in twenty minutes."

Laney winked, stood to hug him. "I'll take care of the glasses. You, Mister Blackwell, better get going. You can buy my morning coffee tomorrow."

*

Lucia needed a change of scenery, was how Laney put it. The outlet stores in Virginia Beach were promoting Saturday sales. Laney came by to pick Lucia up at nine. Lucia whispered in his ear, "We might be a while. Hope you're still around when we get back." Slipped into Laney's passenger seat, tossed her hair and the car was off.

Laney dropped Lucia on Taz's doorstep late that afternoon. She had a dress bag slung over her shoulder. Taz opened the door and Lucia pecked his cheek and trotted into the bedroom, closing the sliding door behind her.

Taz fished a bottle of sauvignon blanc from the refrigerator, found two acceptable wine glasses, sat at the little round table, and poured one for each of them while he waited. The door slid open. Lucia, hands on hips, wearing a pink button-down blouse with a navy-blue tie and a matching, blue-pleated skirt. Taz surveyed her slowly, with a smile. He applauded and offered her a glass. "Definitely the sexiest professor ever." She took a sip and slipped back into the changing room, sliding the door closed behind her.

The second Lucia was a punk, with a shiny nose ring and a black leather vest over a white T-shirt. Taz clapped and hooted, held her glass out for a second sip. She knocked it down in one fell swoop. Tossed her hair back again, slipped back into the bedroom.

After a minute more, Lucia emerged again, this time wearing a red cocktail dress that could set a concert hall on fire. The front was low cut, showing off the raven pendant and leading the gaze towards just a hint of twin delights. The back was cut even lower, both sleek and inviting. The waist hugged hers and then flowed in a relaxed fashion to just above her knees. Taz was stunned.

"Do you like it?"

"Do I like it? On you, it's the most delicious thing I've ever seen. I'd be afraid to take you to a party, though."

"And why is that?" Laughter in her eyes.

"Because every man there, and probably some of the women, would be trying to figure out how to steal you from me."

"You're this far"—thumb and forefinger a half inch apart— "from being arrested for hyperbolic exaggeration. I think that's a thing—"

"That dress would start a riot at a New Year's party."

Now blushing. "Do you think it's too—?"

"No, no, not at all. It's perfect. I think the word that I'm looking for is *vamp*."

"So, you do like it?" A wonderful question just at that moment.

"Well, that's certainly one way of putting it." More blushing. Taz took it in. Now standing directly in front of him, swaying ever so slightly, her hands on her hips.

Looking up past her breasts to her sparkling eyes. "I do like you in that dress. Why don't you take it off?"

"And if I don't want to?"

Taz stepped close enough that his chest was just touching the cloth over her breasts, looked into her eyes. "Then maybe I'll have to do it for you."

"Maybe you'd like to try."

Their lovemaking was primitive, basic, desperate. Later, they were reading in bed. Lucia pulled aside the covers, swung her leg over his, put her chin on the palms of her hands, and gazed at him. Suddenly, her eyes widened in alarm. Taz looked over his shoulder to see whatever had given her the scare, but there was nothing. Meanwhile, she had thrown off the covers and leapt out of bed and rummaged around in the little pile of clothes she had left behind before her fashion show. Finally, she gave a little whoop, turned, and stood, blessedly naked, and holding something in her hand. Did a little skip and then she was sitting next to Taz and smiling.

"I brought you something – but then you were so cute about the outfits, and I forgot it! Bad Taz!" She opened her hand and offered him a little leather pouch. She giggled and gave a little bounce on the bed. "Laney finally went through that little shoe box of stuff they gave us when she picked you up at the hospital. Look what was in it." She clasped her hand and waited, totally still, as Taz opened the draw string and pulled out a leather cord. His jaguar claw was hanging on it.

*

The knot on Salvador's leather necklace cord had come undone. Taz was about to tie it when Lucia drew it gently from his hand. With a warm smile, she leaned towards him, placed it around his neck and re-tied it, all the while nuzzling his ear. Finished, she leaned back and looked him over. She pursed her lips and tapped them gently with her forefinger, looking at him expectantly. Their kiss was light, then warmer and more sensitive, then deep and very satisfying—not unlike the lovemaking that followed.

Afterwards, they lay on their sides perspiring, facing one another. Lucia stroked his chest, then rolled the claw in her fingers. Trained those eyes on his. "There must be a story there. Are you going to tell it to me? Or is this going to be like that damn Tabasco?"

Taz laughed and rolled his eyes. "No. I'll tell you – promise." She smiled. "On the condition that you answer one question first."

"Okay, but this better be good."

"Lucia," he twirled a lock of her hair. "I need to know something about you and your panthers."

She pushed herself a little space away, perhaps to get a better look, to see if he was making fun of her. Her examination complete, she leaned back in. "That's, as you say, a long story."

"What I mean is you have a special bond with them, don't you? You're not just studying them. They mean more to you than that. I can see you know them—deeply—know their behavior, all the little signs. But there's more, isn't there. You had the courage to befriend a cougar. And they accepted you somehow, didn't they? So how did you do it?"

"Haven't you ever run into a love you didn't see coming?" Taz thought it quite an ironic question, considering their present circumstances. "At first it was just the high desert itself. My family was so broken. I needed some other connection. So, I found wild cousins—the ones who called my landscape home. The ones I tracked, the ones I watched—the hawks, ravens, jays, and hummingbirds. The ones I followed—the wandering mustangs. In the end, the ones who found me—the cougars. I guess I was looking for a spirit even wilder than the impulses I felt in my own heart." She gave him a searching look. The blanket had slipped below her shoulder. Taz reached over to pull it back up.

"Taz, you know you can coax a cougar to trust you? Not tame it. Why would you want to? But to trust you enough to nibble the meat you throw near them, or, later, to eat the meat out of your hand, to lie down quietly in your presence. Maybe, if you're lucky, they'll purr, and even accept a scratch under the chin." Taz turned to gaze at her, to absorb the reality of being so close to a mountain lion. Lucia gave him a questioning look—a soft one. "I have this strange feeling that you've had some kind of connection with the big cats. Am I right?"

Taz was trying to decide how much to say.

She reached a tentative hand for his. She turned it palm up, rested her fingers for a moment in the warm center of his hand. Then she pulled back and drew her elbows towards her chest, looking studiously out the window as the trailers passed by on their way to the campground up Beebe Road.

He reached for her shoulder, drew her gently back in his direction. She blinked. Reached to touch the leather string around his neck and pulled up the jaguar claw. There were tears.

"Do you believe in us? Enough to share just a little bit of your soul with me?"

"I . . . it's just that the whole story is so implausible that it's almost embarrassing to tell it—especially to you."

"Try me, Taz. I'm not one of your one-time extravaganzas. I see more than you think." Lucia waited, searched his eyes. "Taz? The big cats all talk to each other in the spirit world. One thing they talk about is which of us two-leggeds they can rely on."

Baffled, Taz had absolutely no answer. He let the silence reign for a moment.

"So, when I was in Acre, underneath the escarpments that step up to the Andes. I was with the young Brazilian I mentioned, the one I want you to meet. He was a doctor who worked among the local villagers, both settlers and the Txai. He heard about the villages in the Javari Reserve that had been raided by illegal loggers. We did our best to help. But in the middle of all that, I got to know a *curandeiro*, a *brujo*. The details don't matter. His name was Salvador Chindoy. It turned out he could speak English as well as Guarani. He invited me to join him on a walk into the forest. Of course, I said yes."

Lucia raised her eyebrows and rolled her eyes. "Oh, of course."

"I had no idea how far we would be going. We slept just off the trail. Two nights, maybe three. I can't remember. The last night he gave me a drink of an herbal brew that turned out to be ayahuasca. Sometime later, I became aware of something circling our campfire. It was a jaguar, quiet as an owl in flight. At first all I could see was the eyes, gleaming green. I thought maybe I was dreaming, like my subconscious was recycling the stories you had told me about your experiences with your cougars. But then the jaguar stopped circling and lay down by the embers, resting on her front paws. She looked to be at least six feet from chest to tail."

"You weren't afraid?"

"I was terrified. But at another level I asked myself what would be the point? Fear is just a pump to raise your adrenaline and get you to run faster. Nobody, and I mean nobody, was going to outrun this jaguar. So no, I didn't feel scared. If anything, I felt some kind of fellowship."

"What did you do?"

"I sat where I was for a long time. She was close enough that I could smell her breath. I thought maybe if I hummed a lullaby, but I couldn't think of any. Then it just popped into my head—"Love Makes the World Go 'Round"—really. So, there I was, humming your song. Lucia, I swear her purr sounded like an idling freight engine. I reached over and started stroking her just under his chin, just like you said. She didn't seem to mind. After a few minutes, she rolled over and stretched her rear legs. All I knew to do was what you would do with a house cat. So, I moved carefully down her ribs and started scratching that little tender zone that makes them so happy."

"And then?" Her eyes gleamed.

"I don't remember much after that. Sometime before dawn, I woke just enough to realize my jaguar had arranged herself to rest on her forepaws like a sphinx. I had gone to sleep with my cheek on her left paw. When dawn finally came, my face was resting on a bed of ferns. I knew for sure I had had a vision. And maybe that's all it ever was."

Her eyes soft. "You don't believe that."

Taz rested his arm on hers and began gently rubbing her shoulder, keeping his eyes locked with hers. "No."

Lucia crossed her arms above her heart, made herself busy snuggling into his side. Taz reached over her shoulder for the side of the blanket and pulled it over them. She sighed and burrowed even closer.

Later, he heard her murmuring in her sleep. Taz leaned close. She seemed to be repeating the same phrase over and over again. "It's like you said it should be, Granma."

*

The morning had been breezy, cool, and beautiful. They knew this because the bedroom windows were open. A little before ten, Taz escaped their rumpled sheets and propped himself with a pillow against the headboard. Lucia gave a petulant squeak and crawled across his thighs to reach for a hand mirror on the bedside table. Now he was watching a scallop boat making its slow way towards the inlet and Lucia was spread-eagled face-down over his hips, looking in horror at the mirror and giving voice to a ringing indictment, the gist of which was that his intemperate attentions had resulted in the most tangled bedhead she had ever had and it was Monday and he knew she had to go to work in an hour and, for God's sake, actually see people and what was he prepared to do about it. One good slap on her already sore and exquisitely bare bottom put an end to that, though she kept muttering in a sort of singsong that Taz found quite endearing. His penance involved making coffee and slathering toast with butter and blackcurrant jam while she luxuriated in the shower. Once she had made short work of brunch, she gave him a light kiss on the cheek, nibbled his earlobe and left to hold office hours and teach an early afternoon seminar. They had made vague plans to go out to dinner and Taz figured she'd be back before the afternoon was over. Plenty of time for him to collect the day's papers and see how they were playing the aftermath of Thursday night's fundraising fiasco.

CHAPTER FIFTY-THREE

One Story Starts Where Another One Ends

THE MEDIA HUBBUB OVER THE fall of Carter Swindell followed the parabola of all such stories. First, a recount of his meltdown, then intrigue and questions, then a recounting of the revelations reported by Eliza and an enterprising podcaster named Shawna Alexander, then further details and follow-ups, then the review of unanswered questions, the human-interest angles, and finally the wrap-ups. Taz was more than happy to fade into the background while the inevitable news cycle played itself out.

*

Lucia pulled into the shell driveway just before five. The day was still warm, dry, and sunny. A light breeze brought a hint of marsh and eelgrass off the bay. They sat on the end of his dock, feet dangling over the water. She appeared more beautiful than ever, but her eyes looked troubled. He turned to face her.

"What's wrong?"

"The feeling I had last night when we made love—I've never felt anything like it before. Never, Taz. The emotion that washed through me. I can't put it into words. Sitting here with you, now, I still feel it. Maybe you do too." He covered her hand with his, locked his eyes on hers and smiled. She continued: "But look at the two of us. Neither of us are cut out for offices and desk jobs. Even in the half year we've known each other, we've been apart more than we have together." Her hand clasped his. "And I don't see how that's going to change. You just got back from Brazil. John White told me about your Arctic work, and there's no telling where you'll have to go next. And the work I love the most, where I can actually do something important, that's in the field as well." She raised his hand to her lips, kissed each knuckle in turn. "There's already some talk about working with the Russian conservation community on a population survey of Siberian tigers. I just need to know if you're alright with that. And whether you've thought about what I said in the Tabard bar. Have you? Do you still want me in your life?"

She looked down at her feet. Troubled the water with her toe, shrugged. Taz stretched to dip his toes in. The bay felt good. Cool, not cold. He slipped all the way in.

"Hey! You've still got your clothes on!"

He stood on the sandy bottom just a foot away from her. The water came up to his chest. He tilted his head and flashed her a smile. "That's funny—you do too. And you know what? I know it doesn't make a lick of sense, but you and I belong together—even when we're apart. Come hell or . . ." He smoothed the surface with his hand. ". . . high water."

He took a step towards the dock and gripped her waist just above the hips. "Taz! What the—?" He lifted her and tossed her over his shoulder into the water. Two seconds later, she shot back to the surface, blouse soaked and clinging, shaking her wet hair and sputtering, "You . . . you . . . I'm going to drown you! And that's if I don't kill you first."

Gleeful. A laughing mermaid.

ACKNOWLEDGEMENTS

WRITING ISN'T AS LONELY a project as some people think. I had lots of help on *Jaguar's Claw*. I have to thank my long-time friend and favorite *editrice* Diane McEachern, who took the first editorial swipe at what was then a very rough draft. Diane's early judgements were astute, sometimes inconvenient, and always impossible to ignore. I also want to expess my gratitude for my gang of 'first readers,' including Diane, Bill Eichbaum, Judith Mills, and the formidable duo of Jonathan and Jane Richstein, all of whom gave me valuable critiques and often, invaluable ideas. Marion Granigan went one step beyond first-readership to clean up the manuscript early on. Jane Stewart's first talent is music, but she's also a magisterial copy-editor. Thanks also to the team at Koehler Books—to John Koehler for our second publishing collaboration, to his daughter Danielle for the cover design, to Joe Coccaro for his good advice and excellent editing, to Anna Torres for her meticulous final copy edit, and to Lauren Sheldon for her invaluable help in final production. My personal thanks to Brenda Kelly for her kind permission to use her husband's lyric from 'Let's Start Again'.

In addition to Bap Kennedy and the inimitable Jerry Garcia, the book's most important musical inspiration comes from the great Ana Moura, the luminous Portuguese singer whose brilliance has brought *fado* to a new generation. A special thanks to her for opening my eyes and ears to a new musical romance.

And finally, my most heartfelt thanks to my partner-in-life Cindy Shogan, who has shaped so many of my ideas and perceptions that her influence is literally in every page of *Jaguar's Claw*. Love you forever.

CPSIA information can be obtained
at www.ICGtesting.com
Printed in the USA
BVHW081810041122
650895BV00001B/1

9 781646 638536